THE EBENEZUM TRILOGY

A Malady of Magicks

A Multitude of Monsters

A Night in the Netherhells

By Craig Shaw Gardner

As bad as it sounded outside of Snurff's House of Degradation, it was much worse inside. Whatever the original purpose of the shop had been, it now looked like its sole purpose was to sell debris. The air was full of dust and the ground crunched and snapped beneath our feet. I drew Cuthbert again from its midnight-blue scabbard, but even the sword's magic light was lost in this gloom. I instructed Snarks to grab hold of my belt, and Hendrek to grasp Snarks's hood, and so on down the line. With the atmosphere this murky, the only way we might stay together was to form a living chain.

"Do I have to be out here?" Cuthbert whined. "I warn you, I tarnish very easily!"

I told the sword to be still. There were other voices up ahead.

"You!" a particularly nasty voice screamed. "You really disgust me!"

"Glurph!" a second, equally nasty voice cried in panic. "I don't think he came here for that!"

"Remember the really bad things your mother used to call you when she was mad at you?" the first nasty voice continued. "Well, she was right! Except she was your mother, so she was being too kind!"

Introduction

Idecided I wanted to be a science fiction writer in the fifth grade, at the Hoover Drive Elementary School in Greece, NY. My teacher, Mr. Fabry, would read to us at the end of the every day; lots of Mark Twain, as I recall, but a smattering of other writers, including, for a couple of glorious weeks somewhere in winter, THE INVISIBLE MAN by H.G. Wells. Whoo, doggies! First off, you have a guy who figures out how to become invisible (neat, huh?) and then he goes crazy (which, to my ten-year-old brain, was even neater.)

I immediately sought out SEVEN SCIENCE FICTION NOVELS OF H.G. WELLS, and read the first five of the seven. WAR OF THE WORLDS! THE TIME MACHINE! FIRST MEN IN THE MOON! THE INVISIBLE MAN (one more time!) And, best of all, THE ISLAND OF DR. MOREAU! Creepy beast men were even neater than being invisible. (The last two in that volume, FOOD OF THE GODS and IN THE DAYS OF THE COMET seemed a bit too dense for me at the time.) I was hooked. I read everything in the school library; the Heinlein "juveniles", and the "Paul French" (Isaac Asimov, actually) books, and bugged my parents to buy me every volume of TOM CORBETT, SPACE CADET. The town of Greece finally built a standing library (before that, we had only had a Bookmobile), and I quickly devoured their collection of sf books as well. In addition, some kind soul had donated all their old science fiction magazines to the library, so I'd bring home half a dozen issues of AMAZING, GALAXY, ANALOG and all the others and read them cover to cover. I moved on to the larger library in downtown Rochester NY. Ace and Ballantine and half a dozen other publishers put out new paperbacks every month. I ended up getting a paper route to support my habit.

So, I got the reading part of it down. But I wanted to write the stuff, too.

Back in the fifth grade, my teacher had the students put out their own mimeographed newspaper. It contained my first published story. "Frankenstein Meets Juliet." In junior high school, I wrote parodies of the stuff that me and my buddies read ("Doc Cabbage, the Man of Chartreuse") and eventually went on to make a couple of silent films, a pair of Tarzan takeoffs starring my best buddy, Glenn Garman, called "Garman of the Grapes" and "Garman Baby."

High school ended. College came and went. I'd write a short story now and then, send it out to the markets I'd find in Writer's Digest, and get rejected. Getting rejected is never any fun. But I realized, some six years out of college, that I wasn't really writing enough (a couple of stories a year) to say I was serious about breaking into publishing.

I attended a couple of science fiction workshops, including one run by Hal Clement, which bolstered my confidence to actually become a writer. As a result of the Clement workshop, I posted a notice posted at the Science Fantasy Bookstore in Cambridge, which led to the first meeting of a writers' group that would get together every couple weeks. Suddenly, I had deadlines and structure.

The second story I wrote in our new workshop was called "A Malady of Magicks." The basic idea came from "What if a wizard became allergic to magic?" But I didn't think the wizard should tell the tale. Instead, I invented a young apprentice, who would tell the great man's story, much like Dr. Watson does for Sherlock Holmes. I submitted the story to all the major markets, from highest paying down to the lowest. And the last, poorest paying market actually bought it – FANTASTIC, edited at the time by Ted White, who would go on to helm HEAVY METAL.

Six months later, the story saw print, and got picked by Lin Carter to appear in THE YEAR'S BEST FANTASY collection. More people read it, and I got requests to submit further Ebenezum stories to a pair of anthologies. Pretty soon I had a bunch of stories, all gently lampooning the fantasy novels I had grown up with. In those days, there were regular science fiction

conventions all year round up and down the east coast. These were great places to get known and to talk to real live science fiction editors. Which I did. It was at one of these conventions (at Disklave, I believe, held outside Washington D.C.) that Ginjer Buchanan, newly hired as an editor for Ace Books, asked me if I had anything she might be interested in. I suggested an Ebenezum trilogy. She liked the idea, and the books ended up selling quite well, going through multiple printings and really launching my funny fantasy career.

Someday, I hope to collect all the other Ebenezum stories that aren't in the original six-book series into a collection of their own. If these books do well in their new e-format, that just might happen.

But, in the meantime, this book is where it all began. I hope you enjoy it.

Craig Shaw Gardner
May 2013

CHAPTER ONE

"A wizard is only as good as his spells," people will often say. It is telling, however, that this statement is only made by people who have never been wizards themselves.

Those of us who have chosen to pursue a sorcerous career know that a knowledge of spells is only one small facet of the successful magician. Equally vital are a quick wit, a soothing tongue, and, perhaps most important, a thorough knowledge of back alleys, underground passageways, and particularly dense patches of forest, for those times when the spell you knew so well doesn't quite work after all."

—from The Teachings of Ebenezum, Volume I

The day was quietly beautiful, perhaps too much so. For the first time in a week, I allowed myself to forget my problems and think only of Alea. Alea! My afternoon beauty. I had only learned her name on the last day we were together, before she went on to, as she called them, "better things." But as surely as she had left me, I knew that we might be reunited. In Vushta, anything might happen.

The wizard sneezed.

I woke from my reverie, instantly alert. My master, the wizard Ebenezum, greatest mage in all the Western Kingdoms, had sneezed. It could only mean one thing.

There was sorcery in the air!

Ebenezum waved for me to follow him, his stately and ornate wizard's robes flapping as he ran. We headed immediately for a nearby copse of trees.

A hoarse scream erupted from the bushes across the clearing.

"Death to the wizard!"

The spear embedded itself in the tree some three feet above my head. ,Half a dozen warriors ran screaming from the undergrowth, blood cries on their lips. They had painted themselves with dark pigments for a particularly fierce appearance, and they carried great swords as long as their arms.

The spear seemed to have a few primitive charms painted on it. Oh, so that was all it was. Just another assassination attempt. In a way, I was disappointed. For a moment, I had thought it might be something serious.

So it began again. By this time, I must admit these assassination things had grown quite tiresome. All thoughts of my afternoon beauty had fled from my mind. As boringly regular as these attacks had become, it would still not do to become too lax in our response.

I looked to my master. The wizard Ebenezum, one of the most learned men upon this huge continent we now traversed, nodded briskly and held his nose.

I placed my hands in the basic third conjuring position. Taking a deep breath, I stepped from concealment.

"Halt, villains!" I cried.

The warriors did nothing to acknowledge my warning, instead bounding across the field toward me with redoubled fury. Their leader's tangled blond hair bounced as he ran, a mobile bird's nest above his brow. He hurled another spear, almost tripping with the effort. His aim was not very good.

I quickly wove a magic pattern with my hands. During the last few days of our headlong flight, Ebenezum had taken what few rest periods we could manage to teach me some basic sign magic. It was all quite simple, really. After you had mastered a few easy gestures, earth, air, fire, and water were yours to command.

Still, I didn't want to try anything too difficult for my first solo endeavor. Another spear whistled through the air, almost impaling the leader of the warrior band from the rear. The leader yelped and stopped his headlong charge. He was close enough that I could see the anger in his pale blue eyes.

Infuriated, he spun to lecture his men on appropriate spear-throwing technique. Ebenezum waved from the trees for me to get on with it. It would be a simple spell, then. I decided I would move the earth with my magic and create a yawning pit in which our pursuers would be trapped. I began making the proper movements with my elbows and left leg, at the same time whistling the first four bars of "The Happy Woodcutter's Song."

The warriors screamed as one and ran toward me with even greater speed. I hurried my spell as well, hopping once, skipping twice, scratching my head, and whistling those four bars again.

The sky suddenly grew dark. My magic was working! I pulled my left ear repeatedly, blowing my nose in rhythmic bursts.

A great mass of orange dropped from the heavens.

I paused in my gyrations. What had I done? A layer of orange and yellow covered the field and the warriors. And the layer was moving.

It took me a moment to discern the layer's true nature. Butterflies! Somehow, I had conjured millions of them. They flew wildly about the field, doing their best to get away from the warriors. The warriors, in turn, sputtered and choked and waved their arms feverishly about, doing their best to get away from the butterflies.

I had made a mistake somewhere in my spell; that much was obvious. Luckily, the resulting butterfly multitude was enough of a diversion to give me time to correct my error. I reviewed my movements. I had spent hours perfecting my elbow flaps. The hop, the skips, the scratch, everything seemed in its place. Unless I was supposed to lift my right leg rather than my left?

Of course! How stupid of me! I immediately set out to repeat the spell and correct my mistake.

The warriors seemed to have won free of the butterflies at last. Breathing heavily, some leaning on their swords, they gave a ragged yell and staggered forward. I finished my humming and started to blow my nose.

The sky grew dark again. The warriors paused in their hesitant charge and looked aloft with some trepidation.

This time it rained fish. Dead fish.

The warriors left with what speed they could muster, slipping and sliding through a field now covered with crushed butterflies and thousands of dead haddock. I decided it was time for us to leave as well. From the smell now rising from the field, the haddock had been dead for quite some time.

"Excellent, apprentice!" My master emerged from his place of concealment among the trees. He still held his nose. "And I had not yet taught you the raining creatures spell. You show a real talent for improvisation. Though how you managed a rain of butterflies and dead fish is beyond me." He shook his head and chuckled to himself. "One could almost imagine you were whistling 'The Happy Woodcutter's Song.' "

We both laughed at the foolishness of that thought and rapidly left the area. I decided I needed to hone my sorcerous skills just a bit before our next encounter, which probably wouldn't be all that long from now. King Urfoo simply wouldn't give up.

A bloodcurdling scream came from far overhead. I looked up in the trees to see a figure, dressed all in green, plummeting in our general direction. The wizard and I watched the man fall some ten feet in front of us, knocking himself unconscious in the process.

Ebenezum and I stepped gingerly around the fallen assassin. Surely another of King Urfoo's minions, incredibly bloodthirsty, and incredibly inept. Urfoo, it seemed, had offered a reward for our death or capture. That alone was enough to attract certain mercenaries. But Urfoo was the cheapest of cheap tyrants, keeping his purse strings tied in a double knot and giving a whole new meaning to the phrase "tight-fisted." The reward for our demise was not all that large, and none of it was payable in advance. Certain mercenaries, by and large, lost interest when they became familiar with the terms. This left only the foolish, the desperate, and the desperately foolish to pursue us. Which they did. In droves.

I looked down at my worn shoes and torn tunic, aware of every noise in the forest around me, careful of every movement I might see out of the corner of my eye. Who would have thought that I, a poor farm boy from the Western Kingdoms, would find himself in circumstances such as these? What would I have done, on that day when I was first apprenticed to Ebenezum, had I known I would leave the peace and security of a small, rural village, destined to wander through strange kingdoms and stranger adventures? Who would think that I might one day even be forced to visit Vushta, the city of a thousand forbidden delights, and somehow have the courage to face every single one?

I looked to my master, the great wizard Ebenezum, boldly marching by my side, his fine tunic, tastefully inlaid with silver moons and stars, now slightly soiled; his long white hair and beard a tad matted about the edges; his aristocratic nose the merest bit stuffed from his affliction. Who would have thought, on that summer's day a few months ago, that we would come to this?

"Wuntvor!" my master called.

I considered making a hasty retreat.

"No, no, Wuntvor. Come here, please!" Ebenezum smiled and waved. It must be worse than I thought.

I had only been apprenticed to the wizard for a few weeks then and, frankly, didn't care much for the job. My new master hardly spoke to me at all and certainly made no attempt to explain all the strange things going on around me. That is, until he became angry with me for something I'd done. Then there seemed to be no end to his wizardly rage.

And now the gruff wizard was smiling. And waving. And calling my name. I didn't like this situation at all. Why had I become a wizard's apprentice in the first place?

Then I remembered that I had a reason now. A very special reason. Just that morning I had been in the forest, some distance from the house, collecting firewood for use in the magician's never-ending assortment of spells. I had looked up from my gathering, and she had been standing there!

"You seem to have lost your firewood." Her voice was lower than I expected from so slender a girl, and huskier as well. She formed each word with a pair of perfect lips. I looked down to the pile of wood at my feet. One look at her long-haired splendor, and my arms had gone limp.

"Yes, I have," was all I could think to say.

"Whom do you gather it for?" she asked.

I nodded toward the cabin, just visible through the trees. "The wizard."

"The wizard?" Her lips parted to show a smile that would make the angels sing. "You work for a wizard?"

I nodded. "I am his apprentice."

Her finely etched brows rose in pleased surprise. "An apprentice? I must say, that's much more interesting than most of what goes on hereabouts." She flashed me a final smile.

"We will have to see each other again," she whispered, and was gone.

I thought on that at the door to the master's studio She wanted to see me again. And simply because I was a magician's apprentice!

Ebenezum called my name once more.

My afternoon beauty! It was a good thing to be a magician's apprentice, after all! I took a deep breath and entered the magician's study.

"Over here, Wuntvor." My master pulled forward a stool for me. "I will show you how to construct a spell." That smile showed again, curling through space between his mustache and his long white beard. "A very special spell."

The wizard's robes swirled as he turned. The stars and the moons embroidered on the cloth danced in the candlelight. Ebenezum pushed his cap to a jaunty angle and walked over to an immense oak table that was almost entirely covered by a huge, open book.

"Most spells," the wizard began, "are quite mundane. Plying one's trade in a rural clime such as this any wizard, even one as experienced as myself, finds most of his or her time occupied with increased crop yield spells, and removing curses from sheep and the like. Now, why anyone would want to curse a sheep is beyond my comprehension"—the wizard paused to glance in his book—"but a job is a job and a fee is a fee. And that, Wuntvor, is the first law of wizardry."

Ebenezum picked up one of two long white candles that sat

at either side of the table. He placed it in the only clear spot on the study's floor. The candlelight illuminated a star, sketched in the dirt.

"The second law is to always stay one step ahead of the competition," he continued. "As I was saying, you'll soon tire of crop and curse spells. As far as I'm concerned, you're not a full-fledged wizard until they really bore you. But in your spare time—ah, Wuntvor, that's when you'll find the opportunity for your wizardry to shine!"

I watched my master with mute fascination. He moved quickly about his study, turning here, kneeling there, fetching a book or a gnarled root or some strange, sorcerous device. I could half imagine his wanderings set to music, like some mysterious dance to herald the coming magic. The whole thing was something of a revelation; like cracking open a piece of slate to find the speckled blue of a robin's egg.

"And now we begin." My master's eyes seemed to sparkle in the reflected candle flame. "When this spell is finished, I shall know the exact position, disposition, and probably future direction of every tax collector in the realm!"

So this is what my master did in his spare time. I imagined there was some greater scheme to the spell that he had just described that I did not yet see, but I judged it a bad time to ask for explanations.

My master pulled back his sleeves with a flourish. "Now we begin!"

He hesitated at the edge of the markings. "But my enthusiasm carries me away. Wuntvor, something seems to be on your mind. Did you have a question?"

So I told him about the bucket.

I mean well, but my hands do not always do exactly what my mind intends. Growing pains, my mother always called them. On perhaps in this case, the thought of the girl I had encountered in the woods. At any rate, I dropped the bucket, without the rope, into the well.

What could I do? I stared dumbly at the length of rope I had wanted to tie around the handle. I should never have set the bucket on the well's edge. I looked down into the well but couldn't see a thing in the gloom. I kicked the side of the well. If only, somehow, the rope could magically tie itself to the bucket, everything would be fine.

And then I realized that the rope could magically tie itself to the bucket. So I ran to the wizard's study to ask for help. That is, if he wasn't too busy.

"Oh, I think I can fit it in," the wizard replied. "You do sometimes have a problem with your hands, Wuntvor. Not to mention your feet, your height, and a few other things. Still, with luck, you should grow out of it."

Ebenezum pulled at his beard. "There's a lesson to be learned here, Wuntvor. If you intend to be a wizard, you must consider your every action carefully. Every action, from the smallest to the largest, might somehow affect your performance of magic, and thus your fortunes and possibly your life. Now let's fetch the bucket and get on with things."

I stood to lead my master to the well. But instead of walking to the door, the wizard took a half step back and raised his arms. His low voice murmured a dozen syllables. Something bumped against my knee. It was the bucket.

"Now—" the wizard began just before he yelled in surprise. "What the—" He leapt forward and turned to face whatever had upset him.

It was smoke, or so it seemed at first; a particularly vile-smelling cloud of bluish gray that hung over the star drawn in the dirt. It swirled about furiously, growing until it almost looked like a human shape.

The wizard pointed to the ground. There was a smudge across the markings on the floor where the mystically propelled bucket had passed.

"The pentagram!" Ebenezum cried. "I've broken the pentagram!"

He grabbed a small knife from the table and knelt by the side of the star. He placed the knife against what remained of the line and used it to redraw the markings up to the point where he was stopped by a huge blue foot. The foot was attached to an even larger body; a body made of almost nothing but spikes, talons, and horns.

"A demon!" I cried.

The thing opened its mouth. Its voice was as deep as an earthquake. "Sound the charge and ring the bells," it said. "You have freed me from the Netherhells!"

Ebenezum's lips curled behind his mustache. "Even worse, Wuntvor. 'Tis a rhyming demon!"

The giant blue thing took a step toward the candlelight. As it approached the illumination, I could make out what in charity might be described as facial features: a knife slash for a mouth, above that a pair of hairy nostrils, and a couple of eyes too small and evil to even be called beady.

The thing spoke again:

"Alas, you humans are out of luck,

For now you face the demon Guxx!"

"Luck and Guxx?" Ebenezum's face became even more distraught. "That's not even a proper rhyme!"

Guxx the demon displayed its dark and pointed claws. "I'm somewhat new at the poetry game. But you'll soon be dead all the same!"

Ebenezum glanced at me. "See what I mean? The meter's all wrong." The wizard pulled at his beard. "Or maybe it's the creature's delivery."

"You try to confuse me with your words!" the demon cried. "But Guxx will shorten you by a third!"

The demon's claws shot out with lightning speed, straight for the wizard's neck. But Ebenezum was every bit as fast as the creature, and the claws only grazed his magician's cap.

"You're getting too complex," the wizard remarked as he pulled back his sleeves. Ebenezum liked both arms free to the elbows for maximum conjuring. "You'd be better to stick to simpler rhymes."

The demon paused in its attack, a deep rumble in its throat. "Perhaps," it said, and coughed into one of its enormous palms.

"Guxx Unfufadoo is my name,

And killing wizards is my game!"

Ebenezum's hands made a complex series of movements in the air as he spoke half a dozen syllables that I didn't understand. The demon roared. It was surrounded by a silver cage.

"You think to stop me with your silver!" Guxx screamed. "But I'll break free and eat your—" It paused. "No. That doesn't work. What rhymes with silver?"

"Orange," the wizard suggested.

"I'll teach you this demon to mock! A few more rhymes, and I'll break this lock!" The creature stared at its cage. The bars shook without it even touching them.

"This demon could be a bit of a problem," Ebenezum said. "Come, Wuntvor. I will teach you a quick lesson in banishment."

"Guxx will win, this demon knows!
For with every rhyme my power grows!"

"Yes, yes. Bear with us for a moment, won't you? That's a good demon." Ebenezum glanced over one of the dozens of bookshelves that cluttered the room. "Ah. The very tome."

He extracted a thin brown volume from the upper shelf. 312 More Easy Banishment Spells was stamped in gold on the cover.

"Now, as I remember it..." Ebenezum paused as he leafed through the book. "In a case such as this, Wuntvor, it is important that you find just the right spell. Saves messy cleanup afterward. Ah, here's the very one!"

"Don't talk of spells, don't talk of mess, for seconds from now Guxx will bring your death!" the hideous creature cried.

"If your power grows with that rhyme," Ebenezum remarked, "there is no justice in the cosmos." The wizard cleared his throat. "At least no poetic justice."

"You make awful jokes at my expense,
But from Guxx's claws you'll have no defense!"

With that, the demon's arms burst through the sides of the silver cage.

"Back, Wuntvor!" the wizard cried.

The demon was on top of Ebenezum. It had moved faster than my eyes could follow it. Razor claws whistled as they descended on the wizard.

My master was in dire peril. I had to do something!

I jumped for the thing's back. Guxx shrugged, and I was tossed aside.

Ebenezum shouted something, and the demon was thrown across the room. The wizard staggered to his feet. His right

sleeve was torn. The arm beneath was bright with blood.
" 'Twill soon be finished, come now, make haste!
A wizard's blood is to my taste!"
The demon smiled.

Ebenezum grabbed a box from the shelf behind him. He tossed the contents at the approaching Guxx. Yellow powder filled the air. And the world slowed down.

Guxx was no longer a blur. You could see the demon's every movement now as its heavily muscled form strained against whatever the yellow powder had done. I could feel the effects as well. Sitting on the edge of the conflict, it took an eternity to turn my head or blink my eyes.

Ebenezum still seemed to be moving at normal speed. His voice cried a tuneless song, and his hands wove swirling patterns upward, ever upward, like two birds seeking the sun.

The demon was moving faster. Its slow progress had become a walk.

Small points of light appeared above the wizard's hands; dancing light that described fantastic shapes as it circled the upper reaches of the room.

The demon flicked aside the great oak table. Its movement was as fast as any man's.

The wizard snapped his fingers, and light flew at the demon's head. The demon cried in pain, its claws splayed out at the open air.

"Death is coming, wizard!" it screamed. Then, a moment later, as if an afterthought: "I'll cut out your gizzard!"

"Gizzard?" The wizard reached for something in his sleeve. "Well, I suppose it's more appropriate than blizzard."

The demon leapt for the mage. And Ebenezum had pulled a short sword from the folds of his cloak.

So it would come to hand-to-hand combat. But the demon was clearly stronger than the wizard. There had to be some way I could help! I stood and almost tripped over the bucket. If only I had a sword as well!

Dagger met claws. And the claws were sheared in half.

Guxx screamed with a rage that shook the floor beneath me. The creature darted away from the wizard and swatted the air with its blunted talons. Holding the dagger before him, Ebenezum stepped toward the demon.

What was my master doing? He had virtually walked into the demon's arms. Guxx's still-taloned hand was behind the wizard now, aimed for the back of Ebenezum's head.

I had to do something. So I threw the bucket.

Bucket met talons, and the claws sliced through the wood as if it were paper. But Ebenezum whirled about as the bucket split. Dagger met claws again, and Guxx had lost all its weapons. Or so I thought before the demon opened its mouth. There were two rows of sharpened spikes where the creature's teeth should be.

It was a frightening sight. The mage backed away from the fiend's gaping maw, but Guxx was faster. The demon's deadly incisors caught Ebenezum's beard.

The wizard tried to call out a spell, but his words dribbled away as he choked in the demon's foul breath, so close to his own. Although the demon's mouth was largely occupied by beard, the corners of the fiend's lips appeared to smile. But only for an instant, for Guxx, too, must have realized the flaw in its demonic plan.

By capturing the wizard's beard, and contaminating the mage's air with its own exhalations, Guxx had put an end to Ebenezum's magicks. But since the demon's own mouth was filled with wizard hair, Guxx could not utter that final, devastating poem that would make it a victor of this sorcerous contest. The demon furrowed its immense brow, causing its incredibly tiny eyes to appear even tinier.

The combatants had reached a stalemate. But Ebenezum could not hold his own for long. Guxx's demon breath prevented not only the wizard's speech, but cut off the mage's supply of wholesome air. Ebenezum was rapidly turning a color not unlike a robin's egg, or certain pebbles I have found at river bottom. It was not a hue that particularly suited him.

If I did not act quickly, Guxx would win by default.

I looked about for a weapon, but all I could see were the broken bucket and a half dozen sheared claws. The claws! What better way to defeat a demon?

I grabbed a pair of the deadly daggers, one for each hand. The claws were the length of my longest finger.

"Take that, fiend!" I cried, plunging them toward the demon's rib cage.

The claws bounced from Guxx's stonelike skin. The demon made a deep sound, like rocks dropped down a well. After a second's hesitation, I realized it was laughter.

So it would be harder than I thought. But I must save my master! I struck again, with redoubled force.

The claws made a scratching sound this time as they slid across the demon's hide. Guxx laughed even louder. He couldn't control the laughter; tears ran out of his pinpoint eyes. Ebenezum pulled back at the fiend's mirth and managed to free a small portion of his beard.

I threw myself at the demon, both claws running up and down its fearsome rib cage. Guxx reared back its head and roared helplessly.

Ebenezum was free!

The mage shouted something, and the demon seemed to grow smaller. It grabbed at the wizard's robes with the remains of its claws. Ebenezum made a series of passes in the air, and Guxx once again turned to blue smoke, which was sucked in turn back into the pentacle from which it came.

The wizard half sat, half fell into the dirt. His beard was matted and ragged. The demon had torn fully half of it away.

"Open the windows, Wuntvor," he managed after a minute. "We need to clean the air."

I did as I was told, and the last bits of the blue cloud vanished with the breeze. That's when the wizard began to sneeze.

It was a sneezing fit, really. My master couldn't stop. He lay on the ground, sneezing over and over again. I remembered his remarks about clearing the air. Even with the windows open, the atmosphere in the study was far from wholesome. I thought I should get him outside, in the open. Which, with some difficulty, I managed to do.

His fit ended almost as soon as we were out in daylight, but it took him a moment to catch his breath.

"Never have I had such a fight," he whispered. "I was

worried there for a time, Wuntvor." He shook his head. "No matter. It is over now."

Unfortunately, Ebenezum was wrong. It was only just beginning.

CHAPTER TWO

Reasoned decision is important, and there comes a time in every wizard's life when he must decide what goal he should pursue to give true meaning to his life. Should it be money, or travel, or fame? And what of leisure and the love of women? I myself have studied many of these goals for a number of years, examining their every facet in some detail, so that, when the time comes to make that fateful decision of which I spoke, it will be reasoned in the extreme.

—from The Teachings of Ebenezum, Volume XXXI

I could no longer bring myself to gather firewood. My world had ended. She hadn't come.

I sat for far too long in the sunlit glade where we always met. Perhaps she didn't realize it was noon, she had somehow been delayed, her cool blue eyes and fair blond hair, the way her slim young body moved, the way she laughed, how it felt when she touched me. Surely she was on her way.

Oh, there had been other women: Aneath, the farmer's daughter; what a child I had been then! And Grisla, daughter of the village tinsmith; nothing more than a passing infatuation. Only now did I know the true meaning of love!

But I didn't even know her name! Only her interest in me—a magician's apprentice. She once called magicians the closest thing to play actors she knew in this backwater place. She said she had always admired the stage. And then she laughed, and we kissed, and—

A cold breeze sprang up behind me. A reminder of winter, due all too soon. I gathered what logs and branches I could find and trudged back to my master's cottage.

In the distance I heard a sneeze. So my master was studying

his tomes again. Or attempting to study them. Spring had turned to summer, and summer threatened to give way to autumn any day, and still his malady lingered. Ebenezum studied his every waking hour, searching for a cure, but all things magical still brought an immediate nasal reaction. In the meantime, he had handled a handful of commissions, working more with his wits than his spells, so that we might continue to eat. And just this morning, he had mentioned something about a new discovery he had made; a magic spell so quick and powerful that his nose would not have time to react.

Yet still he sneezed. Had his latest experiment failed as well? Why else would he sneeze?

Unless there was something sorcerous in the air.

Perhaps there was another reason besides my mood that the world was so dark around me, another reason that she hadn't met me as we'd planned. The bushes moved on my right. Something very large flew across the sun.

I managed the front door with the firewood still in my arms. I heard the wizard sneeze. Repeatedly. My master stood in the main room, one of his great books spread on the table before him. Smaller books and papers were scattered everywhere, victims of his nasal storm. I hurried to his aid, forgetting, in my haste, the firewood that scattered across the table as I reached for the book. A few miscellaneous pieces fell among the sneezing Ebenezum's robes.

I closed the book and glanced apprehensively at the mage. To my surprise, Ebenezum blew his nose on a gold-inlaid, dark blue sleeve and spoke to me in the calmest of tones.

"Thank you, 'prentice." He delicately removed a branch from his lap and laid it on the table. "If you would dispose of this in a more appropriate place?"

He sighed deep in his throat. "I'm afraid that my affliction is far worse than I imagined. I may even have to call on outside assistance for my cure."

I hastened to retrieve the firewood. "Outside assistance?" I inquired discreetly.

"We must seek out another magician as great as I," Ebenezum said, his every word heavy with import. "Though to do that, we might have to travel as far as the great city of Vushta."

"Vushta?" I replied. "With its pleasure gardens and forbidden palaces? The city of unknown sins that could doom a man for life? That Vushta?" All at once, I felt the lethargy lift from my shoulders. I quickly deposited the wood by the fireplace.

"That Vushta." Ebenezum nodded. "With one problem. We have not the funds for traveling, and no prospects for gaining same."

As if responding to our plight, a great gust of wind blew against the side of the cottage. The door burst open with a swirl of dirt and leaves, and a short man wearing tattered clothes, face besmirched with grime, staggered in and slammed the door behind him.

"Flee! Flee!" the newcomer cried in a quavering voice. "Dragons! Dragons!" With that, his eyes rolled up in his head and he collapsed on the floor.

"I have found, however," Ebenezum said as he stroked his long white beard, "in my long career as a magician, Wuntvor, if you wait around long enough, something is bound to turn up."

With some water on the head and some wine down the gullet, we managed to revive the newcomer.

"Flee!" he sputtered as he caught his breath. He glanced about wildly, his pale eyes darting from my master to me to floor to ceiling. He seemed close to my master in age, but there the similarity ceased. Rather than my master's mane of fine white hair, the newcomer was balding, his hair matted and stringy. Instead of the wizard's masterful face, which could convey calm serenity or cosmic anger with the flick of an eyebrow, the other's face was evasive; small nose and chin, a very wrinkled brow, and those eyes, darting blue in his dark, mud-spattered face.

"Now, now, good sir," Ebenezum replied in his most reasonable voice, often used to charm young ladies and calm bill collectors. "Why the hurry? You mentioned dragons?"

"Dragons!" The man stood somewhat shakily. "Well, at least dragon! One of them has captured Gurnish Keep!"

"Gurnish Keep?" I queried.

"You've seen it," Ebenezum murmured, his cold gray eyes

still on our guest. " 'Tis a small castle on yonder hill at the far side of the woods." Ebenezum snorted in his beard. "Castle? 'Tis really more of a stone hut, but it's the home of our neighbor, the Duke of Gurnish. It's a very small dukedom. For that matter, he's a very small duke."

Our visitor was, if anything, even more agitated than before. "I didn't run all the way through Gurnish Forest to hear a discussion of the neighborhood. We must flee!"

"Gurnish Forest?" I inquired.

"The trees right behind the hut," my master replied. "Surely the duke's idea. Everyone else knows the area as Wizard's Woods."

"What do you mean, Wizard's Woods?" the newcomer snapped. "This area is Gurnish Forest. Officially. As Gurnish Keep is an official castle!"

" 'Tis only a matter of opinion," Ebenezum replied, a smile that could charm both barbarians and maiden aunts once again upon his face. "Haven't we met somewhere before?"

"Possibly." The newcomer, who was somewhat shorter than my master's imposing frame, shifted uneasily under the wizard's gaze. "But shouldn't we flee? Dragons, you know."

"Come now, man. I wouldn't be a full-fledged wizard if I hadn't dealt with a dragon or two." Ebenezum looked even more closely at the newcomer than he had before. "Say, aren't you the Duke of Gurnish?"

"Me?" the smaller man said. His eyes shifted from my master to me and back again. "Well—uh..." He coughed. "I suppose I am."

"Well, why didn't you say so? I haven't seen you since you stopped trying to tax me." Ebenezum's smile went to its broadest as he signaled me to get our guest a chair. The duke obviously had money.

"Well, this whole situation's a bit awkward," our honored guest said as he stared at the floor. "I'm afraid I feel rather undukish."

"Nonsense. A run-in with a dragon can unnerve anyone. Would you like some more wine? A nice fire to warm you?"

"No, thank you." The duke lowered his voice even more than

before. "Don't you think it would be better if we fled? I mean, dragons. And I've seen other things in the forest. Perhaps if your powers were—" The duke coughed again. "You see, I've heard of your accident."

Ebenezum bristled a bit at the last reference, but the smile more or less remained on his face. "Gossip, good duke. Totally blown out of proportion. We'll deal with your dragon in no time."

"But the dragon's taken over Gurnish Keep! He's immense, with bright blue and violet scales, twenty-five feet from head to tail. His wings scrape the ceiling of my great hall! And he's invincible. He's captured my castle and beautiful daughter, and defeated my retainer!"

Beautiful daughter? My thoughts returned to the girl of my dreams. Where had she gone? What had kept her away?

"Only a child!" the duke cried. "No more than seventeen. Fine blond hair, gorgeous blue eyes, a lovely, girlish figure. And the dragon will burn her to a crisp if we don't do his bidding!"

Blond? Blue? Figure?

I had a revelation.

"Come now, man," Ebenezum remarked. "Calm down. It's common knowledge that dragons tend to be overdramatic. All the beast's really done so far is to overwhelm one retainer. I assume you still had only one retainer?"

She hadn't deserted me! She was only held prisoner! All the time she and I had spent together, all those long, warm afternoons. That's why she would tell me nothing of herself! A duke's daughter!

The duke glared at my master. "It wouldn't be like that if my subjects paid their taxes!"

A duke's daughter. And I would rescue her! There'd be no need for secrecy then. How magnificent our lives would be!

A fire lit in Ebenezum's eyes. "Perhaps if certain local royalty were not so concerned with extending the borders of their tiny dukedom..." The wizard waved his hands and the fire disappeared. "But that's not important. We have a dragon to evict. As I see it, the elements here are quite ordinary. Dragon captures castle and maiden. Very little originality. We should be able to handle it tidily."

The duke began to object again, but Ebenezum would have none of it. Only one thing affected his nose more than sorcery—money, and the smell of it was obvious in the cottage. My master sent the duke aside while we gathered the paraphernalia together for dragon fighting.

When I had packed everything according to my master's instructions, Ebenezum beckoned me into his library. Once in the room, the wizard climbed a small stepladder and, carefully holding his nose, pulled a slim volume from the uppermost shelf.

"We may have need of this." His voice sounded strangely hollow, most likely the result of thumb and forefinger pressed into his nose. "In my present condition, I can't risk using it. But it should be easy enough for you to master."

He descended the ladder and placed the thin, dark volume in my hands. Embossed in gold on the cover were the words How to Speak Dragon.

"But we must be off!" Ebenezum exclaimed, clapping my shoulder. "Mustn't keep a client waiting. You may study that book on our rest stops along the way."

I stuffed the book hurriedly into the paraphernalia-filled pack and shouldered the whole thing, grabbed my walking staff, and followed my master out the door. With my afternoon beauty at the end of my journey, I could manage anything.

My master had already grabbed the duke by the collar and propelled him in the proper direction. I followed at Ebenezum's heels as fast as the heavy pack would allow. The wizard, as usual, carried nothing. As he often explained, it kept his hands free for quick conjuring and his mind free for sorcerous conjecture.

I noticed a bush move, then another. Rustling like the wind pushed through the leaves, except there was no wind. The forest was as still as when I had waited for my secret love. Still, the bushes moved.

Just my imagination, I thought. Like the darkness of the forest. I glanced nervously at the sky, half expecting the sun to disappear again. What was so big that it blotted out the sun?

A dragon?

But my musings were cut short by a man dressed in bright

orange who stood in our path. He peered through an odd instrument on the end of a pole.

I glanced at the duke, walking now at my side. He had begun to shiver.

The man in orange looked up as we approached. "Good afternoon," he said, the half frown on his face belying his words. "Could you move a little faster? You're blocking the emperor's highway, you know."

The duke shook violently.

"Highway?" Ebenezum asked, stopping midpath rather than hurrying by the man in orange.

"Yes, the new road that the great and good Emperor Flostock the Third has decreed—"

"Flee!" the duke cried. "Dragons! Dragons! Flee!" He leapt about, waving his hands before the emperor's representative.

"See here!" the orange man snapped. "I'll have none of this. I'm traveling to see the Duke of Gurnish on important business."

The duke stopped hopping. "Duke?" he said, pulling his soiled clothing back into place. "Why, I'm the Duke of Gurnish. What can I help you with, my good man?"

The man in orange frowned even more deeply. "It's about the upkeep of the road...."

"Certainly." The duke glanced back at us. "Perhaps we should go somewhere that we can talk undisturbed."

The duke led the man in orange into the underbrush.

"They deserve each other," Ebenezum muttered. "But to business." He looked at me solemnly. "A bit about dragons. Dragons are one of the magical subspecies. They exist largely between worlds, partly on Earth and partly in the Netherhells, and never truly belong to either. There are other magical subspecies—"

Ebenezum's lecture was interrupted by a commotion in the underbrush. Large arms with a thick growth of grayish-brown hair rose and fell above the bushes, accompanied by human screams.

"Another subspecies is the troll/' Ebenezum remarked.

I let my pack slide from my back and firmly grasped my staff. They would eat my true love's father! I had never encountered trolls before, but this was as good a time as any to learn.

"Slobber! Slobber!" came from the bushes before us. A rough voice, the sound of a saw biting into hardwood. I assumed it was a troll.

"Wait!" another voice screamed. "You can't do this! I'm a representative of the emperor!"

"Slobber! Slobber!" answered a chorus of rough voices.

"Let's get this over with!" Another voice, high and shaky. The duke?

Although the voices were quite close now, it was getting difficult to distinguish individual words. It just sounded like a large amount of screaming, punctuated by cries of "Slobber!" I lifted my staff over my head and ran forward with a scream of my own.

I broke into a small clearing, which contained four occupants. One was the duke. The other three were among the ugliest creatures I'd seen in my short life. They were squat and covered with irregular tufts of gray-brown fur, that did nothing to hide the rippling muscles of their barrellike arms and legs. Three pairs of very small red eyes turned to regard me. One of them swallowed something that looked a good deal like an orange-clad foot.

The sight of the three hideous creatures completely stopped my forward motion. They studied me in silence.

"Oh, hello," I said, breaking into the sinister quiet. "I must have wandered off the path. Excuse me."

One of the trolls lumbered toward me on its immensely powerful legs. It was time to leave. I turned and bumped into my master, who was in the midst of making a mystic gesture.

"No slobber! No slobber!" the trolls cried, and ran back into the heart of the woods.

I picked myself up and helped the wizard regain his feet as well. Ebenezum sneezed for a full three minutes, the result of his actually employing magic. When he caught his breath at last, he wiped his nose on his robe and regarded me evenly.

"Wuntvor," he said, all too quietly, "what do you mean by dropping all our valuable equipment and running off, just so you can be swallowed by—"

The duke ran between the two of us. "Flee! Flee! Dragons! Trolls! Flee!"

"And you!" my master said, his voice rising at last. "I've had enough of your jumping about, screaming hysterical warnings! Why do you worry? You were surrounded by trolls and they didn't touch you. You lead a charmed life!" He grabbed the duke's shoulder with one hand and mine with the other and propelled us back to the trail.

"Come," he continued. "We will reach Gurnish Keep before nightfall. There, my assistant and I will deal with this dragon, and you, good duke, will pay us handsomely for our efforts." The wizard deposited us on the trail and walked briskly toward the castle before the duke could reply.

"Look!" The duke pulled at my sleeve. There was a break in the trees ahead, affording a clear view of the hill on the wood's far side. There, atop the hill, was Gurnish Keep, a stone building not much larger than Ebenezum's cottage. Smoke poured from the keep's lower windows, and once or twice I thought I saw the yellow-orange flicker of flame.

"Dragon," the duke whispered. I hurriedly reached into my satchel and pulled out How to Speak Dragon. The time to start learning was now.

I opened the book at random and scanned the page. Phrases in common speech filled one side. Opposite these were the same phrases in dragon. I started reading from the top:

"Pardon me, but could you please turn your snout?"

"Sniz mir heebu-heeba szzz."

"Pardon me, but your claw is in my leg."

"Sniz rnu sazza grack szzz."

"Pardon me, but your barbed tail is waving perilously close…"

The whole page was filled with similar phrases. I paused in my reading. It had done nothing to reassure me.

Ebenezum shouted at us from far up the trail. I slammed the book shut and ran to follow, dragging the Duke of Gurnish with me.

We walked through the remaining forest without further difficulty. The woods ended at the edge of a large hill, called

Wizard's Knoll or Mount Gurnish, depending upon whom you spoke with. From there, we could get a clear view of the castle. And the smoke. And the flames.

The duke began to jabber again about the dangers ahead but was silenced by a single glance from my master. The wizard's cool gray eyes stared up toward the castle, but somehow beyond it. After a moment, he shook his head and flexed his shoulders beneath his robes. He turned to me.

"Wunt," he said. "More occurs here than meets the eye." He glanced again at the duke, who was nervously dancing on a pile of leaves. "Not just a dragon, but three trolls. That's a great deal of supernatural activity for a place as quiet as Wizard's Woods."

I expected the duke to object to the wizard's choice of names, but he was strangely quiet. I turned to the pile of leaves.

The duke was gone.

"Methinks," Ebenezum continued, "some contact has been made with the Netherhells of late. There is a certain instrument in your pack…"

My master went on to describe the instrument and its function. If we set it up at the base of the hill, it would tell us the exact number and variety of creatures from the Netherhells lurking about the district.

I held up the instrument. My master rubbed his nose. "Keep it at a distance. The device carries substantial residual magic."

I put the thing together according to the wizard's instructions and, at his signal, spun the gyroscope that topped it off.

"Now, small points of light will appear." Ebenezum sniffled loudly. "You can tell by the color of-"

He sneezed mightily, again and again. I looked to the device. Should I stop it?

Ebenezum sneezed to end all sneezes, directly at the instrument. The device fell apart.

"By the Netherhells!" Ebenezum exclaimed. "Can I not perform the simplest of spells?" He looked at me, and his face seemed very old. "Put away the apparatus, Wunt. We must use the direct approach. Duke?"

I explained that the duke had vanished.

"What now?" Ebenezum looked back toward the forest. His

cold gray eyes went wide. He blew his nose hastily.

"Wunt! Empty the pack!"

"What?" I asked, startled by the urgency of my master's voice. Then I looked back to the woods and saw it coming. A wall of black, like some impenetrable cloud, roiling across the forest. But this cloud extended from the sky to the forest floor and left complete blackness behind. It sped across the woods like a living curtain that drew its darkness ever closer.

"Someone plays with great forces," Ebenezum said. "Forces he doesn't understand. The pack, Wunt!"

I dumped the pack's contents on the ground. Ebenezum rifled through them, tossing various arcane tomes and irreplaceable devices out of his way, until he grasped a small box painted a shiny robin's-egg blue.

The magician sneezed in triumph. He tossed me the box.

"Quick, Wunt!" he called, blowing his nose. "Take the dust within that box and spread it in a line along the hill!" He waved at a rocky ridge on the forest edge as he jogged up the hill and began to sneeze again.

I did as my master bid, laying an irregular line of blue powder across the long granite slab. I looked back to the woods. The darkness was very close, engulfing all but the forest's edge.

"Run, Wunt!"

I sprinted up the hill. The wizard cried a few ragged syllables and followed. He tripped as he reached the hilltop and fell into an uncontrollable sneezing fit.

I turned back to look at the approaching blackness. The darkly tumbling wall covered all the forest now, and tendrils of the stuff reached out toward the hill like so many grasping hands. But the fog's forward motion had stopped just short of the ragged blue line.

There was a breeze at my back. I turned to see Ebenezum, still sneezing but somehow standing. One arm covered his nose, the other reached for the sky. His free hand moved, and the breeze grew to a wind and then a gale, rushing down the hill and pushing the dark back to wherever it had come from.

After a minute the wind died, but what wisps of fog remained in the forest below soon evaporated beneath the bright afternoon sun. My master sat heavily and gasped for breath, as if all the air had escaped from his lungs.

"Lucky," he said after a minute. "Whoever raised the demon fog had a weak will. Otherwise..." The magician blew his nose, allowing the rest of the sentence to go unsaid.

A figure moved through the woods beneath us. It was the duke.

"Too exhausted to fight dragon," Ebenezum continued, still breathing far too hard. "You'll have to do it, Wunt."

I swallowed and picked up How to Speak Dragon from the hillside where it lay. I turned to look at Gurnish Keep, a scant hundred yards across the hilltop. Billows of smoke poured from the windows, occasionally accompanied by licks of flame. And now that we stood close, I could hear a low rumble, underlying all the other sounds in the field in which we stood. A rumble that occasionally grew into a roar.

The dragon was going to be everything that I expected.

The duke grabbed at my coat sleeve. "Dragon!" he said. "Last chance to get out!"

"Time to go in there," Ebenezum said. "Look in the book, Wunt. Perhaps we can talk the dragon out of the castle." He shook the quivering duke from his arm. "And if you, good sir, would be quiet for a moment, we could go about saving your home and daughter. Quite honestly, I feel you have no cause for complaint with the luck you've been having. Most people would not have survived the evil spell that recently took over the woods. How you managed to bumble through the powerful forces at work here is beyond..." Ebenezum's voice trailed off. He cocked an eyebrow at the duke and stroked his beard in thought.

The rumble from the castle grew louder again. I opened the thin volume I held in my sweating palms; I had to save my secret love.

I flipped frantically from page to page, finally finding a phrase I thought appropriate:

"Pardon me, but might we speak to you?"

In the loudest voice I could manage, I spat out the dragon syllables.

"Snzz grah! Subba Ubba Szzz!"

A great, deep voice reverberated from within the castle. "Speak the common tongue, would you?" it said. "Besides, I'm afraid I don't have a commode."

I closed the book with a sigh of relief. The dragon spoke human!

"Don't trust him!" the duke cried. "Dragons are deceitful!"

Ebenezum nodded his head. "Proceed with caution, Wunt. Someone is being deceitful." He turned to the duke. "You!"

"Me?" the Gurnish nobleman replied as he backed in my direction. Ebenezum stalked after him.

They were squabbling again. But I had no time for petty quarrels. I firmly grasped my staff, ready to confront the dragon and my afternoon beauty.

The duke was right behind me now, his courage seemingly returned. "Go forward, wizard!" he cried in a loud voice. "Defeat the dragon! Banish him forever!"

"Oh, not a wizard, too!" cried the voice from within the castle. "First I get cooped up in Gurnish Keep, then I have to capture your beautiful daughter, and now a wizard! How dull! Doesn't anyone have any imagination around here?"

I came to a great oak door. I nudged it with my foot. It opened easily, and I stepped inside to confront the dragon.

It stood on its haunches, regarding me in turn. It was everything the duke had mentioned, and more. Blue and violet scales, twenty-five feet in length, wings that brushed the ceiling. The one oversight in the duke's description appeared to be the large green top hat on the dragon's head.

I saw her a second later.

She stood in front and slightly to one side of the giant reptile. She was as lovely as I'd ever seen her.

"Why, Wuntvor," she said. "What are you doing here?"

I cleared my throat and pounded my staff on the worn stone pavement. "I've come to rescue you."

"Rescue?" She looked up at the dragon. The dragon rumbled. "So Father's gotten to you, too?"

The duke's voice screamed behind me. "I warned you! Now the dragon will burn you all to cinders!"

The dragon snorted good-naturedly and turned to regard the ceiling.

"The game is up, Duke!" Ebenezum called from the doorway, far enough away so that the dragon's magical odor would not provoke another attack. "Your sorcerous schemes are at an end!"

"Yes, Father," my afternoon beauty said. "Don't you think you've gone far enough?" She looked at my master. "Father so much wanted control of the new Trans-Empire Highway, to put toll stations throughout the woods below, that he traded in his best retainer for the services of certain creatures from the Netherhells, which he'd use to frighten off anyone who stood in the way of his plans."

She turned and looked at the dragon. "Luckily, one of those creatures was Hubert."

"Alea! How could you? Betrayed!" The duke clutched at his heart. "My own daughter!"

"Come, Father. What you're doing is dangerous and wrong. Your greed will make a monster of you. I've been worrying what my future was with you and the castle. But now I know." She glanced happily back to the dragon. "Hubert and I have decided to go on the stage."

The duke was taken aback.

"What?"

"Yes, good sir," Hubert the dragon remarked. "I have some small experience in the field and on talking with your daughter, have found that she is just the partner I have been looking for."

"Yes, Father. A life on the stage. How much better than sitting around a tiny castle, waiting to be rescued by a clumsy young man."

Clumsy? My world reeled around me. Not wishing to be rescued was one thing, considering the situation. But to call me clumsy? I lowered my staff and walked toward the door.

"Wait!" my secret love cried. I turned quickly. Perhaps she had reconsidered her harsh words. Our long afternoons together still meant something!

"You haven't seen our act!" she exclaimed. "Hit it, dragon!"

She danced back and forth across the castle floor, the dragon beating time with its tail. They sang together:

"Let's raise a flagon
For damsel and dragon,
The best song and dance team in the whole, wide world.
Our audience is clapping,
And their toes are tapping,
For a handsome reptile and a pretty girl!"

The dragon blew smoke rings at the end of a line and breathed a bit of fire at the end of a verse. Six more verses followed, more or less the same. Then they stopped singing and began to shuffle back and forth.

They talked in rhythm.

"Hey, dragon. It's good to have an audience again."

"I'll say, damsel. I'm all fired up!"

They paused.

"How beautiful it is in Gurnish Keep! What more could you ask for, damsel, than this kind of sunny day?"

"I don't know, dragon. I could do with a shining knight!"

They paused again.

"Romance among reptiles can be a weighty problem!"

"Why's that, dragon?"

"When I see a pretty dragoness, it tips my scales!"

They launched into song immediately.

"Let's raise a flagon
For damsel and dragon—"

"I can't stand it anymore!" the Duke of Gurnish cried. "Slabyach! Grimace! Trolls, get them all!"

A trapdoor opened in the corner of the castle floor. The trolls popped out.

"Quick, Wunt!" Ebenezum cried. "Out of the way!" But before he could even begin to gesture, he was caught in a sneezing fit.

The trolls sauntered toward us. I bopped one on the head with my staff. The staff broke.

"Slobber!" exclaimed the troll.

"Roohhaarrr!" came from across the room. The dragon stood as well as it was able in the confines of the castle's great hall. It carefully directed a thin lance of flame toward each troll's posterior.

"No slobber! No slobber!" the trolls exclaimed, escaping back through the trapdoor.

"Thank you," Ebenezum said after blowing his nose. "That was quite nice of you."

"Think nothing of it," the dragon replied. "I never sacrifice an audience."

"I finally got our good Lord of Gurnish to listen to reason," my master said when we returned to our cottage. "When I mentioned how close to the palace I might be soon, and that I might find myself discussing the region, the duke saw his way to hire me as a consultant." Ebenezum pulled a jangling pouch from his belt. "The duke will now most likely receive clearance to build his tollbooths. Pity he no longer has the money for their construction."

"And what of his daughter and the dragon?" I asked.

"Hubert is flying the two of them to Vushta this very instant. I gave them a letter of introduction to certain acquaintances I have there, and they should find a ready audience."

"So you think they're that good?"

Ebenezum shook his head vigorously. "They're terrible. But the stage is a funny thing. I expect Vushta will love them."

"But enough of this." The wizard drew another, smaller pouch from his bag. "Hubert was kind enough to lend me some ground dragon's egg. Seems it's a folk remedy among his species; gives quick, temporary relief. I've never found this particular use for it in any of my tomes, but I've tried everything else. What do I have to lose?"

He ground the contents of the pouch into a powder and dropped it in a flagon of wine.

"This might even save us a trip to Vushta." He held his nose and lifted the concoction to his lips. My hopes sank as he drank it down. With Alea gone, a trip to Vushta was the only thing I had to look forward to.

The wizard opened a magical tome and breathed deeply. He smiled.

"It works! No more sneezing!"

His stomach growled.

"It couldn't be." A strange look stole over the wizard's face. He burped.

"It is! No wonder I couldn't find this in any of the tomes! I should have checked the Netherhell Index! It's fine for dragons, but for humans..." He paused to pull a book from the shelf and leaf rapidly through it. He burped again. His face looked very strained as he turned to me.

"Neebekenezer's Syndrome of Universal Flatulence!" he whispered. A high, whining sound emerged from his robes.

"Quick, Wunt!" he cried. "Remove yourself, if you value your sanity!"

I did as I was told. Even from my bed beneath the trees, I could hear the whistles, groans, and muffled explosions all night long.

CHAPTER THREE

Every sorcerer should explore as much of the world as he can, for travel is enlightening. There are certain circumstances, such as a major spell gone awry, or an influential customer enraged at the size of your fee, where travel becomes more enlightening still.

—from The Teachings of Ebenezum, Volume V

Thus we were forced, at last, to leave our cottage and seek outside assistance. My master realized he could not cure his own affliction—the first time, I think, that the wizard had to face up to such a circumstance. So we traveled to find another mage of sufficient skill and cunning, though we might have to travel to far Vushta, the city of a thousand forbidden delights, before we found another as great as Ebenezum.

The wizard walked before me along the closest thing to a path we could find in these overgrown woods. Every few paces he would pause, so that I, burdened with a pack stuffed with arcane and heavy paraphernalia, could catch up with his wizardly strides. He, of course, carried nothing.

Still, all was not right with my master. I saw it in his walk—the same long strides he always took, but something was missing: the calm placing of one foot in front of the other, knowing whatever lay in one's path, a wizard could handle it. He walked too swiftly now, anxious to be done with what I imagined he thought the most unsavory of tasks: asking another wizard for aid. It threatened to affect his whole bearing. For the first time in my apprenticeship, I worried for my master.

The wizard stopped midpath to gaze at the thick growth about us. "I will admit I'm worried, Wunt." He scratched at the thick white hair beneath his sorcerer's cap. "My maps and guidebooks indicated this was a lively area, with much commerce and no dearth of farms and friendly inns. That is the prime reason I took this route, for though we have cash from our recent exploits, a little more wouldn't hurt in the least."

The wizard stared out into the dark wood, his bushy eyebrows knitted in concern. "Frankly, I wonder now about the effectiveness of certain other preparations I made for our journey. You never know what you'll encounter when traveling."

There was a great crashing of underbrush to one side of the trail. Branches were rent asunder; leaves rustled and tore away; small forest creatures cried in fright.

"Doom!" cried someone from within the thicket. Something large fell between my master and myself. Ebenezum sneezed. There was sorcery in the air!

"Doom!" the voice cried again, and the dark brown object that had fallen between us rose again. It was a tremendous club, I realized, for attached to the end nearest the thicket was a large hand, in turn attached to an arm that disappeared into the heavy greenery. Ebenezum fell back a few paces along the path and blew his nose on a wizardly sleeve, ready to conjure despite his affliction.

The club rose and fell repeatedly to crush the underbrush. A man appeared in the cleared space. He was enormous—well over six feet in height, with a great bronze helmet on his head, topped by ornamental wings that made him look even taller. And he was almost as wide as he was tall, his stomach covered by armor of the same dull bronze.

He stepped out to block our path. "Doom!" his deep voice intoned once more. Ebenezum sneezed.

There was no helping it. I dropped my pack and grabbed my stout oak staff in both hands. The armored man took a step toward the helplessly sneezing wizard.

"Back, villain!" I cried in a voice rather higher than I would have liked. Waving the staff above my head, I rushed the fiend.

"Doom!" the warrior intoned again. His barbed club met my staff in midair, shearing the sturdy oak in two.

"Doom!" The fiend swung once more. I ducked to avoid the blow and slipped on a pile of crushed leaves and vines littered beneath my feet. My left foot shot from under me, then my right. I fell into a bronze-plated belly.

"Doo—oof!" the warrior cried as he fell. His helmet struck the base of a tree, and he cried no more.

"Quick, Wunt!" Ebenezum gasped. "The club!"

He tossed a sack at my shoulder. I pushed myself off the armored belly and managed to fit the cloth around the heavy weapon. The wizard let out a sigh and blew his nose.

"Enchanted."

So it was the club, and not the warrior, that had caused my master's sneezing attack. Ebenezum, once the greatest magician in all the forest country, now brought to this by his sorcerous affliction! The wizard leaned against a nearby tree, his breathing deep and ragged, as if his sneezes had robbed his lungs of air. I looked away until he might recover his breath, idly studying the pile of leaves into which I had fallen.

The warrior groaned where he lay.

"Quick, Wunt!" Ebenezum called. "Quit dawdling and tie the fellow up. I have a feeling we have much to learn from our rotund assailant."

The big man opened his eyes as I tightened the final knot on his wrists. "What? I'm still alive? Why haven't you killed and eaten me, the way demons usually do?"

"Indeed?" Ebenezum stared down at our captive, his eyes filled with wizardly rage. "And do we look like demons?"

The huge man paused. "Now that you mention it, not all that much. But you must be demons! It is my doom to always confront demons, my fate to fight them everywhere I turn, lest I be drawn into the Netherhells myself!" A strange light seemed to come into the large man's eyes, or perhaps it was only the quivering of his massive cheeks. "You could be demons in disguise! Perhaps you wish to torture me—slowly, exquisitely— with a cruelty known only to the Netherhells! Well, let's get it over with!"

Ebenezum stared at the quivering warrior for a long moment, pushing his fingers through his great white beard. "I think the best torture would be to leave you talking to yourself. Wunt, if you'll shoulder your pack again?"

"Wait!" the stout man cried. "Perhaps I was hasty. You don't act like demons, either. And the way you felled me. A lucky blow to the stomach! You must be human! No demon could be that clumsy."

"Come, good fellows, I shall make amends!" He tugged at his hands, bound behind him. "But someone's tied me up!"

I assured him it was only a precaution. We thought he might be dangerous.

"Dangerous?" That look came into his eyes again, or perhaps it was the way his helmet fell to his eyebrows. "Of course I'm dangerous! I am the dread Hendrek of Melifox!"

He paused expectantly.

"You haven't heard of me?" he asked after neither one of us responded. "Hendrek, who wrested the enchanted warclub Headbasher from the demon Brax, with the promise it would be mine forever? The cursed Headbasher, which drinks the memories of men? It has given me such power, it has become a part of me! I need the club, despite its dread secret!"

His sunken eyes turned to the sack that held his weapon. "The demon did not inform me of the terms!" The warrior began to shake again. "No man can truly own Headbasher! They can only rent it! Twice a week, sometimes more, I am confronted by demons making demands. I must slay them, or do their fearsome bidding! For Brax did not tell me that when I won the club, I won it on the installment plan!" By now Hendrek shook uncontrollably, his armor clanking against his corpulent form.

"Installment plan?" mused Ebenezum, his interest suddenly aroused. "I had not thought the accountants of the Netherhells so clever."

"Aye, clever and more than that! Poor warrior that I am, I despaired of ever finding someone to save me from this curse, 'til I heard a song from a passing minstrel about the deeds of a great magician, Ebenezer!"

"Ebenezum," my master corrected.

"You've heard of him?" A cloud seemed to pass from before Hendrek's eyes. "Where can I find him? I am penniless, on the edge of madness! He's my last hope!"

I glanced at the wizard. Didn't the warrior realize?

"But he's—"

Ebenezum silenced me with a finger across his lips. "Penniless, did you say? You realize a wizard of his stature must charge dearly for his services. Of course, there is always barter—"

"But of course!" Hendrek cried. "You're a magician, too! Perhaps you can help me find him. I ask not only for myself, but for a noble cause—a curse that threatens the entire kingdom, emanating from the treasury of Melifox!"

"Treasury?" Ebenezum stood silent for a long moment, then smiled broadly for the first time since we began our journey. "Look no farther, good Hendrek. I am Ebenezum, the wizard of whom you speak. Come, we will free your treasury of whatever curse may have befallen it."

"And my doom?"

My master waved a hand of sorcerous dismissal. "Of course, of course. Wunt, untie the gentleman."

I did as I was told. Hendrek pushed himself erect and lumbered over to his club.

"Just leave that in the sack, would you?" Ebenezum called. "Just a sorcerous precaution."

Hendrek nodded and tied the sack to his belt.

I reshouldered my pack and walked over to my master. He seemed to have the situation well in hand. Perhaps my concern had been misplaced.

"What need have you to worry?" I asked in a low voice. "Minstrels still sing your praises."

"Aye," Ebenezum whispered back. "Minstrels will sing anyone's praises for the right fee."

The warrior Hendrek led us through the thick underbrush, which, if anything, became more impassable with every step. The late afternoon sun threw long shadows across our paths, making it difficult to see exactly where you placed your feet, which made the going slower still.

As we stumbled through the darkening wood, Hendrek related the story of the curse of Krenk, capital city of the kingdom of Melifox, and how demons roamed the city, making it unsafe for human habitation, and how all the land around the capital grew wild and frightening, like the woods we passed through now. How Krenk had two resident wizards, neither of whom had been able to lift the curse, so that, as a last resort, Hendrek had struck a bargain for an enchanted weapon but had failed to read the infernally small print. But then their ruler, the wise and kind King Urfoo the Brave, heard a song from a passing minstrel about a great wizard from the forest country. Hendrek had been sent to find that wizard, at any cost!

"Any cost?" Ebenezum echoed. His step had regained the calm dignity I was more familiar with, not even faltering in the bramble patch we were now traversing.

"Well," Hendrek replied, "Urfoo has been known to exaggerate slightly on occasion. I'm sure, though, that as you're the last hope of the kingdom, he'll—"

Hendrek stopped talking and stared before him. We had reached a solid wall of vegetation, stretching as far as the eye could see and a dozen feet above our heads.

"This wasn't here before," Hendrek muttered. He reached out a hand to touch the dense, green wall. A vine snaked out and encircled his wrist.

Ebenezum sneezed.

"Doom!" Hendrek screamed, and pulled his great club Headbasher from the sack at his belt.

Ebenezum sneezed uncontrollably.

Hendrek's club slashed at the vine, but the greenery bent with the blow. The whole wall was alive now, a dozen vines and creepers waving in the air. They reached for Hendrek's massive form. His swinging club pushed them back. Ebenezum hid his head in his voluminous robes. Muffled sneezing emerged from within the folds.

Something grabbed my ankle: a brown vine, even thicker than those that threatened Hendrek, winding up my leg toward my thigh. I panicked and tried to leap away, but I only succeeded in losing my footing. The vine dragged me toward the unnatural wall.

Hendrek was there before me, slashing in the midst of the gathered green. His strokes were weaker than before, and he no longer cried out. Vines encircled his form, and it was only the matter of a moment before he was lost to the leafage.

I yanked again at the creeper that held me captive. It still held fast, but I caught a glimpse of my master behind me as I was dragged the last few feet to the wall.

The vines were all about the wizard, but only pushed at his sorcerous robes, as if the animate vegetation somehow sensed that Ebenezum was a greater threat than either Hendrek or myself. A gnarled tendril crept toward the wizard's sleeve, groping for his exposed hand.

Ebenezum flung the robes away from his face and made three complex passes in the air, uttering a dozen syllables before he sneezed again. The tendril at his sleeve grew brown and withered, dissolving into dust.

My leg was free! I kicked the dead vine away and stood. Ebenezum blew his nose heartily on his sleeve. Hendrek had collapsed in what had been the vegetable wall. Leaves crackled beneath him as he gasped for air.

"Doom!" Hendrek groaned as I helped him to his feet. " 'Tis the work of demons, set on exacting vengeance upon me for nonpayment!"

Ebenezum shook his head. "Nonsense. 'Twas nothing more than sorcery. A simple vegetable aggression spell, emanating from Krenk, I imagine." He started down the newly cleared path. "Time to be off, lads. Someone, it appears, is expecting us."

I gathered up my gear as quickly as possible and trotted after Ebenezum. Hendrek took up the rear, muttering even more darkly than before. I saw what looked like a city before us on a distant hill, its high walls etched against the sunset sky.

We reached the walls sometime after nightfall. Hendrek pounded on the great oak gate. There was no response.

"They fear demons," Hendrek said in a low voice. Rather more loudly, he called: "Ho! Let us in! Visitors of importance to the township of Krenk!"

"Says who?" A head, clad in an ornate silver helmet, appeared at the top of the wall.

"Hendrek!" intoned the warrior.

"Who?" the head replied.

"The dread Hendrek, famed in song and story!"

"The dread who?"

The warrior's hand clutched convulsively at the sack that held the club. "Hendrek, famed in song and story, who wrested the doomed club Headbasher—"

"Oh, Hendrek!" the head exclaimed. "That large fellow that King Urfoo the Brave sent off on a mission the other day!"

"Aye! So open the gates! Don't you recognize me?"

"You do bear a passing resemblance. But one can't be too careful these days. You look like Hendrek, but you might be two or three demons, huddled close together."

"Doom!" Hendrek cried. "I must get through the gate, to bring the wizard Ebenezum and his assistant before the king!"

"Ebenedum?" The head's voice rose in excitement. "The one the minstrels sing about?"

"Ebenezum," my master corrected.

"Yes!" Hendrek roared back. "So let us in. There are demons about!"

"My problem exactly," the head replied. "The two others could be demons, too. With the three huddled together to masquerade as Hendrek, that would make five demons I'd be letting through the gate. One can't be too careful these days, you know."

Hendrek threw his great winged helmet to the ground. "Do you expect us to stand around here all night?"

"Not necessarily. You could come back first thing in the mornin—" The head's suggestion was cut short when it was swallowed whole by some large green thing that glowed in the darkness.

"Demons!" Hendrek cried. "Doom!" He pulled his warclub from the sack. Ebenezum sneezed violently. Meanwhile, up on the parapet, a second thing had joined the first. This one glowed bright pink.

What appeared to be an eye floating above the circular green glow turned to regard the pink thing, while the eye above the pink turned to look at the green. Something dropped from the middle of the green mass and writhed its way toward us down the wall. A similar tentacle came from the pink creature to grab the green appendage and pull it back up the wall. Both orbs grew brighter with a whistling sound that rose and rose, then both vanished with a flash and a sound like thunder.

The door to the city opened silently before us.

The wizard turned away from Hendrek and blew his nose.

"Interesting city you have here," Ebenezum said as he led the way.

There was something waiting for us inside. Something about four and a half feet high, its skin a sickly yellow. It wore a strange suit of alternate blue and green squares, as if someone had painted a chessboard across the material. A piece of red cloth was tied in a bow around its neck. There were horns on its head and a smile on its lips.

"Hendrek!" the thing cried. "Good to see you again!"

"Doom!" the warrior replied as he freed his club from his sack. Ebenezum stepped away and held his robes to his nose.

"Just checking on my investment, Henny. How do you like your new warclub?"

"Spawn of the Netherhells! Headbasher will never be yours again!"

"Who said we wanted it? Headbasher is yours— for a dozen easy payments! And nothing that costly. A few souls of second-rate princes, the downfall of a minor kingdom, a barely enchanted jewel or two. Then the wondrous weapon is truly yours!"

The creature deftly dodged the swinging warclub. Cobblestones flew where the club hit the street.

"And what a weapon it is!" the demon continued. "The finest warclub to ever grace our showroom! Did I say used? Let's call it previously owned. This creampuff of a weapon sat in the arsenal of an aged king, who only used it on Sunday to bash in the heads of convicted felons. Thus its colorful name, and its beautiful condition. Take it from me, Smilin' Brax"—the demon fell to the pavement as Headbasher whizzed overhead—"there isn't a finer used club on the market today. As I was saying just the other day to my lovely—urk—"

The demon stopped talking when I hit it on the head. I had managed to sneak up behind the creature as it babbled and knocked it with a rather large cobblestone. The creature's blue-and-green-checked knees buckled under the blow.

"Easy terms!" it gasped.

Hendrek quickly followed with a blow from Headbasher. The demon ducked, but it was still groggy from the first blow. The club caught its shoulder.

"Easy payments!" the thing groaned.

Hendrek's club came down squarely on the sickly yellow head. The demon's smile faltered. "This may be—the last time—we make this special offer!" The creature groaned again and vanished.

Hendrek wiped the yellow ichor off Headbasher with a shabby sleeve. "This is my doom," he whispered hoarsely, "to be forever pursued by Smilin' Brax, with his demands for Headbasher, which no man can own, but can only rent!" That strange light seemed to come into his eyes again, though perhaps it was only the reflection of the moon on the cobblestones.

Ebenezum stepped from the shadows. "It doesn't seem as bad as all that.... Uh, put that club back in the sack, would you? That's a good mercenary, mustn't take any chances." He blew his nose. "The two of you defeated the demon tidily."

My master pulled his beard reflectively. "As I see it, the effectiveness of any curse depends on how the cursed looks at it. Watching the proceedings very carefully, with a wizard's trained eye, mind you, I can state categorically that once we disenchant the treasury, you'll have nothing to worry about."

A weight seemed to lift from Hendrek's brow. "Really?"

"You may depend on it." Ebenezum brushed at his robes. "Incidentally, does good King Urfoo really consider us the last hope for rescuing his gold?"

Hendrek assured us once again of the importance of our quest, then proceeded to lead us through the winding streets of Krenk to Urfoo's castle. I'd grown up in the duchy of Gurnish, in and around Wizard's Woods, and Krenk was the largest town I had ever seen, with walls and a gate, as many as five hundred buildings, even paved streets! But I saw nothing else as we walked. Where were the taverns, where we could stop and exchange pleasantries with the natives? Where were the town's attractive young women? How could I be prepared when we finally arrived in Vushta, the city of a thousand forbidden delights, if every town was as dead as this?

There was a scream in the distance. Hendrek froze, but the scream was followed by a woman's laughter. At least some were enjoying themselves, I supposed. Was the whole town so afraid of demons?

We came to an open space, in the middle of which was a building twice as grand and five times as large as anything around it. There was a guard standing in front of the palace's huge door, the first human we'd seen since entering Krenk.

"Halt!" the guard cried as we walked into the courtyard before him. "And be recognized!"

Hendrek kept on moving. "Important business with King Urfoo!"

The guard unsheathed his sword. "Identify yourself, under penalty of death!"

"Doom!" the immense warrior moaned. "Don't you recognize Hendrek, back from an important mission for the king?"

The guard squinted in the darkness. "Don't I recognize who? I didn't quite catch the name."

"The dread Hendrek, here with the wizard Ebenezum!"

"Ebenezus? The one they all sing about?" The guard bowed in my master's direction. "I'm honored, sir, to meet a wizard of your stature."

The guard turned back to Hendrek, who was quite close to the door by now. "Now, what did you say your name was again? I can't let just anybody through this door. You can't be too careful these days, you know."

"Doom!" Hendrek cried, and with a speed amazing in one so large, he pulled his club from its restraining sack and bashed the guard atop the head.

"Urk," the guard replied. "Who are you? Who am I? Who cares?" The guard fell on his face.

"Headbasher, the club that drinks the memories of men. He will recover anon, but will remember none of this, or anything else, for that matter." Hendrek resheathed his club. "Come. We have business with Urfoo." He kicked the door aside and stormed into the castle.

I glanced at my master. He stroked his mustache for a moment, then nodded and said: "The treasury." We followed Hendrek inside.

We walked down a long hall. Sputtering torchlight made our shadows dance against huge tapestries that covered the walls. A breeze from somewhere blew against my coat to make me feel far colder than I had outside. This, I realized, was the castle with the curse.

Two guards waited before a door hung with curtains at the far end of the hall. Hendrek bashed them both before either could say a word.

Hendrek kicked this door open as well.

"Who?" a voice screamed from the shadow of a very large chair on a raised platform in the room's center.

"Hendrek," the warrior replied.

"Who's that?" A head sporting a crown peered over the arm of the great chair. "Oh, yes, that portly fellow we sent off last week. What news, what?"

"I've brought Ebenezum."

There was a great rustling as people rose from their hiding places around the room. "Nenebeezum?" someone said from behind a chair. "Ebenezix?" came a voice from behind a pillar.

"Ebenezum," replied my master.

"Ebenezum!" a chorus of voices responded as a good two dozen people stepped from behind marble columns, tapestries, and suits of armor to stare at my master.

"The Ebenezum? The one they sing about?" King Urfoo sat up straight in his throne and smiled. "Hendrek, you shall be justly rewarded!" The smile fell. "Once we take the curse off the treasury, of course."

"Doom," Hendrek replied.

King Urfoo directed us to sit on cushioned chairs before him, then paused to look cautiously at the room's shadow-hung corners. Nothing stirred. The ruler coughed and spoke. "Best get down to business, what? One can't be too careful these days."

"My thoughts exactly, good king." Ebenezum rose from his seat and approached the throne. "I understand there is a cursed treasury involved? There's no time to waste."

"Exactly!" Urfoo glanced nervously at the rafters overhead. "My money involved too. Lovely money. No time to waste, what? I'd best introduce you now to my two sorcerous advisers."

Ebenezum stopped his forward momentum. "Advisers?"

"Yes, yes, the two court wizards. They can fill you in on the details of the curse." Urfoo tugged a chord by his side.

"I generally work alone." My master pulled at his beard. "But when there's a cursed treasury involved, I suppose one can adjust."

A door opened behind the king and two robed figures emerged, one male, one female. "No time to waste!" the king exclaimed. "May I introduce you to your colleagues, Granach and Vizolea?"

The newcomers stood on either side of Urfoo's throne, and for an instant, the three wizards regarded each other in silence. Then Vizolea smiled and bowed to my master. She was a tall, handsome woman of middle years, almost my height, red hair spiced with gray, strong green eyes, white teeth showing in an attractive smile.

Ebenezum returned the gesture with a flourish.

Granach, an older man dressed in gray, nodded to my master in turn, something on his face half smile, half grimace.

"The problem," King Urfoo said, "is demons, of course." He cringed on the word "demons," as if he expected one of them to strike him down for mentioning their existence. "We're beset with them. They're everywhere! But mostly"—he pointed a quivering hand toward the ceiling, "they're in the tower that holds the treasury!"

He lowered his hand and took a deep breath.

"Doom," Hendrek interjected.

"But perhaps," the king continued, "my court wizards can give you a better idea of the sorcerous fine points." He glanced quickly to either side.

"Certainly, my lord," Granach said quickly behind his half grimace. "Although none of this would have been necessary if we used the Spell of the Golden Star."

Urfoo sat bolt upright. "No! That spell would cost me half

my funds! There has to be a better way. Doesn't there?"

Ebenezum stroked his mustache. "Most assuredly. If the other wizards are willing to discuss the situation with me, I'm sure we can find some solution."

"Nothing's better than the Golden Star!" Granach snapped.

"Half my gold!" the king cried. He added in a whisper: "Perhaps you should all—uh...inspect the tower?"

Granach and Vizolea exchanged glances.

"Very good, my lord," Vizolea replied. "Do you wish to accompany us now?"

"Accompany you?" Urfoo's complexion grew paler still. "Is that completely necessary?"

Vizolea nodded, a sad smile on her face. "For the hundredth time, yes. It states directly in the sorcerer's charter that a member of the royal family must accompany all magicians on visits to the treasury."

"Signed right there," Granach added. "At the bottom of the page. In blood."

Urfoo pushed his crown back to mop his brow. "Oh, dear. How could that have happened?"

"If you'll excuse me for mentioning it, my lord," Vizolea said with downturned eyes, " 'twas you who stipulated the terms of the pact."

The king swallowed. "There is no time to waste. I must accompany you?"

Granach and Vizolea nodded. "There's no helping it, without the Golden Star," Granach added.

"And so you shall!" My master's voice broke through the tension around the throne. "We shall inspect the treasury, first thing in the morning!"

Urfoo, who had been slowly sinking in his throne, sat up again and smiled. "Morning?"

Ebenezum nodded. "My 'prentice and I have just completed a long journey. How much better to confront a curse during the light of day with a clear head!"

"Morning!" Urfoo the Brave shouted. He smiled at the court-appointed wizards. "You are dismissed until breakfast, what? Ebenezum, I can tell you are a wizard of rare perception. I shall have my serving girls make your beds and bring you dinner. And in the morning, you will end the curse!"

I sat up straight myself. Serving girls? Perhaps there was something of interest in the township of Krenk after all.

"We must plan, Wunt," my master said when we were at last alone. "We only have 'til morning."

I turned from arranging the pile of cushions and skins that I was to sleep on. My master sat on a large bed they had provided him, head in hands, one on either side of his beard.

"I did not expect wizards." He threw his cap on the bed then and stood. "But the accomplished mage must be prepared for every eventuality. It is of utmost importance, especially concerning the size of our fee, that no one should learn of my unfortunate malady."

The sorcerer paced across the room. "I shall instruct you on certain items that have been stored in your pack. We must keep up appearances. And the business with that warrior's enchanted club has given me an idea. We'll best my affliction yet."

There was a knock on the door.

"I was expecting that," Ebenezum said. "See which one it is."

I opened the door to find Granach. He shuffled into the room, still wearing his grimace smile.

"Excuse me for interrupting at so late an hour," the gray-clad wizard began, "but I did not feel earlier that I had an opportunity to welcome you properly."

"Indeed," Ebenezum replied, raising one bushy eyebrow.

"And I thought there were certain things that you should be informed of. Before we actually visit the tower, that is."

"Indeed?" Both eyebrows rose this time.

"Yes. First, a quick word about our patron, King Urfoo the Brave. It is fortunate for him that the Krenkites prefer epithets added early during a ruler's reign, for since he gave up chasm-jumping at the age of sixteen, Urfoo has spent all his time in the treasury tower, counting his gold. Note that I didn't mention spending. Just counting. If you were anticipating a large return on your services, you might as well leave now. Our ruler should rather be called King Urfoo the Stingy. The payment won't be worth the risk!"

"Indeed." Ebenezum stroked his beard.

Granach coughed. "Now that you know, I expect you'll be on your way."

My master tugged the creases of his sleeves into place. "Indeed, no. A traveling magician, unfortunately, cannot pick and choose his clients in the same way a town mage might. He has to accept what tasks come his way, and hope that what small payment he might receive will be enough to take him farther on his journey."

The toothy grimace disappeared completely from Granach's face. "You have been warned," he snarled from between tight lips. "The payment you will receive will in no way compensate for the danger you will face!"

Ebenezum smiled and walked to the door. "Indeed," he said as he opened it. "See you at breakfast?"

The other magician slithered out. Ebenezum closed the door behind him. "Now I'm sure there's money to be made here," he remarked. "But to business. I shall instruct you as to the proper volume and page number for three simple exorcism spells. I wonder, frankly, if we'll even need them."

He pulled one of the notebooks he was constantly writing in from his pocket and began to tear out pages. "In the meantime, I will begin to prepare my temporary remedy.

"The idea came from Hendrek's enchanted club." He tore the pages into strips. "When Hendrek's club is in the open air, I sneeze. However, when the club is in the sack, my nose is unaffected. It can no longer sense the club's sorcerous aroma. Therefore, if I stop my nasal sensitivity to things sorcerous, I should stop my sneezing!" He rolled the first of the strips into a tight cylinder. "But how to accomplish this, short of standing in the rain 'til I catch cold?"

He held the cylinder aloft so I could get a good look at it, then stuffed it up his nose.

There was another knock at the door.

"High time," Ebenezum said, pulling the cylinder back out. "See who it is this time, Wunt."

It was Vizolea. She had changed from her stiff wizard's robes into a flowing black gown with a low neckline. Her deep green eyes looked into mine, and she smiled.

"Wuntvor, isn't it?"

"Yes," I whispered.

"I would like to talk to your master, Ebenezum."

I stepped back to let her enter the room.

"I've always wanted to meet a wizard of your skill."

"Indeed?" my master replied.

She turned back to me, touched my shoulder with one long-fingered hand. "Wuntvor? Do you think you can leave your master and me alone for a while?"

I glanced at the mage. He nodded rapidly.

"Let me tell you about the Golden Star," Vizolea said as I closer he door behind me.

I stood in the hallway outside the room for a moment, stunned. I had a feeling from Vizolea's manner that she wanted to do more than talk. With my master? I had been known, in recent months, to keep company with a number of young ladies in my home district, but somehow Ebenezum had always seemed above that sort of thing.

But I was still only an apprentice, unaware of the nuances of a true sorcerer's life. I sat heavily, wondering how I could get to sleep on the hallway's cold stone floor, and wishing, for just a moment, that a serving maid of my very own might wander by and make my situation more comfortable.

She wanted to leave.

Wait! I cried. I'm a sorcerer's apprentice. When will you get another chance to dally with anyone half as interesting?

She wouldn't listen. She drifted farther and farther away. I ran after her, trying to shorten the distance. It was no use. She was oblivious to me. I grabbed at her lowcut serving gown, pushed the tray from her hands, begged her to give me a single word.

"Doom," she said in far too low a voice.

I awoke to see Hendrek's face, lit by torchlight.

"Beware, Wuntvor! 'Tis not safe to sleep in these halls! Demons roam them in the wee hours!" He leaned close to me, his overstuffed cheeks aquiver, and whispered: "You moaned so in your sleep, at first I thought you were a demon, too!"

I saw then he held Headbasher in his free hand. "Some nights I cannot sleep, I fear the demons so. 'Tis strange, though. Tonight I've seen nary a one. Grab on to my club!" He helped me to my feet. "What brings you to moans in the hallway?"

I explained my dreams of serving maids.

"Aye!" Hendrek replied. "This place is full of haunted dreams. This cursed palace was built by Urfoo's doomed grandfather—some called him Vorterk the Cunning, others called him Mingo the Mad. Still others called him Eldrag the Offensive, not to mention those few who referred to him as Greeshbar the Dancer. But those are other stories. I speak now of the haunted corridors Vorterk built. Sound will sometimes carry along them for vast distances, seemingly from a direction opposite to where it actually originates. Hush, now!"

I didn't mention that it was he who did all the talking, for there was indeed a voice in the distance, screaming something over and over. I strained to hear.

It sounded like "Kill Ebenezum! Kill Ebenezum! Kill Ebenezum!"

"Doom!" Hendrek rumbled. I took a step in the direction of the screams. Hendrek grabbed my coat in his enormous fist and dragged me the other way through the maze of corridors. He paused at each intersection for a fraction of a moment, waiting for the screams to tell him which way to turn. Sometimes it seemed we turned toward the sounds, other times away. I became lost in no time at all.

But the voices were clearer now. There were two of them, and the one no longer shouted. Both were agitated, though.

"I don't think so."

"But we have to!"

"You want to move too fast!"

"You don't want to move at all! We'll have to wait for years before we get the treasury!"

"If I let you handle it, it will slip through our fingers! We should enlist Ebenezum!"

"No! How could we trust him? Ebenezum must die!"

"Perhaps I should join Ebenezum and do away with you!"

Hendrek stopped suddenly and I walked into him. His armor banged against my knee.

"There's someone out there!"

A door was flung open just before us. I froze, waiting for the owners of the voices to emerge.

Something else came out instead.

"Doom," Hendrek muttered when he saw it crawl our way. It looked like a spider, except that it was as large as me and had a dozen legs rather than eight. It was also bright red.

Hendrek swung the club above his head. Headbasher looked far smaller than it had before.

The creature hissed and jumped across the hall. Something else followed it out of the room. Large and green, the newcomer looked something like a huge, bloated toad with fangs. It jumped next to the spider-thing and growled in our direction.

"Doom, doom," Hendrek wheezed. I considered running, but Hendrek's bulk blocked my only escape route.

The bloated toad leapt in front of the almost spider. Its fangs seemed to smile. Then the red, many-legged thing scuttled over it in our direction. The toad growled and pushed past the dozen legs, but four legs wrapped around the toad and flipped it over. The almost spider moved in front.

Then the toad-thing jumped straight on top of the many-legged red thing. The almost spider hissed, the toad-thing growled. Legs interlocked, they rolled. Soon we could see nothing but flashing feet and dripping fangs.

Both disappeared in a cloud of brown, foul-smelling smoke.

"Doom," Hendrek muttered.

Another door opened behind us.

"Don't you think it was time you were in bed?"

It was Ebenezum.

I started to explain what had happened, but he motioned me to silence. "You need your sleep. We've a big day tomorrow." He nodded at Hendrek. "We'll see you in the morning."

The warrior looked once more at the spot where the creatures had disappeared. "Doom," he replied, and walked down the hall.

"Not if I can help it," Ebenezum said as he closed the door.

CHAPTER FOUR

"Never trust another sorcerer" is a saying unfortunately all too common among magical practitioners. Actually, there are many instances where one can easily trust a fellow magician, such as cases where no money is involved, or when the other mage is operating at such a distance that his spells can't possibly affect you.

—from The Teachings of Ebenezum, Volume XIV

No one ate when we met for breakfast. I sat quietly, running the three short spells I had memorized over and over in my head. My master was quieter than usual, too, being careful not to dislodge the thin rolls of paper that packed his nose. Vizolea and Granach glared at each other from opposite sides of the table, while Hendrek muttered and the king quivered.

Ebenezum cleared his throat and spoke with 'the lower half of his face. "We must inspect the tower." His voice sounded strangely hollow.

"The tower?" Urfoo whispered. "Well, yes, there's no time to lose." He swallowed. "The tower."

Ebenezum stood. The rest followed. "Hendrek," my master instructed, "lead the way."

The mage strode over to the king. "As we go on our inspection, Your Majesty, I should like to discuss the matter of our fee."

"Fee?" Urfoo quivered. "But there's no time to lose! The treasury is cursed!"

Vizolea was by my master's side. "Are you sure you really wish to inspect the tower? There may be things there you do not want to see." Her hand brushed his shoulder. "You do remember our conversation last night?"

"Indeed." Ebenezum tugged his mustache meaningfully. "I have a feeling there are things about this treasury that will surprise us all."

"Doom!" came from the front of the line as the procession moved from the throne room.

"Do I really have to come along?" came from the end.

"The charter," Granach replied.

"Perhaps we are being a bit hasty, what?" The king wiped his brow with an ornate lace sleeve. "What say we postpone this, to better consider our options?"

"Postpone?" Granach and Vizolea looked at each other. "Well, if we must."

They turned and started back for the great hall.

"If you postpone this," Ebenezum said as he caught the eye of the king, "King Urfoo may never see his money again."

"Never?" The king positively shook. "Money? Never? Money? Nevermoney?" He took a deep breath. "No time to lose, what? To the tower!"

We climbed a narrow flight of stairs to a large landing and another thick oak door.

"The treasury," Hendrek intoned.

"Your Majesty. The incantation, if you would," Granach remarked.

Urfoo huddled in the rear corner of the landing, eyes shut tight, and screamed:

"Give me an O! O!

Give me a P! P!

Give me an E! E!

Give me an N! N!

What's that spell?

Open! Open! Open!"

The door made a popping noise and did as it was bidden. No sound came from within.

"Go ahead," Urfoo called. "I'll just wait out here."

Ebenezum strode into the treasury.

The room was not large, but it was not particularly small, either. And it was filled with ornate boxes and stacks of gold, fantastic jewelry, and quite a few unmarked sacks, piled waist high at least, shoulder height near the walls.

We waded into the midst of it.

"Doom," Hendrek murmured. "So where are the demons?"

An unearthly scream came from the landing. Urfoo entered, pursued by the spider.

"The Spider of Spudora!" my master cried. He held his nose.

"Granach!" Vizolea exclaimed. "We didn't talk about this!"

"Your Majesty!" Granach shouted. "There is only one hope! The Golden Star, performed by me!" .

"No, you don't!" Vizolea recited a few quick words beneath her breath. "If anyone recites the Golden Star, it will be me!"

The toad-thing hopped into the room.

"The Toad of Togoth!" my master said.

"Quick, Urfoo!" cried Granach. "Give me leave to perform the spell before it's too late!"

A red claw snapped out of a pile of jewels.

"The Crab of Crunz!" my master informed me.

"Not the crab!" Vizolea shrieked. "This time, Granach, you've gone too far! Bring on the Lice of Liftiana!"

Granach stepped aside to avoid the panting Urfoo, now pursued by the almost spider, the bloated toad, and a grinning crustacean.

"Oh, no, you don't!" the dour wizard cried. "Bring forth the dread Cows of Cuddotha!"

My master flung his hands in the air. "Stop this now! You'll cause a sorcerous overload!"

The air shimmered as the room was filled with a chorus of spectral moos. A sickly yellow form solidified before us.

"Ah, good Hendrek!" Smilin' Brax exclaimed. "How good to see you again. We of the demon persuasion like to check out areas of extreme sorcerous activity; see if we can do a little business, as it were. And boy, is there business here! Perhaps some of you folks would like to purchase an enchanted blade or two, before some of my folks arrive?"

"Doom," Hendrek muttered.

Urfoo ran past. "All right! All right! I'll think about the Golden Star!" A blue cow with bloodshot eyes galloped after him.

"The Lion of Lygthorpedia!"

"The Grouse of Granola!"

"Stop it! Stop it! It's too much!" Ebenezum pulled back his sleeves, ready to conjure.

"How about you, lad?" Brax said to me. "I've got this nifty enchanted dagger, always goes straight for the heart. Makes a dandy letter opener, too. I'm practically giving it away. Just sign on this line down here."

"The Tiger of Tabatta!"

"The Trout of Tamboul!"

"Too much!" Ebenezum shouted, and sneezed the most profound sneeze I have ever seen. Paper showered over the newly materialized devil trout, while the force of the blow knocked Ebenezum back against a pile of jewels.

He didn't move. He had been knocked unconscious.

"Doom," Hendrek intoned.

"Then again," Brax said, looking around the room, "maybe I'd better sell you an axe."

"The Antelope of Arasaporta!"

Someone had to stop this! It was up to me. I had to use the exorcism spells!"Sneebly Gravich Etoa Shrudu—I began.

"The Elephant of Erasia!"

Wait a second. Was it "Sneebly Gravich Etoa" or "Etoa Gravich Sneebly"? I decided to try it the other way, too.

"All right! You force my hand! The Whale of Wakkanor!"

There was an explosion in the center of the room. Instead of a materialized whale, there was a lightless hole.

Ebenezum stirred on his bed of jewels.

Brax looked over his shoulder as the black void grew. "Drat. This would have to happen now, right on the edge of a sale. Oh, well, see you in the Netherhells!" The demon disappeared.

It was suddenly quiet in the room. The two other magicians had stopped conjuring, and all the demon creatures, crabs and cows, tigers and trout, had turned to watch the expanding hole.

Ebenezum opened his eyes. "A vortex!" he cried. "Quick! We can still close it if we work together!"

A wind rose, sucked into the hole. The creatures of the

Netherhells, bats and rats, mice and lice, were drawn into the dark.

Granach and Vizolea both gestured wildly into the void.

"Together!" Ebenezum cried. "We must work together!" Then he began to sneeze. He pulled his robes to his nose, stepped back from the vortex. It was no use. He doubled over, lost to his malady.

The darkness was taking the jewels now, and the sacks of gold. And I could feel the wind pulling me. Granach screamed at it, and he was drawn in. Vizolea cried against it, then she was gone. The blackness reached out for Hendrek and the king, my master and me.

Ebenezum flung his robes away to shout a few words into the increasing gale. A bar of gold skidded by me and was swallowed. Ebenezum made a pass, and the vortex shrank. He gestured again, and the vortex grew smaller still, about the size of a man.

Then Ebenezum sneezed again.

"Doom!" Hendrek cried. King Urfoo, wide-eyed, was skidding across the floor to the void.

The warrior and I pushed against the wind to his aid. Jewels scattered beneath our feet and were lost. I shoved a chest toward the gaping maw, hoping to cover a part of it, but it was sucked straight through.

"My gold!" Urfoo cried as he rolled for the hole. I snagged a foot, Hendrek grasped the other. I struggled for footing on the loose jewels that rolled across the floor to the void. I slipped and fell into the warrior.

"Doo—oof!" he cried as he lost his balance. He fell back into the hole.

The wind stopped. Hendrek stood, half here and half somewhere else. His girth had plugged the vortex.

Ebenezum blew his nose. "That's better." He recited a few incantations, sneezed once more, and the hole sealed up as we pulled Hendrek free.

My master then gave a brief explanation to the king, who sat glassy-eyed on the now bare floor of the treasury. How his wizards had tried to cheat him of half the treasury by inventing a curse when they couldn't get the money any other way, thanks to the sorcerous charter that called for a member of the royal family to open the door. How Ebenezum had discovered this plot, and how he should be amply rewarded for saving the king's money.

"Money?" King Urfoo the Brave whispered as he looked around. Perhaps a dozen jewels and gold pieces were left where once there had been a room of plenty. "Money! You've taken my money! Guards! Kill them! They've taken my money! Urk!"

Hendrek hit him on top of the head.

"They've—what? Where am I? Oh, hello." The king lost consciousness.

"Doom," Hendrek murmured. "Headbasher does its hellish job again."

My master suggested it might be a good time to travel.

We had to wait some hours in the pouring rain before we could get a ride away from Krenk. Ebenezum had thought it best, in case of pursuit, to cover his wizardly robes with a more neutral cloth of brown, and passing wagons were reticent to pick up characters as motley-looking as the three of us, especially with one the size of Hendrek.

"Perhaps," Ebenezum suggested with a pull on his beard, "we would have better luck if we separated."

"Doom!" Hendrek shivered and clutched at the bag that held Headbasher. "But what of my curse?"

"Hendrek." The wizard put a comradely hand on the large warrior's shoulder. "I can guarantee you'll see nothing of Brax for quite some time. The severity of that vortex was such that it shook through at least three levels of the Netherhells. Take it from an expert; their transportation lines won't be cleared for months!"

"Then," rumbled Hendrek, "I'm freed of Brax and his kind?"

"For the time being. Only a temporary remedy, I'm afraid. I have a certain affliction..." He paused, looking Hendrek straight in the eye. "Also temporary, I assure you, that keeps me from affecting a more permanent cure. However, I shall give you the names of certain sorcerous specialists in Vushta, who should be able to help you immediately." My master wrote three names on a page of his notebook and gave them to the warrior.

Hendrek thrust the piece of parchment in Headbasher's bag, then bowed low to my master. "Thank you, great wizard. To Vushta, then." His head seemed to quake with emotion, but perhaps it was only the rain pouring on his helmet.

"We're bound for Vushta ourselves, eventually," I added. "Perhaps we'll meet again."

"Who knows what the fates will?" said Hendrek as he turned away. "Doom."

He was soon lost in the heavy downpour.

Once the warrior was gone, I looked again to my master. He stood tall in the soaking rain, every inch a wizard despite his disguise. If any doubts had assailed Ebenezum on our arrival in Krenk, his actions in the subsequent events seemed to have erased them from his mind. He was Ebenezum, the finest wizard in all the forest country. And in Krenk as well!

Finally, I could bear it no longer. I asked my master what he knew about the plot against King Urfoo.

" 'Tis simple enough," Ebenezum replied. "Urfoo had the wealth that the wizards wanted, but couldn't get to, because of the charm on the door. So they devised the Spell of the Golden Star, through which, by their definition, Urfoo would have to release half the gold from the charmed tower in order for the spell to work. I don't blame them, in a way. According to Vizolea, the king hadn't gotten around to paying them in all the years they were in his service. Unfortunately, they got greedy, and didn't work in unison, and you saw what happened. They even considered working the Golden Star spell three ways; at least Vizolea suggested as much, although"—my master coughed—"I usually don't engage in such activities."

He looked up and down the deserted road, then reached in his damp coat to pull out a bar of gold. "Good. I was afraid I'd lost it in our flight. I have so many layers of clothing on, I could no longer feel it."

I gaped as he hid the gold again. "How did you get that? The floor of the treasury was stripped."

"The floor was." The wizard nodded. "The insides of my

robes were not. A wizard has to plan ahead, Wunt. Sorcerers are expected to maintain a certain standard of living."

I shook my head. I should never have doubted my master for a moment.

Ebenezum gazed off into the never-ending rain. "Things are afoot, Wuntvor," he said after a moment's pause. "I had not thought we would find this much sorcerous activity this soon."

"We've been lucky, then?" I asked.

"Perhaps. We were lucky, too, in the last few months at our cottage. A half dozen high-paying commissions, all somehow the result of the Netherhells. It has sent us on the road to Vushta far sooner than I had imagined."

The wizard glared up at the sky. The water splashed from his cheekbones and ran in rivulets through his beard. "Oh, if I could risk a weather spell! But I have sneezed far too much today. One more sniff of magic tonight, and I fear my nose would jump from my face."

My master made light of his malady, but still I could tell it troubled him. I did my best to change the subject.

"Tell me about Vushta," I said.

"Ah, Vushta, city of a thousand forbidden delights!" The wizard's mood seemed to lighten with every word. "If a man is not careful, the city might change him completely in the blink of an eye."

It was all I had been hoping for. I begged my master to go on.

"Let's hear no more of magic or fabled cities tonight," was all he would say. "Our luck holds with us. Methinks some sturdy tradesman has come to our rescue."

Indeed, a covered cart had pulled to the side of the road. Perhaps we would spend a dry and quiet night after all.

"Need a ride?" the driver called. We clambered in the back.

" 'Tis a dismal night," the driver continued. "I'll sing you a song to lift your spirits. That's what I am—a traveling minstrel!"

Ebenezum looked out from his hood in alarm, then averted his face so that it was lost in shadow.

"Let's see what would be appropriate?" The minstrel tugged the reins of his mule. "Ah! Just the thing for a night straight from the Netherhells. I'll sing you a song about the bravest wizard around; fellow from the forest country up Gurnish way. Um... Neebednuzum, I think he's called. Now, this ditty's a little long, but I think you'll be struck by the fellow's bravery."

Ebenezum had fallen asleep by the third verse.

CHAPTER FIVE

Your average ghost is a much more complex and interesting individual than is generally imagined. Just because someone is dragging chains or has one's head perpetually in flames does not necessarily make them of a lesser class. Some ghosts, especially those with heads attached and mouths to speak through, are actually quite good conversationalists, with other-worldly stories by the score. In addition, ghosts generally subscribe to the happy custom of disappearing completely at dawn, a habit many living associates and relatives might do well to cultivate.

—from The Teachings of Ebenezum, Volume VI (Appendix B)

After our harrowing experience with King Urfoo in Krenk, I think both Ebenezum and myself expected our luck to change. Perhaps we would at last find a wizard great enough to cure my master without having to travel to far Vushta.

But the city of a thousand forbidden delights began to seem more of a possibility with every passing day. What with being chased out of one kingdom and not being particularly welcome in the next two, we hadn't a chance to meet any wizards at all. Then there'd been the mercenaries Urfoo had sent to kill us, and the seven straight days of rain, and the incident with the giant swamp rats. I didn't even want to think of those.

But still my master walked on, proud and tall, toward far, forbidden Vushta. And I would follow him there, and anywhere. Even with his affliction, Ebenezum was the greatest wizard I had ever seen!

I touched my walking stick to my forehead in a silent salute to the man before me. Our luck was bound to change!

It was then that I lost my footing and slid down the hill, colliding with my master.

Our fall ended in a cluster of bushes at the valley bottom. Not looking at me, the wizard stood with a groan that was like the rumble of an approaching storm. He turned much too slowly to face me. I watched the eyes beneath bushy brows and waited for the inevitable.

"Wuntvor," the mage said, his voice like an earthquake splitting a mountainside. "If you can't watch where you put your—"

My master stopped midsentence and stared over my head. I began to stammer an apology, but the wizard waved me to silence.

"What do you hear, 'prentice?" he asked.

I listened but heard nothing. I told him so.

"Exactly," he replied. "Nothing at all. 'Tis the end of summer, deep in the wood, yet I do not see a single bird nor hear an insect. Though I must admit, the absence of the latter does not upset me overmuch." The mage scratched at a pink welt beneath his long white beard. We had had a great deal of experience, ever since the seven days of rain, with clouds of mosquitoes and biting gnats.

"Methinks, Wunt, something is amiss."

I listened for a moment more. My master was right. The forest was silent, the only sounds the breathing of the wizard and myself. I had never heard quiet like this, except perhaps on the coldest days of winter. A chill went up my back, surprising in the late summer's heat.

My master dusted off his robes. "We seem to have landed near a clearing." He nodded down what remained of the hill. "Perhaps we shall find some habitation, even someone who can explain the nature of this place. Until then, we will bask in the absence of mosquitoes." He scratched his neck absently as he started down the hill. "Always look on the bright side, Wunt."

I hurriedly gathered up the foodstuffs, books, and magical paraphernalia that had fallen from my pack and followed my master's wizardly strides. I scrambled after him over the uneven ground, avoiding what underbrush there was. But the brush thinned rapidly as we walked, and we found ourselves facing a large clearing of bare earth, broken only by a ring of seven large boulders in its center.

"Now we've even lost the grasses," Ebenezum rumbled. "Come, Wunt, we'll find the cause of this." He took great strides across the bare ground, clouds of dust rising with every step. I followed close behind, doing my best not to cough.

When we reached the first boulder, something jumped.

"Boo!" the something said. I dropped my pack, but Ebenezum simply stood there and watched the apparition.

"Indeed," he said after a moment.

"Boo! Boo! Boo! Boo!" the creature confronting us shrieked. On closer inspection, I could see that it was definitely human, with long gray hair covering the face and brown rags concealing the body. The person raised frail hands and rushed us on unsteady legs.

Neither of us moved. Our attacker stopped, out of breath. "Not going to work, is it?" she wheezed at last. It was an old woman; her speaking voice was cracked and high.

Ebenezum stroked his mustache. "Is what not going to work?"

"Can't scare you away, huh?" She parted the long hair that covered her face and peered at the sky. "Probably too late for you to get away, anyhow. Might as well sit down and wait." She looked around for a likely rock and sat.

"Indeed," Ebenezum repeated. "Wait for what?"

"You don't know?" The woman's eyes widened in wonder. "Sir, you are in the dreaded Valley of Vrunge!"

"Indeed," Ebenezum said when it became apparent the woman planned to say no more.

"Now don't tell me you've never heard of it. What, do you come from the ignorant Western Kingdoms?" The woman laughed derisively. "Everyone knows of the Valley of Vrunge, and the dread curse that falls upon it once every one hundred and thirty-seven years. Not that this place is all that friendly at any time"—she spat on the parched earth— "but there is one night, every one hundred thirty-seven years, when all hell breaks loose. One night when no one then in the valley will get out alive!"

I didn't like the direction the woman's speech was taking.

I swallowed hard and cleared my throat. "Ma'am, would you mind telling us just when that night is?"

"Haven't I made it clear?" The crone laughed again. "This is the cursed night of the Valley of Vrunge. It begins when the sun passes yonder hills." She pointed behind me.

I followed her arm and looked to the sun, already touching the top of the western hills, then turned to Ebenezum. He stared above me, lost in thought. It appeared our luck was running true to course.

"If we are all due to die," Ebenezum said at last, "what are you doing here?"

The old woman looked away from us. "I have my reasons, which I'm sure would be of little interest to anyone but me. Let us just say that once this land was green and fair, and it was ruled over by a princess as lovely as the land itself. But a dark time came upon the earth, and the sky rained toads, and the princess became afraid. But her suitor, the handsome—" "You are quite right," Ebenezum interrupted. "No one would be interested in that at all. You've decided to die because the sky rained toads?"

The woman sighed and watched the sun disappear behind the hilltop. "Not exactly. I've worn this body out. I'm due to die. I just thought I'd see old Maggie out in style."

"Maggie?" Ebenezum scratched his insect bite thoughtfully. "That would be short for Magredel?" He peered into her ancient face.

"Oh, I haven't used that name in years. Not since I got away from those dull Western Kingdoms. Used to practice witchery thereabouts for a time, that's probably where you heard of me. Didn't specialize much, though. More of a general practitioner." "Maggie?" Ebenezum repeated. "As in old Aunt Maggie?"

Maggie squinted her eyes in turn. "Say, do I know you from someplace?"

There was an explosion directly behind me. All three of us spun to see a tall, pale apparition atop the tallest of the seven stones.

"Greetings, ladies and gentlemen!" the apparition cried with a swirl of its robe. "And welcome to curse night!"

"Greetings to you, too, Death," Maggie replied. "I hope tonight will be up to your usual standards?" Death laughed, a high, echoey sound that came near to scaring the life out of me. When I mentioned it later to Ebenezum, he said that was no doubt the desired reaction.

The apparition atop the stone disappeared.

"That was our introduction," Maggie remarked. "Soon the fun begins."

I was appalled. "F-fun?" I stammered. "How do you know what happens next?"

"Simple." The crone flashed a toothless smile. "I've been through this night once before."

Now that Death had vanished, the silence was again complete. My master cleared his throat.

"Ebenezum!" the old woman cried. "Of course! I'd recognize that nervous cough anywhere. Poor little Ebby, always coughing or scratching or tugging or doing something. He never could sit still." She winked in my direction. "You know, in the whole first year he studied under me, he didn't get one spell straight? You should have seen the things that showed up in our kitchen!" She laughed.

My master cast a worried glance at the rock where Death had stood. "Please, Aunt Maggie. I don't think this is the proper time to discuss—"

"Oh, keep your cap on!" The woman clapped Ebenezum on the shoulder. "We have a little time. It always takes them a while to get organized. When you only have one performance every one hundred thirty-seven years, you tend to get a bit rusty."

"But what's going to happen?" I asked. I noticed my hand hurt from my tight grip on my walking stick.

"Ghosts, ghosts, and more ghosts." The old woman spat on the ground. "Death is fond of games. He plays a game with every living thing, one in which he's always the victor. Some games he likes more than others, and those great conflicts he brings here, to play over and over again in the Valley of Vrunge!"

"The spirits just play games?" I asked. That didn't sound so bad.

"All of life is a game, remember. Death brings along the best of all his games, ranging from a nation at war to two people in love."

She jumped and screamed.

"Tickle, tickle, tickle," said a high voice from nowhere.

"Poltergeists! Boo! Boo! Boo! Away from here!" Maggie waved her hands about wildly. "More and more ghosts will appear throughout the night. And Death will try to snare you in his games. Beware, he always wins!" She screamed and jumped again.

"Boo, boo, boo?" the voice from nowhere asked. "That's passé, lady. These days, long, sensitive moans are much more the thing in ghostly circles."

"So it begins. I'm sorry, Ebby, you had to stumble into this!" She ran and screamed as "tickle, tickle tickle!" chased her around the circle of boulders.

Ebenezum sneezed once and blew his nose on a silver-inlaid sleeve. "Just a minor spirit. Hardly bothers me at all."

I realized then that this was the first time Ebenezum's malady had affected him since we entered the cursed valley. Perhaps the severity of our situation was effecting a cure. Ebenezum had not sneezed once in the presence of Death!

My master shook his head when I explained my theory. "Why should I sneeze? Death is the most natural thing in the world." He pulled at his beard. "And I fear that, should we fail to devise a plan of action, Death will become all too familiar to both of us."

A great wind sprang up. My master had to shout to be heard. "Stay close! If we're separated—"

The wizard sneezed as three ghosts on a sled grabbed him and whisked him high in the air. Ghosts, sled, and sneezing Ebenezum disappeared around the stones.

Night had fallen completely, and I was alone.

But then there was a crowd around me, sitting on long rows of seats, one atop another, as if they were built on a hillside. The crowd roared, and I saw they were watching a group of uniformed men on a green lawn, a few of whom were running, but most of whom were standing still.

A man carrying a big silver box walked up the steps toward

me. "Hot dogs!" he cried. "Hot dogs!"

He wasn't real, I told myself. This whole place was beyond my understanding. I stepped aside to let him pass. He stopped next to me anyway.

"Hot dog, mister?"

It was only with a mental effort that I kept from shivering. I looked down at my stout oak staff. My grip was firm. If the apparition tried anything, I'd swing at him. And then again, from what I'd heard of ghosts, I might swing through him as well.

With some trepidation, I asked: "What's a hot dog?"

"Like I thought"—the spirit nodded sagely—"you're an outsider. So this is your first ball game? Well, you picked a good one, buddy."

I looked out over the field below us. "Ball game," I repeated, struggling to comprehend.

"Yeah," the apparition replied. "The ball game. People had counted the Red Sox out, but they came around. Now Torrez will blow the Yankees away! Seventy-eight is going to be our year. It has to be."

I looked closely at the spirit, hoping that some gesture or facial mannerism would help me to understand his ravings. All I saw was the haunted look, deep in his eyes.

"Has to be?" I asked.

"Well, yeah." The ghost paused. "I mean, the Sox have to win. Otherwise..." He shuddered. "Do you have any idea what it would be like to have to sell hot dogs throughout eternity?"

He didn't wait for an answer but walked up the stairs beyond me. I turned to the "ball game" on the field below. I felt a sudden, near overwhelming urge to be drawn into that game and find out just what could move the hot dog spirit to such a frenzy. I'd watch the shifting patterns of men on the bright green lawn, and sooner or later some great secret would be revealed, a joyous revelation that would make my whole existence take on new meaning!

Something in the back of my head told me to turn away. I remembered Aunt Maggie's warning about Death and games.

The ball game disappeared. In its place stood Death.

"There you are," the creature said in his sonorous voice. "I've been looking all over for you. These curse evenings can be so long and boring, sometimes I like to indulge in games to help pass the time. Tell me, do you know how to play Red Light, Green Light?"

Death stood much closer than he had before. I stared at the thin layer of pale skin pulled tight over his skull, and at the shadows where there should have been eyes. Yet his smile was ingratiating. You wanted to believe in what he told you, rather like a good seller of used pack animals on market day.

"Well?" Death prompted.

"N-no!" I stammered. "I-I don't know the rules!"

"Oh, is that all." Death reached out to touch my arm. "I'll explain everything. I'm very good with rules."

"No! I have to find my master!" I pulled away from the creature's hand and ran blindly.

Suddenly a pit yawned before me. A pit filled with sharpened spikes and a great, roaring monster, all mouth and teeth and claws. I tried to stop, to step backward, but I was over the edge, falling, falling.

Someone barked a command behind me; my master's voice. I found myself on solid ground, standing by Ebenezum. All the ghosts were gone.

Ebenezum sneezed repeatedly, rocking with the force emitted by his nose.

"Temporary exorcism spell," he gasped at last. "Best I can manage."

I did a short jig on the parched earth while my master caught his breath. Ebenezum had freed himself from the sledding spirits! Hope once again rose within my breast.

I asked him how he'd accomplished his escape.

The wizard shrugged. "I sneezed my way free. The ghosts were ready for sorcery, a battle of wits, anything but extreme nasal activity. They simply evaporated before the onslaught of my nose."

"That's wonderful!" I cried. "We'll be free of this cursed valley in no time!"

Ebenezum shook his head. "Death does not make the same

mistake twice. The next set of apparitions will be ready for my malady."

Aunt Maggie appeared around one of the seven great boulders. She staggered over to Ebenezum's feet and collapsed.

She groaned, then turned to look at my master. "It's gone! The poltergeist is gone!"

The wizard nodded solemnly. "Exorcism spell."

Maggie sighed in relief. "It kept taunting me, begging me to tickle it back. You can't give in to those things. It would have been all over." She looked at Ebenezum. "Exorcism? That means you followed your calling and graduated into wizardry! I did hesitate to ask you. In the early days, you were very determined, but your aptitude was sometimes less than—"

Ebenezum cleared his throat. "'Tis only a temporary spell. Death's power is greater than common magic, and the ghosts will push through presently. We must come up with a more permanent solution."

Maggie laughed. "I pulled through this cursed night once, with the aid of magic. Maybe we can do so again. And gain my kingdom back in the bargain!" She slapped my master's shoulder. "So one of my students made good? Let's see you do your stuff. Nothing fancy; a bird out of thin air, water into wine, something to catch an old woman's fancy."

Ebenezum fixed her with a wizardly stare. "We are in peril for our lives. I need to concentrate." He stalked off and disappeared into the circle of stone.

Maggie shook her head and smiled. "A great wizardly manner. He must be raking in the business." She sighed. "Wish I could work magic the way I used to. After a while, the body gives out. Can toss off a spell now and again, when I'm feeling spry. But the big ones are beyond my reach."

I hesitated to tell her that due to my master's affliction, just about all the spells that could save us from our present predicament were beyond his reach as well. Best not to upset her. I was upset enough for both of us.

"But let me tell you my story, and you'll understand why I'm here," she began. "You've already learned of the fair kingdom, and the beautiful princess. And then, of course, there were the raining toads. And did I tell you about the princess's handsome suitor, Unwin, killed on their wedding day? No? Well, that's a good place to—"

"Tickle, tickle, tickle," the disembodied voice chortled. The exorcism spell was over.

A cool breeze blew in my ear. "Hey, big boy," a woman whispered. "What's a fellow like you doing without a date on a night like this?"

I turned to gaze on the most beautiful apparition I had ever seen. I was speechless. She was slender and pale, with long silver hair. And she wore no clothing at all, ghostly or otherwise. At certain angles, you could see right through her, but at other angles she was more than my eyes could bear.

"Oh, the silent type," she said, and took my hand, her fingers intertwining with mine. Her touch was ice. It sent thrills up my arm and across my shoulders. She leaned close, and her breath was the breeze of autumn. Her lips parted, close to mine. I wanted to kiss those lips more than I wanted life itself.

"I know a little game we can play," the full, cool lips said. "It's called Spin the Bottle."

Yes, yes, whatever it was, yes! All those girls I'd known in the Western Kingdoms, even Alea, my afternoon beauty, they were nothing to me now.

But my beloved was pulled away from me and sent spinning through the air, her ectoplasm flying in every direction.

"I can still toss off a spell or two." Maggie smiled. "Got to watch out for succubi. Not good for your health."

"Crone!" Death was before us. "What would you know of love? Your body has been old and withered for a hundred years. An empty shell which can no longer be filled. Or can it?"

Death waved his hand and a young man materialized at his side.

"Unwin?" The old woman's voice was little more than a whisper. "Is that you, Unwin?"

"Magredel!" the young man cried. "What's happened to you?"

"It's not me, Unwin. It's you. You've been away. I haven't seen you in so long!"

The old woman was crying.

"Consider, woman," Death said. "Come with me and you will be together always."

But Maggie turned on him, anger replacing sorrow. "No! You've stolen my kingdom for centuries! I'll be with Unwin soon enough! I must free what was tricked from me!"

"Such harsh words." Death examined his skeletal hand. "I have need of this place. My ghosts must have their exercise." He looked at me, and I shivered where I stood. "Come, Wuntvor. Let's leave these lovers alone while they talk things over. I'll give you the guided tour."

Without thinking, I found myself following him. Death smiled. "Simon says put your hands in the air."

It took all my willpower to keep my hands at my sides.

"We'll find one yet." Death's hands were full of small rectangles, which he fanned out before him. "How about a little Go Fish?"

I found myself staring at the rectangles. I looked the other way.

"My kingdom," Death said.

There were apparitions everywhere. Armies fighting, women laughing, people in costumes familiar and unfamiliar, crawling across the ground, climbing the trees, flying through the air in strange machines.

"Amazing," I said despite myself.

Death nodded. "The paperwork alone is staggering. Yet we pull it off, every one hundred thirty-seven years. It's a shame our audience has to be so small. The Vrunge Curse is my masterpiece. Here are all the greatest moments of humanity, past, present, future, played out over and over again, from men at war to men at play, games of chance to games of love. A pity. Perhaps I should advertise."

Death coughed gently. "Tell me, Wuntvor. Who is the greatest magician in all the Western Kingdom?" Was he trying to trick me? I'd stay firm to my beliefs. "Why, Ebenezum, of course."

"Right!" Death cried as a gong sounded somewhere nearby. "Wuntvor, you've just won an additional five years on your life!"

We were surrounded by bright light. The ghosts all sat in a

large amphitheater now, whistling and cheering. The succubus I had almost kissed stood a little bit to one side, next to a large board that read "5." She was wearing some sort of spangled costume that managed to look more revealing than her nudity had before.

"Okay!" Death smiled broadly. "Now, Wunt, for ten additional years! Tell us, who is the ruler of Melifox?"

The crowd whistled and stamped their feet. Urgent music came from somewhere. The succubus smiled her magnificent smile.

"Uh—King Urfoo the Brave!" I blurted.

"Right, for ten more years!"

The crowd went wild. The spangled beauty flipped a couple of cards over the board to one that read "15."

"All right! All right!" Death raised his hands for silence. "Now it's time for the question we've all been waiting for. Double or nothing!"

The crowd cheered.

"Now, Wuntvor, are you ready to double your life span?"

"Yes! Yes!" The crowd chanted. I nodded my head. Why not? This was easy.

"All right! The big question, Wuntvor, to double your life span or erase it altogether! Who was the famous chamberlain of the Eastern Kingdoms, three centuries ago, who used to mutter to himself, " 'One of these days, one of these days'?"

"What?" I asked. How could I know something like that?

"Quick, Wuntvor! The Quiz Lady has set the clock. You have fifteen seconds to answer, or pay the penalty, on Forfeit Your Life!"

What? What could I do? I didn't know anything about the Eastern Kingdoms. The dramatic music was back, louder than ever. The crowd was roaring. I couldn't think. Why hadn't I listened to Maggie and kept away from these games?

"Ten!" the crowd chanted. "Nine! Eight! Seven! Six! Five!"

"Gangway! Gangway! Boo! Boo! Boo!" The entire crowd turned to look at Aunt Maggie, riding atop Ebenezum's shoulders as the wizard rushed into our midst. And Maggie was holding Ebenezum's nose!

"Batwom Ignatius, Wuntvor!" my master cried. "Batwom Ignatius!"

"Batwom Ignatius?" I replied.

"Is right!" Death exclaimed. "You've doubled your life! Barring illness or accident, of course."

The crowd started to go wild, but Maggie chanted a few syllables and Ebenezum waved his hands. The crowd noise receded.

Ebenezum sneezed once, loudly, as Aunt Maggie climbed down from his back. I asked him how he knew about Ignatius.

"Had to learn it for my wizard finals," he replied. "It's amazing the useless knowledge they make you pack into your skull."

"Such a pitiful spell," Death remarked. "Why did you do it? They'll all be back in a moment."

"I wanted to talk to you alone," the wizard replied.

"Your affliction will come back, too, when they return. Is that what you're afraid of? Come with me, Ebenezum, and you need never sneeze again."

"Perhaps I will." Ebenezum tugged at his sleeves. "I have heard, Death, that you are fond of games. Will you play one with me?"

Death sneered. "You toy with me, wizard. No one toys with Death! Quick, what will it be? Parcheesi? Contract bridge? Fifty-two pickup?"

The wizard pulled on his beard for a moment, then intoned: "Arm wrestling."

Death shrugged. "If you insist." He snapped his fingers, and a table and chairs materialized between them.

"Now the terms." Ebenezum looked Death in the eye socket. "If I win, the three of us go free, and Maggie regains her kingdom. If I lose, I am yours."

Death smiled. "For someone of your eminence, anything. I always enjoy welcoming someone whom the bards sing about. After you." He indicated a chair.

Ebenezum sat. I thought that the ghostly crowd noises were somewhat closer. Ebenezum would have to hurry, or his nose might betray him.

Death smoothed his snow-white robe and sat opposite my master. His smile, if anything, was broader than before.

"Shall we begin, dear wizard?"

Ebenezum put his elbow to the table. Death did the same. Their hands clasped.

The ghostly crowd was definitely closer. I could see pale flickerings across the clearing.

"Now!" Death said, and Ebenezum tensed his whole body. There was no movement beyond the constant quiver where the two hands met.

And then the ghosts were back upon us, all talking and screaming and laughing at once. "I'm hit!" "You're out!" "Got you!" "Hot dogs!" "Tickle, tickle, tickle!"

"Dishonest Death!" Maggie screamed. "This was to be an even contest, without your ghostly consorts!"

Death laughed. Maggie said something else that I didn't quite catch.

And Ebenezum sneezed.

And what a sneeze! Ghosts went flying. Death pulled back in alarm and was caught in the gale, along with his table and chair.

It was silent all around. I saw the first light of dawn in the east.

"Will they be back?" I asked, my voice little more than a whisper.

"Alas, Wuntvor," the wizard said, "I fear they haven't the ghost of a chance." Then he blew his nose.

Ebenezum and Maggie walked over to one of the great stones so recently toppled by the wizard's sneezing attack, while I surveyed in wonder the devastation a single great sneeze could bring to this already bleak land. Ebenezum helped Maggie to sit on the fallen boulder, then seated himself.

"How?" was my only question.

"Ebby never could keep a secret from me." Maggie cackled. "But his aversion to sorcery presented something of a problem if we were to survive the night."

My master pulled at his beard. "I freed you from Unwin, remember."

"All I had to do was choose to talk to you rather than him. Unwin always was impossibly jealous. Flew off in an ectoplasmic snit. Which made you sneeze about five times."

Ebenezum tried to say something, but Maggie kept right on talking. "That's when I had the idea. If he always sneezed around the supernatural, what if he really sneezed! We couldn't take away his problem, so the two of us worked up a little spell that would increase Ebby's nasal power a hundredfold!"

"Indeed," Ebenezum said, rubbing his nose, which was red from blowing.

"And now we're safe. And the kingdom is free. Or is it?" Maggie spat on the ground. "Death is such a trickster. I was so afraid of him when Unwin died, I gave in and let him give me five lifetimes for what he termed 'occasional use of my kingdom.' What he didn't tell me was that nothing could live in the kingdom between the times he used it." She looked around her. "Has he kept his word? If only there was a sign."

She slapped Ebenezum's shoulder. "But you still haven't heard my story."

Ebenezum looked out over the hills. "Alas, teacher, we have a long way to travel. Shoulder your pack, Wunt. We'd best move before the sun gets too high."

"You'll sit here and listen!" Maggie commanded. "Ebby never did have any manners. From the beginning. Once there was a beautiful kingdom, and a fair princess. But all was not well, for one day came the dreaded rain of—"

"Ow!" I yelled. Something had bitten my arm. Ebenezum jumped up. "Biting gnats! They're all over us!"

Maggie threw her hands up to the heavens. "My kingdom is saved!"

"Drop us a note when 'tis a little better developed!" the wizard called over his shoulder.

And we were once again traveling, somewhat more rapidly than before, with frequent slapping of arms and legs, in the general direction of Vushta.

CHAPTER SIX

A wizard cannot do everything; a fact most magicians are reticent to admit, let alone discuss with prospective clients. Still, the fact remains that there are certain objects, and people, that are, for one reason or another, completely immune to any direct magical spell. It is for this group of beings that the magician learns the subtleties of using indirect spells. It also does no harm, in dealing with these matters, to carry a large club near your person at all times.

—from The Teachings of Ebenezum, Volume VIII

My master sneezed at last. I had been expecting it for quite some time. Ever since we had begun our descent into this new valley, three days' distance from our harrowing experience in the Valley of Vrunge, I had once again noticed a general deterioration of the surrounding landscape: a tree uprooted here or there, an occasional house or barn pounded to splinters, whole sections of farmers' fields gouged from the earth. It looked altogether unhealthy.

I think that by this time, neither my master nor myself were particularly surprised by this turn of events. Sorcery seemed to follow us wherever we might go on the trail to Vushta. Still, as Ebenezum had remarked as we sat by our last evening's cookfire, we had not fared badly so far in the midst of all this magic. Indeed, in some cases we had made a fair profit from our sorcerous dealings. In fact, should certain magical events continue to occur on the course of our travels, we might arrive in Vushta as truly wealthy men.

"There is more than one way to look at luck," Ebenezum had concluded as he settled himself down to sleep. "Never look a gift spell in the runes, Wunt."

But that had been easy for the wizard to say the night before, while we were still far away from this present magic. Now, all Ebenezum could do was sneeze.

There was a tremendous crash in the distance. The wizard's sneezes echoed the chaos.

Someone was calling to us. It was a young woman, close to my age. Her long dark hair streamed behind her as she ran in our direction.

"Hide!" she called. "Quickly, hide before Uxtal finds—" She stopped short a few paces from us, a look of consternation on her beautiful face. "You're a wizard!"

Ebenezum stroked his beard and knitted his bushy brows. "How very observant. How may we serve you, my dear?" His sneezing fit seemed to have disappeared behind his veneer of professionalism.

"You can get those robes off as quickly as possible!" Her deep green eyes looked from side to side, taking in all of the valley. "Maybe we can find some old rags to disguise you as a peasant. Does the inlay of silver stars go all the way through to the other side of the fabric? Maybe, if you wore them inside out, we could pretend you were a monk!"

"Young lady!" My master's eyes glowed with sorcerous indignation. "You want me to hide my wizardry?"

"No, no," the woman said impatiently. " 'Twould be best to hide if you were just common folk. Being a wizard, 'twould be best if you fled the valley altogether."

It was then that I saw the giant.

The giant roared. He was huge, towering over the tallest trees, his feet spread on either side of a broad, rushing river. His hair was matted, his beard long and unkempt, and he showed uneven, yellowed teeth when he growled. Teeth so large they would have no trouble snapping a person in half.

"Fo fo fum fee," he rumbled. "I don't like these other three." He then tossed a rather large boulder he happened to be holding in our direction.

Ebenezum tried to free his hands from the folds of his robes for a quick conjure, but the presence of the giant threw him into a prolonged sneezing bout before he could even straighten his elbows. I moved toward the young lady, hoping to carry her away from the path of the rapidly descending rock. But she pushed me away.

And said a spell herself.

The boulder flew back toward the giant.

"Fee fo fum fi!" he shrieked. "Time for me to say good-bye!" The giant crashed down into the valley and was soon lost from sight.

I stared at the woman. I realized my mouth was open. I shut it. So beautiful and so talented! I wondered what it would be like to marry into the profession.

"I saw that!" A small man scurried from behind a ruined stone wall. Ebenezum blew his nose mightily.

The small man hopped across the stony field. He wore some sort of bright-colored uniform, alternately yellow and green, an outfit complemented by the livid red of his complexion.

"You know magic is strictly forbidden!" he shrieked. "Practicing magic means your death!"

The woman looked to where the rock had flown. "It would have meant my death if I had not used magic."

"Technicalities!" the small man screamed. "Twill not save you from the hangman's noose!" His eyes darted to my master. "You. You're wearing wizard's robes!"

"Indeed. Everyone in your valley is very observant." My master sniffed.

"Well..." The man paused, tongue poked in cheek. "You've yet to conjure. With luck, you'll only get twenty years hard labor."

"But they've just entered the valley!" the woman exclaimed. "How could they—"

"Ignorance of the law is no excuse!" The man caught a silver whistle dangling around his neck and blew a mighty blow. "I've called my minions to take you away."

The minions appeared from behind the same stone wall that produced the government official. They were of much the same size as the first man, though of decidedly different origin; mud brown in color, with barbed tails, long taloned arms, and small heads dominated by wide, grinning mouths. They hummed, ominously and in unison.

"Take them to the dungeon in the hill!" The small man managed to shriek and laugh simultaneously.

The dozen minions spread out before us. Their humming grew louder and fiercer as they approached. Ebenezum was lost to us, sneezing somewhere deep within his voluminous robes.

The woman stepped valiantly forward, her hands extended to call magical aid. But would such meager aid as she could summon instantly be enough to defeat a squad of demon-things? Something had to be done.

I stepped to her side and raised my stout oak staff.

"Aha!" the man in uniform cried. "The old man has surrendered, yet you two still resist. Do not cross me!" He, too, waved his hands in front of him in standard conjuring position. "I will show you my power! I warn you, I have been practicing!"

The hands moved through a complicated pattern as the man chanted beneath his breath. He laughed. "See how you contend with this!"

He pointed both his hands at us. For a moment, nothing happened. Then a pair of white birds emerged from his sleeves.

"I didn't want birds!" The man's uniform flapped as he jumped up and down. "Minions! Take them away!"

The muddy demons approached. Their humming was all around us. Both the young woman and I took an involuntary step backward and bumped into each other. I turned to stammer an apology, and the demons were upon us.

"Yanna!" she cried. "Nothalatno! Away!"

I struck out with my stout oak staff. My master, attempting to recover and come to our aid, rolled against my foot. From the corner of my eye, I saw a demon grab the woman's hair.

"Look out!" I cried, and swung the staff at the demon without thinking. But the arc of the blow was too great. My feet stumbled against the still sneezing wizard as the staff bounced from the demon's head with a resounding thwack!, then ricocheted from the woman's shoulder. She yelped in surprise and fell against me. I completely lost my balance in turn and collapsed atop the stricken mage. Before I could untangle myself, we were all three rolling down the hill.

Ebenezum shouted something as we rolled. When we hit the ground at valley bottom, it felt like a pillow. My master had managed a spell again. At least, I thought it was my master.

"Quick thinking!" the woman said. "My spells were virtually useless. Only brute action of the type you employed could save the day."

" 'Twas nothing," I said, humbly studying the rocky ground on which we had landed. "Any magician's apprentice would have done the same."

The young woman mentioned we had not been properly introduced. Her name was Norei.

"Ebenezum," my master said before I could speak. He brushed and straightened his robes. "Mage of the West. My apprentice is Wuntvor."

I bowed slightly and almost fell over. I was, perhaps, still a bit dizzy from our fall. I looked up, and Norei was smiling.

" 'Tis fortunate you have come," she said. "We have need of two more heads that are good with spells. My mother, Solima, will be glad for the help. As you see, terrible things are happening in this valley. Things that threaten to destroy not only this community"—she paused, and her voice dropped to a whisper—"but also the very reality in which we live."

What could be so awful as to destroy reality? I looked at my master, but he stared far beyond the hills to either side of us.

"Solima," he whispered.

Norei led us into the woods that seemed to cover much of the valley floor. I followed close at her heels, while Ebenezum trailed some distance behind. She led us down a winding path, well marked in places, overgrown with weeds and brambles in others, until, deep in the forest, we came to a small clearing. A tiny cottage was nestled in one corner of the open space.

"My home," Norei said as she led us through the open door.

"Solima!" my master cried.

A woman of middle years looked up from the pot she was tending and stared at my master. She wiped her hands on her gray robe. "Ebenezum? Is that you?"

"Indeed." My master doffed his wizard's cap. "All the

way from the Western Kingdoms. I had heard you might be practicing in the area, but I had little hope of meeting you."

Solima offered my master a sad smile. "It's good to see you, Eb. That white beard fits you; it makes you look less of a scoundrel. Alas, the rest of what you say isn't quite true. Situations have arisen in this valley that may prevent me from ever practicing magic again."

"We met Tork on the way here, Mother."

"So you've met the prince!" Solima pulled a pipe out of her sleeve and knocked it against the long table that filled the center of the room. "Was he hospitable to the newcomers?"

"He tried to arrest us!" Norei replied.

"For Tork, that's hospitality." She snapped her fingers, and smoke rose from the pipe bowl. She puffed at the stem. "Did you tell them anything of our plight, daughter?"

"I was too worried Tork might find us again."

"Quite so. Let me tell you about our liege lord."

"Solima." Ebenezum took a step forward. "Let me tell you about your eyes."

"Ebenezum! It's been years!" She glared at the wizard with the same green eyes she had given her daughter. "Besides, you're changing the subject. Prince Tork is not a matter to be taken lightly."

My master sighed and shrugged. "Indeed. He was the wizard we met?"

"Well, he fancies himself a wizard. He's never gotten one spell straight that I know of. But he's jealous of all those who can conjure rightly, and so has banned all other wizardry but his throughout the valley."

"He's got everything backward!" Norei added. "His evil spells come out good, and his good spells come out evil!"

"Luckily for us," Solima continued. "Tork's nature is such that he seldom contemplates a good spell. Still, he has managed to conjure all sorts of creatures from the Netherhells, including a giant with a rather foul temper."

Ebenezum scratched at his beard. "It does sound serious. Yet if he is so inept, couldn't you cast a spell to neutralize him or banish him somewhere?"

Solima sighed. "If we had realized in time, it would have been easy. But Tork is such a buffoon that we ignored him, until suddenly he came marching to our door with an army of demons to take my two sisters captive."

"Blackmailed by an inept wizard..." My master's brow furrowed in thought. "There's no way to overcome his allies from the Netherhells?"

"None that I can think of. You know the way my family has always made magic, Ebenezum. 'Tis a collective process, with every woman joining in. That's when our witchery is most powerful. With my two sisters gone, that power is greatly diminished. There's still Norei and Grandmother, of course—"

"Grandmother?" A certain dread had crept into the wizard's voice. "She's still alive?"

Solima nodded. "She lives in the attic."

"Would she remember me?"

"Grandmother forgets nothing."

"Perhaps," Ebenezum said, "my apprentice and I should rest a while. Perhaps in a barn or some outlying field."

"Don't worry. She seldom comes downstairs." Solima banged her pipe against the table again. "Besides, we haven't told you the worst part of Tork's incantations."

Ebenezum glanced at the ladder leading above. "Perhaps if we discussed it while we walked outside? I could stand to stretch my legs."

"Nonsense. Listen to me now. Every time a spell does not work, Tork gets a little more frustrated. And with every frustration, he decides he must tackle a somewhat more complicated spell to prove himself. This disturbing tendency has escalated to such a point that, probably this very night, Tork will attempt Fisbay's Grand Forxsnagel."

What little blood remained in Ebenezum's face vanished entirely. "The Forxsnagel? But should that fail..."

"Exactly. I should imagine that this valley would become the eighth Netherhell. And who knows? Perhaps the whole world would follow."

There was silence for a long moment, then Norei spoke. "Perhaps, Mother, the wizard's suggestion is best. We should let the two of them rest. Then, when the Forxsnagel begins, both wizard and apprentice can join us, five strong, to battle it."

Solima puffed on her pipe for a moment, then nodded. Norei led us from the tiny cottage to an even tinier shed in back. Ebenezum followed quietly.

He spoke the instant Norei had left. "She does have the most beautiful green eyes, Wunt. We had our moment together, back when I was near your age. But her grandmother!" He coughed.

I had never seen my master quite like this before. For want of something to say, I asked him about the Forxsnagel.

"Mm?" The question seemed to bring the wizard back to his senses for a moment. "Oh, 'tis the Overspell, the one great conjure that will make the whole world yours for the taking. It's purely theoretical magic, of course, never been attempted before. Ah, but those green eyes, Wunt! I came this way on our journey toward Vushta to see if Solima still lived here. She is a great witch, fully my equal. But when I saw her eyes again, I forgot my malady, the reason, I thought, I had come. Ah, if only the old woman weren't alive!"

I was beginning to seriously worry for my master. His usual professionalism seemed to have vanished with one glance from Solima. He had neglected to tell either of the witches that his ailment prevented him from even being in the presence of wizardry, while I was probably the world's only magician's apprentice who had never been taught any magic. Yet in a matter of hours, we were expected to rally against the greatest spell ever conjured.

An earth tremor shook the shack. There was a giant's foot outside the window.

"Fee fi fo fum! Uxtal for revenge has come!"

The magician held his nose. " 'Tis up to us now! Open my pack and get out the red book! Page forty-six!"

I ruffled as rapidly as possible through the jumble of books and arcane equipment. Finally I spied a thin red tome beneath a bundle of dried herbs. I pulled the book from the pack and examined it. Sorcery Made Simple was stamped on the cover in large gold letters. Beneath that, in smaller script, were the words "E-Z-Spell Library #6." I rapidly turned to page forty-six as my master finally sneezed.

"THE BANISHMENT OF GIANTS," bold block letters proclaimed across the top. This was followed by a brief description of types of giant—from what little I read, Uxtal seemed to be a Northern Blue—and three short spells for their removal.

That's when Uxtal tore the roof from the shack. Ebenezum's hands flew about his sneeze-racked body, and I found myself encircled by thick gray smoke.

"Fee fi fum fo! Where did those two mortals go?"

I heard Uxtal somewhere above us. Someone grabbed my sleeve and pulled. I stumbled after him.

Then the wizard sneezed again, sending the cloud in all directions.

"Fi fo fum fee! I'll teach you to hide from me!" The giant reached for us. I still held the red book in my hand but had lost my place. I leafed through frantically, wishing I could remember the page number.

Then I heard the singing. It came from the front doorstep of the cottage, where Norei, Solima, and a wizened old woman I had never seen before stood. It was a strange song, sometimes sounding like a choir of angels had come to earth, other times resembling nothing more than certain yodeling ditties I had been fond of at the age of three. But the song was a spell, and a glowing ball of orange light grew above the three women, then rapidly sped in the direction of the giant. Uxtal turned and ran so fast he didn't have time for parting words.

My master blew his nose.

"You're safe, then!" Norei called. "Would we could get rid of Tork as easily as we subdued Uxtal."

"That the one?" the old woman said as she pointed to Ebenezum. "I remember him! Looks like he's got a cold. He's spreading disease. Mark my word, it wouldn't surprise me if he were carrying the plague!"

"Now, Grandmother," Solima chided.

"He's probably never worked a day of his life! And look at that beard! Norei, get me some eye of newt and toe of frog! We'll teach him to come skulking around here!"

"Grandmother's a traditionalist." Norei leaned close to me and whispered in my ear. My heart raced. "She's never liked wizards much, either. She always thinks they bad-mouth witches."

"Just a second here, and I'll fry up a couple of lightning bolts!" the old woman proclaimed. She rubbed her hands rapidly. "Then I'll zap you back where you came from!"

"Grandmother!" Solima scolded. "You know we can't use magic unless it's absolutely necessary. Tork will find us!"

"This is necessary!" the old woman shouted, her hands still rubbing together. I heard something crackle between them.

"Grandmother! Ebenezum is my friend! I will not have you zapping him!"

"Friend? After what he did to me? I'll show him what I think of his chicken-feather spell!"

"Grandmother! Up to your room!"

The old woman glowered for a moment, then scooted up the ladder. Ebenezum blew his nose.

"You showed great restraint with Grandmother this time, Eb. I do agree that that spell with the chickens was a bit much, especially after all those dead fish. But she was right about your cold, wasn't she?"

Ebenezum looked at me, then at Solima and Norei. His face was drawn and tired. "Alas, 'tis worse than that." And he told them the story of his malady.

"You poor dear!" Solima said when he was through. "You've managed valiantly, though. I always knew you were a man of character, Eb." She walked over to my master and put her hands on his shoulders. "Give me an hour or so to check my books. I'm sure there are certain herbs that can be used to ease a condition such as yours, and if I'm not mistaken, certain healing sprites can be called to visit an area which would remove your condition completely! Face it, you old codger: you haven't been cured because you have not visited a good witch!" She kissed him on the forehead. "Now I want all three of you out of here. I have to do my research!"

The wizard took me aside as soon as we had quit the cottage.

"Vulnerability, Wunt. Always good as a last resort. Brings out the mother instinct. You still have the red book?"

I showed my master where I had tucked it in my shirt.

"Good." He twirled his mustache. "Who knows? Soon I may even be able to use it."

Norei stepped from the door we had just left. "Wuntvor? May I speak to you for a minute?"

I looked to my master. He pulled his beard reflectively.

"Indeed," he said after a moment. "There are matters I must attend to as well." He walked to the remains of the shack, more bounce in his wizardly stride than I had ever seen before.

Then I turned to Norei. My world was Norei—her oval face, framed by long dark hair. And those large green eyes. Eyes to get lost in.

"Wuntvor? What's the matter?" she said with some concern. "Do I have a bug on my nose? You just got the strangest look."

I cleared my throat and stared at the forest floor, assuring her it was only fatigue from my journey.

"Tired you may be, but you have to put that behind you!" She grabbed my arm above the elbow. I looked up. Her face was close to mine. "Your master is ill, my mother close to collapse, Grandmother unwilling to help because of something your master did long ago involving fish and chickens! It's up to the two of us to be strong. We have to be the center around which the magic grows to defeat Tork's Forxsnagel!"

I nodded. Yes, everything she said was true. I would do anything for her. So what if I'd only tried three spells in my life and none of them ever quite worked out? With Norei as my guide, our magic would be strong.

She kissed me lightly. I could hear my brain hum. When she screamed, I realized it wasn't my brain, but the demons. They surrounded us, and their humming was fierce.

"So!" Tork called from the rear of the demon brigade. "Playing with magic this afternoon, were you? I can deal with you now!"

Ebenezum came running from the cottage, followed by Solima. Grandmother hopped quickly behind.

"The only dealing you'll do, fiend," Ebenezum exclaimed, "is with me!"

"Careful, Eb!" Solima cautioned. "I'm not sure of the potency of the herbs. Perhaps we should work our collective magic before they wear off."

"He'll never listen," Grandmother shouted from the rear. "Let the scoundrel go! Give me some foxroot and duckwort, and I'll show them all!"

In the midst of this, Tork tried to conjure. Frogs fell from his sleeves.

"No! No!" he screamed. "Very well! You've sealed your doom! The Overspell! Forxsnagel!"

The earth shook.

"Fee fi fo fum! I will stamp on everyone!"

Uxtal was above us. Norei ran to her family. The three of them began a chant. Glancing back, Ebenezum joined in as Prince Tork screamed incantations and jumped through a series of extremely acrobatic positions.

"Fi fo fum fee! No one's even watching me!" The giant growled and lifted his great foot into the air.

I looked back and forth at the two groups of combatants: leaping Tork surrounded by demons, the three witches and Ebenezum weaving a vocal tapestry. Uxtal, I reasoned, would stomp the singers first, but the four were so involved in their song they would never see the descending foot.

Twas then I remembered the book. I pulled it all too rapidly from my shirt. It spun from my hands and landed on the ground. When I picked it up, I noticed it had opened to the proper page!

I knew then that I was fated to best the giant. I glanced rapidly over the three spells printed across the bottom of the page. I chose what appeared to be the simplest: "Shrinking the Giant Down to Size." A six-foot-tall giant would be no problem at all!

But I had forgotten the demons! They were all upon me, ripping and tearing at my clothes, their awful hum close against my ears. I shouted out the spell, the book ripped from my hands as the final syllables escaped my lips.

The demons fell away from me. I looked up to the giant. He was getting smaller!

But my exhilaration was short-lived. For some reason,

everything else was getting smaller, too.

I realized my mistake. In my haste, I must have jumbled the syllables of the spell. Instead of Uxtal shrinking, I was growing!

I looked about me as I grew to Uxtal's size and more. It gave me a whole new view of the countryside; the ruined half of the valley where we had descended, and the area around me, which, besides a few spots like the demolished shack, seemed still to be the rolling forest and picturesque farmland this whole valley must have been before the coming of Uxtal.

I noticed then that my stout oak staff had grown with me. Far below, I could hear Prince Tork's screams, counterpointed by four voices weaving in and out, punctuated by shrill whistles and wild whoops. None of them seemed in the least aware of the giant's foot hovering over them.

"Fee fum fo fi! I will crush you by and by!"

I hit his foot with my staff. Uxtal looked up in alarm.

"Hey!" he said in a low voice. "You trying to spoil my act?"

"Away, fiend!" I bellowed. I was surprised at how loud my voice was.

"Away, fiend? What kind of line is that? It doesn't even rhyme! I was only trying to scare the folks. It's part of the contract!"

"A contract with demons!" I cried. I walked toward Uxtal. Things crunched and crashed beneath my feet. I looked down to see my gigantic boots had left a trail of decimation through the forest.

"Say," Uxtal said, his eyes narrowed to slits, "are you nonunion?"

He was trying to confound me with Netherhell double-talk! I decided, rather than risk destroying more of the valley bottom, I would stand my ground and thrash the villain soundly with my staff. I swung the stick with a cry.

And Uxtal jumped out of its path. He was awfully limber for a giant. The staff swept empty air, and I lost my balance. I found myself falling, straight toward Ebenezum and the witches.

Frantically, I tried to twist away. I crashed, scant yards away from the whooping and whistling assembly, demolishing the witches' cottage instead.

I rolled away from the witches' clearing, flattening another couple of acres of forest, and struggled to my feet. Now I was mad! I growled at Uxtal.

"You had better get out of here!"

Uxtal was looking down at the others. A great ball of light had formed above the witches, while Tork had created a large area of total dark above himself. Light and dark moved together.

"I think you're right." Uxtal waved and in four strides had disappeared over the rim of the valley.

Dark and light met.

It turned very cold, and all the color seemed to drain from the world. There was no sound; only gray shapes in silence. I could see the four still singing, and Tork dancing among his demons.

But something was wrong with Ebenezum! He was down on his knees. Even though there was no sound, I knew he was sneezing.

The world was going a deeper gray. Ebenezum tried to rise but fell, quivering in his robes. I tried to move, to help my master, but was somehow glued to the spot.

The world went dark.

In an instant, there was light. The three witches lay on the ground, unconscious. Ebenezum had somehow managed to stand, and now faced Tork and his demon minions, who all hummed triumphantly.

"The Forxsnagel is mine!" Tork cried. "I can have anything I want! Already I have defeated the power of these three witches. You ceased your spells just before the blow and were spared. But that, dear wizard, is a temporary condition! By the power of the Forxsnagel, I claim your wizard's skills!"

Dark lightning flashed from Tork's fingers. Ebenezum threw out his hands to conjure himself, but the lightning threw him back.

Tork laughed, raising his balled fist to the heavens. "Power! All of magic is mine!"

Then he began to sneeze.

Norei and I kissed. A young witch and a magician's apprentice, in a world made new again.

The witches had managed to return the valley to normal in a surprisingly short time. Solima's sisters were rescued from their prison, the demons exorcised from the land, and rebuilding had begun. My master and I should have left a week before to continue our journey to Vushta, city of a thousand forbidden delights and a cure for my master. But here we stayed. Which was fine with me.

I kissed Norei. Her lips were very sweet.

It was a shame about Ebenezum's cure, though. When Tork had achieved Forxsnagel, he had tried to drain off my master's abilities and received Ebenezum's malady in the bargain. Now Solima was afraid to summon such sprites as might cure my master, in case they cured Prince Tork as well. There were still the herbs, of course, though Solima warned against using them too frequently. They had taken their toll on Ebenezum already; he had slept for most of a day after his battle with Tork. And Solima told us that after two or three ingestions, the body built up immunities to the medicine, and the malady would return, as bad as or worse than ever. We would have to go to Vushta after all.

Norei's cool hand brushed the hair from my eyes. "What are you thinking of, Wunt?"

"Fate," I replied. "How we met, and suffered, and triumphed. How we both have our whole lives ahead of us, and how my future has changed, knowing you."

Norei's green eyes looked heavenward. "You do talk funny sometimes, Wuntvor. We've just met. Don't go planning our lives yet. Who knows what will happen to us?" She kissed my cheek.

"Who knows?" I agreed. "For now, my master seems content to stay here." I looked back at the rebuilt cottage, half-hidden by what trees still remained standing in this part of the wood.

There was a rumbling crash.

"Ha, ha, ha! I knew the duckwort would work!" It was Grandmother's voice. "I'll teach you to lay about the house sweet-talking my daughter!" Ebenezum came running full speed from the cottage. Solima held her grandmother back from following. Fire sprouted from the old woman's fingertips.

"The spells may take a little while, but the old ways are the best!" the old woman called. "Stand your ground and let me boil your blood!"

My master tossed me my pack. "Quick, Wunt! It's off to Vushta!" He sneezed and looked back at Solima. "I'll be back when I've found the cure!"

"I look forward to it!" Solima replied, still grasping the struggling oldster.

"We'll all be waiting for you!" Grandmother waved her flaming hands.

I stood, pack in one hand, staff in the other. "I guess I'm off to Vushta, then."

"Oh," Norei replied. "Well, good-bye."

Is that all she had to say? After all the time we spent together? "Norei," I whispered, "come to Vushta."

She looked at me and smiled.

"They call it the city of a thousand forbidden delights."

"Well, maybe I will, someday." She stood and kissed me lightly.

"Now I'll zap you, scoundrel!" Grandmother had broken free from Solima and was coming toward us rapidly. Her fire fingers singed the shrubbery as she ran. "I'll teach you to sully the name of good, honest witches! Fish and chickens, indeed!"

I was off down the road, after my master.

"No matter how ideal the circumstances of one's present location," he remarked as I caught up with him, "there is always something to be said for a change of scene."

CHAPTER SEVEN

There are those who claim that magic is like the tide; that it swells and fades over the surface of the earth, collecting in concentrated pools here and there, almost disappearing from other spots, leaving them parched for wonder. There are also those who believe that if you stick your fingers up your nose and blow, it will increase your intelligence.

—from The Teachings of Ebenezum, Volume VII

After that, of course, our luck got worse. It wasn't just the assassins, although Urfoo's paid minions kept appearing with greater and greater frequency. It was probably all those minstrels that made us so easy to find. When one's fame is being sung in every village in the kingdom, it is difficult for one to travel incognito. Before our present arrangement, we seemed to be always on the run.

Then the earthquakes began.

At first, they were only small tremors, a moment's shifting of the earth beneath our feet. But they grew greater day by day. I worried that Prince Tork had recovered from his inherited malady and would soon visit the Forxsnagel upon us again. When I told my master of my fears, he dismissed them, at least as far as so inept a wizard as Tork was concerned. Yet as to the earthquakes being caused by the Forxsnagel... well, there might be some truth to that. He would speak no more on the subject until we were free of our present company. Until then, he only scratched the hair beneath his cap.

Our conversation was cut short by a commotion in the distance.

There must have been twenty of them, each one attempting to scream louder than his or her companions, all running full tilt down the dirt path that passed for a road in this rural clime. On my master's instructions, we stepped to one side of the lane and watched them pass.

"Indeed," Ebenezum intoned as the cloud of dust caused by the commotion settled down again upon the road. He allowed a hand to stroke his beard and made clicking sounds deep in his throat, a sure sign of wizardly thought.

"I do believe they would have run us over!" Old Dame Sniggett quivered, her pale hands fluttering amongst her black robes. "They can't be from around here! Not civilized at all!"

"Now, now, Auntie." The beautiful Ferona took her elder's hands in her own steady grip. In the two days that the women had been our traveling companions, I had been repeatedly impressed by the young woman's ability to remain calm in the face of any crisis.

"I'm sure there is some logical explanation for their behavior," she continued. "Perhaps they are some sort of religious order, making a hasty pilgrimage to their holy shrine. Whatever their purpose, it is not for us to worry about. Not when we are so close to the safety of our home."

The wizard turned to regard the two women. "We are almost there?"

Ferona smiled, an expression so brilliant on her freckled face, surrounded by her red hair, that if you watched her long enough, you might forget the sun. "Aye, good sir. We are nearly in shouting distance. 'Tis only a couple more hills down the road. Come on, Nanny. Let's all of us walk so we can get home and rest properly."

It was then my master sneezed. I hoped, for a foolish instant, that it was only a reaction to the dust on the road. But I knew, somewhat closer to my soul, that my master's sneeze boded far more ill than that.

The wizard sneezed again. A lone man ran toward us this time, his shadow flung far across the road by the late afternoon sun.

"The sun is setting!" the newcomer cried, his voice cracking from the weight of emotion. "The sun is setting!"

"We thank you for that information," my master replied

when it became apparent the man had finished his speech. "Is there anything else you'd like to add?"

"But—" The man came closer still. I could now see the horror in his eyes. "'Tis the first night of the full moon!"

The wizard scratched at the snow-white hair beneath his cap. "This is also true." He glanced at the ladies. "If you have no more information to impart, I think we should be on our way."

"Bork, you are talking nonsense!" Dame Sniggett stepped forward. "Pardon the intrusion, oh learned sir, but I know this man. He's one of my farm hands. I almost didn't recognize him, acting so." She sniffed. "He's usually so civilized."

"Oh, my lady!" Bork fell to his knees. "I'm so afraid of the beast, I didn't see you. So much has happened at the farm since the change came over Greta."

The elder pulled herself erect, her once watery eyes afire with outrage. "Something has happened to Greta?"

"No, nothing," Bork whimpered. "That is, nothing beyond…" He glanced at my master and myself, and his voice trailed off to nothing.

Ferona looked to Ebenezum, an apologetic smile lighting her face. If only she would smile that way at me! "Greta is my mistress's prize pullet."

My master pulled at his beard. "There is an illness among the chickens, then?"

"Chickens?" Dame Sniggett's voice reached a volume and timbre that I previously would have thought impossible in a woman so frail. "Greta is no—" Her mouth refused to form the word. "Greta is an East Kingdom dandy!"

"Mistress!" Ferona urged. "Your nerves!"

Dame Sniggett glanced, startled, at her young charge. The air seeped from her body in a rush, and she returned to being bent and frail. "Forgive me, good sir," she whispered to my master. "When I hear my Greta is in trouble, all sense leaves me."

"No need for alarm, dear woman," Ebenezum said with the same warm smile and soothing voice that had won a thousand paying clients. "We all have those things that are very dear to us."

The woman glanced at him and quickly looked away. She giggled, a most unexpected sound. "We are fortunate," she said softly, "to be traveling with a man who knows the proper manner in which to view things."

"It's a wizard's duty to place things in perspective. My lady, if you and your ward will accompany me, we will escort you to the safety of your home." With that, Ebenezum led the way down the road once again. I took up the rear as usual, the paraphernalia-filled pack on my back somewhat hindering my movements. Bork struggled to his feet as I passed. "But the beast—" he cried.

Somewhere in the distance, a wolf howled.

The pounding started sometime after they deposited my master and myself in the massive front hall of the estate. Occasionally, the pounding would be accompanied by screaming.

Dame Sniggett would flutter through the hall from time to time, fragments of explanation trailing her rapid movements. "The rooms aren't quite proper yet.... I like everything just so.... It was so much more civilized." Ferona would glide after her every now and then, and spare a smile for my master. I tried to get her to smile at me but once again couldn't quite catch her eye.

No one mentioned the pounding and the screams.

Both seemed to come from just the other side of the great oak door that formed the entrance way to the massive estate that housed Dame Sniggett and Ferona. In a quiet moment, I asked the wizard what he thought all the commotion might be. My master thought for a bit, then replied in a low tone: "The rich do have their quirks. Most likely 'tis a deranged uncle they keep locked in the tower. Pretend not to notice, at least until they've given us dinner."

At last a young woman appeared to tell us we could now enter the main hall and all would be explained. She introduced herself as Borka, sister to the mistress's other servant. My master turned from his study of the elaborate carvings that lined the walls, especially those inlaid with gold, and pulled at his robes to properly straighten the lines. I gathered up my pack and stout oak walking staff, and followed the wizard into the Great Hall.

Our eyes immediately fixed upon the dozen golden chicken coops that lined one wall of the huge room.

"Welcome to my little nest," Dame Sniggett cooed.

She stood at the end of a long table made of dark wood, Ferona at her side. They had changed from their simple but elegant traveling clothes to somewhat more resplendent finery, the mistress of the house dressed all in black lace, her lovely charge dressed in a gown that showed all the colors of spring. This time I thought Ferona smiled at both of us. I wished again I could get her to smile just for me.

My life had changed in the two days since we had chanced to meet the two women in a roadside inn. Praise the assassins that Urfoo sent against us, for they made it necessary for us to find traveling companions! And thus far, it had worked. The last two days had passed assassin free. But far more than that had happened to me. Before, I had been merely Wuntvor, a magician's apprentice content with following my master on his quest for a cure. But on that day when Dame Sniggett had requested the wizard's aid, my life had grown to include Ferona. There had been a few other women, surely, but their memories were like wisps of smoke, burned away by Ferona's fiery beauty. Well… there were some times, late at night, when I thought of Norei, and the way she kissed. But she had her own life to lead. That was something she had made very clear. After that, I shouldn't have thought about her as much as I did. But then there was Ferona!

Ferona! How had I existed before I had known that name? I hadn't yet been able to get her to talk to me, but that was a small matter, now that we had met. Now, my life had purpose.

A chicken clucked. It was probably in response to the immense quantity of pounding and screaming still going on outside, so loud now we could hear it clearly in this inner room.

"Now, now, Greta," Dame Sniggett soothed. "I want you to meet a very important man." Her watery eyes blinked at my master. "Tall, handsome, and a wizard besides!"

"Indeed," Ebenezum rumbled. He glanced briefly at me before returning to examine the hen. I could tell immediately that he was not pleased at being introduced to a chicken. Even with all her money, Dame Sniggett might go too far.

"Borka. Take Greta from her cage."

The wizard grimaced. He expected the worst. He might even have to hold it.

"Yes, ma'am." The serving woman curtsied and grabbed the chicken by the throat.

"Gently, gently," the dame chided. "She is very special to me." I could see the idea of being chased by assassins appealed more to Ebenezum with every passing moment.

"You see, Greta is a very special chicken." Dame Sniggett's voice fell to a whisper. "She has the ability to produce gold."

The smile reappeared on Ebenezum's lips, unfolding like a flower as it catches the warm rays of the sun.

"It's always been possible in theory," the wizard remarked, "though I've never seen a spell that made it happen. She actually produces golden eggs?"

There was an embarrassed silence. Finally, Borka cleared her throat. "Well, you see, the gold really comes out of another part of the chicken entirely."

"How improper!" Fire blazed in the mistress's eyes again, but the look softened as she gazed at her hen. "Yet poor Greta can't help it. All the creatures of the world must perform such functions, even humans. Cursed with such a fate, we should be thankful when it comes out gold!"

Borka looked up from where she held the chicken. Her face grew suddenly pale. " 'Tis getting dark. I must go close the shutters!"

She thrust the chicken back into its cage and ran from the room. The pounding outside seemed to redouble with the approaching darkness, although by now the screams had gotten quite hoarse.

"Now that you know about our Greta," Dame Sniggett said, "I can tell you the real reason I've asked you to come to the estate. When I saw you were a wizard, new hope rose within my bosom. Tell me, dear, dear Ebenezum, might there be a spell by which you could change the orifice through which Greta's gold appears?"

"An interesting point." Ebenezum sniffed. Being in the same room as an enchanted chicken did not seem to be enough to make my master sneeze, although it did make his nose run. I imagined that if Greta decided to make gold any time in the wizard's presence, his malady would return full force. "Many magicians have proposed spells for the laying of golden eggs," he continued, "but no matter what the process proposed, the results always proved to be economically unfeasible. That is, more magic went in one end than gold came out the other." Ebenezum blew his nose.

"But it might be done?"

"Certainly possible, with the head start your hen has. It's just a matter of fathoming the proper spell of transference."

"Then I must insist you remain here as my guests!" Dame Sniggett's watery eyes shone like pools beneath the moon. "Ferona will show you to your room, civilized in every respect! It belonged to the master of the house, Ferona's late uncle. Oh, and your apprentice can sleep in the barn."

A sudden commotion seemed to have replaced the pounding and screaming that went on in the hallway. Bork staggered into the room.

"Why didn't you answer the door? The beast would have gotten me!"

Dame Sniggett stared at him in silent indignation.

"How were we to know you would return?" Ferona replied. "We thought the knocking was yet another pilgrim, looking for a handout for his holy cause." She glanced at Ebenezum and myself. "All the pilgrims around here know that Auntie has money."

A sudden chill wind blew into the room. Bork, Ferona, and Dame Snigget looked at one another, an expression of terror on their faces.

"The door!" Bork whispered.

Something leapt into the room with a horrible, shrieking growl. Dame Sniggett cried out, Ferona and Bork leapt away.

Ebenezum was sneezing now. The creature was sorcerous! Although one look at the thing's near human height, its face full of fangs and coarse gray hair, should have been enough to tell me that. The things would kill us all, unless someone acted quickly. I leapt forward, swinging my stout oak staff.

The creature grabbed the swinging wood and wrenched it from my grasp as if the force behind my blow had been nothing. Talons bit into the skin of my right hand. With a cry I pulled myself free, but the creature was on top of me. It forced me to the floor, its breath hot on my neck. I caught a glimpse of razor teeth. Behind us, the chickens shrieked in dismay.

The beast paused and looked up, sniffing the air. As fast as it had floored me, it leapt away to grab the nearest chicken. Hen in mouth, it ran from the room.

As I stared dumbly at my bleeding hand, I heard Ebenezum blow his nose. Dame Sniggett tossed a napkin in my direction so that I might mop up the blood, her face a mask of distaste. Ferona sighed and shook her head.

"It happens all the time."

CHAPTER EIGHT

Even for a wizard there will often come times when someone close to you, perhaps even your spouse, criticizes your habits by comparing them to those of animals. This is distinctly unfair to the animals, who have far better habits than we in many areas. When, for example, have you seen a frog collecting taxes or a squirrel running for electoral office? Present arguments like these to those people who criticize you. If they still do not see the wisdom of your ways, you may then feel free to bite them.

—from The Teachings of Ebenezum, Volume IX

"There are certain problems with this estate," Dame Sniggett admitted after we had eaten and she had sufficiently calmed.

"Indeed. Like werewolves." Ebenezum stroked his beard. So that was what it was! I had heard of such strange creatures—humans that turn to animals under the full moon. My hand ached in remembrance.

"No," Ferona interjected. "What Auntie is trying to say is that magic collects here, producing all manner of strange and wonderful things. Only in such a place could Greta produce gold. Unfortunately, there are negative sides to the magic as well."

"Yes, yes, but that's why we've brought a wizard here!" The aunt smiled at my master. "Good Ebenezum, surely you can try to dispel the negative magicks that lurk about this farm."

"I can but try," the wizard replied. Apparently, no one had noticed my master's total helplessness during the werewolf's attack, and the mage, sensing a fee, was not eager to bring the matter up. "Now, we have had a long and trying day. Perhaps you would be good enough to show us to our rooms?"

"Certainly. Ferona, take Ebenezum up to the master's suite. After that, Bork can point out the way for Wuntvor to walk to the barn." Dame Sniggett studied her black lace sleeve for an instant. "Oh, incidentally, good wizard, just so there are no more surprises, I should tell you to totally ignore the ghost. He's quite harmless, really."

"Ghost?" I saw my master's eyes cloud with wizardly rage. Dame Sniggett had gone too far at last. His right hand shot out to pave the way for a major denunciation. His fingers banged into the golden chicken cage.

The wizard hesitated, the touch of precious metal bringing him back to his senses.

"Beg pardon, madam, but I cannot sleep with a ghost present. My magical senses are too finely tuned; I would get no rest at all. Give my apprentice the master's quarters. I shall sleep in the barn."

Dame Sniggett frowned. "That's hardly proper! Still, who am I to criticize the methods of a practicing wizard? I'm sure, in time, we'll all be able to make the necessary adjustments." She waved her hand. "Bork, show the young man the way upstairs."

Somewhat dejectedly, I followed the servant. I had hoped that Ferona would escort me. I stumbled into the huge bedroom Bork led me to and fell upon the massive bed. My recent fight had exhausted me. Bork departed, closing the door after him. The room was left in darkness.

"Hey," a voice whispered in my ear. "Hey, buddy."

My mind floundered on the edge of sleep. "Wha?"

Encouraged, the voice got louder. "Hey, buddy, ever hear the one about the farmer's daughter and the traveling tinsmith?"

"What?" I was wide awake now. "What are you talking about?"

"All right, all right, so you've heard that one," the voice said, suddenly defensive. "How about this: How many monks does it take to empty a cistern?"

"I was trying to sleep!" I cried. It then occurred to me that I had no idea who or what I was talking to. Ice rolled down my spine. A valley full of ghosts came to mind, a valley where I had almost become a ghost myself.

"Who are you?" I whispered.

"Oh, I'm a ghost. Peelo's the name. Formerly jester to the court of King Zingwarfel, some four hundred years back now. I had the misfortune to make a joke about the king's name, and was put instantly to death. Now I'm forced to wander these halls endlessly, trying to make people laugh. But hey, you don't want to hear about this. It's showtime!"

I had no idea what this creature was talking about. It didn't seem dangerous, but with ghosts you could never tell. "Why can't I see you?" I asked.

"What, you want me to manifest myself? I usually save that for the big boffo conclusion. But hey. Tell me this. Why did the hippogriff cross the road?"

"I don't care!" I pounded the bed with my fists. The right one throbbed painfully. "Ghosts, werewolves, magic chickens. What's going on here?"

"Hey, buddy, calm down. It's all just part of the package. You know, standard Netherhell grab bag: one gold-producing spell, a werestone, a giant Grak—although heaven knows where it's gone—one slightly used ghost. I'm sort of the M.C. of this troupe, forced to walk these halls until I can make someone really laugh. If only somebody would give me some new jokes! Do you know how difficult it is to milk laughs out of four-hundred-year-old material?"

"I'm sure it's hard," I said. I was too tired to care. I lay back on the bed.

"But hey, no more boring stories! On with the show! Did you hear the one about the unicorn and the tavern keeper? Well, this unicorn goes into this tavern, see, and orders a mug of ale from the tavern keeper. The tavern keeper brings the ale, and says, 'That'll be a hundred gold crowns.' Then he adds, 'You know, we don't get many...' "

It was all too much for me. I fell asleep.

I found my way to the barn and told Ebenezum my ghost story early the next morning.

"Indeed," he said when I was finished. "There's more here than meets either the eye or nose. I have a feeling that Dame Sniggett is attempting to extract a great deal of work from us for a very low fee." He cleared his throat. "I imagine she would think that sort of thing proper."

"Either that," I added, "or she's afraid a spell that took away the bad might take her beloved chicken, too."

"A good point." Ebenezum fingered his long white mustache. "Perhaps there's hope for you, yet, Wuntvor. Whatever happens, we'll have to charge for the spells as piecework. Expensive that way, but they can afford it."

"But—" A sudden awkwardness kept me from finishing the sentence. Who was going to cast the spells? My master's malady left him in no condition to conjure. He had tried innumerable methods of blocking up his nose or somehow diverting the sorcerous smells during the course of our travels. The only common element in all these methods was that none of them worked. None of them, that is, except one. Solima's cure!

My eyes wandered to the vial of herbs Ebenezum had kept by his side this past week. The wizard shook his head. "No, Wunt. This job is nowhere near important enough for me to use my only remedy. It will have to wait for a more serious occasion."

Ebenezum pulled at his beard and stared off into the hayloft. "There are a number of supernatural factors at work here. Yet each one, taken separately, is manageable with a fairly simple spell. A werestone must be destroyed, a ghost banished, perhaps another thing or two exorcised. After that, we'll repair Dame Sniggett's chicken. And you, Wuntvor, will be the one to perform the magic."

I stared at my master for a long moment. "Close your mouth, lad. A good wizard always has his mouth firmly closed."

I complied.

"In the past," my master continued, "you have learned to use some simple spells to extricate us from difficult circumstances. Perhaps they haven't always worked exactly as planned, but we are still alive and on the road to Vushta, which is all that really matters. In the next few hours, you will learn a group of

spells so simple as to be child's play. After that, all that will be
required is the proper timing."

I was overwhelmed. Never had my master placed such faith
in me!

"I hope I will be worthy."

Ebenezum raised one eyebrow. "So do I. There's a large fee
involved."

When Ferona came to the door of the barn, I hardly looked at
her. My head was filled with General Banishment Spell #3, Ork's
Rule of Universal Exorcism, and The Great Foudou's Chant for
the Realignment of Bodily Parts.

"Excuse me," she said. "Is Ebenezum about?"

She had spoken to me! All the spells flew from my head.
At last, what I had dreamed of for so long had come to pass. I
searched my thoughts to come up with a reply worthy of her
beauty.

But there was no reply that magnificent. I told her, therefore,
that Ebenezum had gone out for a walk about the estate.

"A pity," she replied. "Tell me, Wuntvor, what do you think
of marriage?"

What was she saying? I had known, deep in my heart, that
once Ferona and I spoke, everything would change. But this
quickly?

"It can be a good thing," I prompted.

Ferona nodded absently. "Do you think Ebenezum would
consider marrying a woman as young as I?"

I found myself at a loss for words.

"Please close your mouth, Wuntvor," Ferona said. "There
are flies in the barn. It could be unhealthy." One of her
magnificently formed feet scuffed at a small pile of hay. "You're
surprised I want to marry a wizard. It's just that there's such
a concentration of magic around here that we'd all feel more
secure with a magician about."

I couldn't help myself then. My emotions had risen above
reason. "What about me?" I blurted. "I'm a magician, too. Much
closer to your age."

"And much less experienced than your master." Ferona

frowned. "Let me tell you, Wuntvor, there is another reason that I need an older wizard. There is a curse upon me. Any man under the age of thirty that I kiss dies in three hours!"

I took a step backward.

"I used to have a dozen suitors knocking on my door day and night. It was only after the third one expired that I realized the true horror of my affliction."

"What happened to the other nine?" I asked weakly.

"Oh, they all became pilgrims. I'm afraid there aren't many job opportunities for young men in the Eastern Kingdoms these days. Fortunately, there always seem to be some openings in being holy." She sighed wistfully. "If only one of them were kissing me now!"

I thought for one wild moment about taking their place, but then I remembered the curse. I'd have to learn a spell to lift that as well.

"A curse, too?" Ebenezum had come to stand in the door as we spoke. "Young woman, I think you need to explain the entire situation."

And Ferona told the story of how her uncle thought himself a clever businessman and made a deal with the Netherhells for what seemed to be a limitless supply of gold. But, as is almost always the case in such dealings, he had missed the small print (it is usually so small that people mistake it for a dust mote in the lower left corner of the contract) and, besides a gold-producing chicken, received a ghost, a curse upon his niece, a stone that regularly turned one member of the household into a werewolf, and a large, dark bird that immediately carried Uncle away.

"As you can imagine, we were a little upset over this turn of events," Ferona continued. "However, Auntie insisted that there was a proper way out of this dilemma. All we had to do was bring in an expert in the field, and until then, leave things pretty much the way they were at Uncle's hasty departure, in case he should suddenly return."

"Indeed," Ebenezum replied. "That way you might be able to keep the magic elements from unsettling even further. And do you have a copy of this contract?"

"Alas, no. It was carried away with Uncle when the creature got him."

"A typical Netherhell ploy!" Ebenezum strode back and forth between the haystacks. "Well, we can't face the ghost until nightfall, nor will we see the werewolf. The werestone is another matter entirely. We must find where the demons put it!"

"Oh!" Ferona said brightly. "The demons put it on a mantelpiece in the Great Hall."

The wizard stared at the young woman. "And you've done nothing with it?"

"Well, Auntie's afraid to move anything in case Uncle won't recognize the place when he returns. Besides which, if you don't bother the werewolf when it bursts into the room, all it does is steal a chicken and run away again."

"Don't you fear for Greta?"

"A little, but so far the werewolf grabs one of the chickens at either end. As long as we keep the prize hen toward the middle, she seems to be fine." Ebenezum frowned at the fading light outside the barn. My instruction in magic had taken most of the day.

"If we don't hurry," the mage said, "we will be face to face with the werewolf all over again. We'll destroy the werestone now. My assistant, incidentally, will do the actual work while I supervise. Wuntvor needs the practice."

"All right." Ferona looked doubtful. "But we should hurry. The last person the werewolf caught playing with the werestone got his throat torn out."

I swallowed hard and followed my master toward the house. I repeated the three spells, a word for every step I took. There could be no mistakes this time. I had to remember every one, or I would be minus a throat.

"You're sure nothing will happen to Greta?" Dame Sniggett cooed in the direction of her prize hen. The chicken, for its part, ignored the people in the room entirely, pecking away at a pile of dried corn.

"Reasonably sure," the wizard replied. "It depends on the degree of interconnection between the different spells from the Netherhells. Rest assured we will take every precaution."

Ebenezum held his nose. "Wuntvor, open the box."

I did as I was told. A small green stone lay in the middle of the box's plush purple interior. It looked harmless enough. One could hardly imagine it was capable of doing the things Ebenezum had described earlier in the day.

"The werestone," my master explained, "is a particularly fiendish invention of the Netherhells. It causes people who touch it to be driven out into the wilds in the full moon, and the first lower animal they contact, they become like that animal every time the full moon returns. One imagines this particular stone had an additional curse on it, so that the first person to come in contact with it would be forced to seek out a wolf. Otherwise, the person would just have likely turned into a wererabbit."

Ebenezum sneezed behind me. "The spell!" he called. "The spell, Wuntvor!"

I began to recite the neutralizing spell. Somebody screamed when I was halfway through.

"Hey, folks!" an all-too-familiar voice cried out behind me. "It's showtime! Tell me, how many Vushtans does it take to do something forbidden?" I could see a pale jester's scepter out of the corner of my eye. Peelo seemed to have manifested himself for the occasion.

I tried to push the ghost's bad jokes out of my mind. I had to finish the spell! Ebenezum was sneezing with a vengeance now. His nasal whoops threatened to drown out an interminable story on the ghost's part concerning two hairy dogs and a large quantity of mulled wine.

"They're interconnected!" my master managed between sneezes. "Try the"—sneeze—"strongest"—sneeze—"Banish! Banish!"

So I was to go all out! The banishment spell it would be, then. I carefully phrased the first line, making sure I hit all the guttural stops.

That's when I heard the growl behind me.

I leapt to one side as the werewolf lunged and heard cloth tear as the claws grazed my leggings. The creature would kill me now. I needed a weapon.

My stout oak staff was still across the room, near the spot

where I had jumped away. The wolf circled the room, running perilously close to the golden chicken coops and the huddled forms of Dame Sniggett and Ferona. Would the beast devour Greta as well? If only there was something to stab, to hit, to throw. Ebenezum could be of no help now. The appearance of the wolf had made his condition even worse. He lay on the floor, a pitiful mass of sneezing flesh.

I had to get my staff! I took a step across the room, but the wolf was in front of me, its fangs bared in a half-human smile. It was stalking me now.

I would have to use my hands. There was nothing else to defend myself with. Then my eye caught the werestone.

In a single motion, I grabbed the thing and flung it at the wolf. It bounced off the creature's head, throwing it off-balance. Stone and wolf both fell against the huddled women.

I hadn't meant to do that. I started across the room in an attempt to rescue someone, when I saw the stone take its effect on the other two. Both Ferona and Dame Sniggett had grown dark, coarse hair all over their bodies. Where once there was one werewolf, now there were three.

Still, I would continue to fight! Though the odds were great against me, I would give my last ounce of blood to protect my master. Let the werewolves do their worst!

It occurred to me then that I had also touched the werestone. Should a werewolf touch me now, I would also turn into a hairy beast. There'd be no hope for Ebenezum then. The wolves, myself included, would tear him apart.

The creatures were on Ebenezum! The wizard flailed at them with his fists, but he could barely control his movements. A small vial fell from among his robes. The herbal remedy!

I dove beneath a clawed hand and tossed the vial back to my master. My momentum carried me on headfirst into the golden chicken cages.

I felt the change come over me then. My nose and mouth grew together and became hard. I felt my arms sprout feathers. I knew then the horrible truth. I was turning into a werechicken!

A wolf sprang at me, and I pecked it savagely with my beak. Startled, the wolf backed away. It had obviously never dealt with a six-foot chicken before. Surprise was on my side for a moment. But once the wolves regrouped, their teeth and claws would tear me apart in an instant.

My chicken eyes saw movement. Ebenezum placed the vial to his lips and swallowed.

There was a crash of breaking glass, and a great, dark bird entered the room. "Ladies and gentlemen!" Peelo the ghost cried. "The return of the Grak!"

I saw then that the Grak was carrying a small, balding gentleman. "Home at last!" the balding man cried.

The wolves rushed me. Ebenezum was on his feet, conjuring mightily. As they ran, the wolves transformed to Borka, Ferona, and Dame Sniggett.

The bird circled overhead. It was too much for my master, even with the medicine. He collapsed again, sneezing.

"Feerie!" cried the man dangling from the dark bird's claws. "Borkie! Sniggie! How good to see you again! I thought I'd never escape the Netherhells. They have awful, torturous things there. Traffic jams! Aspirin commercials!"

But even the uncle's babbling could not deter Peelo. His four hundred-year-old material just kept on coming.

"Ladies and gentlemen!" he cried, pointing at me. "A practical demonstration! Why did the chicken cross the moat?"

Ferona took one look at me and laughed. I clucked in indignation. Didn't she realize who helped save her?

"A laugh," Peelo whispered. "An honest laugh. We're free to leave this dull estate! Back to the excitement of the Netherhells. I tell you, the old jokes are always the best!"

With that, the ghost disappeared. As did all other things supernatural.

The long silence was broken by Greta's frantic clucking. I turned to look at the chicken and noticed that the feathers had left my arms. Seeing what Greta had deposited in the bottom of her golden cage, I realized the magic had deserted her as well.

"It comes to this," Dame Sniggett wailed.

"Didn't anybody miss me?" inquired the bald-headed man.

"I assume, good sir, that you are the uncle," Ebenezum said after a particularly hearty nose blow.

"And who might you be, sir?" the bald-headed man replied. "Sniggie, you haven't been going around hiring any extra servants?" He examined Ebenezum's silver-embroidered robes. "Unless you aren't—Sir, just what are you doing alone in this house with my wife!"

"Indeed," Ebenezum rumbled. He stooped to gather up my pack amidst the now scattered chicken cages, then thrust it in my arms. He turned, his wizardly strides taking him quickly from the room.

I risked a final glance at the lovely Ferona, but she was lost to me, crying over a mound of gray brown where once there had been a pile of gold.

"You'll pay for this!" Dame Sniggett shrieked at my master's retreating back. "This is not proper at all!"

"Enough of that lot," the mage muttered when we were free of the house. "May all their gold change in turn." He nodded at a man in the robes of a monk who walked toward us. "Rather we should use our magic to aid the pilgrims the girl was always going on about."

"I agree entirely." The monk smiled and pulled back his cowl. Even with the shaven head, I could tell it was Bork.

"Decided it was time for a change," he said to our inquiring glances. "A quieter life, free from the petty pursuits of the material world. Besides"—he tugged at his sleeve—"these fine, thick robes come with the job."

Brother Bork chose to walk with us a ways, and Ebenezum summarized the events that had transpired after his departure.

"You are holier than I," Bork said at last. "You banished every last bit of the curse, and used up the only remedy known to prevent your malady, then left the estate without any sort of payment whatever?"

"I didn't say that," Ebenezum replied. He poked the pack I carried with two fingers. Something clucked.

"A chicken?" Bork asked.

"Dinner." Ebenezum nodded. "Would you care to join us?"

I blanched. Somehow, the thought of a chicken dinner did not appeal to me at all. Quite understandable, I should think, considering what I had been through, even though the werespell over me had vanished with the rest of the gifts from the Netherhells. No, no chicken for me. I would content myself with the bag of dried corn I had brought with me from the estate. Amazingly enough, before this afternoon I had never realized how incredibly tasty dried corn could be.

But we were out in the open, on our way to Vushta again. Quite naturally, it was only a matter of moments before we were attacked by yet another band of assassins.

CHAPTER NINE

Wizards, like all mortals, need their rest. Casting spells, righting wrongs, and putting a little away for your old age can all be draining occupations. The true wizard must therefore always insist on a good night's sleep, and a few days' respite between tasks. After some particularly grueling work, a couple of weeks in the country are not out of line. In the aftermath of truly major assignments, of course, nothing less than a seaside vacation will do. And what of those situations in which a wizard's work affects the very world around him, perhaps the fabric of the cosmos itself? Well, be advised that prime accommodations in Vushta must be reserved at least two months in advance.

—from The Teachings of Ebenezum, Volume XXIII

It was all too much. I could barely support the pack upon my back. Its weight had surely increased fourfold. I leaned on my stout oak staff with such force that it bent each time I put my weight against it. I was sure it soon would snap. My feet barely lifted from the ground as I walked, and I stumbled over hidden rocks and roots as we made our slow way down what passed for a path. Sometime during our exhausted flight, we seemed to have wandered entirely away from the main highway and now found ourselves on a trail so overgrown that even the forest animals seemed to have given up on it.

As tired as I was, Ebenezum was more exhausted still. His head was bowed, his back was bent. His once wizardly strides had shortened to a very unwizardly hobble.

When we had first departed Dame Sniggett's after the successful resolution of her chicken problem, all had seemed well with my master. The tiredness that had ensued after his first use of the remedial herbs seemed to have passed him by entirely on the second application. The wizard began to talk expansively about the possibility of a cure, especially after we obtained another quantity of the healing poultice.

But my master spoke prematurely. His second reaction to the drug came after we had been on the road two full days and was fully four times worse than his earlier reaction. His first response, after our battle with Tork, had been exhaustion. His response after our chicken incident made exhaustion seem like a highly active state.

Then, of course, there were our constant encounters with assassins. And did I mention the increasing incidence of earthquakes? At first I thought it was my balance going, following my muscles into the blanket of fatigue. But no, we were plagued by ever-increasing tremors, as if giants were stomping foothills into the earth. These left us shaken at the least, and often not standing at all.

Ebenezum stumbled forward, managing at last to stand reasonably still. He paused and turned to me, his eyes once so capable of wizardly rage and sorcerous persuasion now no more than red and tired.

"Rest," was all he said.

I pointed to a likely group of stones on the far side of the path where we might sit for a while. We made our way over to them as best we could. I removed my pack with rather less grace than I would have liked. I decided not to look inside it just yet. I would discover what had broken at some later time.

Ebenezum didn't even notice the noise. He was too busy sitting down, which, like everything else just then, occupied a great amount of his time. He groaned and exhaled at the same instant, as if in the process of sitting he might release all his problems to the four winds.

We sat for a long moment in silence. My master's labored breathing softened over time. At last, he pushed back his cap to look at me.

"I was afraid of this," he said. "A second use of that potion has drained all the vitality from my body. 'Twould kill me to use it again." My master paused to regain his wind.

"What are we to do?" I asked before I realized that the wizard had again dozed where he sat.

I knew then it was up to me. Ebenezum was exhausted beyond all imagining. I must find someplace he could rest and recover.

"Pardon?" said a voice from across the road.

I looked up quickly. Two heavily cloaked figures stood a scant yard away.

"Did I say something?" I inquired.

"Oh, no." One of the cloaked figures stepped forward. Only his hands were visible, but they waved about wildly as he spoke, as if they wished to escape the cloak that hid the rest of him.

"I said 'pardon,' " he continued, "for I wish to speak with you. You must excuse me, for I have not the social graces of conversation. For you see, I am but a poor hermit, and seldom speak at all."

The speaker pulled back his hood, revealing a round, bald head that shone in the afternoon sun.

"Oh," I replied after I deciphered his conversation. "And you wished to say something to me?" "Most assuredly, yes." His hands darted about to indicate his chest. "As I have stated, I am but a poor hermit and religious seeker, Heemat by name, pledged for twenty years never to utter a word. Yes, for twenty years these lips are sealed, never to groan in pain or laugh with joy. But that is of no consequence, for when I saw the two of you by the side of the road, I found 'twas time to break my vow."

Heemat continued to smile. I looked to my master, but the wizard snored lightly upon his rock. He had managed to sleep through all of this. It was only then that I realized how truly fatigued Ebenezum was.

Well, tired though I was in turn, someone would have to see this situation through. And I would do it in a way that would make my master proud. I stared at this bald, smiling fellow. Something about him struck me as peculiar. Now, I thought, how would Ebenezum handle this?

"Indeed," I said, determined to seek this hermit's true nature. "You are a religious seeker?"

"Yes," Heemat replied, lifting his hands to the skies. "I

follow the lesser deity, Plaugg the Fairly Magnificent."

"Indeed." I decided I would leave this particular point for the nonce. "And are you sworn to silence for twenty years?"

"Well, yes, more or less. But as we walked down this road to see the two of you in such obvious need..."

The hermit's voice trailed away. Such obvious need? I coughed.

"We were just resting."

"Your companion looks like he might rest for the next dozen years."

I looked over at Ebenezum. He had managed, somehow, to curl up on top of his boulder. His snoring grew louder.

"Just a short afternoon nap," I replied, trying to keep the anxiety out of my voice. How was I to wake the wizard up, short of kicking him?

"Well, perhaps you need a place to stay until his nap is completed?" Heemat waved to his left. "Our hovel is just down the road a bit."

That's it. Now I knew what was bothering me. I stroked my chin thoughtfully. "Indeed," I remarked. "You say you are a hermit, sir."

"That's correct."

"Well." I coughed gently. "Since when do hermits have traveling companions?" I had to keep myself from smiling. What logic! My master would have been proud of me.

"I see." Heemat's hands retreated within his robes at the very hint of impropriety in his conduct. "I believe custom is somewhat different here than wherever you come from. I can tell you are a traveler."

I was completely undone. "In this country, hermits travel in pairs?"

"Come, come. There's no reason to belabor the obvious. How come you to this place?"

"Well, we seem to have wandered off the main road somewhere back there," I admitted before I regained my composure. "A second! Why does your companion not speak? Has he taken a vow of silence as well?"

"Snarks, here?" Heemat laughed, the smile fully across his

face again. "No, no, he's never taken a vow in his life. He just doesn't like to talk. Isn't that right, Snarks?"

The other figure nodded and said something from deep within his folds of cloak. It sounded like "Mmrrpphh!"

Somehow, all these explanations were doing nothing to reassure me. "What did your friend say?" I demanded.

"Sounded like 'mmrrpphh' to me." Heemat rubbed his belly happily.

There really was something all wrong here. I cursed my lack of experience. Maybe I should go over and shake Ebenezum awake.

With that, the wizard rolled off his boulder bed into a mass of brambles immediately behind the stone. His sleeping form sank from sight, but his snoring grew louder still.

"Our hovel is just down the road." Heemat shrugged. "Of course, he could sleep in the brambles all night, if that is your preference."

I looked from the hermit to his cloaked companion. Snarks waved his gloved hands above his head and shouted something like "Vrrmmpphh!" Someone tapped me on the shoulder.

An attack from the rear! I spun about all too quickly, almost losing my balance in the process. So, after all this talk, they would finally make their move! These fiends were everywhere! If only I could discern the true nature of their hellish schemes. I knew magic now! I would fight them if I must, whether they numbered two or two hundred!

The newcomer was a good two feet taller than myself, dressed entirely in black. His shoulders were incredibly broad as well. You could have fit two normal men side by side and just matched the width of his frame. His face was pale and without amusement. He spoke in the deepest voice I had ever heard.

"I need some assistance."

With that, a new earthquake hit. If the earlier quakes had been a giant stamping his foot, this one was the annual giant's dancing social. We were, all but the tall man, tossed to the ground by the severity of it.

It was over in a second. I glanced at the boulders. Apparently, Ebenezum was still asleep.

A great, trumpeting cry came from the depth of the woods. The large man spun about with the grace one might expect of a dancer or a professional eel catcher.

A huge wild boar broke from the underbrush. The creature was larger than I was tall, with great, sharp tusks that seemed pointed straight in my direction. It bellowed again as it raced across the clearing, intent on its frenzied attack. My stout oak staff suddenly felt very puny in my hands.

The large man stepped in the wild boar's path. The boar kept coming straight for him. The man in black grabbed the two tusks as if the huge pig were offering them rather than attacking. He calmly flipped the creature over as he stepped aside. Before the boar could recover, the large man had placed his immense hand around the pig's equally huge neck and lifted the beast aloft. The boar roared, then made an odd, choking sound as the large man squeezed its windpipe. When the boar stopped struggling, the large man casually tossed it back into the woods.

"I do like strangling wild pigs," he remarked. "It's such a satisfying feeling." He flexed his muscles absently.

Then again, perhaps fighting with this fellow wasn't such a good idea. But I couldn't run away, either, and leave Ebenezum snoring in the shrubbery.

"Indeed," I said.

"Well, no matter," the large man said. "I seem to have wandered off the main road somehow, and it will interfere with my duties."

"Alas, another lost traveler!" Heemat exclaimed. "Perhaps we can be of service."

"Who's this?" the large man asked softly.

"Only Heemat, good sir." Heemat spread his hands before him. "A poor hermit and religious pilgrim, pledged to Plaugg the Moderately Glorious. I have only recently broken a vow of silence to aid—"

"That's enough." The large man lifted a very large hand by his large head.

Heemat's smiling mouth snapped shut.

"Who's this?" The large man nodded toward the hermit's cloaked companion.

"Wvvxxrrgghh." Snarks took a rapid step to the rear.

"That is Snarks, sir," I quickly interjected. "Heemat's traveling companion."

"Wait a second," the large man said. "How can you be a hermit and have a traveling companion?"

Heemat's well-clothed form grew rigid. "I will not be swayed by the narrow-minded dictates of society!" he cried.

"Very well." The large man shrugged his incredibly broad shoulders. Heemat smiled apologetically.

"I am known as"—the large man made a sound like an elderly woman being bludgeoned to death by an unwilling snake—"although very few people can pronounce that. I am known, more simply, as the Dealer of Death."

"Indeed," I replied, recalling the great speed with which he had dispatched the rampaging pig. "And what can we do for you, Great Dealer of Death?"

"My friends call me the Dealer," the Dealer replied. "I am on a sacred quest, to find and kill the enemy of my employer, King Urfoo the Vengeful." Casually, the Dealer cracked his massive knuckles.

King Urfoo? A chill went down my spine as a certain clarity began returning to my head. My tired feet suddenly felt capable of running once again. King Urfoo?

"Ah, a sacred quest." Heemat nodded his head knowingly.

"Bzzgllphfll," Snarks added.

"Yes, I must find a certain wizard."

"A wizard?" I inquired. The chill seemed to have spread across my entire rib cage. I was, at last, fully and most completely awake.

"Ebenezum is his name," the Dealer remarked.

"Indeed?" My voice had suddenly become much higher. I thought it best to cease speaking altogether.

The Dealer of Death turned to the hermit and his companion. The muscles in the Dealer's neck rippled as he spoke.

"You know of no one by that name?"

"Wsspklblgg," Snarks mused.

"No, sir, we are not personally acquainted with the gentleman," Heemat added as he backed away.

"Alas." The Dealer sighed. His rib cage danced as the muscles contracted. "My quest must continue."

A particularly loud snore came from amidst the brambles.

"What is that?" The Dealer looked about him, a grim smile playing about his lips. "Another wild pig that needs to be strangled?"

"No, sir!" I cried. " 'Twas nothing! Just a forest bird!"

Ebenezum moaned in his sleep, then snored again.

"You're sure it's not a pig?" the Dealer asked wistfully. "Sounds too deep for a bird. I do rather enjoy strangling pigs."

We paused for a moment but heard nothing but birds and the rustling of small forest animals. Ebenezum was mercifully silent.

"Oh, well, I must get back to the main road, then." The Dealer snatched a passing butterfly and ripped it in two. "Not as much fun as killing a pig," he muttered.

Heemat gave the large man directions on how to regain the highway. The Dealer waved to us all and started back the way he came, his stride three times that of a normal person. My breathing began to return to normal.

"Well, Snarks." Heemat waved to his companion. "Apparently no one wants our hospitality."

"A minute!" I cried, turning away from the rapidly retreating Dealer. "I have reconsidered. We shall make use of your hospitality after all."

"Ah, splendid!" Heemat clapped his hands together. "You realize, of course, that there is a small fee involved."

I nodded absently. I had made my decision at last, and I would not sway from it. Ebenezum was in no condition to travel, and though I still could not quite bring myself to trust the hermit, whatever his hovel offered had to be better than facing the Dealer of Death.

"I don't imagine we can wake your friend." Heemat nodded in the general direction of the brambles. "No matter. We'll get him there. Of course, this entails a slight portage fee."

I nodded again. With the Dealer of Death gone, I found my weariness was quickly returning. The three of us walked to the back of the stone.

"Come! We shall carry him!" Heemat and Snarks proceeded to disengage the wizard from the surrounding brambles.

There was a firm tap at my shoulder.

"Excuse me," the Dealer of Death said, "but I seem to have gotten myself turned about completely. Oh! Here's someone I haven't seen before. Aren't those wizard's robes?"

Ebenezum woke up and sneezed.

CHAPTER TEN

The common folk have many sayings, all about it being darkest before the dawn and clouds with silver linings and suchlike. We in the magical trade like to express our opinions of these matters somewhat differently. A lifetime of experience will have taught the average sorcerer that no matter how hopeless the situation seems, no matter how painful and fraught with danger his options may be, no matter how close he may be to an indescribably hideous death and perhaps even eternal damnation, still, the good wizard knows, it can always get far worse.

—from The Teachings of Ebenezum, Volume XLVI (General Introduction)

"Msstplckt!" Snarks cried.

"Gesundheit," the Dealer added as the hermit's companion ran away.

"Thank you." Ebenezum blew his nose on his sleeve. "And whom do I have the honor of addressing?"

"This is the Dealer of Death, master," I hastily interjected, "sent on a mission by one King Urfoo."

"Indeed?" Ebenezum struggled up to a sitting position, pulling a dozen briers along with him. "Help me up, would you, Wuntvor?"

I did as I was asked.

"So you're the Dealer of Death?" the wizard reiterated.

The Dealer made the woman-being-pummeled-at-some-length noise again. And Ebenezum repeated it.

The Dealer said he was impressed by my master's facility. Ebenezum remarked that he had some small learning. Wasn't the Dealer an acolyte of the respected "noise-rather-like-a-group-of-chickens-being-attacked-by-a-dozen-rakes" sect?

The Dealer was overjoyed that Ebenezum had heard of his order and began to talk rapidly about his teachers, all of whom had names that sounded as if someone were being strangled and torn to shreds simultaneously. The relief I had felt at my master's sudden recovery was once again turning to anxiety. I had very pointedly dropped Urfoo's name into the conversation when I had introduced them. Still, it was quite possible that the wizard did not know the great degree of danger he was in. How could I warn Ebenezum without giving his identity away to the large killer he now spoke to?

"But enough of this cheerful gossip!" the Dealer cried. "I do not even know your name. What knowledgeable man am I now addressing?"

"My good sir," Ebenezum said. I tugged violently at his sleeve. "Not now, Wuntvor, I'm talking. As I was saying, I am—"

The earth shook once again. The giants' social dance had become a once-a-year gala festival. Even the Dealer fell this time.

There was a roaring in the woods. Eagerly, the Dealer of Death regained his footing.

A very large brown bear crashed through the undergrowth. The Dealer smiled. He raised a hand as if he would wave at the eight-foot-high, fear-crazed beast. The bear, sensing an easy target, rushed him.

His hand came down sharply on the bear's skull as the beast approached. There was a sharp crack. The Dealer stepped back to avoid the bear's still-swinging claws. The bear, now deceased, fell to the floor of the clearing.

"That's quite impressive," Ebenezum remarked. "It was nothing," replied the Dealer, wiping bear's brains from his hand with a fallen leaf. "But when we were so rudely interrupted, you were introducing yourself?"

"Ah, yes." Ebenezum smiled as he straightened his robes. The end was near. I held my breath as I waited to hear the wizard's last words before his very speedy assassination. I wondered absently if his brains would be a different color from those of the bear.

"As I was saying," the wizard continued, "I am unable to

divulge that information at this time. Like you, sir, I am on a mission."

The Dealer nodded his head. "I knew you were a kindred spirit all along."

"We are all kindred spirits!" Heemat cried, waving his hands to include the whole group of us and perhaps the entire forest beyond. "That is why Snarks and I stumbled upon you, and began this whole remarkable chain of events."

This was just too much. With the recent dramatic occurrences, I had almost forgotten the hermit and his cloaked companion. I began to say so when the wizard waved me to silence.

"We are quite assured of your importance," Ebenezum remarked. "Isn't it time you led us to your hovel?"

Heemat clapped his hands. "Of course! It's a very nice hovel, you'll see. Quite worth the pittance I ask for your stay."

I was astonished that my master would trust these two strangers so completely.

"Wunt, gather up the packs," my master instructed before I could say another word. In a lower voice, he remarked: "They are even more important than they think. And I do need my sleep."

I glanced up at the Dealer as I reassembled our gear. He, in turn, had furrowed his muscular brow as he gazed at the late afternoon sky.

"I think I shall come along as well," he remarked. "I do not care to be out alone after dark."

"Good! Good! A full hovel is a happy hovel!" Heemat cried as he turned to lead the way.

Ebenezum waved Snarks away as the hooded figure approached. "Keep your distance, would you? That's a good fellow. I need some space for proper contemplation." He wiped his nose on his sleeve, then paused for me to come abreast. "It has been an interesting trip so far," he whispered to me, "but I fear it will become far more interesting still, before the day is out."

I nodded and continued to walk down the path after Heemat. I found myself not so much interested as thoroughly confused. I was glad that Ebenezum was once again alert and in control.

With that thought, I felt the earth shift beneath me again.

"Wsstppllkt!" Snarks cried as a fissure opened at my feet. I found my stout oak staff torn from my trembling hands as the small cloaked figure ran down the length of the crack in the earth, swiping at things that tried to rise from the dust-filled fissure. The things cried out as they were struck, inhuman squeals of outrage, guttural cries of anger and pain.

The earth shook again and the fissure closed. Snarks walked back over and handed me my staff.

"Vllmmpp!" he remarked.

"Anytime," I replied, still somewhat shaken.

'Most interesting," Ebenezum mused behind me. "Just what I thought."

With that, the procession resumed its march in the fading evening light, winding its way along the barely existing path to Heemat's.

"All hail Plaugg, the Reasonably Grandiose!" Heemat intoned. "Welcome to my humble hovel." He waved as two women dressed in forest garb passed us in the front hallway, then stopped abruptly as we reached a table, behind which stood a third man wearing a hermit's cloak. Heemat studied the wall beyond the third hermit, then turned back to us.

"I'm afraid the only cells that I have to offer you are way over in the south wing. 'Tis the busy season in the forest, after all. They're quite nice accommodations, mind you, just don't get as much sun as those cells in the east and north. I'll block your rooms all in a group, so you may continue your discussions!"

He turned back to the third hermit. "Maurice, see what you can do for our guests, won't you?" He waved to all of us as he walked away. "Maurice will show you your rooms." He coughed delicately as he passed through one of the surrounding doorways. "He will, of course, also make arrangements for payment."

With that, he was gone. I noticed that Snarks had disappeared somewhere as well, so that only Ebenezum, the Dealer, and myself stood before Maurice, a thin man with a mustache, who proceeded to read us rates from a large red ledger. The

Dealer claimed to be without funds, as was the practice of his sect. Perhaps, I hoped wildly, we could be free of him at last. Ebenezum reached into one of the many folds in his wizardly robes and paid for all three of us.

I did my best not to show my dismay. The black-clad man followed us down the hall, idly squashing insects that here and there crawled along the walls. Was my master trying to kill us all?

"I am indebted to you," the large man rumbled as Maurice opened the door to our suite of cells. The mustached hermit hovered behind us as we inspected our new quarters, as if he expected something more from us. A single, dark look from the Dealer sent Maurice on his way.

"Again," the Dealer addressed Ebenezum, "thank you for your generosity. Most times my sect has little need for money. Gold, like all worldly things, would interfere with our art."

By way of emphasis for the last remark, the Dealer leapt in the air, twisted about in a somersault, and landed facing us on the room's far side.

"Very impressive." The wizard stroked his beard. "Still, it might be better if you ceased your demonstrations until you were once again outside. I believe you have landed on the room's only table."

The Dealer looked down at the splinters that clustered about his feet. "Once again, I am in your debt. Most times, my sect has little need for furniture. Tables, like all worldly things, would interfere with our art."

"Indeed," Ebenezum replied. "But you pursue your art now, do you not, on a sacred mission?"

The Dealer kicked what remained of the table out of the way. "You are a man of understanding, sir. For I have signed a contract with King Urfoo to kill a wizard and his two traveling companions." A grim smile lit the fellow's broad and muscular face. "And when my sect signs a contract, the dividend is death." He began to move his arm as if he might punch through the wall, then stopped himself.

"Excuse me," he remarked. "I become overly enthusiastic when discussing my art."

"Perfectly understandable," Ebenezum said as he sat in a rough-hewn chair, the room's only remaining piece of furniture. "But I am curious. How does one sign a death pact?"

The Dealer smiled gleefully. "One negotiates. You must be very clever. It is the final lesson of my sect."

"Indeed. It must be difficult to negotiate with royalty."

The Dealer nodded, still smiling.

"Especially with someone like Urfoo. I hear he is very tight with the purse strings."

"He is a clever bargainer, no doubt about it. But we Dealers of Death are cleverer still. After I kill the wizard and his two assistants, one very young, the other very fat, I need only return to Urfoo and pay him ten pieces of gold!"

Both Ebenezum and I stared at the large man for a moment. So this was how Urfoo, stingiest of monarchs, finally hired a qualified assassin!

"I was very clever," the Dealer continued. "Originally, Urfoo only had me pay a single gold piece for each of the three I kill. But the job is worth far more than that!"

"Indeed," Ebenezum said softly. "You are paying Urfoo so he can have you kill three persons?"

"Why, yes, those are the terms of the contract." The Dealer's well-muscled mouth turned downward. "Isn't that the proper method? Do you mean..."

He frowned deeply, then stamped his foot in frustration. The room shook. "Wouldn't you just know it! It was almost graduation. Who would blame anyone for skimping a little on the final course of study? I did learn all the definitions, just had a little trouble with addition and subtraction. I pay him, he pays me, what does it matter? A contract is a contract. Negotiations interfere with my art!"

The Dealer punched his fist into the ceiling. His knuckles left indentations in the rock. "I find this place confining. I will return in time for dinner." With that, the large man was gone.

When I was sure the Dealer was well away from the room, I asked my master just what he was doing.

"There are many kinds of problems, Wuntvor," Ebenezum intoned. "There are small ones that occur every day, and are easily dealt with. Then, there are the larger problems, that one must plan in order to conquer. Finally, there are a few problems so enormous that the only way to deal with them is to ignore them completely and go about your other business. Our friend the Dealer falls into this latter category."

How could my master be so calm? "But shouldn't we run away?"

"The minute we run, he will realize who we are. We are far safer as his friends. You see, I know even more about his sect than I discussed with the Dealer. They are commonly known as the Urracht."

"The Urracht?"

Ebenezum nodded. "The sound the victim makes after they see the assassin. The last sound they make."

"Urracht," I repeated. The word felt cold in my throat.

"Very efficient assassins, trained for years in the arts of death. Every effort is turned toward murder, so much effort, in fact, that there is little room in their lives for anything else."

I pondered my master's words.

"Do you mean they are somewhat deficient in wit?"

"Much as a large fern is deficient. Or perhaps a multifaceted piece of quartz. Every time they look for their feet, their shoes get in the way. In other words, yes. And as long as we act as a nonsuspicious pair, rather than the fugitive trio the Dealer is looking for, I imagine we will be quite safe."

The room shook again.

"Then again," Ebenezum remarked, "life is not so predictable as our assassin."

I braced myself, waiting for the quake to come. But the room shook in a way different from the tremors we had felt for the past few days. The shocks came with a regular rhythm, as if someone were trying to pound through the walls. And there was a voice, crying something far away, a single word over and over again.

It took me a long moment to recognize that word, but once I did, I knew the voice as well.

Deep and sepulchral, it rang in my ears:

"Doom! Doom! Doom!"

CHAPTER ELEVEN

Nothing is quite so unexpected as the truth. If, for example, you find your spells inadequate to defeat the local dragon, immediately go to your employers and apologize profusely. They should be so taken aback by your show of humility that you will have plenty of time to hastily vacate the areaf allowing the dragon to eat your employers rather than you, and thus halt any ugly rumors they might have spread about your competence.

—from The Teachings of Ebenezum, Volume XXXIII

The wizard and I looked at each other for a long moment, the only sound the warrior's distant, muffled cries. So Hendrek was lodging here as well! But what if Hendrek ran into the Dealer of Death? From our former dealings with Hendrek, we knew he was not a subtle man. And should the Dealer of Death see the three of us together... well, even the large Urracht assassin couldn't be that stupid, could he?

"Doom!"

Ebenezum sighed, his eyes still half-shut with fatigue.

"Wuntvor," he whispered. "See what can be done."

I left the room as Ebenezum sat heavily on the bed. It was up to me, then, to find the large warrior and silence his cries.

"Doom!"

The word echoed down the corridor. I turned left, headed toward the sound.

"Doom!" I prayed the Dealer had by now found the forest and a brace of pigs to be strangled. Truly, Hendrek could not make his presence more well known if he had painted arrows along the corridor. He cried out again, and the sound reverberated against the walls. What would make the big man shout that way?

Demons, of course.

I slowed my headlong rush to meet the warrior. I had run into the midst of sorcerous dealings before. I did not wish to repeat my error. Perhaps stealth was called for here rather than haste.

A small, sickly-colored creature, dressed in a checkered suit, stepped in my path. It waved a cigar in my direction. It was Smilin' Brax.

"Ah, we meet again," the demon intoned from behind the broadest smile I had ever seen. "Never forget a potential customer. Rule number one of demonic commerce. And believe me, young sir, never have you needed the services of a charmed weapons dealer as you do now."

The conviction in the demon's voice chilled me. I temporarily forgot my quest to stare at the cheerful creature. What terrible secret could make Brax that happy?

"And you notice that I call my weapons charmed.' Brax took a puff on its cigar. "Because my previously owned weapons are truly charming. And you, good sir, are in luck! I'm overstocked! I've just received a huge inventory from a tribe of nature worshipers. I don't know what came over me! I don't have room for them in my warehouse. I'm almost giving weapons away!"

Hendrek's voice echoed again from somewhere in the hermit's massive hovel. Brax's smile faltered for only an instant. The demon waved the cigar in my direction.

"You look like a young man of unusual intelligence," the creature remarked. "And I'm about to make you an unusual offer. You won't be sorry you listened to me. I see you carry a walking staff. Small stuff, I assure you. Have you ever thought really big? Why walk around with a puny branch, when you can own an entire magic tree?"

"Magic tr—" I began.

"I see the idea appeals to you! Yes, just think of it, a magic tree, straight from the nature worshipers of the North. And just barely broken in, I can assure you, only used for an occasional human sacrifice, and those only on the solstices! Someday, young man, you will be a sorcerer. Just think of the amazing tactical advantages if you came to your sorcerous battles accompanied by a tree!"

"Doom!" The cry was far closer now.

"Yes, yes, of course, we also carry more conventional weapons," Brax added hurriedly as he edged toward the middle of the hall. "Perhaps there is some question in your mind about obtaining something as large as a tree for your first mystical weapon. Although, may I assure you, the surprise value alone of such a weapon—"

Headbasher came flying down the hall.

"Urk!" the demon cried as it dodged the club. Hendrek followed his weapon at a run.

"Doom!" he cried as he spied us both.

"Friend Hendrek!" the demon replied in a somewhat less friendly voice than before. "I must protest your business practices! I have told you before, I will not accept a return of your enchanted weapon, no matter how forcefully"—the demon dodged Headbasher, now in Hendrek's hands—"you attempt to thrust it upon me. A contract is a contract."

Hendrek's club crashed into the wall quite close to the demon's head. I ducked as stone shards flew over me. I heard other voices in the distance, then the sound of running feet. Our little altercation seemed to be attracting some attention.

"Really, good Hendrek." Brax spoke rapidly, dodging the warrior's blows with even more dexterity than the last time I had seen them meet. "I am not unsympathetic to your plight. So you did not read the fine print on your contract." The demon dashed between the warrior's legs, temporarily freezing the large man. "A purely human error, nothing you should blame yourself for. But I, after all, am in the business of human error. And I urge you to pay your contract."

Hendrek regained his bearings and spun on the small fiend in checkerboard garb.

"I have done all I can, yelp!" the demon cried as the weapon grazed his shoulder. "All I ask is that you depose a minor ruler or assassinate a fairly ineffectual high priest. That would be payment enough for now. If you continue to refuse, I'm afraid the matter will be out of my hands. I'll be forced to send the Dread Collectors!"

Hendrek paused in his attack.

"The Dread Collectors?"

The demon nodded silently. "My hands are tied. There is nothing else I can do."

"I didn't know about the Dread Collectors," Hendrek whispered. "Doom."

The running footsteps grew closer. I glanced around to see Heemat and Snarks speeding toward us, their robes flapping with their haste.

"Yzzzgghhtt!" Snarks cried.

"You!" Brax replied, his smile replaced by a look of pure loathing.

"Doom!" Hendrek replied, once again raising his club above his head.

"Excuse me," an even more sepulchral voice intoned by my side. I jumped involuntarily. Suddenly, the Dealer of Death had appeared silently in our midst. "Somehow, in trying to find the exit, I lost my way in this vast maze of hallways." He glanced at Hendrek. "Ah! A fellow warrior!"

Club still over head, Hendrek regarded the newcomer with some suspicion.

"And what have we here!" Heemat jumped into our midst. "A large number of guests at my humble hovel, all engaged in social discourse!" He smiled at us all, his hands rubbing together fast enough to generate heat. "But I venture that few of you have yet experienced a number of the humble pleasures available at our little retreat. Have any of us visited the lower level yet today? No? Well, let me recommend our fabulous casino tavern, with entertainment nightly by the Hovellettes. And what of our temperature-controlled swimming pond—"

"Fellow warrior?" the Dealer of Death mused. "You wouldn't happen to know someone named Hendrek, would you? About your size, from what I understand."

With an unearthly shriek, Brax jumped upon the heavily cloaked Snarks.

"And have I mentioned our sun roof?" Heemat continued.

"Trrf blggllzz!"

"You have cost me too many sales, demon!" Brax screamed. "They were too kind to merely banish you from the Netherhells!

Now I shall banish you from this world as well!"

"Excuse me," the Dealer of Death murmured to Hendrek. "We should continue our conversation in a moment. It occurs to me that I haven't strangled a demon in some months."

Before I could see him move, his hand was around Brax's throat.

"Urracht!" Brax cried. "That's a very powerful grip you have there, sir."

The Dealer smiled. "Prepare to meet your death, demon."

"Have you considered how much more powerful you'd be with an enchanted weapon in that hand?"

The Dealer tightened his grip.

"Urk! Just asking! Easy credit terms!"

With a soft pop, the demon disappeared.

The Dealer grunted as his hand closed into a fist.

"That's the trouble with demons," he muttered. "You just get a good strangle started, and they disappear. No manners at all."

"There, there!" Heemat beamed. "Nasty things, demons, but it's gone now. Why don't we retire to the Hovel Lounge, where we can play a quick game of Hovelo?"

The Dealer flexed his fingers. "An awful feeling, losing something midstrangle. Makes you want to grab the nearest free creature and throttle him just so the effort isn't wasted."

"Hovelo is a fascinating game," Heemat continued. "And so easy to play! A bean is placed in one of three identical cups…"

He paused as the Dealer placed a hand on his shoulder.

"It takes a great effort of will not to strangle something," the Dealer whispered. "I would appreciate some quiet."

"Certainly!" Heemat's hands flew back within his robes. "Snarks, we should go and prepare this evening's entertainment."

A voice even more muffled than before mumbled something from the corner of the hallway. The small hermit seemed to have become completely entangled in his robes during his battle with Brax. Head and feet were absolutely indistinguishable within the mass of torn fabric. Some part of him bumped repeatedly against the wall.

"Llffmm," Snarks cried weakly.

"Doom," Hendrek replied. "The little fellow may be suffocating! Quick. Help me free him from his robes."

"No, no!" Heemat cried. "You don't understand, his sacred vows..."

But his protests were too late, for the immense warrior and the Dealer of Death had rushed to either side of the fallen hermit and were pulling the small man's clothes away in opposite directions.

There was a long, loud rip. Snarks's head popped out of what had once been his clothing. His head was green and had a pair of horns, one above each ear.

"A demon!" the Dealer cried.

"Doom!" replied Hendrek.

"This is not what you think—" Snarks the demon began. Hendrek's club smashed into the pile of formerly occupied robes. The now naked Snarks was halfway down the hall.

The demon cleared this throat politely. "You'd do better, you know, if you anticipated your opponent's movements before blindly striking."

"Doom!" Hendrek cried even more loudly. He twirled the enchanted Headbasher above his head until the warclub sang.

"And you know," Snarks continued as he ran, "you could stand to lose a little weight."

"Doom!" Hendrek bellowed so loudly that I had to cover my ears. His immense bulk rushed the retreating demon.

"And do you mind if I ask you when the last time was that you managed to take a bath?"

Hendrek's rage went beyond words. The demon disappeared around a bend in the corridor, the warrior in heavy pursuit.

"Our shame is known!" Heemat cried, wringing his robes with both hands. "Snarks is a demon, but he is a different demon. He could not help it! When he was a small demon-child, his mother was frightened to death by the promises of a group of politicians. You can imagine the damage done to his impressionable young mind. He became everything those demon politicians were not. Yes, friends, now Snarks is ruled by a great compulsion to tell nothing but the truth! The absolute truth, in great detail, and at great length, exploring every nuance that might occur to him, but the truth!"

" 'Tis no wonder you keep him heavily cloaked."

I looked up to see Ebenezum standing at the same bend in the corridor where Snarks and Hendrek had disappeared. The wizard blew his nose.

"Yes," Heemat admitted sadly. "Praise Plaugg the Moderately Exhalted, sometimes Snarks was too much for even a humble hermit such as myself. Why, do you know that one time he said I should stop moving my hands...and those things he inferred about my smile, and my haircut!" The hermit coughed softly. "Suffice it to say, heavy robes were preferable to a strangled throat."

"That," replied the Dealer of Death, "is a matter of opinion."

Ebenezum yawned. "Now that the excitement is over, I think I shall return to my nap." He glanced at Heemat, his great bushy eyebrows knitted in concern. "It is something of a trial to sleep in this place. I expect this to be reflected in our bill."

The hermit waved his shaved head in dismay. "I assure you, this is most unusual! My hovel is usually the most quiet place imaginable, a combination of the best the forest has to offer with a few innovative ideas Snarks brought with him from the Netherhells! Together, they make a truly unique experience. Just wait for tonight and the entertainment!"

"I would like some entertainment now," the Dealer whispered. "Could you show me the way to the forest?"

"Most assuredly! Follow me." The hermit bustled down the corridor.

"I will feel better when I have strangled something," the Dealer remarked as he silently followed the huffing Heemat.

Ebenezum turned to me when they were gone. "Quickly, Wunt, you must seek out Hendrek and calm him before he squashes Snarks. A demon who tells only the truth could be very useful in the time to come."

"Time to come?" I asked. "Do you mean Vushta?"

The wizard shook his head. "No. If we are ever to travel to Vushta, first we must survive this night." He tugged at his beard. "Wuntvor, I must get my sleep. While my affliction prevents my practice of sorcery, my wizardly intuition is still intact. That intuition, as much as anything, has kept us alive during our travels. And that intuition tells me that we must prepare today, for tonight none of us here will have time to sleep at all. Now go find Hendrek!"

I ran down the corridor, listening for the warrior's low cries and the boom of Headbasher hitting rock, rather than demons.

CHAPTER TWELVE

It is a mistake to think of all demons as being exactly alike. Some are short while others are tall; some are yellow, others are blue; some are nasty and others are extremely nasty. Some of the nastiest are quite fast as well. Should you encounter one of these, it is a mistake to think at all. Much more appropriate are such responses as running, screaming, and the very rapid formulation of a last will and testament.

—from The Teachings of Ebenezum, Volume IX

The noise was deafening. Three quick, thundering crashes followed by a wild scream.

"Doo—doo—doo!"

I heard another voice talking quietly in the midst of all the chaos. As I ran toward the melee, I could make out phrases between the thuds and shouts.

"Really, if you just held that club... time you rested, you're getting rather..." "a really good diet plan, even if it does come from the Netherhells..."

The crashing and screaming stopped. Again, I ceased my headlong run and peaked cautiously around the corner.

Hendrek sat in the hallway, his massive form propped against the far wall. His eyes stared through me, far beyond the limits of the hall.

"D-d-d-d-da," he whispered.

Snarks frowned and shook his head at the inert warrior.

"Your friend has become distraught," the demon remarked solemnly. "If he could have sat still and just heard me out, he might have realized I meant him no harm. But with these big fellows, it's always attack, attack, attack! Soon they simply work themselves over the edge. Pity."

Hendrek's great bulk quivered like pudding. He collapsed upon the floor with a thunderous crash. I ran to his side. Mercifully, he appeared to have lost consciousness.

The large warrior began to snore.

"Persistent fellow, isn't he?" Snarks brushed off his green-scaled arms. "Oh, if only he could see himself as others see him."

I approached the small demon warily, my stout oak staff held close to my chest. "What do you want?" I asked.

The demon sighed. "What does anyone want? Someone to love, the respect of one's peers, perhaps to achieve something special in one's brief span. The first two, I fear, are now beyond my grasp. My extreme honor has caused me to be banished from among my fellows. You know, you don't have to hold that staff of yours so tightly. I am no threat whatsoever. You weren't so cautious of me when my face was hidden by hermit's robes, were you?"

The demon was right. I relaxed my grip on the wood.

"And you know," the demon continued, "you could manage to stand up a little straighter. It would do wonders for your overall appearance."

I felt my fingers tighten again on my staff.

"Ah, there I go again, don't I?" Snarks shook its head sadly. "It really is quite out of my control, you know. Not only am I a demon, I'm a cursed demon. It all seems rather redundant, doesn't it?"

The demon turned, shaking its head sadly, and walked away down the hall. I took a step to follow, but the floor was no longer where I expected it to be.

When the tremor subsided, I picked myself up from where I had fallen. This new quake had been sharp and fast, and seemed to have left less damage than the last couple I had experienced. Still, it took me a moment to fully regain my balance.

Snarks waited patiently for me at the next bend in the hallway. The demon yawned.

"Of course," it said, "I knew this would come as well."

Before I could ask the demon just what it meant by that remark, it launched into a long and vivid description of my complexion and the various problems it perceived therein. Without thinking, my hands went to my face. I couldn't look that bad, could I? I had a large red blotch where? There were certain remedies, the demon continued, poultices concocted in the Netherhells for conditions even as severe as mine. Why, Snarks had used one of the formulas very successfully. In just a few days it had completely shrunk the pus-filled hillocks that had marred his countenance, and it had had the unexpected additional benefit of turning his skin an attractive shade of green.

We had reached the door to Snarks's cell at last. I wondered absently if there might be a large sack about somewhere that I might place over my head.

But I collected my thoughts as the demon clothed itself. There was far more at stake here than a few unsightly blemishes. I would take this far-too-honest creature to my master. Ebenezum would know what to do.

I told Snarks we must go see the wizard.

"Good!" it replied. "It is best if you are completely honest with me as well. An eye for an eye, as the old saying goes. But take it from one who knows: it is just amazing how the truth facilitates communication." The demon adjusted its robes as it spoke. "Just a moment here, and I shall be rrddrrff gglmmphggl."

The hood once again totally covered the demon's face.

I grabbed a portion of the hooded demon that I took for an arm and pulled him from the room. The sooner we saw Ebenezum, the sooner I could forget my problem skin.

"Doooooooom." A low moan came from the corridor where we had left Hendrek. Placing myself between him and Snarks, I approached the fallen warrior, who had managed to regain a sitting position.

"Doooom!" Hendrek fumbled for his enchanted warclub, but Headbasher was still beyond his enfeebled grasp. "A demon hermit! They are all around me! They haunt me wherever I go!"

"Kkssbrffmm!" Snarks replied.

Hendrek growled in response. I realized Heemat was right. By now, without Snarks's muffling robes, the immense warrior would once again be in a rage.

"No, Hendrek," I replied. "This demon is different. It was banished from the Netherhells. Now, like it or not, it is one of us."

"Trrff," added Snarks.

"Doom," Hendrek said shortly. He retrieved his club at last and used it to help him stand. Even that exertion seemed almost too much for him. He swayed perilously for a moment on regaining his feet, but somehow his large boots remained on the floor. He made no move to attack but glowered in the demon's direction.

"Doom," he added again.

"I'm taking our friend here to the wizard. He'll know what to do about this." I grabbed Snarks and once again led the way. Hendrek nodded glumly and followed.

Snarks removed his hood for a moment. "I expected all this, you know." One brief glance at Hendrek, and the hood was hastily back in place.

Feet ran rapidly down a side corridor. I turned to see Heemat approach.

"Praise Plaugg the Somewhat Omnipotent! The three of you together, walking as friends!"

"Doom!" Hendrek whispered to me. "These corridors seem a maze, and yet we encounter a new person every fifty paces. 'Tis an enchanted place. I would not be surprised if I were to turn a corner and run into myself!"

Hendrek was right. I had felt a growing sense of uneasiness, too. For an establishment of this size, we seemed to be having random encounters impossible within the laws of chance. But then, Heemat had mentioned that some of this place had been built according to plans from the Netherhells.

"But we must plan tonight's entertainment," Heemat continued. "If our gracious guests could excuse Snarks now, he could give me some much needed assistance in the preparations."

I was about to object when I smelled the sulfur.

"Doom!" Hendrek cried again, his warclub poised unsteadily over his head.

Brax stood in the hallway before us. The demon flicked a bit of cigar ash on the floor.

"Last chance, Hendrek."

"Doom." The warrior did not move.

"Very well," Brax replied. "You shall meet the Dread Collectors."

With that, the chessboard-costumed demon disappeared, and in its place stood something extremely large and incredibly ugly. It appeared to have at least nine heads of different shapes and sizes. All the heads, however, had very sharp looking teeth. Perhaps, it occurred to me, this thing was actually a "they."

It, or they, scraped half a dozen feet equipped with razor claws along the floor, gouging rivulets in the hard-packed earth. The heads spoke as one.

"We have come to collect you," they said. "Will you come quietly, or do we have to rend and tear?"

All nine heads smiled as they finished the sentence. I had the sudden feeling that rending and tearing were two of their favorite forms of recreation.

"Doom!" Hendrek replied. "Before you rend and tear, you will feel the wrath of Headbasher!"

The nine heads laughed as one. I did not find the sound cheerful in the least.

"Shall we?" one head, vaguely in the center of the monstrous mass, asked.

"After you," the remaining heads replied. As one, nine demonic mouths opened and howled.

That howl was like nothing I had ever heard, the death cries of a hundred birds, or a thousand rodents screaming as they are crushed underfoot. The sound hit us like a wave from one of the Great Seas, pushing me back down the hall. I felt as if the wailing force would tear the flesh from my body and only leave the bones behind. I realized, in that instant, that the Collectors might have come for Hendrek, but they would take the rest of us as well.

The sound filled my head. All I could think of was the wailing. The things were coming for us, a blur of motion, all claws and teeth and long, sharp, razor things; tails, perhaps, or maybe something else that had no name.

I managed to lift my staff. Perhaps I could beat back a head or two before they overwhelmed me. I was aware of the others around me. Although the fiends rushed toward us, I felt that time had slowed, allowing me to regard each of my fellows in turn and ponder some on my life as well.

Hendrek, grim and silent, held his club at the ready. Snarks had pulled back its hood and was staring at the approaching demon-thing with a look of contempt. The evil eye, I thought. Maybe our honest demon would give the Dread Collectors indigestion. I did not see Heemat until Hendrek moved, revealing the hermit's hiding place.

The howling rose in pitch. It would push my eyeballs straight back into their sockets. The things were almost on us now, their slavering jaws as wide as my staff was long. I prepared to strike.

Words carried over the howling, words punctuated by sneezing.

The shrieks of demon rage became shrieks of fear. The heads turned on each other, snapping and biting, scratching and clawing. A dark, foul-smelling liquid sprayed through the air. It was demon blood.

There was an explosion like thunder, just overhead. The Dread Collectors vanished.

"Doom," Hendrek murmured.

The wizard sat at the far end of the corridor, his eyes closed, his breathing rapid. Ebenezum was still far from being at his best. But his magic had saved us again.

It occurred to me then that I might have been able to use sorcery against the Dread Collectors as well. I stared blankly at my stout oak staff. I was so used to confronting demons with brute force that my use of magic in a situation such as this never entered my head. True, I still only knew a few spells, and I imagined a rain of dead fish would have done little to slow the Collectors' attack. Still, there might have been some other bit of magic I might have used, far more effective than the piece of wood I held in my hands. I would have to start thinking like a wizard.

Ebenezum groaned and slid farther onto the floor.

"Hendrek!" I called to the large warrior, who still stared blankly at the spot where the Dread Collectors had disappeared.

"Help me get my master to his room. I fear Ebenezum still needs his rest."

"Excuse me," a voice said by my side.

I spun before I could think, my body still full of the fear brought by our recent demonic encounter. My staff held the full force of my weight behind it as it rammed into the Dealer's shoulder.

The staff shattered as if it were made of glass. Splinters littered the floor. The Dealer of Death seemed not to notice.

"Excuse me," he repeated. "I believe the time for proper introductions is in order. If our companions here"—he smiled graciously at the large warrior and the fallen wizard—"are Hendrek and Ebenezum, you, I imagine, must be named Wuntvor?"

I did not reply. My tongue felt like ice within my mouth.

"Come come, now," the Dealer chided. "If we have to conduct business here, the least we can do is remain on friendly terms. You'll find me a very reasonable man. I'll give you a much more colorful death than you ever imagined. You'd be amazed at the large number of options available."

Somehow, I didn't find the Dealer's reassurances at all comforting.

"There are, of course, the popular standards: strangulation, beheading, impalement, suffocation... You know, the classic deaths. But my cult features a large number of novelty murders as well. Take 'The Troll and the Shepherdess,' for instance. That's a very popular number, let me tell you." Hendrek could take no more. His face, normally flushed, was now crimson with anger, in stark contrast to the paleness of his knuckles where they gripped the doomed warclub, Headbasher.

He rushed the Dealer in silence. Headbasher sought the assassin's skull, but the Dealer deflected the club with a skillful fist. There was a crash when club met fist, like stone against stone.

The Dealer winced and smiled as he blew on his hand. "Ah. A worthy opponent. I shall have my entertainment at last."

"Doom," was Hendrek's sole reply as his club once again flew through the air. The Dealer deflected the new blow with an open palm, the sound of a small boulder falling on paving stone. The Dealer of Death lashed out with a foot aimed at Hendrek's great armored stomach. The foot met Headbasher instead, which Hendrek had somehow twisted to protect his vitals. I heard the sound of a tree crashing in the forest.

The Dealer tried to distract the warrior with his fists, but wherever the assassin mounted an attack, Headbasher was there first. The club seemed almost a part of the large warrior's arms, an extra joint that Hendrek could flex, giving him twice the power and speed of a normal man.

Or mayhap, I thought, the club controlled the man. In my previous experience with the vast warrior, Hendrek had always had a tendency to lumber. Now, though, his great club flashing in his hands, parrying constant blows from the Dealer of Death, the huge man seemed to dance, pirouetting from one impossible defense to another unlikely attack, then back to defense again. With the club in his hands, the warrior himself appeared enchanted. The Dealer of Death was an extremely well trained assassin; but when he faced Hendrek, he faced magic.

The Dealer of Death seemed to be enjoying himself immensely, however. He would laugh with every blow of Headbasher, and his face was lit by a smile as innocent as a child's.

"Urracht against enchantment!" he cried at last. " 'Tis a fair game, 'twould seem, but I fear it's time to change the rules!"

He laughed, jumped to one side, landed on his hands, then sprang to his feet behind the large warrior. Hendrek spun to defend himself again, but the Dealer now stood over the unconscious Ebenezum.

"If I cannot kill the enchanted warrior," the Dealer remarked, "I shall kill the enchanter instead. You have to be flexible in my profession."

Hendrek raised his club threateningly.

"I do believe I can fend you off and kill someone else at the same time," the Dealer continued. "In fact, I consider it a bit of a challenge." He smiled down at the prone wizard.

Hendrek approached the Dealer of Death warily as the assassin knelt and placed a very large hand around my master's neck. Both paused, however, to look my way as I began to flap my elbows and whistle "The Happy Woodcutter's Song."

Large quantities of haddock appeared some inches below the hallway's vaulted ceiling. I had not lost my touch. Haddock, three-day-old dead haddock, rained on the Dealer, and Hendrek, and Ebenezum, and myself, and everywhere else the eye could see. Heemat and Snarks seemed to have disappeared. I realized I hadn't seen them since our battle with the Collectors.

I had to act quickly, while the others were still surprised, and before the odor of massive fish death overcame us all. I slipped and slid my way through a mountain of scales, over to where I had last seen the wizard.

The Dealer was no longer there. He had apparently fled in a vain search for air. But I heard the wizard groan from somewhere deep within the odiferous mound. A warclub rose and fell on the other side of the hallway as Hendrek hacked a passageway through the amassed fish flesh.

"Quick, Hendrek!" I cried. "Help me get Ebenezum to safety."

Hendrek erupted from the haddock with volcanic force, his enchanted warclub held high.

"Doom!" he cried as I burrowed my way down through the haddock toward the buried Ebenezum. But soon he was at my side, and together we pulled the wizard free of the fish corpses.

"We'll have to get him back to the room," I grunted, taking his feet.

"Nay!" Hendrek replied vehemently. "We should quit this hellish place. That dark assassin is lurking about here somewhere. The sooner we are away from here, the safer." He lifted up Ebenezum's head and shoulders as I might pick up a piece of parchment, quickly and without effort. The warrior turned and led the way through the haddock.

Ebenezum groaned again and opened his eyes. When he spoke at last, his voice was a hoarse whisper.

"The Happy Woodcutter's Song," was all he said.

I nodded. "It's all I could think to do in the circumstances."

The wizard glanced at the floor. "Apparently, your efforts were successful." He snuffled. "It is only at times like this that I am thankful for my malady."

I had been doing my best not to think about the odor, bad enough when I first used the spell in an open field, but quite overpowering in this enclosed space. In fact, I had been doing my best not to breathe at all. If I did not get fresh air in a moment, the fish and I would be much closer.

"Look!" Hendrek cried. "A stairway!" The warrior led us to a dark portico in the wall, which indeed led to a staircase that descended into further darkness.

Ebenezum insisted upon walking. So we set him down between us, keeping the large bulk of Hendrek in the lead. The darkness deepened as we went down, stairs worn smooth by years of use. I was forced to hold on to Ebenezum's robes as he kept a hand against Hendrek's armor-plated back. When at last we reached a landing, the darkness was total.

Hendrek bumped against something wooden and hollow-sounding.

"Doom!" he said.

A door was flung open before us. We were blinded by brilliant torchlight.

"At last!" I heard Heemat's cheerful voice ring in my ears. "Our guests have arrived! Let the entertainment begin!"

CHAPTER THIRTEEN

Casual amusement can be one of a wizard's greatest problems. After all, when one can conjure virtually anything, what can one do to 'get away from it all?'

Different wizards arrive at different solutions for their entertainment. A sorcerer of my acquaintance decided to increase his physical prowess through a vigorous program of exercise but found that his new muscles were wont to rip his robes midconjure. Another mage decided to develop the interplay between tongue and teeth so that he could exactly reproduce any insect noise imaginable. He became so successful at this that they discovered his corpse one midsummer's eve, suffocated by six thousand three hundred and two amorous katydids. And of the wizard who tried to start personal communications between humans and sheep... well, the less said the better.

—from The Teachings of Ebenezum, Volume XLIV

One of Heemat's many assistants led us to a table deep within this new room. The place seemed very large. Torches had been placed every twenty paces or so around three sides of the room's perimeter, but little light reached the area we now traversed. The room seemed full of people, some hermits, others travelers like ourselves. I had never seen so many people in one place in my entire life. I found it made me almost as nervous as being surrounded by ghosts. My mind caught at a fleeting doubt: Would Vushta be like this? What if I were surrounded by five hundred people upon entering that city of a thousand forbidden delights? Even worse, what if I were surrounded by five hundred women, all young and beautiful, with long red hair cascading across their backs and shoulders, and all of them, every single one, making demands of me?

Well, I would bear it somehow, if only for my master.

"Your table, sirs." Our hooded guide indicated three empty chairs to one side of a small, round table. A chair on the table's far side was occupied. Even in the almost nonexistent illumination, the seated man's size and stature told me at once who he was. We had found the Dealer of Death.

"Doom," Hendrek rumbled.

Heemat bustled over in our direction. "My most honored guests!" he cried, rubbing his stomach happily. "You are among the very privileged few to witness the full, true, and historically accurate saga of Plaugg the Adequately Overwhelming, related through an inspired mesh of dramatic reenactment, dancing, and song! And at the same time and for only a negligible fee, you'll be able to sample the first sacrament of our order. Pastry!" Heemat patted his stomach for emphasis as another hermit wheeled over a cart laden with cakes, pies, and cookies.

Heemat bowed, then shuffled away. "Make your choices quickly. Soon, you will be entertained!"

My eyes were becoming accustomed to the light, so dim after our confrontation with the torches at the entrance. I could see the Dealer smile. He nodded in my direction.

"I shall be entertained," he said.

But before he could speak further, there was a crash of cymbals, and a pair of heavy drapes parted before our table. Seven figures stood before us, all covered completely by monastic robes. Jaunty music began somewhere. The seven figures formed a line and started to kick. From the shapes of their legs I guessed the seven were female. Their singing voices confirmed my supposition:

"Seven happy hermits are we,
And we hope you all will see,
You've been brought here by the hand of fate
To hear about Plaugg the Moderately Great!"

Ebenezum leaned over and tapped the Dealer on the shoulder. "Might we discuss the terms of your contract for a moment?"

The assassin's smile disappeared. "I would rather not. I've become a bit sensitive about the matter. I only neglected one course of study, after all!"

"Indeed," the wizard hastily interjected. "I by no means

wish to criticize. Actually, should you think on it, a talk might be to your benefit as well. Your vocation is artful death. Consider how much more satisfying a murder might be if it followed a truly satisfying discussion."

The Dealer nodded his head slowly. " 'Tis true a good discussion might help to round my character. I have neglected things for my art."

Ebenezum stroked his beard and smiled. "Indeed. I knew you were a man of reason. I might humbly add that I am a man of some learning, and a discussion with me might help bring out some nuances of thought to aid you in your work."

The Dealer leaned toward the wizard, his gaze intent upon the mage. Ebenezum, for his part, stroked his beard absently, as if lost in deep and sorcerous conjecture. I turned back to the stage. The dancers and singers had vanished, replaced by an old monk who read from a great book:

"And lo, the masses turned unto Plaugg and entreated him to help them in their hour of need. And Plaugg heard them, for his throne was not so great or not so high as to escape the voice of the masses, and was made of second-rate materials besides, studded with elaborate baubles made of adequate cut glass. And Plaugg looked down upon the throng, and speaketh. And lo, he sayeth unto them: 'Not today. I do not feel up to it.' "

"Pray tell," Ebenezum said to the Dealer, "in your current contract, is there a time limit on the delivery of our deaths?"

The Dealer's eyes narrowed. "That is private information. A contract is a sacred..."He paused. "Well, perhaps not this contract. No such limit was stipulated."

"Good!" Ebenezum beamed. "We will have time for a really detailed discussion."

The Dealer relaxed. "Yes, perhaps we shall. I have slighted myself in some areas of study. A few hours of discussion could do no harm."

"Indeed!" Ebenezum removed his cap and placed it on the table. "Then 'tis time to get down to business. We are very lucky we met, you and I. I am quite skilled in the art of discussion; ask either of my compatriots. We can cover many of the areas neglected in your education. If you'll just give me a day or two to prepare, I'm sure I can devise a truly rewarding course of study. Then, in a few months, only weeks, really, you shall become a fully rounded individual!"

The Dealer stared long and hard at the wizard. A new group of singers and dancers had moved on the platform before us. They were doing a strange dance that seemed to consist of jumping wildly about for a few seconds, then sitting absolutely motionless for minutes at a time. One of the singers, off to the side, exhorted the others to "do the Plaugg." The crowd around us seemed quite taken with the performance.

"Your suggestion has a certain merit," the Dealer murmured, so low as to be almost lost in the crowd noise. "I shall think."

"But you haven't had any pastry!" Heemat had once again appeared tableside, rolling a cart laden with frosted edibles. "You do not want to offend Plaugg, praise his somewhat exalted name!" The hermit heaped pastries before Ebenezum, then moved on to do the same for the glowering Hendrek. "For it has been spoken that Plaugg has a moderately hideous wrath." He quickly ate something small and gooey, then moved on to fill the space before the Dealer. "Of course, no one has ever actually witnessed Plaugg's wrath, praise his fairly magnificent name. But there have been some very strong rumors about what might happen if we were to finally get him mad."

Heemat moved on to me. "It has been written that in a time of moderate crisis, Plaugg shall return. But what am I saying? You've been watching our dramatic presentation. You probably know more about Plaugg now, praise his reasonable significance, than I do!"

He chuckled to himself about his little joke. I, for one, had absolutely no idea what he was talking about. The performers before us had jumped about and sung a great deal, but there seemed to be no dramatic unity at all to what I'd seen. Of course, my mind had not been entirely on the players. I was somewhat more concerned with the drama that transpired at our small table: the Dealer still lost in thought over my master's proposal; Hendrek munching sullenly at some long, narrow sugar-thing; my master smiling and convivial, casually watching the not-yet-paid assassin's every move.

The Dealer's eyes bored into the layer cake before him, "I have thought," he said after a moment's pause, "and I have decided to accept your offer."

Ebenezum nodded solemnly, no hint on his features that he had just been granted a reprieve from death. I couldn't believe it! The Dealer of Death had accepted the wizard's offer! If my master could talk the Dealer into delaying assassination now, he could surely talk the Dealer out of killing us altogether in a few short days. I vowed never to distrust my master again. I wanted to jump up and down and shout. Still, that would not be businesslike. I filled my mouth with a frosted cupcake instead.

"You are a man of learning, and subtle powers of speech," the Dealer continued to my master. "You are correct. I must become flexible if I am to improve myself, both within and without my craft."

"Bravo!" my master intoned. "We will immediately begin—"

The Dealer held up his hand for silence. "Unfortunately, you are the only person included in this bargain. Your apprentice and the warrior will, of course, be killed immediately."

My half-eaten cupcake jumped in my throat. I tried to cough and swallow at the same time. Hendrek rose to his feet in a rush, the doomed Headbasher scattering delicacies before it as it skidded across the table. The Dealer yelped in surprise as he was assaulted by a sugar-filled deluge. He managed to dodge all but a single cherry pie.

The assassin wiped sticky red from his eyes. "Two can play at this, warrior," he whispered.

"Doom," Hendrek replied.

"Hendrek, wait!" I cried as I saw the immense man once again raise his warclub. I had had a revelation as the pie hit the Dealer's face. Hendrek could do no better than hold the assassin at bay with his enchanted warclub. But if we were to work together, using the wizard's wits and my beginning spells, we could break through the Dealer's defenses, as the pie, aided by a rain of pastry, had found its mark.

But my master was lost within his robes, hiding from the effects of the enchanted warclub, and Hendrek was full of battle lust and was beyond listening. The warrior dodged a chocolate cake lobbed easily across the table. But the Dealer had only thrown the cake as a decoy, for his right hand held three large, cream-filled eclairs, which shot across the table with deadly force. Yet club was faster than pastry, and I found a large, sodden chocolate mass deflected into my face.

"Gack!" I cried, quite beside myself. Bits of cupcake still lined my throat, and now icing obscured my vision. I expected the hands of the Dealer to descend on me at any moment and tear me into a dozen frosted pieces.

"Blasphemy!" Heemat's voice cut through my panic like a knife dividing a pie into sections. What could happen next? Expectant, I licked the remains of a missile from about my mouth, then wiped away enough cream filling to see.

Heemat stood before a huge crowd, all wearing the same monastic robes. There must have been a hundred hermits gathered there, all staring at the Dealer and myself. Maybe our commotion had interrupted the play.

I was relieved that whatever had occurred, the Dealer had temporarily ceased his attack. However, looking at the grim jaws and cold eyes of the assembled hermits, I had the feeling that what happened next might not be a marked improvement over recent events.

"Blasphemers!" Heemat repeated, his eyes darting back and forth between the Dealer and myself. "In your folly, you have sinned. You have taken what must be eaten, and used it for false purposes. Heathen interlopers, you have profaned the pastry!"

"Profaned the pastry," chanted the crowd of monks behind Heemat.

Heemat shook his head sadly, his eyes looking to the ceiling. "Sometimes I forget." His voice was a hoarse whisper, choked with emotion. "Sometimes my expansive nature gets the better of me. I ask people to be my guests, and share my custom!"

"Share our custom!" the chorus replied.

"And what do you do to thank me for all this?" Heemat waved his arms wildly above his head. "I, who have taken a twenty-year vow of silence, but feel such a compulsion to be friendly to the likes of you that I have managed to fulfill only six weeks of my pledge? Yes, yes, you! We invite you into our homes, give you the very best our humble order has to offer, and you—you—you stamp on the very name of Plaugg the Conservatively Overwhelming!"

"Conservatively Overwhelming," repeated the others.

"Indeed," Ebenezum said, stepping between me and the hermit horde. "I am sure we are all very sorry for departing from established custom among your sect. But we are new here, and perhaps a bit shaky as to the finer points of local tradition. I myself am recovering from a long, severe illness, and must spend much of my time sleeping. The large warrior at my side is possessed by a cursed warclub, and cannot be held responsible for his actions. And what of my apprentice? He is but a youth, and has not yet reached his majority. Surely you cannot blame him for a childish prank or two? We are, all three, quite innocent of malice." He coughed gently into his palm. "As to the gentleman in black... well, he will have to speak for himself."

The Dealer's eyes blazed at Ebenezum. "You would so lightly end our agreement, then? Well, my answer is this!" He reached behind him to grab an immense kuchen that covered the entire pastry cart.

The crowd of hermits gasped as one. Apricot filling oozed through the Dealer's fingers.

"No!" Heemat cried. "I will have no more of this! Take them!"

In an instant, a dozen monks swarmed over the Dealer. Another instant and the crowd had broken past Ebenezum. Monks surrounded me. I found my arms pinioned behind me, the Dealer similarly trussed at my side. Heemat stood before us both.

"Now listen, blasphemers, and I shall tell you of Plaugg's judgment, praise his reasonably enormous name!"

"Reasonably enormous name," the crowd replied.

"We are a strict sect, but we are fair," Heemat continued. "Before you are put to death, we will give you a trial, and it is possible that through this trial you may be redeemed. We have three trials within our sect. The first is trial by water."

"Trial by water," they all chimed in.

"Unfortunately, being in the middle of the woods, we are

rather lacking in moats, lakes, and other bodies of water suitable for the task."

"Suitable for the task," the others said.

Heemat rubbed his hands together. "And then, of course, there's that traditional favorite, trial by fire."

"Trial by fire," the hermits echoed.

"Unfortunately, we have discovered a side effect of this trial. Often, the fire gets a bit out of hand, and we find our hovel burning down as well."

"Burning down as well," the hundred chanted.

"How much better, then, our third form of judgment. And how much truer to the central spirit of the minor deity that we worship: Plaugg, bless his insubstantial glory!"

"Insubstantial glory!" they parroted.

Heemat leaned so close to me that I could smell his sugar-tainted breath. "Now, interlopers, you shall see the truth. Now, you shall have to face—trial by custard!"

"Trial by custard!" everyone cried.

I was grabbed by two-dozen hands and bustled through the curtains onto the stage. My last sight of the room was Ebenezum waving to me. They had not taken him or Hendrek; perhaps, I guessed, because neither of them were covered with pastry.

But Ebenezum was free! That meant he could help me! Didn't it?

I was carried into darkness.

CHAPTER FOURTEEN

Religion is a personal matter, and those of us in the sorcerous profession would do well to steer clear of it. Still, you will find some situations, say a spell accidentally demolishing someone's holy temple, where you will be given the choice of (one) conversion to their belief, or (two) being sacrificed to their deity. It is only at times like this when one realizes the true depth and beauty of religions, at least until one can find some way out of town.

—from The Teachings of Ebenezum, Volume XXXI

They had bound my hands and feet and left me in the dark. After some time had passed, the door to my cell opened and a lone hermit bearing a candle entered. He silently closed the thick door behind him, then approached the bed on which I lay. He placed the candle on the room's only table, then used both hands to remove his voluminous hood.

It was Snarks.

The hooded demon motioned me to silence. "I should not be here," it whispered, "but somehow I have taken a liking to you. You seem like one of those rare mortals who can be trusted. Perhaps it's your awkward manner and bumbling gait that endears you to me, or the fact that your hair is never properly combed, or the way you misbutton your shirt, or those complexion problems we discussed—but no matter. Whatever it is, you have touched my demon heart. I have decided to help."

I studied Snarks in the dim light. I wasn't sure whether to be grateful or scared out of my mind. Just what came out of a demon heart, anyway?

"Soon," Snarks continued, "the performance will be over in the Great Hall, and it will be time for your trial. Your blasphemy was a lucky break for Heemat, let me tell you. It gives him a much better climax for his evening's entertainment. Before that, all he had planned was another of those big musical numbers. You know: 'Listen to the dancing feet, praising Plaugg the Kind of Neat!' That sort of thing."

I nodded somewhat warily. Thus far, Snarks was not improving my outlook. I wondered if I should call the guards.

"But trial by custard!" the demon exclaimed. "It can be a terrible ordeal if you are unprepared. You and the other blasphemer will each be lowered into one of two vats of custard, each two feet higher than the top of your head. What happens next... well, suffocation by custard is a hideous death!"

The demon shivered. "There is only one escape. You must lift your head and eat your way to the surface! I have used my influence to have you dropped into the lemon-filled vat. It is somewhat lighter and less filling than the butterscotch. Once you have a hole to the surface, simply untie your hands and feet, and swim to the doorway at the vat's side. Then you will not only have survived trial by custard, but—"

There was a shuffling noise in the hallway, as if some great weight were being dragged across the cobblestones.

"The other blasphemer is being taken to the Great Hall. I must go. I cannot be seen here!" The demon swallowed hard. "I have no appetite for custard."

Snarks replaced its hood and moved to the door, opening it a crack. The demon looked both ways, turned to me, and waved.

"Grrffmmj!" it called. Then the demon was gone.

Eat my way to the surface? Untie my hands and feet? Snark's words spun through my mind. I had had no idea of the true nature of my ordeal until—

The door to my cell was flung open with such force that it smashed against the wall.

"Now, blasphemer!" Heemat's voice cried, high and full of rage.

And the room began to shake. It was a good quake this time, solid and deep, with a large amount of booming, crashing, and frightened voices in the background. One of the best ones we'd had, actually. I gave it eight out of ten. I wondered absently, tied up on the slab, when I had begun to rate these disturbances.

Heemat picked himself up from the floor when the quakes had finished. He brushed perfunctorily at his robes.

"As I was saying: Now, blasphemer! We will see just what you are made of! Guards, take him away!"

Four burly hermits rushed into the room and lifted me from my pallet. I imagined, in a few short minutes, that I should be made largely of custard.

"Let the trial begin!"

The curtains opened before us. I stood on a high platform, hands and feet tied, a burly hermit guard on either side. A few paces away, the Dealer of Death stood on a similar platform. The ropes around the Dealer appeared somewhat thicker than mine and covered his body in great loops from his chest to his ankles. A dozen burly hermits crowded to either side of him. Between the platforms were two iron vats, each large enough to contain three men. The one closer to me was filled with a quivering bright yellow. The contents of the other were more of a light brown.

The roar of the crowd drew my attention away from the vats. The curtains were open now, revealing an audience that filled the Great Hall.

Was this the room that I had sat in mere moments before? It looked different from my new vantage point, high above the crowd. It was still quite the largest enclosed space I had ever seen, mind you, but from where I stood now, it was definitely just a room, bordered by well-defined, torchlit walls, rather than the limitless vista it had felt like before. And as many people as there were down there, they seemed very small from my platform vantage. For a brief moment, I felt above them, removed.

And then I realized they were all here to see me. Me and the Dealer of Death. We were the attractions here, hundreds of people studying our faces, looking for signs of fear or guilt or even holy reassurance. I knew, somehow, far away, that perhaps I should be afraid. I was, after all, to be dumped into a vat of custard at any moment, and a part of me, deep inside, was screaming in a very tiny voice.

But they had me bound and guarded. There was nowhere to run, no place to hide. And the audience was out there—for me.

They all applauded. It felt wonderful. No more helpmate to the great Ebenezum. I was the center of attention now.

Would it be like this when I was a full-fledged wizard?

I bowed stiffly and lost my balance. Guards grabbed me from the rear, hauling me back from a premature meeting with the custard.

I looked up. The audience was silent. My near accident had caused the assembled masses to gasp as one.

Then, out of the silence came a lone voice, whistling "The Happy Woodcutter's Song."

I looked down to see Ebenezum and Hendrek, seated at the same table the Dealer and I had been spirited away from such a short time ago. Hendrek glowered at the crowd around him and played with the pouch that held the doomed club, Headbasher. Ebenezum shook his head firmly, then pointed to me. I nodded to him, and he touched his whistling mouth.

Did he wish me to whistle as well? Then again, what did I have to lose? If I was about to die in a vat of custard, there were worse ways to go out than whistling.

I began to whistle "The Happy Woodcutter's Song" as well. Ebenezum nodded enthusiastically. So he did want me to whistle!

The wizard had a plan.

Heemat glared at my master, but Ebenezum had stopped whistling and now seemed content to flap his elbows.

"O Plaugg, who may be among the Great Ones above, or may not, please hear our plea. These two you see before you have blasphemed your name in the midst of our most relatively holy ceremony. So we have brought them to trial before you now, and beseech you to aid us in judging them with your adequate wisdom!"

I noticed that Heemat was staring at me rather fixedly. Perhaps it was because I had whistled "The Happy Woodcutter's Song" during the entirety of his oration.

Heemat clapped his hands.

"Into the vats!"

Strong arms pushed me into the yellow pool. I barely had time for one quick breath before the sticky mass engulfed me.

I had closed my eyes when my feet hit, but my nose told me I had sunk into the mire. A strong scent of lemon, and then I could no longer breathe at all. I floated for an instant within the thick custard, my hands and feet tied, totally helpless. I fought down a rising panic and tried to remember what Snarks had bade me do. My feet hit the bottom of the vat, and I lifted my head toward the heavens, knowing I must eat now as I had never eaten before.

I opened my mouth, and custard poured in, too much, too fast! I forced my teeth closed, doing my best not to choke, and then, with an effort of will, swallowed. There. That wasn't too bad. Quite tasty, really.

It was just that there was so much more to go.

But I would not panic. I would persevere, for my master, and my future as a wizard, and for Vushta, the city of a thousand forbidden delights. So I ate again, quickly, efficiently, aware that every bite I took might be my last.

For my master! I thought. Ebenezum would be proud of the way I forcefully ate my custard.

For my future! How noble of character a wizard would be if he overcame a challenge like this in his youth. I swallowed a second mouthful, and then a third.

For Vushta! Dear, forbidden Vushta. Surviving an ordeal like this would only make me more prepared for that great city where a single glance might mark a man for life. I opened my mouth wide and let the custard pour.

My teeth closed on air. Air! I swallowed quickly and began to breathe. Air! Sweeter than all the lemon custard in the world! I laughed and began to whistle "The Happy Woodcutter's Song."

But something covered my mouth again. Had the custard shifted? My panic returned. I opened my eyes to see insect feelers waving above my nose.

It was a butterfly.

There was a crash as the vat, burdened with me, hundreds of gallons of custard, and thousands, perhaps millions, of butterflies, could no longer support the weight. I found myself floating off the stage on a river of custard.

Snarks called from the platform overhead:

"He has survived the trial by custard!"

"But—" Heemat began, rather flustered. "He can't—" He rubbed his bald head and smiled. "I suppose he can."

Hendrek waded into the yellow torrent and grabbed me before I could be swept beyond the wizard's table. He placed me on a seat above the now dwindling custard tide. Ebenezum, of course, was still sneezing.

When my master composed himself, I thanked him for not using the haddock spell.

Ebenezum nodded happily. "Butterflies were all that was needed. And it was better that I saved you without alienating our hosts. Undo Wuntvor's bonds, would you, Hendrek?"

The large warrior did as he was asked. In the meantime, Ebenezum went on to explain what a great thing it was that we had accomplished—collaborative magic. I had whistled, he had flapped and wriggled, and the magic had still occurred. That was important, since in flapping and wriggling, he wasn't doing anything sorcerous. Thus, the magical implications did not affect his malady until the spell was already successfully completed, whereas if he had tried to accomplish the entire spell himself, he would have collapsed in a sneezing fit halfway through the song.

"So you see what this means?" Ebenezum concluded. "Whole vistas of magic are open to me again. Together, Wuntvor, we might even find a cure!"

A cure? This was all too much. First, almost drowning in a vat of custard, and now this! I pictured myself fated to return to Wizard's Woods without the slightest chance of seeing Vushta for years to come.

Ebenezum was much too excited to notice my mood. "And it was never so important as now to muster our magical resources. While you were preparing for your ordeal, I have had discussions with Hendrek. His demonic tormentors were able to locate him much too quickly after our escape from Urfoo."

"Doom," Hendrek added.

"Which fits the pattern we began to see on our journey to Vushta. Wuntvor, there are far too many demons loose in the world. Something new is coming from the Netherhells. And now, Wuntvor, that certain inconveniences are out of the way"— he nodded to the stage and the still-upright vat of butterscotch custard—"we can find out just what that something is."

In my relief at being alive, I had quite forgotten what was still transpiring on the stage. By now, the live butterflies had all flown out among the audience, and they had swept the dead butterflies, custard, and broken bits of vat away.

Heemat stood, arms outstretched, on one of the platforms. His eyes surveyed the audience. He cleared his throat.

The remaining vat tipped over sideways, and the Dealer of Death tumbled out. The vat rolled about so that its innards faced the audience. There was no custard left in there at all. The iron sides had been licked clean.

The Dealer burped.

"Certain inconveniences appear to have returned," Ebenezum remarked. He tugged at his beard thoughtfully. "But perhaps it will take him a few minutes to digest. We must talk to Snarks, and quickly. He has knowledge of the Netherhells that is important to our guest and, yes, may be important to our very lives."

The Dealer groaned and tried to stand. His stomach appeared somewhat larger than it had before. Heemat ran back and forth across the upper platform, his hands rubbing together so fast that I expected to see sparks.

"Two have passed!" he cried. "Two! Two! Never in the history of the worship of Plaugg, bless his mundane magnificence, have two survived the trial! We must—we must—It is time for a conference!"

A heavily cowled figure scooted past our table. Hendrek grabbed his hood as Ebenezum held his wizardly nose. The doomed warrior had been correct in his assumption. It was Snarks.

"Good Snarks!" Ebenezum managed, doing his best not to sneeze. "We must speak—we must— spee—sp—" He quickly grabbed his cap and sneezed therein. "Pardon. Something is happening with the Nether—with the Ne— Ne— N—" Three sneezes this time, in rapid succession. Ebenezum held his cap at arm's length with some distaste. "Snarks, you mu— mus— Drat! Wuntvor! 'Tis up to you!"

The wizard fell beneath the table, lost in a sneezing fit.

"Indeed," I began. What should I ask this all-too-honest demon? I wanted to make my master proud! But there wasn't much time. Already the Dealer of Death was leaping about the stage, involved in a complex series of calisthenics designed, I was sure, to aid digestion and free custard-stiffened muscles.

"Indeed," I said again. "I believe you come from the Netherhells?"

"No, no, no," Snarks replied. "Actually, you know for a fact that I come from the Netherhells. You should think more before you speak, you know. Inexact language, inappropriate questions. Sometimes I don't know how you humans make it from day to day."

"Snarks!" I cried, a bit more loudly than perhaps I should. I would not be upset by his demon tongue. "We have reason to believe there's a plot afoot in the Netherhells!"

"And good reason it is, too," Snarks replied. "There are always plots afoot in the Netherhells. It's part of the charm of the place. But I imagine, in your bumbling way, you're asking me if there's one particular plot, a large, dangerous plot, perhaps, that could threaten all of humankind. Is that what you want to ask of me?"

I nodded my head. Perhaps it was best not to speak at all and just let the demon talk.

"Well, the answer is yes. Now, if you'll excuse me, I'm late for the conference."

"Doom!" Hendrek remarked as Snarks leapt up onstage. Ebenezum blew his nose.

Heemat had already turned away from the huddled monks and once again began to address the audience.

"Ladies and gentlemen, fellow believers, and our guests. Never in the history of Plauggdom has such a modestly blessed event as this occurred. Two in our midst have been tested, and found reasonably worthy. Even Plaugg himself, bless his marginal magnificence, must be looking down from his moderate height and—"

A small gray storm cloud appeared over Heemat's head, the kind that meant a moment's rain before it disappeared. Heemat paused midsentence to gape as the cloud took on the shape of a man, wearing rumpled gray robes and a distracted expression. The disheveled floating man squinted out into the audience.

"Pardon me," he muttered in a timorous voice. "I'm not so sure I should be here."

Heemat, his fellows on the stage, and all the hermit-monks in the audience had fallen to their knees. The assemblage looked to the rumpled man overhead and spoke with one voice.

"Plaugg!"

CHAPTER FIFTEEN

*So you think you know great, nail-biting excitement, you think
you know truly abject fear, think you know total and complete despair,
you think you know the incredibly degenerate underside of this world
we live in, and the ridiculously despicable lengths that your fellow man
can sink to, more rotten, more putrid than the lowest form of fungus....
Oh. You are a sorcerer as well. Then perhaps you do.*

—Further Conversations with Ebenezum, Volume III

"Oh, maybe I'm a little early," Plaugg said, seemingly to
himself. "Yes, of course, that must be it. I'm early!"

Ebenezum watched the minor deity with some trepidation.
Once again, the wizard held his nose.

"Oh, come now, come now," Plaugg said, singling the wizard
out. "I won't let you sneeze around me. It's the least I can do."

The wizard looked up at the gray, rumpled deity. He
breathed in and out without ill effect. "Do you mean to say,"
the wizard said cautiously, "that you have the power to cure my
affliction?"

"Well, that's a problem, isn't it?" Plaugg clasped his hands
together. "Not exactly, no. We minor deities can only do so
much, you know. Unfortunately, I can only cure your affliction
with regard to myself."

"Oh." Ebenezum frowned. "Pity."

"Yes, isn't it," Plaugg agreed. "It's one of the problems with
being a minor deity. You only get so much power, and oh, the
responsibility that comes with it! You could hardly imagine.
Always having to please the faithful. After all, what do you
imagine I'm doing here now? Although come to think of it, that
hasn't happened yet, has it?"

"O reasonably beneficent Plaugg!" Heemat cried from the platform.

"Yes, yes, I'll be with you in a moment," the minor deity remarked. "As soon as I finish talking with this gentleman here. You wouldn't believe how long it's been since I've had a good talk. It's one of the problems with my profession, I'm afraid. You get a lot of worship in my position, but very little good conversation."

Ebenezum nodded. "What would you like to talk about? You wouldn't want to tell us why you're here?"

"Oh, that." Plaugg sighed. "Duty. I do sometimes get tired of all that. Being a minor deity is really more trouble than it's worth. Your worshipers never look you in the eye, and should you even attempt to speak to them, they start sacrificing things to you. Sacrifices and more sacrifices, at the drop of a hat. Now I ask you, what use have I got for a dead goat?"

"Plaugg, do you demand a sacrifice?" Heemat queried.

"See what I mean?" The deity frowned. "Oh. Don't get me wrong. Heemat and his group are a perfectly nice bunch of worshipers. There are just certain problems with being a minor deity. For one thing, there's very little chance for promotion. And the hours! I've been thinking seriously about getting into another line of work."

"What do you wish from us, Adequate One?" Heemat continued.

"Mostly that you stop asking questions," the deity replied. "Believe it or not, I am here for a reason."

There was silence in the Great Hall. All was still. I noticed that sometime after the appearance of Plaugg, the Dealer of Death had managed to quit the stage. I decided to search the room for him, but I didn't have to look far. He stood just behind Ebenezum. He smiled at me.

"Oh," Plaugg said as the silence lengthened. "I suppose you want to know why I'm here. Well, that's a reasonable request, and you are my worshipers, after all. Very well. I am here to band us together through the coming crisis."

The coming crisis? I did not like the sound of that. Hendrek muttered darkly at my side.

A hermit directly below the deity pulled back his hood. It was Snarks.

"You mean the attack from the Netherhells?"

"Why, yes, didn't I say that?" Plaugg rubbed at his balding pate as he stared in the distance. "Oh. I suppose I didn't." He looked down at the ground beneath our feet. "Here it comes now."

It started more as a feeling than a sound. Deep, far deeper than any of the quakes we heard before, as if it started at the center of the world.

"Now I want us all to be ready!" Plaugg cried, his voice much stronger than before. "In a few minutes, we're going to see all kinds of demons! But they've never dealt with anyone like Plaugg's hermits before!"

The noise grew beneath our feet.

"Doom," Hendrek intoned. He unsheathed the doomed club, Headbasher. Ebenezum backed away to a safer distance.

"Now I want every one of you to do your utmost!" the deity encouraged. "Drive those demons back where they came from. Do it for Plaugg!"

The rumbling had become a vibration in the floor. It was difficult to remain standing. The Dealer walked up to me.

"It appears I must once again postpone your deaths," he said behind his childlike smile. "Oh, well. This is the most fun I've ever had, ever!" He flexed his muscles and stared expectantly at the floor.

I was glad someone was having a good time. The quake was quite loud by now. Plaugg had to shout to be heard.

"Okay." He pointed a quivering finger at the middle of the audience. "I imagine the Netherhells will break through just about there. And I'm pretty good at guessing these things, let me tell you. Comes with the job, I suppose. So everyone should spread out to the corners of the room. And pile those tables up in front of you, why don't you? It'll protect you from some of the molten debris."

"What, are some of you leaving?" Plaugg shook his balding head. "Now, you don't want to get me angry, do you? My wrath may not be in the big leagues, but it is moderately great, let me tell you! Oh, weapons? You need weapons? Well, all right, then. I do sometimes get carried away with myself. You'll have to excuse me."

I looked to my master, and he turned away from the deity, a bemused smile on his face.

"We find ourselves in the middle again, Wuntvor," remarked the mage. He held his nose as Hendrek approached.

"Doom," the large warrior intoned. "We shall be overwhelmed by those things!" He shifted the great warclub nervously from hand to hand.

This whole situation seemed to have gotten totally out of control. "Perhaps we should relocate," I suggested delicately.

Ebenezum shook his head. "I fear we should have to relocate to another world entirely. I think that for the first time in our travels, we have stumbled on something that is truly serious."

I swallowed hard. My hands ached for my stout oak staff. This was serious? Then what were all our battles and narrow escapes of the past few weeks? For a brief moment, I even longed for the utter peace and boredom of our home in the Western Kingdoms.

"Okay, now, they're almost here!" Plaugg shrieked at the top of his lungs. The rumbling had redoubled again. I tried to speak to my master, but I couldn't even hear myself. "Is everybody ready? I know you can do it! Just do what you do best!"

The deity paused to look at Ebenezum and myself. "Now, I will ask you folks not to do the fish trick. I know it has worked before, but this situation is different. And I simply refuse to work around large quantities of dead haddock. I'm sorry, but we all have our limits.

"Here they come! Here they come!" Plaugg was beginning to sound really excited. "Let's hear the call and defeat them all! Do it for Plaugg!"

That's when the earth really began to shake. I was thrown off my feet and bounced across the room. I tried to follow Plaugg's advice and crawl toward the wall.

And then the ground was ripped in two. I grabbed onto a table just to hold on to something solid. The table shifted and dragged me along with it toward the crack that widened in the floor. I was sliding straight for a pit that dropped all the way down to the Netherhells! I could hear the death screams of those who fell before me; screams that started loud and shrill, then faded with distance. I tried to find something else to grab onto, but everything was slipping away with me.

And then it stopped, as suddenly as it had begun. I found myself face to face with a troll.

"Slobber!" the troll remarked.

I hit the troll with the table. The table broke.

"Slobber!" the troll repeated.

"Oh, if my teachers could only see me now!" A large hand appeared before me and plucked the troll off the ground. An incredibly cheerful Dealer of Death stood at my side.

"This is the first chance I've had to strangle a troll," the Dealer enthused.

"No slob—" was all the troll had time to say.

A great, deep voice spoke somewhere behind me:

"Come on, my minions!
Grab all of them!
And tear every one of them
Limb from limb!"

Dust filled the air. It was impossible to see more than a few feet. Still, I had a cold feeling in my stomach about that voice. Only one poet could be that bad.

"Roar for the Netherhells
Let your colors unfurl,
In a matter of hours
We will rule this world!"

Dimly, I could see a great blue form standing above the rubble. Yes, it was the demon Guxx.

"We'll rule this world
With pride and pomp,
And so for the moment
Let's Stomp! Stomp! Stomp!"

This was terrible! There were demons everywhere! Every second the dust cleared, there seemed to be more of them, as if they sprang from the dust itself. If someone didn't do something quickly, we were all going to die. Worse yet, the last sounds to assail our ears would be Guxx's doggerel verse.

But then a higher voice cried out from across the room:

"Give me a P!"

A few ragged "P"s were shouted here and there.

"Give me an L!"

I cried, "L!" with the others. The response was stronger now.

"Quickly now!" Guxx screamed back at us.

"Don't let them rally! We need a death count we can tally!"

But the other voice would not be silenced.

"Give me an A!"

The dust had settled enough now so that I could see halfway around the room. A small red demon jumped for my throat. I still held a table leg, all that remained of the weapon I had used on the troll. I batted the small demon high in the air.

"A!" I cried.

Hendrek was at my side. His warclub wove a fantastic pattern in the air, knocking the senses from a dozen demons in as many seconds. Cries of "What?" "Who am I?" and "What am I doing here?" could be heard from those demons who were still conscious, evidence of Headbasher's hellish powers.

"U!" Hendrek cried with the rest of us.

I looked about for my master.

"Give me a G!"

The Dealer of Death stood at my other side, moving so fast that he made Hendrek's attack look like a Sunday stroll. Demon arms and legs were all around him. Sometimes they had demons attached.

"G!" the Dealer cried with the others. He laughed and began to whistle.

I spotted Heemat and Snarks as part of a circle of about a dozen hermits. Each of them held a stick a bit thicker and a little shorter than my usual stout oak walking staff. They were using them quite effectively to hold off a horde of demons and doing occasional greater damage among the fiends as well.

"Give me another G!"

"Another G!" they cried together joyously.

And then I saw my master. He had backed up against a pile

of rubble, holding his nose with both hands.

A particularly large and hairy troll advanced upon him.

"Slobber," the troll said in its gravel voice.

"And what does that spell?" came the voice from on high.

Ebenezum's face had become an odd shade of purplish red. His head reared back involuntarily. He could no longer hold his malady within.

The troll felt the full force of the nasal blow. The muscular creature jumped and screamed, shaking mucus from its legs and arms.

"No slobber! No slobber!" it cried as it ran back to the pit that led to the Netherhells.

"Plaugg!" a hundred voices joined together to shout.

"What's that spell?" the first voice prompted again.

"Plaugg!" We all joined in this time, a thousand voices strong.

"One more time!" The voice sounded delirious with joy.

I saw Ebenezum take a deep breath and join in.

"Plaugg!"

The world froze around us. Or, more specifically, the demons froze, in whatever position they had assumed when we had let loose with our final cheer. What dust remained in the air had vanished as well. Our surroundings were as cool and clear as a spring morning.

Plaugg hung where we'd left him in the middle of the air.

"There," he said. "That's much better, isn't it?"

Guxx screamed in rage from atop a large pile of dead hermits. Apparently he was the only demon unaffected by our chanted magic.

"You think to stop Guxx and his demons,
But I will find a way to free them!"

Ebenezum blew his nose. "Beware!" he called to Plaugg. "His power grows with every rhyme!"

"Even that one?" The deity shook his head in disbelief. "But who am I to judge? I don't make the rules. Or at least not many of them."

The large blue demon flexed its muscular arms. Its claws had grown back since its fight with Ebenezum.

"You try to stop Guxx with your jokes,

But I will live to see you choke!"

I saw the demons nearest me twitch slightly. Guxx's poetry would bring them back to life!

"My, you are a serious fellow, aren't you?" Plaugg replied. "Just a second, now, and I'll nicely send you back where you came from."

Ebenezum began to sneeze again. The demon's magic was returning!

Guxx bared its razor fangs.

"You'll not have a moment!
You'll have no time at all,
For me and my demons
Will cause your downfall!"

All the demons nearby definitely quivered.

"Oh, this fellow can be tiresome, can't he?" Plaugg replied. "Give me a moment, won't you? I hardly ever do these physical manifestations, and usually they only allow me to show up as burning moss. I'm not high enough up on the ladder to do bushes, you know. But do I mind?"

Guxx leapt up and raked the air with its claws. You could tell the demon was feeling better with every passing moment.

"You've had your chance,
You heavenly fool,
But now 'tis time
For demons to rule!"

I saw the demon closest to me blink repeatedly.

"Name calling, is it, then?" Plaugg retorted. "It's no longer a gentleman's game, I see. If I wasn't having so much trouble figuring out just how to make things work in this form, you wouldn't even have time to carry on this way. Perhaps I should have shown up as the burning tree moss after all. It's not very intellectually stimulating, though, let me tell you."

"I've had enough of your lies and talk!
Fellow demons, arise, to work!"

The frozen demons didn't move.

"Ahem," Guxx remarked. "Not good enough, huh? Well, let's try this:

"Come on demons, arise, dig in,
For we have a world to win!"
A few of the demons yawned and stretched.
"O reasonably mighty Plaugg!" Heemat cried. "Do something. Please?"
"I'm sorry," the deity replied. "I can't be rushed. Oh, wait a second. Is this it?" He shook his posterior three times. Nothing happened.
"Arise demons! Come now, make haste!
For we have a world to waste!"
The demons awoke en masse.
"Quick! Do something!" Heemat screamed. "Er... we beseech you! Please!"
"Yes, yes, I'll have it soon." Plaugg bit his lower lip. "You'll just have to handle them for a moment or two."
"This one is mine!" the Dealer of Death called, launching himself toward Guxx. "I always wanted to strangle a really big demon!"
Guxx struck out at the approaching assassin, but the Dealer was too fast. Guxx held nothing but itself in its claws, and the Dealer held the demon in a stranglehold from behind.
"Demons, demons, to work, to work!
We must overwhelm these pitiful—urracht!"
The Dealer tightened his hold.
"Wait a second!" Plaugg cried as the demons once again began to rend and tear. "I have it!" He shook his posterior three times and snapped his fingers.
Trumpets sounded from on high. I heard the flutter of wings above us, too, as if the air were filled with invisible birds. An even larger hole appeared in the middle of the room. The denizens of the Netherhells shrieked as one as they were pulled back to their home.
When the hole had closed, Heemat and ten other hermits rose from where they sat on Snarks.
"Can't risk losing a convert." Heemat smiled.
"Vsspllthmm Quxx!" Snarks replied.
"There's one left?" Plaugg frowned. "But I quite specifically remember getting an exact count."

It was then that I realized the Dealer was no longer among us.

"Well," Plaugg said. "It's been nice. Don't call me, I'll call you. I need a vacation. It's a problem with my position, you know. Do you think they give me any time off at all?"

And with that, Plaugg was gone as well.

Ebenezum blew his nose.

"Now our real work begins."

CHAPTER SIXTEEN

Beginnings and endings are, for the most part, artificial constructs. You say you begin when you are born, but what of those months spent growing in the womb? Endings are hazier still, for further things may occur that extend and enlarge the earlier story. And that is my final sentence on the subject. Or perhaps this one is the final sentence. No, most assuredly what I write now is the final word on the matter. But now that I think upon it, perhaps this—

—from The Teachings of Ebenezum, Volume LVII (Abridged)

"What do you mean, you won't pay?"
Ebenezum stared evenly at a scarlet Heemat.

"As you recall, good Heemat, we paid for basic room and board on arrival. At that point, you gave us no indication of the extent of additional charges we might entail."

"But surely you must realize that a hovel of our standing—"

The wizard glanced through the three sheets of parchment, each one filled with a list of charges written in a tiny hand. "Now, I see you list a broken table among the charges. That, at least, is a reasonable request. I suggest that you contact the man who broke said table. He is, I believe, currently residing in the Netherhells." He slapped the bill before him. "Ninety-six gallons of lemon custard? You would dare charge us—" Ebenezum became speechless with wizardly rage.

Heemat shrugged. "Someone has to pay it."

"Indeed." The wizard spoke all too evenly. I had seen my master like this before. I stood as far back as I could possibly get.

"I will say the following only once," the wizard remarked. "Sir, how would you feel if you were turned into a frog?"

"A frog," Heemat repeated. He looked down at his feet. Perhaps he imagined them webbed. He looked back at Ebenezum, in full sorcerous regalia.

"A frog," he said again. He snatched the bills from Ebenezum's grasp. "Well, perhaps there are a few mistakes herein. Occasionally, our accountants do become overzealous. I shall review the account personally."

"Please do so." The wizard's voice had grown considerably calmer. "We will, of course, be taking Snarks with us as well."

"You're taking Snarks?" The color returned to Heemat's face. "You cheat me of my rightful monies, and then you demand my best assistant? I'll have you know—"

"I understand the lily pads are very nice this time of year," Ebenezum interjected.

"Lily pads." Heemat went white. "Too long have I neglected my vow of silence. It is high time I reinstituted my most holy pledge, this very instant." Heemat clamped his lips together tight.

"I have always admired holy men," Ebenezum replied as Hendrek joined us. The large warrior had Snarks in tow.

The demon hermit removed its cowl. "They are right, friend Heemat," it said. "I saw what was going on before I was expelled from the Netherhells. There are certain demons down there who are tired of being constantly under the earth. They would like to see what it feels like to control the surface as well. And these factions are finding greater demonic favor every day."

"Far too true," Ebenezum agreed from a safe distance. "My 'prentice and I have seen a massive overabundance of sorcerous activity in our travels to fabled Vushta, and I have long feared consequences such as these. So the four of us, Wuntvor, myself, Snarks, and the warrior Hendrek, must continue to Vushta in all haste. At first, I wished to visit this city for personal reasons. Now, though, I must make preparations to warn the great Wizard's University, and help them prepare for the tremendous sorcerous battle that is to come."

Heemat nodded silently.

"So you actually will keep to your vow of silence," Snarks remarked. "It will make up for all the times you talked too much. And you know, friend Heemat, you, too, could stand to lose a few pounds. And of course, I would be remiss if I did not mention grrllp xxzzttff krll."

Hendrek had replaced the cowl on the demon's head.

"Doom," the warrior remarked.

Heemat, who seemed on the edge of saying something, glanced at the wizard and did not.

"We appreciate your reasonableness in this matter," Ebenezum continued to the hermit. "And due to the severity of the matter, we have taken the liberty of borrowing a horse and cart from your stables. Oh, have no fear! They'll only be gone for a few months at most! That is, so long as we're not attacked by demons. Still, I want you to know that all four of us appreciate your sacrifice, so that we may get some much needed rest on our way to Vushta."

He pointed to the kitchen. "Wuntvor, go and fetch those two sacks of provisions I had put aside."

I did as I was told, doing my best to ignore Heemat, who had once again turned the red of a truly spectacular sunset.

And so we were on our way once again to Vushta, city of a thousand forbidden delights that could truly mark a man for life. I couldn't remember the last time I was in such a good mood. A light rain fell as the cart made its way through the woods, as refreshing a cold, light rain as I had ever felt. I hummed to myself as I urged the horse forward. Coming from a farming background, I had as much experience as anyone with animals.

Ebenezum sat on the seat next to me on the cart. It was plain that the wizard was still exhausted. Every minute or two he began to nod, until the bumps of the cart jarred him awake. Hendrek sat directly behind us, glowering as usual. Snarks sat even farther back in the cart, under the canvas covering, doing whatever Snarks did deep within those robes.

A bloodcurdling scream came from the bushes. A man dressed only in a loincloth rushed toward the cart, dagger held before him. His bare foot hit a rock as he ran up the road. He tripped. Somehow, he managed to impale himself on his own weapon.

"Another assassin," I remarked absently as we rode by the corpse.

"Indeed," Ebenezum replied. "It's all rather comforting, isn't it?"

And indeed it was. Ebenezum finally fell to sleep in earnest, and I continued to drive the cart, to Vushta and destiny.

Oh, what a wonderful world!

A MULTITUDE OF MONSTERS

Book Two of the Ebenezum Series

Introduction

I decided I wanted to be a science fiction writer in the fifth grade, at the Hoover Drive Elementary School in Greece, NY. My teacher, Mr. Fabry, would read to us at the end of the every day; lots of Mark Twain, as I recall, but a smattering of other writers, including, for a couple of glorious weeks somewhere in winter, THE INVISIBLE MAN by H.G. Wells. Whoo, doggies! First off, you have a guy who figures out how to become invisible (neat, huh?) and then he goes crazy (which, to my ten-year-old brain, was even neater.)

I immediately sought out SEVEN SCIENCE FICTION NOVELS OF H.G. WELLS, and read the first five of the seven. WAR OF THE WORLDS! THE TIME MACHINE! FIRST MEN IN THE MOON! THE INVISIBLE MAN (one more time!) And, best of all, THE ISLAND OF DR. MOREAU! Creepy beast men were even neater than being invisible. (The last two in that volume, FOOD OF THE GODS and IN THE DAYS OF THE COMET seemed a bit too dense for me at the time.) I was hooked. I read everything in the school library; the Heinlein "juveniles", and the "Paul French" (Isaac Asimov, actually) books, and bugged my parents to buy me every volume of TOM CORBETT, SPACE CADET. The town of Greece finally built a standing library (before that, we had only had a Bookmobile), and I quickly devoured their collection of sf books as well. In addition, some kind soul had donated all their old science fiction magazines to the library, so I'd bring home half a dozen issues of AMAZING, GALAXY, ANALOG and all the others and read them cover to cover. I moved on to the larger library in downtown Rochester NY. Ace and Ballantine and half a dozen other publishers put out new paperbacks every month. I ended up getting a paper route to support my habit.

So, I got the reading part of it down. But I wanted to write the stuff, too.

Back in the fifth grade, my teacher had the students put out their own mimeographed newspaper. It contained my first published story. "Frankenstein Meets Juliet." In junior high school, I wrote parodies of the stuff that me and my buddies read ("Doc Cabbage, the Man of Chartreuse") and eventually went on to make a couple of silent films, a pair of Tarzan takeoffs starring my best buddy, Glenn Garman, called "Garman of the Grapes" and "Garman Baby."

High school ended. College came and went. I'd write a short story now and then, send it out to the markets I'd find in Writer's Digest, and get rejected. Getting rejected is never any fun. But I realized, some six years out of college, that I wasn't really writing enough (a couple of stories a year) to say I was serious about breaking into publishing.

I attended a couple of science fiction workshops, including one run by Hal Clement, which bolstered my confidence to actually become a writer. As a result of the Clement workshop, I posted a notice posted at the Science Fantasy Bookstore in Cambridge, which led to the first meeting of a writers' group that would get together every couple weeks. Suddenly, I had deadlines and structure.

The second story I wrote in our new workshop was called "A Malady of Magicks." The basic idea came from "What if a wizard became allergic to magic?" But I didn't think the wizard should tell the tale. Instead, I invented a young apprentice, who would tell the great man's story, much like Dr. Watson does for Sherlock Holmes. I submitted the story to all the major markets, from highest paying down to the lowest. And the last, poorest paying market actually bought it – FANTASTIC, edited at the time by Ted White, who would go on to helm HEAVY METAL.

Six months later, the story saw print, and got picked by Lin Carter to appear in THE YEAR'S BEST FANTASY collection. More people read it, and I got requests to submit further Ebenezum stories to a pair of anthologies. Pretty soon I had a bunch of stories, all gently lampooning the fantasy novels I had grown up with. In those days, there were regular science fiction

conventions all year round up and down the east coast. These were great places to get known and to talk to real live science fiction editors. Which I did. It was at one of these conventions (at Disklave, I believe, held outside Washington D.C.) that Ginjer Buchanan, newly hired as an editor for Ace Books, asked me if I had anything she might be interested in. I suggested an Ebenezum trilogy. She liked the idea, and the books ended up selling quite well, going through multiple printings and really launching my funny fantasy career.

Someday, I hope to collect all the other Ebenezum stories that aren't in the original six-book series into a collection of their own. If these books do well in their new e-format, that just might happen.

But, in the meantime, this series, which started with *A Malady of Magicks*, is where it all began. I hope you enjoy it.

Craig Shaw Gardner
May 2013

CHAPTER ONE

When traveling, the sages say, one must always be prepared to accept local customs. Yet there are areas of this very kingdom where one might find it customary to tax a wizard into poverty; to insist a wizard should not be paid, for magic exists only for the common good; or even to tar and feather a wizard unsuccessful at his task. Contrary to the sages, when one is traveling in these areas, one should be prepared to avoid local customs altogether.

—from The Teachings of Ebenezum, Volume VI

I had walked through dark forests before, but never one as dark as this. The massive trees we passed between rose high above our heads, their branches meeting hundreds of feet in the air to weave a green blanket above us. They let so little light to the forest floor that half the day we seemed to march through evening, and the rest of the day was blackest night.

I had walked through treacherous undergrowth before, but none more treacherous than this. Despite the fact that little light seeped through the leaves above, the ground about our feet was littered with bushes, low things with pale leaves that looked as if they thrived on darkness rather than light. The leaves held sharp edges as well, and hid sharper brambles beneath that would stick to your leggings, and draw blood if you touched them.

I had walked through chill climates before, but none where the cold seeped right through muscle and bone the way it did here. Not only did the leaves above banish sunlight, but also any memory of warmth that the sun might bring. I felt that the blood on my bramble-sore fingers might freeze if the temperature were to descend the slightest degree.

My master, the wizard Ebenezum, once the greatest mage in all the Western Kingdoms, turned to regard the rest of our procession. He stretched his arms out beyond the sleeves of his wizardly robes, black silk tastefully inlaid with silver moons and stars, a bit soiled and torn from the rigors of our trip, perhaps, but still the sign of a serious sorcerer. He yawned and scratched at his full white beard.

"Oh, what a bracing morning," the wizard remarked.

"Doom!" a voice called behind me. Without turning, I could tell it was the warrior Hendrek, his grip tight about the sack that held his doomed warclub, Headbasher. Hendrek, it appeared, felt much the same as I.

"Yztwwrfj!" added yet another voice, this one belonging to the demon Snarks, so deeply clothed in layer upon layer of robe that anything he said was completely indecipherable. Still, did I sense disquiet in the tone of his voice?

"Oh, come now." The wizard stroked his mustache contemplatively. " 'Tis not as bad as all that. We have not had to deal with a demon attack for well over two days. We are making good time through this forest; in a few more days we shall reach the Inland Sea. And on the other side of that sea lies Vushta!"

Vushta? I must admit, even in that gloomy forest, the name alone cheered my spirits. Vushta, city of a thousand forbidden delights, a place where, were he not the soul of caution, a man might go mad with myriad desires. Vushta, where a young lad such as myself had to be doubly careful, lest he be dragged unwillingly to one of the city's fabled pleasure palaces, and there forced, no matter how he might protest—

An explosion disturbed my thoughts.

"Eh?" the wizard remarked. "Well, perhaps I was mistaken."

"Doom!" Hendrek repeated. The large warrior stepped to my side. His whole body quivered with anticipation; a fearsome sight to see, for he was almost as wide as he was tall. His hand clutched convulsively at the bag that contained his enchanted weapon. "We are in the presence of some dread magic!"

I glanced up, wondering if I should correct him. I knew, for the moment at least, that Hendrek was wrong. There was no great magic here yet. My master had not sneezed.

As I have said, Ebenezum was once the greatest wizard in all the Western Kingdoms. And really, he was still a mage without peer, save for one problem. A few scant months ago, due to a small error on his part, the wizard found himself fighting for his life with Guxx Unfufadoo, one of the most powerful demons the Netherhells has ever seen. Ebenezum defeated the demon, and banished it to the Netherhells once again, but his battle was not without its cost. From that day forward, should he even be in the presence of magic, the wizard would begin to sneeze violently and uncontrollably.

Now, a malady of this sort might defeat many a lesser wizard. But not Ebenezum! He continued to ply his trade, using his affliction to sniff out sorcery wherever it might lurk, while at the same time seeking a cure among his learned tomes. At last, however, even a wizard as great as Ebenezum had to admit he could not cure his malady alone. He would have to seek outside assistance, even though he might have to travel to far and fabled Vushta, city of a thousand forbidden delights, before he might find another wizard with skill sufficient for this enormous task.

So to Vushta we journeyed. And as we journeyed we encountered demons and dragons, giants and ghosts, trolls and enchanted chickens! There was sorcery everywhere we turned. Far too much sorcery.

It was when we were staying in a hermit's very large and palatial hovel that we learned the truth; only as we were attacked again by Guxx Unfufadoo, the very demon that caused my master's malady! The Netherhells, not content with an occasional bit of demonic intervention, had mounted a campaign to take over the surface world as well and turn it into an extension of their foul domain!

Ebenezum and I, with the help of many others, managed to win that first battle. But we knew it was only the beginning of the war. Now, it was even more imperative that we reach Vushta and its College of Wizards. The future of the whole world was at stake!

Since then, we had redoubled our endeavors to complete our journey, aided by our two companions, Snarks and Hendrek. But even in our daily travels, we had to observe extreme caution.

Besides an occasional attack by human assassins, hired by a ruler Ebenezum had managed to slightly offend some time ago, we were constantly being set upon by demons and demonic magic, and 'twas only through our combined efforts that we managed to survive.

There was another explosion, much closer this time. The earth shook at our feet.

"Doom!" the large warrior repeated. "The demons attack again!"

"No, no, good Hendrek," my master corrected. " 'Tis not demons, yet. As least not in any force. My nose would not be able to withstand such an assault." The wizard stepped hastily back, drawing up his robes to cover his lower face. With the third explosion, Hendrek had drawn Headbasher from its protective sack.

"Doom!" Hendrek swung the warclub above his head so quickly that the air screamed with its passing. Headbasher was an enchanted club, and when the large warrior held it in his hands, he became like a man possessed. But Headbasher's magic was a curse as well, for Hendrek had obtained the club from the demon Brax, who neglected to inform the warrior as to the exact terms of sale. To his everlasting horror, Hendrek soon learned that Headbasher was a club no man could own, but could only rent!

Snarks had pulled his sickly green demonic head free of his concealing robes. He stood next to Hendrek, staring at the site of the last explosion.

"The wizard is right," Snarks hissed. "No demon has done this. It is something far worse!"

There was an explosion by Snarks's right foot. The demon screamed.

"Oh, excuse me!" a small voice exclaimed. "Pardon, pardon, pardon!" A very diminutive fellow dressed all in brown stood in our midst. He brushed distractedly at his sleeves. "I don't quite have that trick down yet. I'm very close, though!"

Hendrek squinted in the newcomer's direction. " 'Tis some kind of Fairy...."

"What!" The little man glared at the large warrior. "I am

nothing of the kind! The very idea!" He took a deep breath, drawing himself up to his full height (just under a foot and a half). "Gentlemen, I am a Brownie!"

"Brownie?" Snarks murmured. The look of distaste on his countenance turned to one of pure horror. "Brownie?"

Hendrek smiled at the Brownie. "Well, little man, 'twas a natural mistake. You know how everyone talks about Fairies and Brownies."

"Fairies and Brownies! Fairies and Brownies!" The little man stamped his feet in indignation. "It's never Brownies and Fairies, no, no, no, never the other way around! Well, we Brownies have had enough! We're not going to take it anymore!"

"Indeed," Ebenezum said behind the folds of his robe. "Would it be impolite to ask just what you were not going to take?"

The little fellow shook his head sadly. " 'Tis a longstanding truth that Brownies have always been taken for granted. Well, it's partially our fault, I'll be the first to admit that. My ancestors did a lot of hiding from you big folks, and it's always been the Brownie Way to get most of our work done after dark. Well, believe me, the days of the invisible Brownies are over! From now on, when we do good deeds, you'll darn well see them. Up with Brownies!"

Snarks shuddered, clearly appalled by the very thought. I studied our green companion with some concern. With his thorough knowledge of the Netherhells, Snarks had been of invaluable assistance in our battles with demonic forces. Could he perhaps sense something sinister in this small man's speech?

In a whisper, I asked the demon what was wrong.

Snarks looked at me, misery in his eyes. If anything, his sickly green complexion was even more sickly and more green than usual.

"You know," he whispered hoarsely, "that I have been banished from the Netherhells, for, due to demonic politicians scaring my mother while I was in infancy, I can speak nothing but the truth. And, for the most part, I have come to accept my lot in life—forced to wander the surface world, the enemy of my kin and kind, most of whom would kill me on sight. And still… and still…"

Snarks choked back a ragged sob. "It is just too much! I may have been driven from the Netherhells... but I still have some standards. He's so, so..." Snarks gagged. "So... CUTE!"

I looked back at the Brownie. I could see the demon's point. There was something about that foot-and-a-half high fellow, jumping up and down and saying positive things about Browniedom, that was absolutely nauseating.

"Where are the Fairies now, let me ask you that?" the little man was saying now. "You think they don't know about the plans that the Netherhells have for these parts? No, no, no, those Fairies know everything about every demon that's ever set foot in the realm! But do they do anything about it? No, not the Fairies! They're too frightened! They go into hiding! Well, now it's the Brownies' time. We're not going to go into hiding again. We're going to wait right here, and show the demons and everybody that the Brownies have come to stay! Fairies and Brownies, indeed!"

"Indeed," Ebenezum replied. "Very commendable."

"In fact," the Brownie beamed, "that's the reason I've come. There was this young lady I just met, back in the forest a bit, who had a very important message for you!"

"Young lady?" I asked.

"Yes, yes, her name began with an N I think. Well, an N or an M." The Brownie shook his head. "There's something to be said for that mode of transportation. It's certainly good if you're in a hurry, but I must say those explosions shake one up a bit."

"An N?" I queried. "Was the woman's name Norei?" Could it be true? Was my true love trying to find us? Perhaps, dare I hope, she could not exist another minute without me?

"It might have been an S. Excuse me. It's this ringing in my ears, you know. But it's one of those for sure, either an M or an N, or possibly an S. It's got to be one of those, I'm quite certain of that."

Couldn't this Brownie be more specific? It had to be Norei! Didn't it? Perhaps, I thought, the message she had for us would give me some clue.

"What did she have to say?" I demanded. "Did she mention Ebenezum?" For a second, my voice caught in my throat. "Did she say anything about... Wuntvor?"

"Well, she may have used one of those names. Yes, I think she did. Now, what did her name start with?"

"I see." This was obviously all too much for my master. He strode forward, his great, bushy eyebrows knitted with concern. I must admit, I was relieved to see the wizard take a truly active role in this interrogation. His sorcerous wiles could get to the bottom of anything. Magic or no magic, he'd get an answer from this forest spirit.

"What did the young woman tell you?" He sneezed briefly, then turned away to blow his nose.

"Well, let's see," the Brownie said. "You know, I can't tell you just now. It's that name thing. Funny how something small like that can just get in your way, but when I get bothered like that—was it an M?"

The wizard stepped forward to try again. "Can you find out what the young woman told you?" He sneezed twice this time.

"Well, I could go back and ask her her name. I bet it'll all come back to me then. You've got to give me a chance here. Us Brownies are going to take a more active role in this world than ever before. We're really set on doing that. But, we're a little new at it. You've got to give us a little time to grow. I promise I won't let you down. This is our Brownie Pledge: We'll keep on doing it until we get it right."

Ebenezum managed only one word before the sneezing fit took him: "Go!"

"Oh. Pardon me. Yes, I guess I'd better. Well, remember, Brownies do it better!"

He closed his eyes and stamped his feet.

Snarks yelped as the air exploded at his feet.

The Brownie smiled weakly. "Sorry. Still having a little trouble finding the range." He frowned. "Whatever that young woman had to say, I know it was important. What was it? Oh yes, a matter of life and death. That's what she said. Life and death. Or was it life or death?"

There was another explosion. This time, the Brownie was gone.

CHAPTER TWO

There are as many styles of magic as there are magicians. While much of magic is gaudy, noisy, and easily appreciated by the masses, it goes without saying that some of the finest sorcery is also the most subtle; small, delicate changes in the fabric of being that often can only be discerned by another wizard's practiced eye. Occasionally, even a wizard as learned as myself will experience a twinge of regret that I have not yet conquered some of the most delicate aspects of my art; that, for example, I have not learned the Eastern finger magic, where, by the turn of a knuckle, the mage may make the flowers sing. And perhaps some day my fingers might learn that art, on the day they become tired from constantly carrying about the large amounts of gold I receive for performing the more gaudy and noisy magic that pays so well.

—from The Teachings of Ebenezum, Volume VII

"Norei!"

The word escaped my lips as the Brownie disappeared. Norei! The greatest love of my life. How could I describe her? Her face, her hair, her skin, the way she smiled? No, mere words could not do justice to the way I felt about her. Norei! And if the Brownie could be trusted, she was coming to join me!

Some would say we were too young to be so in love. But appearances are often deceiving. I will admit that there were times, in my earlier life, when I thought I was in love and it was not so. There was a certain rich farmer's daughter, and another girl, who, instead of remaining with me, decided to pursue a career in show business with a singing dragon, and, now that I think of it, perhaps five or six others. But you must understand that it was only through meeting Norei that I discovered true, true love. Yes, it was only through knowing Norei that I discovered that everything before was nothing more than youthful infatuation.

Now, though, my life was different. I was a man of the world, on my way to Vushta, city of a thousand forbidden delights. Even a magician's apprentice grows quickly on a journey such as this. When traveling to Vushta, one had to be ready for anything.

"I do not trust the Brownie."

I glanced up. The demon Snarks had moved to my side as I stood lost in thought. He had tossed back his hood so that his whole green-scaled head was exposed, horns and all. His large, well-fanged mouth was turned downward into one of the most miserable looking grimaces I had ever seen.

"Why, friend Snarks," I inquired, "what could a Brownie do that might cause us harm?"

"The very point!" the demon cried. His red eyes peered intently into my own. "Just what do Brownies do? Very little, as far as I can tell. Oh, there's this piffle about them fixing shoes in the middle of the night. Sounds like a cheap way for shoemakers to gain some unwarranted sales! Enchanted Brownie shoes, phfahh! I wouldn't be surprised if the shoemakers and the Brownies were in this together! I tell you, Brownies are just too quiet for their own good!" Snarks kicked a medium-sized rock out of the path before us. The demon glowered with an intensity only possible for one raised in the Netherhells.

"Doom!" The great warrior Hendrek moved to my other side. "There was something about that Brownie, then? 'Tis true, no one should look that cheerful without good reason." Hendrek nervously fingered the sack that held Headbasher. He glowered with an intensity only possible for one possessed by an enchanted warclub.

I glanced back and forth between my two companions. How they had changed in our two weeks of traveling together! When first they met, I was afraid each would tear the other limb from limb. Hendrek had gained his cursed warclub through demons, and thus had no great love of the species. And Snarks, in his desire to tell all the truth all the time, seemed to take particular delight in informing the very large warrior as to the efficiency of certain diet and exercise programs. But Snarks had been indispensable in his knowledge of demonic strategy during our recent skirmishes with the Netherhells, and Hendrek was no less useful with his flashing warclub, Headbasher. The two, at last, realized that they needed each other. Now, while they were still not the best of friends, they did manage to speak occasionally, and I no longer feared the imminent murder of one at the hands of the other.

There was a loud harummph from the path before us.

"If you wish to continue your private discussion," the wizard remarked, "the least you might do is march at the same time. We have much ground to cover before this half-light fails us." Ebenezum glowered with an intensity only possible for a great mage cut off from his art.

I realized then that my master was feeling the ardours of our journey as much as the rest of us. There was exhaustion in his voice, and creases about his beard that I hadn't seen before. My master, the wizard Ebenezum, seemed to handle the march, and the occasional battle that came with it, with such aplomb that I sometimes forgot that he, too, could grow weary. He was unable to approach us any closer, for, if the wizard should close upon Snarks without the demon's protective hood, or if the mage should be in the vicinity of Headbasher when the club was drawn from its sack, the great Ebenezum would be totally lost to a sneezing attack. As I thought about it, I realized it could do him no good to be further cut off from conversation with his fellows due to the severity of his malady. I told him of our concerns.

"Indeed." The wizard stroked his beard thoughtfully. " 'Tis but one way to see if the Brownie is playing us true or false. We must make our own magic to contact the young witch!"

Magic! Alas, at that point in my young career, I knew far too little about it. During the time of my early apprenticeship, back in the Western Woods, Ebenezum had been too busy to instruct me in much more than sweeping and bucket carrying. Then, with the arrival of his malady, and our subsequent discovery of the fiendish plots of the Netherhells, things became far more hectic. Well, we needed new magic, and Ebenezum suggested we try some. I listened attentively. I may have been ignorant of spells, but surely my eagerness would more than make up for any knowledge I lacked.

"Indeed," Ebenezum remarked, noting my extreme attention with a single, raised eyebrow. "I suggest a communication spell. Very effective and very simple. Wuntvor should be able to master it in no time."

Holding his nose delicately, the wizard pulled me aside.

"Wuntvor." My master spoke softly, but with great feeling. "I believe we have come to a turning point in our journeys. Once we left Heemat's behind, we left civilization as well. We will not see another town before the edge of the Inland Sea." He paused a moment to stroke his long white mustache. "I sense some dissent between our companions. Both have proved their worth on this journey, as I am sure they will continue to do. But both will be of much more worth if we give them leadership. And magic is what makes us leaders. As we've seen, I can still manage a spell or two under duress, but it takes far too much out of me. And we need more than that. Simple spells, everyday things to keep our spirits up. This, Wunt, is where you can be invaluable."

The wizard coughed discreetly. "I know I have been remiss in the past in teaching you your craft. I apologize for that. You know about the circumstances. Now, though, I must teach you the spells that will serve us from day to day. Whatever happens, we must continue to appear to be in control of our situation here."

So he had heard us after all. I agreed with him totally. We would only be able to succeed if we kept our spirits up. It was the one way Hendrek and Snarks would make it through. He did not have to mention how much he and I needed it as well.

"Wuntvor," my master intoned. "I remember a spell that you should have no trouble with at all." He clapped me on the shoulder. "We have need of the contents of your pack."

Quickly, I removed the heavy burden from my back. When we had left from our home in the Western Kingdoms, Ebenezum had brought what learned tomes and magical paraphernalia we might have use of on our journeys. As his apprentice, it was of course my duty to carry these important belongings, especially since, as my master had so often told me, a wizard should keep his hands free for quick conjuring and his mind free for sorcerous conjecture. Heavy as these items were, they had already proved indispensable on a number of occasions, and I had begun to think of the weighty pack as almost a part of me, especially since I could depend on my stout oak staff to help support the weight when the going got rough, and to keep me from pitching forward when we traveled downhill.

Ebenezum briefly outlined his plan and, after a moment's rummaging through the crowded sack, I found just what the wizard requested: the Spring issue of Conjurer's Quarterly. I could tell at a glance that it was just what we wanted, for, in the bottom right-hand corner of the bright yellow cover, just below the painting of the attractive, smiling witch, were the words, printed in an even brighter red, Five Simple Spells Even Your Apprentice Can Master. This was for me! I quickly turned to the appropriate page.

And there it was, right after "Basic Cleaning Spell" and just before "Basic Romance Spell" (I'd have to come back to that one later), "Basic Communication Spell: Communicate Better Through Visual Aids!"

The wizard frowned thoughtfully in my direction. "So Wuntvor. Do you think you are up to it?"

I nodded eagerly. "Yes, master. We will speak with Norei in no time!" The spell was little more than a series of pictures. If using this spell meant I could speak with my beloved, I knew I would not fail!

"Good, 'prentice." The wizard scratched thoughtfully beneath his cap. "I shall be nearby if you require advice. Or at least as nearby as I deem safe." My master quietly moved a few paces away.

I returned my attention to the learned periodical.

"Think of magical thoughts as you might think of birds," the instructions began. "Your thoughts may fly through the air as birds may fly, and they may land miles and miles from that point at which they began their flight. To best use this spell, you must picture yourself as a bird in flight, a noble hawk, perhaps, which brings tidings of great import, or a gentle dove, bearing a message of love."

Beneath these words were a series of drawings: a hawk in flight; a swan upon a lake; a dove carrying a rose in its beak. "Look at one of these images, or look at a real bird in flight, and concentrate. Your thoughts are that bird, flying to a perch of your choosing. But remember, concentration is the key! Let nothing distract you—"

"Doom!"

Hendrek's cry startled me from my reading. Then Ebenezum sneezed, and I lost my place completely.

A cloud of sickly yellow smoke was congealing a few feet away from the large warrior. Hendrek's club was free of its restraining sack. Snarks had thrown back his hood, his head now free to see and speak the truth. We needed all our wits about us now.

"Easy payments!" the just-materialized demon cried.

"Along with your hellishly small fine print!" Snarks hissed back.

"So, you are still here, traitor?" The newly materialized demon continued to smile broadly as it ducked a blow from Headbasher. It brushed the dust from its orange-and-green checkerboard costume, and puffed on a foul-smelling cigar. Brax, for it was the Salesdemon, pointed at Hendrek. "Of course, my most honored client here should not believe a single word this despicable demon has to say. After all, how can you trust someone with his origins?"

"They are your origins as well, merchant Brax!" Snarks cried.

"See what I mean?" Brax flicked some cigar ash into Snarks's robes. "This creature has absolutely no sales awareness." The salesdemon sighed melodramatically. "Who would have thought someone raised in the Netherhells could be so dull, pedantic and boring."

"Me, dull? Me, boring?" Snarks retorted. "Only if the truth is boring!"

"Ah, so we at least agree on that," Brax rapidly replied. "Which brings me to the reason for my visit. I trust, Hendrek, you have so far been satisfied with the performance of your enchanted weapon?"

Headbasher crashed noisily against the rocks where, only a moment before, Brax had stood.

"Doom!" the larger warrior intoned.

I realized with a start that someone was tugging on my robes. I looked about to see my master, enveloped in his robes, doing his best not to sneeze.

"Wuntvor," he managed. He nodded his head towards a place somewhat farther up the path.

I rapidly followed my master to the point he had indicated. Ebenezum sneezed once, then blew his nose voluminously on a corner of his sleeve.

"Good," the wizard remarked, once he had caught his breath. "We must be wary of further distractions. Did it not cross your mind, Wuntvor, that the coming of the demon Brax might be the very event Norei has attempted to warn us about?"

I looked back in horror at Brax, who was offering the warrior a line of warclub accessories which, the demon assured Hendrek, "would make Headbasher even better!" Actually, the wizard's surmise had not crossed my mind for an instant. Brax was always coming around to annoy Hendrek, and to demand that the warrior do this or that foul deed in partial payment for the enchanted club. It was one of the things I had come to depend on in our travels. But then, what more fiendish plot could there be than something from the Netherhells that we had grown to expect?

"Yes!" Brax shouted as he once again dodged Headbasher. "You'd be able to crush me easily if you had a Netherhells Extendoclub (patent pending) attached to your weapon! Here's how the little marvel works—"

"Therefore," the wizard continued, drawing my attention back to the matter at hand, "it is imperative that we contact Norei without further delay. Have you sufficiently studied the spell?"

I told my master I would have it in a minute. I found my place again in the learned periodical. It did seem simple enough. Essentially, you had to envision yourself as a bird. Well, I had once been turned into a bird by a spell that had gone the slightest bit wrong. True, the bird had been a chicken, and chickens aren't generally known for their powers of flight, but that was a minor quibble. I remembered the experience very well, and, in fact, would on occasion still get an overwhelming urge to eat dried seed corn. I would just have to use my imagination and transfer my experience to a bird with a better wingspan.

After that, one merely had to picture that person with whom one desired to communicate, recite a simple phrase or two, and the spell was complete. As the learned article said, "Concentration is the key." It didn't seem like any problem at all.

I looked at the picture of the hawk. That would be nice. I would become the noble hawk, and fly to my beloved.

"Shoddy workmanship?" Brax screamed. "What do you mean, shoddy workmanship?"

"Admit it!" Snarks retorted. "You remember those singing swords that couldn't carry a tune!"

"Well, yes, that was a problem," Brax admitted. "I could only sell them to clients who were tone deaf."

"And what about those love potions that attracted insects?" Snarks cried triumphantly. "Imagine how upset people got, surrounded by hordes of amorous mosquitoes?"

"Quality control is not my department!" Brax cried, clearly on the defensive. "Besides, I deal exclusively with used weapons. If you have a complaint about that, you have to direct it to Potion Control! They're open, I think, every third Tuesday...."

It was no use. I simply couldn't concentrate on being a noble hawk with all this racket. I decided I would imagine myself as a sleek, white dove instead. How romantic, to visit my true love in the image of a dove!

"Doom!" Hendrek's warclub came crashing down where Brax had been.

"Wuntvor," my master whispered. "Hurry! We must find the true reason for Brax's arrival!"

The wizard had a point. "Concentration is the key." Somehow, though, I couldn't quite get a picture of a dove firmly in my mind.

"Good Hendrek!" Brax cried as the demon leapt above a low swing of Headbasher. "You misunderstand me! I have only your best interests at heart!"

"Foul fiend—," Hendrek began to bellow, but then he hesitated. "Yes, you do often arrive just before a battle. Why do you always warn us?"

Brax's smile grew even broader. "Simply good business practices, friend Hendrek. We have to make sure you remain alive until we see sufficient return on our investment. How would we demons ever get paid if we didn't warn people?"

"Doom!" Hendrek cried, Headbasher once again flying through the air. "I will never fulfill your hellish contracts!"

"Oh come now. It's not as difficult as all that." Brax waved its cigar at Snarks. "What say, as the first payment, you eliminate a certain green and sickly fellow in a hood? Just reach out with your weapon, and no one will ever tell you to diet again!"

"Doom! Doom! Doom!" Hendrek attacked Brax with redoubled fury.

"Listen—urk—" Brax paused to somersault out of the way. "Like I said, good Hendrek, you're an investment. Eeps! A little close there. Just think of us—urk—as having a long and endearing friendship. Like we always say in the Netherhells, 'No money down, a lifetime to pay.' "

"Wuntvor!" Ebenezum whispered, again urgently. Yes, yes, my master was right! I could no longer let the drama at the other end of the clearing distract me. I had to succeed, for my master, for Norei! But images of hawks and doves flitted away every time the noise level rose. Somehow, I needed to clearly see a bird in my mind's eye.

The doomed warclub, Headbasher, struck a tree with a resounding thump. A bird flew from an upper branch with a harsh cry of protest. A bird! It was truly a sign. I concentrated on the fowl's deep brown feathers. I would use this bird's image, common and workmanlike, to be my messenger. What need had I for distant hawk and dove? The sturdy grackle would be my guide!

Quickly, I set my mind to its task. The wizard exhorted me one final time to gain Norei's message. I nodded, reciting the short, mystic spell. "Concentration is the key!" Fly thoughts! Fly like a grackle, brown wings beating against the air. Fly to my beloved Norei!

Norei! I saw her then, far below me, as if I did fly through the air. Her hair was a brilliant red in the midday sun. She looked up as I approached, her beautiful green eyes filled with wonder.

"Wuntvor?" Her perfect lips spoke my name.

She spoke my name! All thoughts of grackles fled my head. I blinked. Ebenezum stood before me, hands covering his nose. Norei was gone!

"Well, Wuntvor?" Ebenezum asked.

"Don't say I didn't warn you!" Brax called and waved. "Don't worry! You've got a friend in Brax. After all, I've got my investment to worry about! I'll be seeing you!"

The demon popped out of existence.

A terrible cry rose all about us. We were in the midst of a demon attack!

CHAPTER THREE

In magic, as in all true professions, there are rules by which you must play. At least, you must play by them until such time as you can get away with something else.

—from The Teachings of Ebenezum, Volume I (PREFACE)

There was an explosion at my feet.

"Pardon me," a small voice said. "We Brownies like to arrive with a bang! I have good news for you!" The fellow's little eyes gazed about in amazement. "My, my, what's going on here?"

What was going on here was that, once again, all of the Netherhells had broken loose. I suppose that, after a time, one should get used to this sort of thing. Heaven knows we had seen enough demon attacks in the last few days. Somehow, though, there was something about being attacked by a large number of creatures equipped with tearing claws and rending fangs that never lost its ability to startle.

"Bllrorowr!"

The dark, hairy thing attacked me again. I should never have looked at the Brownie. I swung my stout oak staff at the place where the thing's face should be. The fiend had too much hair for me to discern most of its facial features. The only thing I was able to see was far too many teeth.

The hairy thing backed away with a scream. I must have hit something vital! I wished I knew what it was so I could do it again. I risked a moment to see how my fellows were faring.

Snarks was caught up in battle with a purple mass of muscle, while Hendrek fought off a dozen creatures with the thwacking Headbasher. Ebenezum was sneezing somewhere deep within his robes, but he was safe for the moment. We seemed to be keeping this horde of fiends at bay. I guessed that, like anything else, all this practice was sharpening our skills at fighting the Netherhells! I swung my stout oak staff at the hairy thing once again. The creature leapt back in alarm. Take that, I thought, foul fiends! The worst hordes of the Netherhells don't stand a chance against Ebenezum's noble band!

A large, slavering thing leapt straight for the Brownie.

"Oh, is that all?" the Brownie remarked. The small fellow winked three times as he did a small dance.

The large, slavering thing disappeared.

"How did you do that?" I said with some astonishment.

The Brownie glanced at his feet. "I believe it's called the fox trot." He winked in my direction. "That, of course, combined with Brownie Power!"

"Doom!" Hendrek cried, bonking the only demon that still faced him.

"Urk!" the demon cried as it disappeared. The demon confronting Snarks shrieked and disappeared as well. I realized then all the demons had vanished. "Pretty nifty, huh?" The Brownie was all smiles. "Don't give the little fellow too much credit," Snarks remarked. "That was a simple Netherhells' Multiplication Spell. It is child's play to reverse something like that."

The smile vanished from the Brownie's face. "That's right, belittle us. I mean, we are called the little people, after all. We're short, why should anyone pay any attention to us?"

"My thoughts exactly," Snarks agreed. "And now that we've gotten this fellow out of the way, perhaps we can get about our business?"

"Out of the way?" the Brownie shouted. "Let's see you try to put Brownie magic out of the way!" The little man began to dance furiously.

"Doom!" Headbasher came crashing down in the space between Snarks and the Brownie. Hendrek glowered darkly at the others.

"We fight demons," the large warrior asserted. "We do not fight among ourselves."

"And what do you mean?" I interjected. "What's a Netherhells' Multiplication Spell?"

"Oh, it's a typically shoddy piece of Netherhells chicanery," the Brownie remarked casually. "They use it when they don't have enough demons to go around. It's purely a last-chance diversionary spell."

"You mean," I asked, "that we weren't attacked by a horde of demons?"

"Only if you define horde as any group containing two or more," the Brownie replied.

I tapped my stout oak staff on the ground in disbelief. I remembered the feel of the weapon in my hands as it whistled through the air toward the hairy thing, the satisfaction as the creatures leapt away in fear. We could best anything the Netherhells sent against us!

"That's all that were there?" I asked. "Two?" "Yes," the Brownie replied cheerfully. "Those spells can keep you occupied for hours. Then they vanish. By that time they've kept you away from whatever goal you've been trying to reach until it's far too late. Or maybe they've just kept you standing in one place long enough for the real nasty stuff to arrive!"

"I could have told you that!" Snarks cut in. "I know all about that sort of thing! And I can tell a demon from a phantom as well as the next magical creature!"

"Yes," the Brownie replied. "But did you?"

"Listen, short stuff!" Snarks was shouting now. "I would have if you hadn't been doing all this grandstanding. It's getting so an honest demon can't get a word in edgewise. Why don't you talk about things you know about, like making shoes?"

"There we go again!" the little fellow cried. "Brownie stereotyping! I'll have you know—"

"Doom!"

Headbasher crashed between the two again.

"What did I tell you two about arguing?"

"Arguing?" Snarks shrugged his cloaked shoulders. "Why, friend Hendrek, 'tis nothing more here than a simple difference of opinion, a discussion of definitions, if you will. But arguing?" Snarks patted Headbasher gently.

"Doom," Hendrek replied somewhat more gently. "We must repair to Vushta with all speed. Our very lives depend on it."

Ebenezum called to us from some distance away. "The warrior is right. I, too, discerned the deception on the part of the Netherhells, but was unfortunately too incapacitated to act. Whatever the reason for the multiplication spell, it bodes ill. Quickly Wuntvor, you must tell us. What news did you gain from Norei?"

Norei! In the ensuing madness, I had quite forgotten my one, shining moment of contact. She had spoken my name! Of course, my concentration had slipped a bit in that moment. Whose would not have? Now, how best to explain it to the wizard...

Norei! Of course—the Brownie had come back! He had the message!

"Quickly, small fellow!" I cried to the Brownie. "Tell us what words the woman had for us!"

"What?" The Brownie started, as if the very idea of a message was news to him. He scratched his tiny head. "Oh, yes. The message. I remembered the young woman's name! It was Norei!" The Brownie nodded and smiled, obviously waiting for approval.

Norei! My beloved's name came close to dissolving my resolve. But no! I must find out from the Brownie what I had failed to ask of her.

"Indeed," I said, emulating my master. "We are very glad you now know the young woman's name. Would you please give us the message as well?"

"Message? Oh, yes." The Brownie coughed. "The message. Oh dear. My, my. I knew I'd forgotten something."

"See?" Snarks cried triumphantly. "What did I tell you? Brownies! Get them away from their shoelaces—"

"Sir!" the Brownie said sharply. "We Brownies will not be intimidated. We make shoes, yes, but we make very good shoes. Remember sir, the Brownie Creed: We are short, but we are many."

Snarks shivered. "Thousands of tiny shoemakers, stretching to the horizon—" The demon paused as he watched Hendrek nervously finger Headbasher. He turned back to the Brownie. "Well, perhaps I am snapping at you too soon. Anything is possible with a few years of practice."

The Brownie held up his hands. "All right, all right. I admit that my performance has been just a tad spotty up to now. Like I said, we Brownies are a little new to public performance. I tell you what. There's none of those wimp Fairies around, right? Well, take my word for it, those guys go into hiding when there's a thunderstorm. Something like this and you'd have better luck finding a tax collector on refund day. See? I do know the ways of mortals."

The Brownie leapt to a nearby tree stump to give himself some height. "I hearby make a pledge!" His tiny fist pounded his tiny chest. "We all know what Fairies are good for. You know, the three wishes bit? Well, I'm here to show you that Brownies do it better!"

His voice lowered to a more confidential tone.

"Listen, I know you fellows are in some trouble. It's not only that message from the young girl, would that I could remember it. I mean, we Brownies have eyes, you know. Any time you drop in on a group and they're in the middle of a pitched battle with the Netherhells, you can be sure they've got problems. Well, I tell you what I'm going to do for you. For the first time ever on this subcontinent, you folks are going to be the recipients of three wishes from—not Fairies—but Brownies!"

"Brownie wishes?" Snarks smiled a demon smile. "I take a size twelve."

The little fellow looked grieved. "Some day, when you've been saved by Brownie magic, you'll regret these remarks."

"Yes," Snarks replied. "But I have the feeling it will be a very small regret."

"Doom!" Headbasher once again flew through the air.

"Wuntvor?" the wizard called from where he stood in the distance. "May I see you for a moment?"

So this was the moment of truth. No longer would my master simply watch this drama unfold. There would be an accounting for my actions.

"Wuntvor." My master spoke softly as I approached. "I

need to speak with you in earnest." He nodded toward a small rise nearby. "We can talk with more privacy on the far side of yonder hill."

Oh no. This was far worse than I first imagined. I had experienced wizardly rage before. Did Ebenezum wish to take me far enough away so the others would not hear him shouting?

The wizard turned. I followed him over the hill.

"All right!" the Brownie was shouting behind me. "I'll prove what I can do. I'll give you a little wish for free."

"I can think of a little wish," Snarks replied.

"Doom!" cried Hendrek.

"I'll behave! I'll behave!" Snarks shouted.

There was a crashing sound.

The noises behind us became muffled by distance.

"At last." Ebenezum paused and turned to me. "We can talk with some privacy."

The wizard cleared his throat. Quickly, I began to speak. Perhaps, if I explained what had happened with Norei before he asked, I could defuse the wizard's anger.

"Indeed." Ebenezum pulled at his beard. "Wuntvor, it is no wonder you cannot concentrate, with all that is going on on the far side of this hill. That, 'prentice, is the real reason I brought you here."

The wizard continued, his tone barely above a whisper. "I have noticed some problems with our current mode of travel. To be frank, our new companions seem to be rather more of a hindrance than a help."

I mentioned to my master the help the others had been in our battles with the Netherhells.

"True enough," the mage agreed. "But every battle has two sides, and that is true for all concerned. A few moments ago, Hendrek spoke about reaching Vushta with all haste. That is most assuredly true, and most assuredly a goal we are having great trouble attaining.

"There are certain things wrong with our party. If the Netherhells are looking for us, we definitely make an embarrassingly large and easy target. The only things moving with haste around here are the mouths of our companions."

The wizard sighed and scratched at the hair beneath his skullcap. " 'Tis true that all of our companions have their uses. Hendrek is quite good with that doomed club of his. Snarks knows things about the Netherhells that even I had not found out. And the Brownie..."

He hesitated for a moment, gazing back over the hill where our companions continued to argue. I think, at first, Ebenezum had wanted to dismiss the Brownie as just another of those peculiarities we had encountered in our travels. However, I could tell that the little fellow's remark about tax collectors had given the Brownie new respect in my master's eyes.

"No, we would be better off alone," he concluded. The wizard blew his nose briefly. "As you have no doubt noticed, I have another problem with our company. My malady reacts to all things magical—things such as Hendrek's club and the demon Snarks. It is troublesome to maintain allies when one is trying desperately to restrain a sneeze. The addition of the Brownie makes even that restraint impossible. For the sake of my nose, we must travel alone.

"Shoulder your pack, Wuntvor."

The wizard shrugged his robes back into place along his shoulders, and turned to walk down the path, away from the hill and our companions. " Tis better to move quickly to Vushta, and arrive there alive. Once we are among the company of magicians, we can do far more to help the likes of Snarks and Hendrek than we can in constant battle with the Netherhells."

I did as my master instructed, supporting myself with my stout oak staff as the wizard walked briskly before me.

"Master?" I asked hesitantly. "About Norei's warning? What if it has something to do with the two of us alone?"

The wizard pulled solemnly at his beard. "One way or another, we shall know soon enough. Come, Wuntvor. We need to gain some distance."

And so we walked again as we had through most of our journey, the wizard lost in sorcerous thought, while I brought along our belongings on my back—the arcane paraphernalia that had saved us a dozen times from death; a change of clothes; and lunch. I had to admit, there was a familiarity to this mode of travel that I found comforting. We set a sure pace with my master in the lead, and the forest seemed quieter with every step we took.

At length we reached a clearing. My master paused.

"Now, I think we have put sufficient distance between ourselves and our distractions. It's time, Wuntvor. We must speak with Norei."

I looked about the clearing. There didn't seem to be any birds at all in this part of the woods. But if my master wanted a communications spell, he would surely get one. It was so quiet in this spot, I could do nothing but succeed.

I thought of a grackle. A great brown bird, its feathers shining in the sun. I whispered the proper mystic phrases, and launched myself from an imaginary branch, cawing at an imaginary sky. Norei! I was aloft, soaring above the clouds. Norei!

I saw my beloved's red hair, far below. I swooped down to be near her, plummetting through the air with tremendous speed. This time, I would learn her warning!

"Wuntvor?" Norei turned her face to the sky.

"Yes!" I cried, almost overcome with joy. "I—"

The wizard sneezed.

"Norei!" I called.

The earth shook at my feet. A fair quantity of dirt and pebbles showered both the wizard and myself.

No! Not now!

But there was no helping it. All thoughts of birds and Norei flew from my head. Insidiously foul demons! They attacked when we were at our weakest!

My master still sneezed uncontrollably. It was up to me, then, to handle the demons until the mage was sufficiently recovered to recite a spell. I waved my stout oak staff at the dust cloud that had risen with the explosion.

"There they are!" said a high, lilting, and all-too-familiar voice.

The dust lifted first from the ground, revealing a short fellow, about a foot-and-a-half high, dressed in a brown cloak and hood. To one side of him was someone in a long cloak; to the other, a pair of massive feet, legs and thighs.

The Brownie's legs were wobbling badly. He sat abruptly. "Excuse me, fellows. Just need to rest a moment."

"Doom!" a great voice boomed. "The Brownie has done what he promised!"

"Yeah, yeah," another, grating voice answered. "It isn't the gentlest way to travel, is it?" The dust was clearing now. I could discern the form of Snarks, trying to shake even more dirt from his robes.

"Now see what you have done!" Hendrek, spying my master, hastily replaced Headbasher in its protective sack. "Whatever fiendish plans of the Netherhells separated us from the wizard, the Brownie has reunited us, though it has taken all the strength in his tiny form!" He glowered at Snarks. The demon retreated behind his voluminous robes.

"Gzzphttx!" Snarks replied.

"Doom," Hendrek murmured softly. He turned to the wizard and myself. "Thank the gods we have found you. Apparently, the plans of the Netherhells are even more nefarious than we imagined. They will separate us, and cut us down brutally, one by one!"

My master stroked his long, white beard. "Indeed," he remarked. "We must be continually more vigilant."

Hendrek pointed the sack containing Headbasher at the little fellow sitting in the dirt. "Thank the gods we have this noble Brownie as our companion."

"Oh no!" the Brownie cried and leapt to his feet. "That wasn't big enough to be a wish! You folks had asked for a demonstration or two. I just wanted to show you the full extent of Brownie Power! The three wishes come next!"

I looked to my master. This quiet corner of the forest had suddenly become as noisy as every place else. We had lost our solitude, and our chance to learn Norei's warning. Yet my master stood in the midst of it all, stroking his beard, the picture of calm. All in all, he seemed to be taking it very well.

" 'Tis true," my master remarked when there was finally a pause in the conversation. He cleared his sorcerous throat. "We are in a perilous situation, the true extent of which is not yet known. For the good of us all, we may have to make some special arrangements."

"Doom," Hendrek remarked. "What do you mean, great wizard?"

"Oh, only that we should spread out a bit so that we do not form such an obvious target for the plots of the Netherhells." The wizard sniffed. "But that is only the second most important thing we must remember."

The large warrior looked suspiciously around the clearing. "And the first?"

"That, no matter what, we keep walking." The wizard turned and marched out of the clearing. "If there are no objections?"

"Snrrzbffl!" Snarks lifted his robes and pointed to what appeared to be a new pair of shoes upon his demon feet.

"Oh, did I make the shoes a little bit too tight?" The Brownie shook his head in sympathy.

"Gffttbbll!"

"No, no, the one thing Brownies really know about are shoes. You said that yourself." The Brownie ran to follow the marching wizard.

"To Vushta!" Hendrek cried, falling in close behind the Brownie's tiny feet.

I shouldered my pack and gripped my stout oak staff. Grumbling deep within his hood, Snarks took up the rear. We were marching at last, on to our goal. Nothing would stop us now.

Then, at the edge of the forest, we saw the unicorn.

CHAPTER FOUR

There is talk in some learned circles in our major cities about whether or not satyrs, centaurs, griffins and certain other fantastic beasts really exist, or are only the product of the popular imagination. As a wizard, I, of course, tend to side with the satyrs, centaurs and griffins, especially when these beasts begin to doubt the existence of any learned circles in our major cities.

—from The Teachings of Ebenezum, Volume XXXVI

The unicorn ran in our direction.

I forgot to walk. All I could do was stare.

"Doo—oof!" Hendrek exclaimed loudly as he walked into my overloaded pack. He began a loud and complicated curse.

I placed a hand upon his shoulder to quiet him, and pointed at the approaching beast. Hendrek's complaints stopped midsentence as his mouth opened, unable to form further words. All of his attention, and mine as well, was drawn to the newcomer.

How do I describe that creature? Its golden hooves would stamp upon any words I might use, grinding them to inconsequential dust. Still, what can humans do but try?

Imagine a horse, if you will, a horse of pure white, its color that of the snow as it falls fresh from the clouds, before it is sullied by the common air. It is a swift horse, in its prime, lean but powerful. Its muscles ripple beneath its coat as it leaps through the stillness, and, when its hooves touch ground, the earth shakes with its passing.

Ah, but this creature is more than a mere horse, for atop its white head, before its wildly cascading mane, is a golden horn as long as my arm. The horn is not quite straight, and yet not truly curved, as if neither the line nor the circle were special enough to give it form. And it rises above the creature's head as if it were reaching for the sun.

I spoke of the sun. It had, in fact, appeared before us. We had come to a clearing. The close trees that we had toiled through for the past few days spread apart to reveal a good-sized meadow filled with flowers and long, deep green grass. Patches of light shone upon this field through broken clouds, as if the sun had sewn a quilted pattern upon the earth.

How I had complained about the dank and dreary forest we had labored through for so long! How dearly I had longed to see true sunlight! But now, I only noticed the sun because it reflected off the back of the approaching beast. And the white of the unicorn's coat seemed as bright as the sun itself.

Somehow, it was only proper. If we were to see the sun for the first time after so many days, it should be at a wonderful moment such as this. How else could we do honor to such a regal beast?

The unicorn reared up before us. It was even more astonishing to look at close at hand, the very heart of magic brought to life. It stood but a dozen paces away, magnificent, the essence of peace and bearing, contentment and beauty. Except that there was something about the way the creature blinked its large and soulful eyes.

"How could they!" the splendid creature exclaimed.

Ebenezum blew his nose. He moved a few steps to the left, careful, I was sure, to remain upwind of the magnificent beast.

"Indeed," the wizard remarked quietly. "How could they what?"

The unicorn eyed us warily, then glanced rapidly back over its grandly beautiful shoulder. "Well, I barely know where to begin. There I was, minding my unicorn business, when they attacked me!"

The perfect beast snorted in dismay.

"Pray continue." The wizard pulled reflectively upon his long beard. "You were attacked? By demons?"

"No, no!" the unicorn cried. "Far worse than that! Mere demons I would have gored and tossed aside! But to be attacked by such as these!" A tremor passed through the beast's stately frame.

"What they did! I can barely speak about it even now. They tied my golden hooves, these hooves meant to run free over the green and verdant sward! They covered my golden horn, the center of my beauty and my defense against injustice! They bound it round with common pillows, saying, 'We don't want any accidental stabbings, ha ha.' Pillows about my magnificent golden horn! And, and—" The unicorn paused, swallowing deep within its splendid throat. Its voice lowered to a whisper. "And they mussed my stately, flowing mane!"

"Indeed?" my master replied.

"My flowing mane!" The unicorn nodded its head vehemently. "Can you imagine, handled roughly like that? They have no respect for my species at all. And not a virgin among them, either! Well, you know, that's not at all surprising in this part of the forest, but still..."

The unicorn snorted mightily. It appeared too overwhelmed to go on.

A large shadow passed over our heads.

The unicorn screamed.

" 'Tis them!" the stately beast cried. "They have found me!" The unicorn glanced nervously aloft. "You weren't listening, were you? I'm distraught! I didn't know what I was saying! I didn't mean what I said about virgins! Honestly!"

The shadow was gone.

"Indeed." My master spoke in his most reassuring tone, honed to a fine art through years of use placating rich clients and distracting tax collectors. "Whoever they were, they seem to be gone now. If you are in distress, perhaps we can help you. Tell me, is there any money involved?"

"What use have magical creatures for money?" The unicorn tossed its perfectly formed head to and fro in despair. "How could I ever expect mere humans to understand?"

"Okay. It's time for an expert." The Brownie stepped forward. "Enchanted creature to enchanted creature, we will learn the truth. And I won't even count it as a wish. That's Brownie Power for you!"

"No, no, I've said far too much already!" The unicorn shied away from its small interrogator.

The Brownie stepped even closer, undaunted by the splendid beast's greater size. "All right!" the small fellow said. "Let's get to the heart of the matter. What's all this guff about virgins?"

"What?" The unicorn shook its head. "Why, it's just something unicorns do. It's expected of us, you know, like Brownies making shoes."

"And we're going to change all that!" the Brownie cried. "Brownies do it better!" The little person cleared his throat. "Pardon. Just hit a sore spot there." He shot an accusatory look back at Snarks, still hidden deep within voluminous robes. "I've always been interested in this. Do unicorns really seek out virgins?"

"Actually, no," the snow-white beast replied. "I've always thought the unicorn's essential task was to frolic through distant fields while looking ethereally beautiful. Virgins are really a sideline. But we know one when we see one. There's one here, in fact."

All around me there was an intake of breath.

"Yes. Somebody's a virgin. I can always tell, you know. It's something we unicorns are very good at." The beast tossed its head jauntily. "Of course, we unicorns are good at so many things!"

"Wait a second," I interjected, somewhat unsettled by this line of conversation. "Don't virgins have to be female?"

"A popular misconception. No, a virgin is a virgin, male or female, and I scent one nearby." The unicorn looked from Hendrek to me and back again.

"Doom," the large warrior intoned.

The creature's scrutiny was very discomforting. Just what was this overmuscled animal implying? Snarks made a low, snickering noise deep within his hood.

"Well." The wizard once again stepped forward, his robes discreetly covering his nose. "I'm sure this is all very interesting, but could you tell us exactly who you are running from?"

"Running?" The unicorn stamped its golden hooves upon the earth. "Unicorns run from no one! Well, that's not quite

true. Let's just say the intelligent unicorn knows who to avoid."
The beast glanced nervously overhead.

The wizard blew his nose. "And who, indeed, might that
be?"

The unicorn lowered its gaze from the sky. "I have said far
too much already." It turned its head slightly to look at all of us,
then pointed briefly with its horn. "Just don't go that way."

The beast's horn pointed toward Vushta.

"I have said all that I can. May you be blessed with a
unicorn's luck." The mighty beast reared up, then galloped into
the dark forest from which we had come.

"A unicorn's blessing!" Snarks had removed his hood. "If
what that fancy horse has been through is unicorn luck, it
should be as much use to us as three Brownie wishes!"

The demon rapidly replaced his hood as the Brownie
approached.

"Doom," Hendrek intoned. "Dare we go farther, to face
whatever dread thing yon beast has escaped?"

"We must," the wizard insisted. "Put your club away, would
you? That's a good fellow. In this instance, I believe friend Snarks
has made a valid point. Information, the wise man knows, is
only as good as its source. A source whose main concern is how
much its mane has been mussed is hardly any source at all."

"Whatever happens," a small voice piped, "you have a
Brownie at your side!"

"Indeed. And I am sure we will be properly grateful when
the time comes."

"But what of Norei's warning?" I asked. "Could the unicorn
have seen something?"

"Would that I knew, Wuntvor." The wizard stared up at a
sky filled with skittering clouds, hoping, perhaps, to see what
had frightened the unicorn so. "If this were a perfect world,
I might take some time and study this matter, using the full
body of my learning and experience to reach a learned, truly
wizardly decision. Unfortunately, this world appears to be
getting less perfect every day. Things are happening much too
fast to depend upon wizardly conjecture."

My master tugged his robes into more aesthetically pleasing

lines. "We must rely, therefore, entirely on wizardly intuition! Wuntvor, shoulder your pack! On to Vushta!"

So saying, Ebenezum led us across the clearing to another stretch of nearly impenetrable forest. I paused for an instant, savoring a last glimpse of golden sunlight before we were once again surrounded by great, dark trees.

Far behind us, I heard the unicorn scream.

"I have an idea what you can use for your first wish."

I jumped at the sound of the Brownie's voice.

"Sorry!" the small voice piped. "I do tend to be enthusiastic. Part of my overall Positive Brownie Image, you know."

I looked back in the direction of the unicorn's cry, but the trees blocked my view.

"Can you wish us out of here?" I asked.

"Sorry. We just tried that, bringing your friends here." The Brownie frowned and shook his head. "Puts too much strain on the magic muscles."

The Brownie paused. I realized belatedly that he was expecting me to keep up my end of the conversation. I was too busy listening for the unicorn, or whatever the unicorn had seen.

"What wish did you have in mind?" I asked at last.

"That's more like it!" the Brownie replied. "You have to get in the spirit of this three wishes thing, you know. My job is to make the wishes happen! I don't have time to think them up as well! "

I nodded. The Brownie certainly had a point. Somehow, though, things had been too busy lately for me to think about wishing for anything.

"I know, I know," the Brownie went on. "My performance up to now has not been exemplary. That's why I feel I have to push the wishes bit a little. Remember the Brownie Creed: It's not magic—it's Brownie Power!"

The Brownie continued in a whisper. "I have been observing your master. A sad case, a great wizard like that, unable to perform magic because of a malady of the nose. See? We Brownies notice things like that! And this Brownie knows a cure!"

I turned to look at the small fellow. A cure? Hope rose within me like the sun lighting a summer dawn. If Ebenezum could regain his powers, we would reach Vushta in no time at all!

"I know it will work." The small one's voice became softer still. "It has to do with shoes."

My hope plummetted like a winter storm. This was the Brownie who had trouble remembering people's names, let alone the messages they had given him. Maybe Snarks was right about him after all.

The little fellow glanced somewhat apprehensively at the demon, who was walking now at Hendrek's side. It was almost as if the Brownie had read my mind.

"Some may laugh at me," he continued in a whisper, "but always start with what you know best. That's what His Brownieship says."

His Brownieship? I decided not to ask.

"Anyways, I can make a shoe big enough to protect your master from magical influences." The Brownie paused and tapped his tiny foot. "I can see that you're skeptical. Well, just wait 'til you see it! Hands-on experience, that's what we need here. I just have to have a little while to get my notes together, and, next time we have a crisis, one Brownie shoe special will do the trick!"

My master began to sneeze.

"Doom!" Hendrek bellowed, looking in the trees overhead.

"It's time for the shoe!" I cried to the Brownie, but my voice was drowned out by the beating of gigantic wings.

CHAPTER FIVE

A wizard must do his best not to judge any person or thing on their first appearance. Many a human or other intelligent creature will have hidden depths to their personalities which you will only discover as you get to know them and work with them; and hidden cash reserves, which you can bill them for regularly as this aforementioned knowledge process takes place.

—from The Teachings of Ebenezum, Volume LVI

I was pushed to the ground. Something grabbed me. Something as hard as rock. I was lifted into the air as I might lift an insect from a leaf.

I looked down at the rapidly receding earth to see Snarks, Hendrek and the Brownie staring up in horror. Where was my master?

There was a sneeze close by my left ear. I managed to turn my head against the wind, and saw my master, clasped within a giant yellow claw. I looked down at the hard yellow ridges that contained me, and realized that I was held by a claw as well.

The thing had me clutched facing down. I found it impossible to crane my head any farther to discern the true nature of our captor. Perhaps, considering the size of the claws, ignorance was bliss. I could only look at the rapidly moving ground far below and wish that I had not eaten such a heavy lunch.

We were moving at fantastic speed. I felt as if the wind might tear the clothes from my already-chilled body. It roared in my ears and made tears stream down my face. I cried out against the wind, full of fear and anger. What could be worse than this?

And then the thing's claw began to open.

I clutched for a hold on the horny yellow flesh. Rather we

should be carried aloft and windblown forever than be dashed among the trees far below! But the trees were getting closer. In my panic, I had not noticed how far the thing had descended.

Suddenly, we were above a clearing filled with milling people. No, no, they weren't people. They were something else entirely.

That's when the claw let me go.

As I picked myself up, my first thoughts were for my master. But there he was beside me, his deep blue wizard's robes in disarray. His fine magician's cap was gone, but otherwise he seemed to have survived intact. He was, of course, sneezing profusely.

Something roared mightily nearby. Instinctively, I reached for my stout oak staff. It was nowhere around me. I realized with a chill that both my staff and pack were gone!

It would have to be my fists, then. I stared at the ground for an instant, calming myself, steeling my resolve to battle until my last ounce of strength was gone, for Ebenezum, and Vushta!

I looked up into the face of the strangest creature I had ever seen.

"Do you have any gold?" the face rumbled. It was the face of a very large eagle. The body of the creature, however, was not birdlike at all, but was rather that of a lion. Was this what I had heard roar before? It had not been a very friendly sound. Then, of course, there were the creature's great wings, not to mention the tail, which looked like the latter half of one of the longest snakes I had ever seen. All in all, I was understandably taken aback.

The creature growled, obviously upset that I had not answered him.

"I repeat," it said, "do you have any gold?"

What could I say? I had no idea whether we had any gold or not. Ebenezum always handled all our money matters. But being in the presence of what was obviously an enchanted beast, my master's sneezing fit now consumed him entirely.

The beast's serpent tail began to twitch in an agitated manner. The creature opened its beak and emitted a sound far worse than words. It began as the cry of an eagle and ended as the roar of a lion, embodying the harsher characteristics of both calls. All in all, it was quite unpleasant.

"Oh, Pop, come off it!" Another magical beast, this one with the head and wings of an eagle and the body of a horse, galloped between us. "Can't you see you're scaring the pants off this guy?"

"There are certain customs that must be observed," the father said stiffly. "Griffins always look for gold."

"But we're here to change all that, remember?"

"Ah, yes." The Griffin made a strangled noise deep in his throat. "We'll talk about it later, when we're alone. He's a bright lad," it said to no one in particular. "A little headstrong, but bright."

"But Pop! You have to tell them!"

The Griffin turned and roared at its son.

"I don't have to do anything!"

"But Pop! Why else would we bring them here?"

"Ah, yes." The Griffin paused again. "That is true." The beast turned to me. "You have been abducted for a reason."

The eagle/horse walked over to my still-sneezing master.

"You know, Pop, this guy looks like he's in a lot of trouble."

"Do you have to keep interrupting me!" The Griffin raked its claws through the tall grass before him. The grass became considerably shorter. "Youngsters! Nothing's good enough for them anymore! Well, let me tell you something, son. I've had more than enough of your interference!"

"I was just trying to help!" The youngster stamped its left forehoof. "It takes you forever to do anything!"

"No respect!" The Griffin growled deeply. "When I was your age, nobody wore his feathers that long! You're a disgrace to the mythical community!" Ebenezum covered himself with his robes. The sneezing continued unabated.

"We've really got to do something with this guy." The youngster nudged Ebenezum gently with its beak. "It doesn't do any good to talk to them if they're dead."

"Oh, very well." The Griffin turned back to me. "Are you sure you don't have any gold?" It nodded its beak at a couple of nearby creatures. "Shake them up and down and see if they clink."

The younger creature was right. Ebenezum was in sad shape. I didn't think a good shaking would improve his health. Hurriedly, I remarked that, even if we had had any gold, we would have lost it during our ride here.

The Griffin sighed. "True enough. That's one problem with the Rok. He's fast enough, but he's not very bright." The beast stared at me with an eagle eye. "He's the exception, of course. Most of us are quite talented." "Maybe we should let them rest awhile," the youngster suggested gently. "There's that old shack over—"

"Be quiet and let your elders think! Youngsters!" The Griffin paused, then raised a wing in triumph. "Of course! There's that old shack over there! It's out of the wind. The sneezing human can get warm and dry. After a few hours, he'll be ready to talk!"

"You mean listen, don't you, Pop?"

The Griffin caught itself midroar. "Ah, yes. My son is right. We'll have our meeting tomorrow then, at dawn." It shook its head sadly. "Why is there never any gold? It's hard on an old Griffin, let me tell you."

A couple of creatures with the bodies of horses and the chests, heads and faces of men helped hoist the helplessly sneezing wizard onto the back of the eagle/horse. Apparently, even though the Griffin was still muttering about the lack of gold and his place in society, we weren't supposed to pay any attention to him anymore. Certainly nobody else was.

"Centaurs," the youngster said to my confused expression. He took off at a good trot. I had to run to keep up.

"Excuse me," I ventured, trying to make sense out of this whole thing. "Is that what you are? A Centaur?" Somehow, I had the feeling that this creature's head was all wrong for that classification. I added lamely: "You're not a Griffin, are you?"

The youngster laughed heartily. 44Boy, you don't have your mythology down at all, do you? I'm a Hippogriff. Actually, I'm the Hippogriff, as far as I know."

Was that something my master should have taught me? Perhaps every apprentice worth his name automatically knew what a Hippogriff was. On occasion, when we found ourselves in difficult situations such as these, I did wish I had made it just a little further with my wizardly apprenticeship.

"You're the only Hippogriff, then?" I replied, doing my best to seem polite. Though it is difficult to feign interest when your master may be sneezing his life away. "What," I added after a moment, "is there not much call for the job?"

The Hippogriff looked at me far more soberly. "On the contrary. Since I'm the first, writing the job description is up to me." It looked down proudly at its hooves. "I am unique, the product of true interspecies romance."

"Interspecies romance?" I asked. I realized as soon as the words were out of my mouth that this matter might be too delicate for common conversation.

"Of course." The Hippogriff fluffed its wings out proudly. Well, the creature didn't seem to mind, then. Still, I would have felt on much firmer ground in this situation if I could have told just when an eagle was smiling. "You've met my father. My mother was a horse. All in all, I would say a fine combination."

"You mean," I asked, temporarily taken aback by the very thought, "that you can have—uh—romantic interludes with any animal that interests you?"

"Certainly. Birds and fish, too!"

The whole idea left me momentarily speechless. I was all too familiar with the problems presented by romance with human females. Romance with nearly anything that moved was a truly overwhelming concept. A wizard's apprentice needs to be ready for all occurrences. Still, having a love affair with a trout was virtually beyond my comprehension.

"You seem a bit taken aback," the Hippogriff remarked. "Trust me, it's a truly liberating experience." The creature's voice lowered to a more confidential tone. "I tell you, right now there's this little ocelot I have my eye on. Woo Woo!" The Hippogriff smacked its beak.

"Ah! Here we are!" The Hippogriff sat, depositing the bundle of still-sneezing wizard at the front door of what could in charity be called a dilapidated shack. The boards of what once were sturdy walls sagged inward on all sides, as if the shack was trying hard to return to its earlier state of being as a pile of lumber. There was something that might once have been a window on one side of the structure, plus a couple of even more ragged holes elsewhere that appeared to have occurred sometime after the shack was built.

"Our best accommodations," the Hippogriff remarked. "This should give your friend here a chance to rest. It's away from the hustle and bustle of the rest of the beasts. Your only neighbor is the unicorn we've got penned up just beyond those trees. What a bore, that unicorn, always going on about virgins. Who knows anything about virgins?"

I agreed hastily.

"Oh, by the way," the Hippogriff added, "please don't think of escaping. There's a lot of beasts among us who are very good at finding humans, and some aren't as gentle in their transportation as our friend the Rok. Have a nice night." The Hippogriff turned and galloped away.

My master took a deep breath and, for a change, did not sneeze. He groaned instead. I looked at the clouds gathering in the late afternoon sky. I decided I should get him inside what little shelter the shack would provide.

A piece of frayed rope was tied to the door. I pulled, praying the crumbling hemp would hold long enough for the door to swing out. There was a rending noise. I tossed the door, now free of its hinges, aside and carried my master into the shack's interior. The place had a dirt floor. I placed my master in the very center of the small room, as far away from the crazily leaning walls as possible.

Ebenezum groaned again, then raised himself to his elbows and blew his nose.

" 'Tis a nightmare, Wuntvor," was all he could manage before he had to catch his breath.

I asked my master to rest. There must be a stream nearby. I would pop out for a minute and bring us back some water.

I stepped to the door, and startled two winged creatures. They flew up with cawing screams that ran down my spine like ice. Their appearance had unsettled me almost as much as I had frightened them. The things had the bodies of vultures, but the heads of beautiful women.

I almost stumbled over the buckets they had left behind. One was filled with water, the other with something hot and steamy that looked like stew. Well, I reflected, at least our captors were taking care of us. If what I had seen so far was indicative of the rest of them, I hoped they would continue to take care of us from the greatest distance possible.

I grabbed a bucket in each hand and took them inside to my master.

Ebenezum had sat up in my absence and, besides the fact that he had lost his cap, looked reasonably well composed.

"Indeed," he murmured as I placed the two buckets before him. He pulled two wooden spoons from the stew and handed one to me. "All the comforts of home."

The wind gusted outside. The shack creaked horribly.

"As temporary as our home may be," Ebenezum added as he spooned a mouthful of stew.

The food was bland but palatable, with many vegetables and some sort of thankfully unidentifiable meat. As my stomach filled, I considered that it had probably been prepared to satisfy the needs of the greatest variety of creatures possible. Satiated at last, I inquired how my master felt.

"Remarkably well, all things taken into account," Ebenezum replied when he was done licking his spoon. "One feels much better when one can breathe. The first bout of sneezing tends to clear the nasal passages." He rubbed his nose absently. " Tis a little sore, but, with a good night's sleep, I will survive."

The wizard rubbed his stomach. "Indeed," he said after a moment's pause. "We seem to have but one or two small problems here. First, there is far too much magic about here for my malady. I do not think these creatures necessarily mean to do us harm, for they took note of my sneezing, and gave us accommodations so that I might recover." He glanced absently at the swaying walls. "Then again, perhaps they put us here to be rid of us altogether. I don't think this shack would survive a summer shower."

The wizard pulled his gaze away from the creaking wood and turned back to me. "Second, they have separated us from the rest of our party, although that may, in a way, be more blessing than curse. Still, along with our companions we have lost both personal belongings and some very important magical gear. With the limits of my sorcery of late, I had come to depend more and more on my arcane paraphernalia. I shall miss it."

My master paused again. His fingers, which had been playing absently with his beard, tightened into a fist.

"Third, and by far the most serious, we are no longer able to travel to Vushta. The world seems to be unravelling faster than any of us can hold it together. Tonight I must sleep. Tomorrow, we will listen to what these beasts have to say, but we cannot stay here longer. If they do not let us leave freely, we will escape in the night."

I shivered involuntarily.

My master nodded. "And we will have to deal with whatever terrible things they send after us. We must, to defeat the Netherhells!"

So we sat for a minute, listening to the shack complain at an occasional gust of wind. I realized that, much to my surprise, it was perfectly quiet. For the first time in half a day, I thought of my own true love.

"I must talk with Norei," I said. "I think I can do it now."

"An excellent plan, Wuntvor! While it is hard to imagine us in more difficulty than we are at present. Still, my age and wisdom tell me that it can get far worse. At this juncture, any assistance from any source would be most welcome." My master rubbed his nose again. "Except, may I suggest that when you perform the necessary magic, you do it outside our shelter?"

It was little enough to ask. I stepped through the doorway, and looked about in the twilight for the piece of rotting wood I had discarded before. I propped it as best I could against the doorway, shutting my master away as much as possible from the outside world and the magic that I was about to perform.

The wind had died, as it often does at evening, and the world seemed strangely serene. Clouds still covered a good part of the sky, but where they broke I could see the stars. It was nice to be outside, on my own, in the quiet dark. But I should not let a temporary feeling of well-being distract me from my task. Every moment I dallied was another moment the

Netherhells could further their plans. I would contact Norei, and gain what knowledge and help that I could.

After a moment's thought, I decided to move a bit farther from the shack in which my master slept. The greater the distance, I thought, the kinder it would be to his nose. I would not go too far; the clouds above made the night very dark. Still, there was a copse of trees nearby. If I were to perform my magic just beyond that natural barrier, I would be able to find my way back handily when the task was done. I walked slowly across the field, careful of sinkholes and hidden roots. Already, my mind was filled with thoughts of flying grackles. I would make my master proud of me!

I passed through the trees even more carefully, lest I trip over some bush or sapling in the blackness. Soon, though, I had won my way through to the other side, where I came to a wooden fence. It was a sturdy piece of construction, and held my weight well when I leaned against it. I decided I would prop my back against it as I said my spell.

I said the magic words and thought of a grackle.

Once again, my thoughts took flight, this time through the night sky above the clouds. It was a new world up here, awash with countless points of pale light which made the clouds below into rolling hills, like the world must have looked before the coming of man and beast. As I flew, I felt like I was a small star myself, brother to all the other stars in the heavens.

Some sense given me by the spell guided me on my way. I was near. I spread my wings and dived through the clouds, confident I would see my true love anon.

I couldn't see a thing. The clouds had grown together as I flew, blotting out the stars. How could I find my true love's flaming red hair when there was no way in the blackness to tell red from green or purple? I cried out my despair; the rough caw of a grackle.

"Wuntvor!" The voice was far away. I did not so much hear it as feel it in my mind. But I knew the voice was Norei's.

"Beloved!" I cried in return, being careful to keep the grackle's image firm in my mind. This apprentice was not going to make the same mistake twice! "Norei! Where are you?"

"Follow my voice!" she cried, and I obeyed gladly. "I am beneath the trees!" I swooped lower, skimming the treetops. The forest went on forever!

"Here!" she called. "I can sense you near!"

I plunged through the leaves. Where was I? There was rustling all around me. I was so close now! I couldn't get lost in the upper branches! I flapped my wings, and broke through to clear air beneath the trees. And there, before me, stood Norei!

She smiled up at me. Her perfect lips opened and she called, "Well done, Wuntvor!"

It was enough to make all my feathers stand on end. I cawed with happiness! Oh, if only my magic beak would turn to lips, I would kiss that perfect mouth 'til all the breath had left my mortal form!

"Wuntvor, please!" Norei laughed, the sound of tiny bells ushering in springtime. "Wuntvor, stop! Your feathers tickle!"

I pulled up short, and almost lost the grackle in my mind. My magical form had far more substance than I had imagined. I started to stammer out an apology.

"There's no time for that now!" Norei replied. "We must talk while the spell holds us together!"

Yes, yes, talk! Norei, my beloved! How long had I wished to see your sweet face—

"Wuntvor!" My beloved's voice had developed a stern edge. "You are sweet, but sometimes—" She sighed. "Your spell is far too delicate. It's liable to be broken at any moment! We must talk about the Netherhells!"

Yes, yes, of course, she was right. I was here to get her message, the important warning the Brownie had told us about!

"Wuntvor, the Netherhells have embarked on the most diabolical plan in the history of the world!"

Yes, yes, my beloved! Ebenezum discerned this as well! The Netherhells wish to take the surface world and make it their own! That's why we must rush to Vushta and rally our strength!

Norei paused. Was that the limit of her message? I felt a brief disappointment. Had I anticipated this moment for so long, only to have Norei tell me something I already knew?

"I see," she said at last. "Then do you know about the Forxnagel?"

Not the Forxnagel! The shock was so great, I once again nearly lost my grackle form. The Forxnagel was the overspell. He who successfully completed it would control all magic everywhere. We had once defeated an inept magician who had attempted this all-powerful magic. But the denizens of the Netherhells were far from inept! This was much worse than I imagined!

"What, you knew that, too?" Norei had taken my shocked silence for silent indifference. Vexation was entering her voice. "Maybe I shouldn't have even spoken to the Brownie! Well, how about this, then? It's the most important part. Do you know about the fate the Netherhells have particularly planned for the Wizard?"

"What?" I cawed in alarm.

"Well, good. I'm glad I didn't call you for no reason whatever. It's a shame to waste magic." Norei smiled ever so slightly before her earnest expression returned.

"They're very specific about it. Ebenezum has quite an enemy in the Netherhells, a powerful demon named Guxx Unfufadoo."

A chill went down my feathered spine. The warning had to do with Guxx? The situation was becoming more desperate with every passing moment.

"Guxx has plans for your master," Norei continued. "Hideously demonic plans. Listen carefully, if you wish to save his life—"

"Yes, my belov—I began. I felt a pain in my chest. No, not the chest of the magic grackle, but my human chest, so many miles away from Norei.

I was being stabbed!

CHAPTER SIX

There comes a time when every wizard should retire, and pass the mantle of responsibility on to younger shoulders. It behooves us, then, to teach our successors well, so that the new wizard may do honor to our names, attract the very best of clients, and be well enough paid to support our retirement home in Vushta.

—from The Teachings of Ebenezum, Volume LXXI

It was the unicorn. It stood across the fence from me, its golden horn pressing into my chest.

"Oh good," the magnificent beast said. "You're awake. You seemed to be having the strangest dream. Tell me. Do you often caw in your sleep?"

I stepped back from the horn. This is what had startled me away from my beloved, just as I was about to receive her true message!

"Why?" I asked, struggling to form words, my head still half-full of grackle. "What do you want?"

The beast sighed. "Unicorns, beautiful though we are, get lonely, too."

"You woke me up because you were lonely?" I was incredulous.

"Yes." The unicorn fluttered its dark, soulful eyes. "That, and I was looking for a virgin lap somewhere, to lay my head."

"Get away from me!" I cried. This was too much!

"Come on now," the unicorn pleaded. "Here I am, trapped by a bunch of uncouth beasts, unable to roam the verdant fields as is my right. Do you know how tedious it can get, all by yourself with no one to admire you?"

I wanted to scream. I had lost Norei because some creature

wanted me to admire it? My beloved hadn't told me her message! I had to go back. I did my best to think of a grackle.

It was no use. I was too upset. Anger killed my concentration. How could things get any worse?

It started to rain.

The shack survived the summer shower. It did so by leaking in every conceivable location. I perceived, at last, why the shack was still standing. Water could not damage the old structure, since the old structure simply let the rain pass on through, straight down upon us.

In short, we did not have the most restful of nights.

Something pounded on our door around dawn.

"Wake up! Rise and shine! We're all waiting for you!"

We? Waiting for what? I realized that I had talked to the Hippogriff for quite some time yesterday without learning anything of substance. Well, there was always interspecies romance, but I didn't feel that was appropriate to our present situation. At least, I hoped it wasn't.

The door fell in. It hit the muddy earth with a sickening plop.

Ebenezum rolled over and groaned. The Hippogriff stuck its eagle head inside.

"My, my," the creature said. "All right, we'll give you a few minutes to pull yourselves together. You're guests of honor, you know."

Ebenezum sat up and sneezed.

"I'll wait a respectful distance away," the Hippogriff said, withdrawing its head. "I know how you humans value your privacy."

"Wuntvor," Ebenezum said hoarsely after the Hippogriff had gone. "I cannot go out there."

I looked to my master. This trip had been more than hard on him. He had rallied above his difficulties time and time again, saying spells to remove us from danger even though he might sneeze for hours thereafter. But our adventures had taken a toll upon the wizard. A half-dozen times on our journey thus far, my master's ills had overwhelmed his sorcerous spirit, and his aura of wizardliness would leave him for an hour or two, leaving only an old man behind.

Now, I could see that fatigue about his eyes once again. The day before had been far too taxing on his constitution. He needed rest desperately. He needed to be kept far away from anything that would cause a nasal reaction.

Now the Hippogriff was going to take us to a meeting of monsters. And, as far as my master's malady went, the assemblage out there was ragweed season. If my master took that trip out there today, I feared it would be the last trip he would ever take.

"I will handle it myself," I proclaimed. Before my master could protest, I walked out to meet the Hippogriff in the yard.

"Where's the other one?" the beast inquired.

"I'm the one who makes decisions," I lied. "The other one is old, and you saw that he was sick. If we need him, we can talk to him later."

The Hippogriff considered my words. "But, isn't he the wizard? I mean, I'm not really up on human attire, but those were wizard's robes he was wearing, weren't they?"

The Hippogriff had a point. I had to think fast. How could I convince the beasts that Ebenezum was unimportant, so that they would let the wizard rest and regain his strength?

"Well, the old fellow was a wizard, once. Quite a good one, too. He still can conjure a trick or two, on his better days. We let him keep the robes. It's an honorary sort of thing. But you notice he doesn't have a hat. Only full-fledged wizards can have hats."

"You, then, are a full-fledged wizard?" the beast asked.

I nodded solemnly.

"So where's your hat?"

My hand involuntarily brushed my hair. "Well, yes, indeed. A bit embarrassing, that. I'm afraid I lost it when the Rok brought us here."

The Hippogriff shrugged its equine shoulders.

"All right, I guess. It's a bit of a problem with the Rok, always losing things. Even passengers, sometimes—" The Hippogriff nodded solemnly, as if carefully reviewing the situation. "You'll just have to explain it to Pop. I'll warn you, though, should you in any way try to play him false. Griffins have a very low tolerance for lies."

I waved away the Hippogriff's warning with the back of my hand, as if to say, "What need has a wizard to fear a Griffin's anger?" I did my best to walk by the Hippogriff's side without my knees buckling beneath me from fright.

My master must recover. Otherwise, we would never see Vushta, and the world would be lost to demons.

I told myself that over and over again as we approached the crowd of monsters.

"You know, of course," the Hippogriff remarked, "we observed your party for some time before we requested your presence before our assembly."

"Indeed?" I replied. Had they observed us long enough to realize I was nothing more than an apprentice?

"Yes, our organization wants to be careful in how we are presented to the human world. We wanted the best possible spokespeople to carry our story beyond the Enchanted Forest."

"Indeed!" I said, as firmly as possible. Perhaps I shouldn't be worried after all. We must have made a pretty good impression. My legs seemed firmer beneath me now, my feet striding boldly along the path. If they thought that much of me, I must walk like a wizard.

"Of course, finding any spokespeople at all was a bit of a problem in the Enchanted Forest. For some reason, this is the sort of place people tend to avoid. Probably has something to do with a large number of our membership having a taste for human flesh."

My knees threatened to go altogether. I cleared my throat. "Indeed," I managed after a moment.

"Don't worry, though. The membership has sworn off eating humans until the end of this campaign. Well, at least most of them have, and I'm sure we can crush any dissidents before they have time to nibble more than a toe or two. So really, you have nothing to worry about. You just keep your part of the bargain, and you'll be perfectly safe."

I nodded my head, trying to look far more sure of myself than I felt. What bargain, where? Safe from what? My voice had died in my throat. I couldn't even manage another "indeed."

"So there we were," the Hippogriff continued, "looking for

spokespeople, when who should come crashing through the forest but you five. Now the Rok can only carry two at a time, so we had to figure out who it was best to invite. Luckily, it didn't take long to make that decision. The older wizard and you seemed to be the only ones actually doing anything."

I thought on that for a moment. "Well, the others are very good talkers."

"You got it!" The Hippogriff nodded to the assembled masses before us. "Wait a moment, and you'll see that we, too, are great masters of rhetoric."

The Hippogriff led me through the assembled creatures and monstrosities to a raised platform in their midst. I was aware of a thousand eyes upon me, the eyes of birds and beasts and men, although the bodies that went with those eyes were often of a different species altogether. I glanced about briefly as we moved through the assemblage. I—who had seen a thousand demons, each one different from the last, and who had witnessed other wonders uncountable in my travels toward Vushta—I saw any number of creatures I'd never seen before. I got a sense of every sort of fur and feather, small eyes hidden behind shaggy manes, large eyes on the ends of stalks, and, of course, large teeth and even larger teeth, claws and pincers and long, barbed tails. I did not let my gaze linger too long on any of the beasts, lest some fearsome sight should totally destroy my resolve. Besides, I thought it impolite to stare.

"Only one?" The Griffin stared down at me from the raised platform. "Only one deigns to come to our meeting. Well, I suppose it will be all right." The Griffin paused. "If you brought some gold."

"Pop!" The Hippogriff picked me up in its enormous beak and tossed me onto the platform. "Is that any way to treat a guest?"

"Excuse me," the Griffin said as I stood and brushed myself off. "Every so often, my upstart offspring makes a valid point. All this gold business—well, you know how it is with us mythological beasts, when instinct rears its ugly head. We haven't had much direct, one-on-one contact with humans before. But we mean to change that now."

"I've had direct contact with humans before!" a voice called from the audience. "Straight down the gullet to my stomach!"

There was laughter and shouting out in the crowd. Some seemed to be decrying the remark, saying things like, "Give the human a chance!" On the other hand, others were discussing just how much salt and oregano should be used to truly enhance my flavor. The group before me was, as my master might refer to them, a "rough audience." For the first time, I wished I had Ebenezum by my side to give me advice.

"They're a bit rowdy out there," the Griffin remarked. "We'll have to let them settle down. This is something of a convention, you know."

"Indeed," I said. I thought that if I could control my breathing, at least I could appear calm.

"Yes," the Griffin continued. "You should be very honored. You are the first human ever to attend a meeting of the Association for the Advancement of Mythical and Imaginary Beasts and Creatures. Or, as we like to call it, AFTAOMAIBAC."

The Griffin turned to me, its eagle eyes piercing in their intensity. "Before we address the meeting, however, you and I are going to have a little talk."

"Indeed?" Instinctively, I backed toward the corner of the platform. It took an effort of will to keep my feet from going any farther.

It was all or nothing. I cleared my throat. Ebenezum wasn't here and I had to fill his shoes. I had to persevere, for my master, and Vushta!

"Be careful, sirrah!" I said in my best deep voice. "You are dealing with a wizard!"

"Why, yes, that's our point now." The Griffin's lion claws brushed against my feet. Its eagle breath was hot against my face. It smelled as though it had been eating rodents.

"We know we're dealing with a wizard," the Griffin continued. "But we're wondering why he didn't show up this morning?"

So I would have to go through all this again.

"Oh," I said nonchalantly. "You mean the old man. He may look like a wizard, that's true, but—" I waved the rest of the sentence away impatiently. "I've already explained this to your son!"

"Yeah, Pop, it's true!" the Hippogriff volunteered. "This guy says the old geezer used to be a great wizard, but now is a little gone in the head, you know?"

"But," the Griffin objected, "he was wearing wizard's robes—"

"Yeah, but no hat. Only real, full-time wizards can have hats!"

The Griffin turned to me. "Well, where is your hat, then, wizard?"

"Oh, Pop, you know how the Rok is. He lost it on the trip over here!"

The Griffin nodded grimly. "Have to have a talk with that Rok. Always losing things. Very well. You'll have a chance to prove your wizardly prowess a little later on. I still don't know about this older wizard. Would a retired human so desperately hold on to his old robes?" "I'd believe it in a snap," the Hippogriff replied. "I know how stubborn certain mythological beasts can be when they get older."

"I beg your pardon!" There was battle lust in the Griffin's eyes. "Kindly explain to me, young beast, exactly what you mean—"

"Pop—" The Hippogriff waved its beak at the crowd. "The meeting?"

"Yes. Ahem. I forget my priorities." The Griffin shot me a final, withering glance. "This is the most important day of your life. Let us pray it is not your last."

"Pop!"

"Sorry. Old habits die hard. We are rewriting history here, and you will be a part of it." The Griffin reached out a comradely wing in my direction. "No longer will you be a mere human, forced to eke out a common destiny in the mud."

"Mere human?" How would my master handle this? I had stood here and listened to this beast go on for far too long. To make this work, I needed to adopt a truly wizardly manner. "I have told you, sirrah, I am skilled in the sorcerous arts."

"I'm sorry. You look much more skilled at carrying buckets

and cleaning out cow stalls. That older fellow, now..."

I started to object, and found a lion's paw entwined with my shirt. The Griffin spoke very quietly:

"I will accept the fact that you have no gold. Lies are another matter entirely."

The Griffin turned to the assemblage.

"Brothers, sisters, and indeterminates! We are gathered here today to write a new page in mythology! Too long have we taken a back seat to dragons and unicorns, giants and Fairies! From this day forward, Griffins and Centaurs, Harpies and Satyrs will be on the tip of every tongue, and find a place in every heart!"

And us Chimeras! Don't forget us Chimeras!"

"And what about us Kelpies!"

"How about us Nixies?"

"Yes! Yes!" the Griffin shouted above the crowd. "Chimeras, Kelpies, Nixies, everybody! We'll force mythology down their throats!"

The crowd went wild. They shouted some word, over and over. I strained to make it out.

A voice, much louder than the rest, called from the edge of the clearing:

"But nothing for Bog Womblers?"

The Griffin stopped, openmouthed.

"Bog Womblers?"

A large, gray thing sitting by the river raised its pseudopod. "Yes! Everyone forgets the Bog Womblers!"

"Yes, of course," the Griffin said, recovering rapidly. "Uh—Pookas, and Sphinxes, and Bog Womblers, too!"

The crowd went wilder.

"Uh, Pop?" the Hippogriff said softly.

The other beast glanced back irritably. "Yes, what is it now?"

The youngster nodded its head toward the far edge of the clearing, beyond the Bog Wombler, where a number of near-naked women were wheeling carts into the crowd.

"Just that the refreshments are here."

"Is it that time already?" The Griffin shook its head angrily. "I've spent far too much time with this—human here! And I was just hitting my stride!"

It turned back to the assembled monsters. "Fellow mythical beasts! I know how deeply we all want to complete the business at hand. But our minds won't be at their best if our stomachs are empty, will they?"

The Griffin's remarks brought on a new chorus of shouts from the crowd. A couple of the larger creatures smiled my way. I was not sure if their large, toothsome grins and repeated licking of chops were all in all a sign of friendly good fellowship.

"Nymphs!" the Griffin called. "Bring on the refreshments!"

I was startled for an instant. The beasts were going to take a momentary pause in their strange ritual to refresh themselves. This could be just the chance I needed. Maybe I could discern what was really happening here, and what was expected of me. Maybe I could escape, and take Ebenezum with me. I looked around the dais on which we stood, but could see no gap in the tightly packed monsters.

The Griffin strode up to me on muscular cat feet. "Human. You have a few minutes to yourself. Step down and get to know some of our membership, if you will. We want to put you at your ease."

At my ease? Perhaps, I thought, I was needlessly worried. Perhaps this Griffin was merely a slightly overbearing father figure, and I was here to spread the news about this ritual back among humankind. Perhaps I imagined things, and half the crowd did not fantasize about how I would taste in a light cream sauce. I did my best to smile at the Griffin in a comradely way.

"Oh," the Griffin added as an afterthought, "and after this break, you will have your chance to prove your mystic powers to the assembly."

CHAPTER SEVEN

A wizard's reputation is his bond, or so the sages say. And, as all learned men know, a reputation is difficult to build, and all too easily besmirched. The wizard with a fallen reputation is often led to less savory forms of employ, and, while these sometimes pay better than whatever the wizard was doing before, they are not the sort of thing one writes home to Mother about. The successful wizard, therefore, should develop three or four reputations simultaneously, and then, happily, will have one for every occasion.

—from The Teachings of Ebenezum, Volume XIII

Perhaps, on the other hand, escape was a very good idea. I looked again, out over the multitude of monsters. A dozen scantily clad women were pushing large wooden carts through the crowd. The carts appeared to be refreshment wagons, filled with large kegs of mead, trays full of biscuits and small sandwiches, and little, squirmy things that squealed loudly when the creatures swallowed them.

I could but hope that if they ate those things, they would be less hungry for me. There was nothing for it but to go out amidst the crowd.

"Hey! It's the human!"

I was already attracting notice.

"Do you think he's a wizard?"

There was a coarse laugh. "Sure, and I'm a Pooka!"

"Wait a second. I thought you were a Pooka!"

"No, I'm a Nix! Good heavens, don't you have any eyes in that Chimera head of yours?"

"What do you mean? I'm not a Chimera!"

I lost track of the conversation when one of the voluptuously attractive, and nearly naked, women stood before me.

"Hello, big boy," she said huskily.

"Why—um," I replied. She took my hand as I spoke. Her pink tongue moved slowly across her white teeth.

"Would you like a little something?" the husky voice asked.

"Why—um," I replied. I seemed to have broken into a heavy sweat. I did not realize the day was so warm.

"Hey! Keep your hands off our Nymphs!" A short fellow with a pointy beard stared angrily at me.

"Who are you?" I had the awful feeling that a wizard would know more about mythical beasts than I did. What little I had learned came from conversations with Hubert, a dragon of my acquaintance who was pursuing a career in vaudeville. And Hubert hadn't talked at all about short fellows with pointy beards.

"Get a load of this guy!" The pointy-bearded fellow, who also appeared to have hooves and a tail, sneered. "You know what a Satyr is, don't you?"

Oh. I was on safe ground now. This was something I had discussed with Hubert. "Sure," I replied. "That's a form of comedy, right?"

"Who is this guy?" The bearded fellow searched the heavens above us. "No. Satyr. S-A-T-Y-R! You know, the pipes of Pan! Frolicking and disporting with Nymphs among the spring flowers! That sort of thing!"

"Why, certainly." I dismissed my foolish error with a wave of my wizardly hand. "Now that you say so, of course. It's just that I have a few things on my mind...."

"And your mind is where they're going to stay!" The Satyr glanced at the nearly naked Nymph. "Scoot, Nymphie. We'll do some frolicking and disporting later on, okay?"

The Nymph showed me a final smile.

"Maybe I can get you something sometime, big boy." Her voice, if anything, was lower and huskier than before.

"Why—urn," I replied as I watched her retreat through the crowd.

"You keep shaking your head like that, you'll get sick," a deep voice said nearby. I looked up to see a massive wall of gray flesh. "Us Bog Womblers know all about sick."

So I had made my way through the throng to the Bog Wombler. That meant I was almost to the edge of the clearing. Perhaps I could escape after all.

"Indeed," I replied, doing my best to act wizardly. "Here I am, taking a stroll, to get some air."

"Not a bad idea, with that crowd," the huge creature intoned. "Bog Womblers don't like crowds."

"Indeed," I stated.

"There's a stream just behind me. You might want to refresh yourself. If we don't have a stream around, we Bog Womblers are in big trouble."

"Indeed?" I answered, barely able to contain my elation. A stream? I wondered if any of the creatures came by boat. My escape was beginning to seem more possible with every passing minute.

Still, I shouldn't appear too eager. I would engage in small talk for an instant, then saunter away.

"Pardon me," I said, "but I don't know what a Bog Wombler does."

"You're not alone. No one ever knows." It paused and sighed, fixing me with a single, bloodshot eye.

"We womble," it said at last.

"Oh," I replied. "Indeed. How interesting. I think I'll go and get that drink you suggested. Awfully nice meeting you."

I skirted the Bog Wombler and headed for freedom.

The stream was not as deserted as I had hoped. Another two dozen strange creatures, many with extremely fishy characteristics, lounged in and about the water. Possibly, if I were to wander downstream a bit... I gave a wide berth to the nastier-looking fish-things. With some reluctance, I passed the Mermaids by without a second glance.

The trees grew larger and thicker as I walked downstream, which suited my purpose perfectly. No one had tried to stop me. Even if I couldn't find a boat, the foliage might give me sufficient cover to escape on foot.

Somehow, though, I would have to double back and rescue my master. And while I might be able to move quickly through the forest for hours on end, I doubted if the wizard was yet up to it. For that reason alone, a boat would be very useful.

I came to a bend in the stream. There, moored in the shallows, was a canoe.

My luck got better with every passing moment! At this rate, Ebenezum and I would be well on our way to Vushta by nightfall.

The boat was tied by a line to a sturdy oak. It took me a moment to undo the knot, fiendishly tied, I imagined, by some hands that were not quite human. I gave a muted cry of satisfaction as the final strand pulled free. Now I would push the canoe silently downstream, and hide it somewhere to avoid detection until I had rescued Ebenezum and brought him back to the craft.

I squatted to push the canoe fully into the water.

The canoe didn't move.

Something was keeping it from moving. I now took note of the fact that the boat seemed to contain a horse's hoof.

"Hi there," the Hippogriff said.

Panic struck me. Clearly it was time for a change of plans.

"Well, excuse me!" I cried, doing my best to conjure up wizardly indignation. "It appears I can't have any privacy at all! I'll have you know that even we wizards have certain bodily functions that we have to take care of."

"In a boat?" The Hippogriff shook its eagle beak. "Guess you'll just have to hold it in now, won't you? It's time for the meeting to begin."

The beast looked aloft and whistled. "Oh, Rok!"

There was a great fluttering of wings.

The Hippogriff fixed me again with its eagle stare. "You've been a naughty human, wandering away like that when we needed your wizardly skill. But you're the guest of honor. Spare no expense, right? So we'll get you an express ride back to the podium."

Something very large landed next to me.

"Hey," the huge bird drawled. "What's happening?"

"Got another job for you, Rok," the Hippogriff said. "We need to get this guy back to the podium in a hurry."

"Hey," the Rok replied. "That's cool."

"And, Rok?" the Hippogriff said somewhat tentatively. "I've got a request from my father, the Griffin? It seems you dropped some of this fellow's things last time you carried him. My pop was wondering if you'd kind of be a little more careful?"

The huge bird focused its eyes for the first time. It glared at the Hippogriff. "Hey, horse, I got big claws. Sometimes things slip away. Sometimes they don't." It flexed a claw idly, crushing a tree. "Dig?"

This was terrible. There had to be some way that I could get away.

"Excuse me?" I asked, trying to sound a bit more humble than before. "I really could use a bush somewhere."

"You should have thought of that earlier," the Hippogriff replied. "Now, it's showtime!"

The Rok's claws surrounded me.

"Listen, if it gets really bad," the Hippogriff added, "there's a crawl space under the stage."

The beast waved its wing as the Rok carried me aloft. "Nothing is too good for our guests!" were the last words I heard before the Hippogriff, too, took flight.

The crowd didn't seem to notice us passing overhead. I heard snatches of conversation as I flew by.

"Would you stop changing your shape every two minutes? It's very difficult to concentrate—"

"How can I tell you're the Sphinx?"

"How about a riddle? I've got a million of them. What's yellow, has four wings, weighs two thousand pounds and goes—"

I had grabbed on to the claws and had a much better view than the first time I'd traveled this way. That's how I managed to see something out of the corner of my eye. Something dark and fast-moving, and maybe as big as the Rok. It was too high in the sky to tell. Maybe what it was was something that hadn't been invited to this convention. Whatever that could possibly be...

The Rok deposited me on the dirt by the stage. The Hippogriff landed nearby.

"About time you got back," the Griffin growled. It removed its claws from where it had been shredding a corner of the stage.

"Pop, I think I saw—" the Hippogriff began worriedly.

"Here we are"—the Griffin cut the youngster off—"at the most important moment ever in the history of mythological beastdom, and you two are galavanting around. Don't give a thought to the old Griffin, oh no. I'm merely the one running the show. Who cares if I'm kept informed?"

The Griffin leapt six feet straight into the air, grabbing a small bird in its beak. It crashed back onto the stage, crunching and swallowing noisily.

"Haven't even had time for a decent meal," it mumbled.

There might be a way out of this yet. Perhaps I could get on this beast's good side. If it had a good side.

"Indeed," I said, "the weight of responsibility upon you must be terrible."

The Griffin nodded solemnly.

"How did they pick you to be the leader, if I might inquire?"

"Quiet down out there!" The Griffin raked its claws through the air so fast it made the wind sing. The crowd got considerably quieter. "Oh, I know exactly how to deal with creatures. I always thought it was my Griffin's keen sense of humor and personal style. Keep them laughing, that's what I always say." It raised its voice to the crowd again. "Are you going to be quiet out there, or is there going to be trouble?"

The crowd got quieter still. "You're to be commended," I added. "You've really gathered quite a variety of creatures."

"Yep, got almost everybody," the Griffin replied. "We're still waiting for the Phoenix. He keeps promising to show up."

Could that be what I saw? A Phoenix? Then why wasn't he here?

The Griffin looked wistfully at the sky. "You'd think there'd be more birds. I don't work well on an empty stomach. Oh well, it can't be helped." The beast sighed. "We have history to make."

"Fellow mythological beasts!" The Griffin's voice rang out over the throng. " 'Tis the time for decision! Bring out the unicorn!"

The crowd began to chant the phrase that had puzzled me

before. It sounded like "Half-past three! Half-past three!" Was someone keeping track of the time?

"Yes, that's right!" the Griffin continued. "This is our moment in history. No longer will we have to take a back seat to unicorns, dragons and the like. We're here to see that we get our fair share of tapestry space!"

The crowd was on its feet, or wings, or fins, or, in the case of the Bog Wombler, whatever.

"That's right, mythical beasts! Our fair share of tapestry space! And a maiden for every monster!"

The crowd was at it again. "Tap-es-try!" they called. "Tapestry! Tapestry!"

Oh, that was it then. Tapestry. Quite simple, really.

Hoots of derision rose from the audience. The Hippogriff was leading in the unicorn.

"Here, then," the Griffin was saying, "is our chief competition."

Shouts of "Nyah-nyah-nyah!" and "Who's the walking hat rack?" followed the unicorn through the crowd. Somehow, the magnificent beast seemed above it all.

"Now, what has this beast got that we don't have?" the Griffin asked. "A golden horn perhaps. A magnificent coat, maybe, a stately bearing? Even—hah!—a way with virgins? Not enough, I say! Why are tapestries so crowded with unicorns? How come dragons have cornered the damsel-in-distress market? It sets a mythological beast to thinking, let me tell you!"

The Griffin waved a wing grandly in my direction. "That's why we invited a wizard here today. True, he may not be much of a wizard, but we're operating on very short notice. Still, we are here to show the wizard the wisdom of our course, and to let him use his magic to spread the word!"

A voice came from the crowd. "Then can we eat him?"

"Only if he doesn't do his job!" The Griffin made a short, barking sound that might have been a laugh. "But all kidding aside, fellow creatures! No longer will maidens flock solely to unicorns and dragons! Once we're done, every Kobold and Hob and Fruich among you will have a dozen tapestries, and maidens beating down your door!"

"Tap-es-try!" the crowd chanted. "Tap-es-try!"

A mournful voice cut through the melee.

"What about us Bog Womblers?"

"Bog Womblers, too! When we are done, every Bog Wombler will be covered with maidens!"

That many maidens? It was an awesome thought. From the size of the thing, I would guess a Bog Wombler would take up a tapestry all by itself.

"How about Satyrs?" somebody cried. "Satyrs already get maidens!"

One of the pointy-bearded fellows jumped forward. "We do not! We get Nymphs. It's another thing altogether. You have to spend all your time chasing them around the forest." The fellow shook his fists with frustration. "And have you ever tried to have an intelligent conversation with a Nymph? All they want to talk about is the weather and flower arrangements!"

"Yes, yes!" the Griffin agreed. "Maidens for everyone!" The beast turned to me. "Are you ready?"

I cleared my throat. "Indeed?" I managed. "Ready for what?"

"For the big moment, of course. Oh. We haven't explained that, have we? So much to do, so little time. You'll forgive me for not telling you this before, won't you? That's a good human."

"Now wait a minute!" I shouted. "You get a big bird to drag me and my master to this place, plop me down in a leaky, drafty shack, throw me out here without any breakfast, and expect me to perform for everybody? I will do no such thing!"

They had finally done it. I was angry.

"Hmm," the Griffin mused. "Perhaps this fellow is a wizard after all." The beast turned to the Hippogriff. "Son, see if you can find some—oh, whatever it is humans eat!"

"Sure, Pop!" The Hippogriff galloped off the stage. The Griffin turned back to me. "Now that we have addressed your needs, we can get down to business."

"Fellow mythological creatures! Our guest, the wizard, has asked for a few minutes to prepare his spells before he broadcasts our message to wizards everywhere. A reasonable request, I think, and one that will give him a chance to hear more about our noble purpose!"

Shouts of "Yeah, wizard! That's tellin' him!" and "Let's eat the unicorn!" drifted in from the crowd.

"In the meantime," the Griffin continued, "I will explore some of the finer points of our seventy-two demands, to be presented to all of humanity, as well as the world below."

The world below? Was this creature talking about the Netherhells? Now that I thought of it, I remembered Ebenezum once telling me that magical beasts were only partially of this world, and partially Netherhells-inspired. That meant they might have connections who would know the Netherhells' fiendish plots!

"You're talking about the Netherhells!" I interrupted loudly.

The Griffin paused in its oratory.

"Yes?"

"But the demons have concocted some fantastic scheme to rule the world above ground, too!"

"Oh, yes, of course," the Griffin said. "We know all about that."

"You know what the Netherhells intend?" I cried. "You have to tell me!"

"Sorry." The Griffin shook its head. "We have an understanding with the Netherhells. They're fantastic creatures, too, you know. Besides, it would hurt our bargaining position."

I started to object, when the Hippogriff galloped back on the stage. The creature dropped a bundle at my feet.

"Sorry, fella," the beast said. "Best I could do on short notice."

The bundle was moving and making mewling noises. "No time to cook anything, I'm afraid." The Hippogriff shrugged its wings.

I decided not to look inside. "Indeed," I muttered. "I'll eat it later."

"Fellow creatures!" The Griffin had returned to its oratory. For the moment, I had lost my chance. My mind raced. What could these strange creatures know about the foul schemes of the Netherhells? And how could I get them to talk?

"The time has come," the Griffin continued, "to promote ourselves before the unlearned masses. 'Tis a sad fact that Sphinxes and Hippogriffs rarely crop up in everyday conversation. Hobs and Kobolds are talked about even less. We are going to change all that!"

Some members of the crowd cheered.

"Our first order of business today is to devise phrases that will help the unwashed masses identify us. I will give you an example:

"If one of the masses should describe something as 'As lovely as a unicorn,' or 'As deadly as a dragon,' no one hearing them would think twice. They know all about unicorns and dragons. They see them on tapestries. They're constantly having to go out and rescue maidens from their clutches! Unicorns and dragons are a part of their everyday lives!

"But what of Chimeras and Centaurs? I have gone up to a member of the unwashed and said that word—'Chimera!' And what did they say to me? I'll tell you! They said 'Gesundheit!'

"Let me assure you, this is a situation we can no longer tolerate. If unicorns and dragons are known by their slogans, the rest of us will have slogans as well!" Now the crowd went wild.

The Hippogriff brought the unicorn up onto the stage.

The Griffin glanced at the brilliant white creature with the golden horn. "I brought this unicorn before us for a purpose. We can look at this beast and know that it is no better than any of us."

The unicorn snorted and shook its magnificently flowing mane. Taut muscles rippled beneath its perfect coat. Its golden horn glinted in the sun.

"Well," the Griffin added, "perhaps it is a little better than some of us, but I'm sure that we all have hidden attributes that a unicorn couldn't even dream of!"

The Griffin spread its wings. "All right now! We need to start somewhere, and I have decided that I shall volunteer, to demonstrate one approach we might take. To begin, I look down upon my physical form, and catalogue my various positive features."

The creature flapped its wings with slow majesty. It brought a welcome breeze to the platform. Whatever was in the sack the Hippogriff had brought me was starting to smell.

"First, I have the wings and head of the great eagle, predator of the skies!"

The Griffin then roared and waved a lion's claw with talons extended. It seemed to be getting somewhat carried away. I took a step back for safety's sake.

"Next, I have the body of the mighty lion, king of the beasts!"

The tail that looked like half a snake whipped across the stage, knocking my intended lunch out into the crowd. At least now, I hoped, I would not be expected to eat it. Politeness or no, there are certain limits even a wizard's apprentice has to observe.

"Lastly, but no less mighty, is my serpent's tail, powerful enough to crush the life from half the creatures of the forest."

The Griffin paused for dramatic effect. "What does this all indicate? Yes, yes, I can feel you thinking it! Nobility. Therefore, we will add one phrase to the common speech: 'As noble as a Griffin!' "

The Griffin shot a look at the unicorn, who had snorted at an inappropriate moment, then turned back to the crowd.

"There, you see how easy it is? All right. Who's next?"

The pointy-bearded fellow in the front row waved his triangular-shaped whistle. "What about Satyrs?"

"Satyrs already get maidens!" somebody insisted.

"I'm sorry," the Griffin interjected. "Maidens were dealt with earlier on the agenda. Yes, what about Satyrs? We need a slogan to make you, too, a common, household name."

"Say, Pop!" the Hippogriff called. "Try 'As sly as a Satyr.' "

The Griffin considered it. He glanced at the fellow with the pointy beard, who appeared to be frowning.

"No, no, that has some negative connotations, doesn't it? Maybe 'As sexy as a Satyr'?"

The pointy-bearded fellow shifted uncomfortably. He cleared his throat. "Please, we're trying to downplay certain aspects of our image."

"Very well," the Griffin said impatiently. "Do you have any suggestions?"

"Yes!" The fellow smiled. "I have catalogued my body parts as you did, and I've come up with a phrase that's ideal!" He cleared his throat again.

"As noble as a Satyr!"

The crowd applauded enthusiastically.

"Oh. Yes. I see," the Griffin murmured. "Well, then, 'As noble as a Satyr' it will be!"

The motion was passed to popular acclaim.

A mournful voice came from the audience.

"What about us Bog Womblers?"

"Bog Womblers?" the Hippogriff muttered.

"Simple, but éffective!" the Griffin cried, stepping forward. "As noble as a Bog Wombler!"

The crowd went wild.

The Griffin turned to the Hippogriff. "This is not going quite as well as I had hoped. 'Tis time for the wizard."

It took me a second to realize that they meant me. I had quite forgotten, what with the grand sweep of oratory going on before me, that I was supposed to prepare myself for my task.

The Griffin turned to me. "Come now and prove your sorcerous skills. Spread the word about AFTAOMAIBAC to wizards throughout the world!"

"Pardon me," I said, "but I'm not sure my magic works that way."

The Griffin grumbled deep in its throat. It fixed me again with its eagle eye.

"I, and the collective beasts of our brotherhood, have been lenient, considering your situation, but I am afraid our patience is almost spent. It is time to make our organization known to the world!"

"If not, of course," the Hippogriff added in a more reasonable tone, "there are those among us who would be glad to eat you."

"Yeah!" someone called from the audience. "Waste not, want not!"

"Come now," the Griffin reproached. "You've spent far too long in your preparation. 'Tis time to prove your mettle."

The beast turned to the throng. "Come, fellow creatures! Let us cheer the wizard on. Soon, every sorcerer will know our name! AFTAOMAIBAC! AFTAOMAIBAC! AFTAOMAIBAC!"

A ragged cheer arose from the crowd as they attempted to repeat the group's name.

So I would be eaten at last. Unless—could I dare hope? There was one thing that might work. What if I contacted Norei and somehow got her to speak through me to the assemblage? I could then convince the magical beasts that I had spoken with another sorcerer. Yes! I had to talk with Norei again, anyway! It was a brilliant stroke. Maybe I would survive this after all.

I began to think of grackles.

"AFTAOMAIBAC! AFTAOMAIBAC!"

It was hard to concentrate with the cheering of the crowd. I looked at the Griffin, leading the throng. Its serpent tail whipped fearsomely back and forth in time with the cheers, as its lion's claws ripped boards from the platform and tossed them amidst the crowd. Its eagle beak turned to regard me.

My grackle thoughts went flying aloft.

Norei! I called. Norei!

"Wuntvor? Is it you?"

I saw her below me, marching across an open field. My grackle thoughts flew swiftly to her side.

Yes, my red-haired beauty. Yes! I need your help desperately!

"Oh," she said with a certain amount of disdain, "and about time. So you've finally come back to learn the fate the Netherhells have planned for your master?"

Yes, uh, and no! I admitted. You see, there's this large group of monsters—

"Monsters? There's no time for that now, Wuntvor. I fear the Netherhells suspect our communication. You have used this spell too openly, and too many times. I feel the demons are taking steps against us, even as we speak."

My grackle form cried in alarm: We must talk hurriedly, then, my love. I need a sign from you, if I am to retain my life. You see, I've found myself captured by this convention of mythological beasts—

"Convention of what? Wuntvor! Sometimes your playfulness can be very inappropriate! Listen now to what I have to say. I fear the Netherhells will come between us, and we will never have a chance—"

My beloved screamed. I could no longer see her.

Another face swam before my eyes. A demonic face, with many, many teeth.

With a start, I realized it was Guxx Unfufadoo, the dread, rhyming demon who was the cause of my master's malady.

"We've had enough of your pitiful spell,

For the time has come for your death knell!"

I heard myself scream. I blinked, and found I was back among the monsters.

"So," the Griffin said, sharpening its claws on the remains of the stage. "When do you begin your spell?"

There was a massive explosion.

"Heads up, kiddies!" a high voice cried. "It's Brownie time!"

The smoke set me to coughing. Through watery eyes, I saw that two things had materialized near me on the stage. One was the Brownie.

The other was the largest shoe that I had ever seen.

CHAPTER EIGHT

Wizards encounter periods of crisis from time to time. It comes with the job, right along with the robes and the pointy hat. Now, some wizards thrive on crisis, and there is quite a bit of gold to be made, should the magician survive, by thrusting oneself into the thick of things. The more experienced mage, however, makes ample use of soothsaying spells, so that he may collect the monies, reassure the populace, and still have time to leave the area before the thick of things arrives.

—from The Teachings of Ebenezum, Volume IV

The shoe spoke to me.

"Wuntvor! Tis I!"

It was my master's voice! My first thought was that the Brownie had somehow transformed my master into a giant shoe. After a moment, I regained my wits, however, and realized that the shoe had been built large enough to house Ebenezum. And now he was here, by my side, in the midst of all this magic, and he was not sneezing!

"Master!" I cried joyfully. "You are cured!"

"In a manner of speaking," Ebenezum replied dryly. " 'Tis only a matter of my spending the rest of my life inside a shoe."

"But how did you get here?" I asked.

"Through Brownie magic, apparently. It all started when our Brownie showed up at the shack where I was resting. He'd brought this other little fellow along that he kept calling 'Your Brownieship'—" The wizard paused. "But what's going on here? It's hard for me to see through the buttonholes."

"Well, this is a convention of mythological beasts," I began hastily. "And they wanted me to contact another wizard, or they were going to eat me, and—"

"Who dares to disturb the first regularly scheduled meeting of the Association for the Advancement of Mythical and Imaginary Beasts and Creatures?" the Griffin interrupted with a roar. "A talking shoe?"

"Careful, Pop," the Hippogriff chided. "He may be eligible for membership."

The Brownie walked up to me, all smiles.

"Is this a wish or what?" he said proudly. "We Brownies are new to this game, but once we get going—"

"Would an enchanted shoe be mythological?" The Griffin glared at its offspring. "I'll have to check the bylaws."

The leader of the beasts coughed and turned to us. "One thing I do know, however. Fairies are definitely not welcome at our gatherings!"

"Fairies!" the Brownie cried. "Fairies! Could a Fairy do this?"

The little fellow closed his eyes and shuffled his feet. The shoe floated in the air for a minute, then returned to the stage with a resounding crash.

"Indeed," the wizard's voice came from deep within the leather. "If I might make a suggestion—"

"Little enough magic! A Griffin could move that shoe with even less effort!"

"Please," the wizard began again. "If you might just hear me out—"

The Griffin's tail slithered under the shoe, tossing it two feet in the air. It fell to the stage with an even louder crash.

"Enough!" the wizard called from within. A single, dark-robed hand emerged from inside the shoe leather. A lightning bolt shot down from the sky, searing the space midway between Griffin and Brownie.

"Oh wow!" the Hippogriff exclaimed. "Yes, I think the enchanted shoe has an excellent case for immediate membership."

"If you will listen to me now?" Ebenezum's muffled voice remarked.

"Listen up!" the Hippogriff shouted. "The enchanted shoe has the floor!"

"Very well. First, let me say that this little fellow here is not a Fairy at all. He is, rather, very much a Brownie."

"Really?" the Hippogriff interjected. "You know, Brownies could be eligible for membership, too."

The Brownie thanked my master.

"Don't mention it. Indeed, 'twas the least I could do. Second, I am more than what I seem. Rather than being an enchanted shoe, I am a wizard in disguise!"

The crowd roared in surprise.

"I see." The Griffin had gotten over its shock at almost being singed, and had stepped forward to once again take control, "It's a shame, really. An enchanted shoe would have made such a colorful member. But Brownies now, there's an awful lot of you, aren't there? You know, of course, that there's an entrance fee. And then there're the annual dues. But, what a membership can do for you!"

"Your pardon," the wizard said. "I am not done speaking."

Everyone was silent. I marveled at what a lightning bolt could do for crowd control.

"I am a great wizard," Ebenezum said, "called by my compatriot here to—" My master paused. I had not been able to tell him any more of my plight! "—to do whatever I have been called here to do!" he finished majestically. Somehow, coming from his mouth, the words all made sense.

"Doom!" A voice carried from the edge of the silent crowd.

The Griffin ignored it. "So this fellow really is a wizard after all? I tell you, they must have simplified the entrance exam since I was a hatchling." The beast paused, glanced at the sky, and flapped its wings defensively. "Sorry! Just voicing my opinion. I'm sure I know as little about wizards as wizards know about Griffins!"

Ebenezum's hand emerged from the shoe again.

"Not to say that wizards lack knowledge—"

"Pop!" the Hippogriff whispered. "Get a hold of yourself! We're supposed to tell the wizards our demands!"

The wizard's hand felt about for another buttonhole and extracted a cloth from it. The hand disappeared within the shoe again. I heard the faint sound of a nose being blown.

"I know exactly what I'm doing!" the Griffin snapped. "That's

the problem with youngsters today. No sense of diplomacy. And
the things they bring home to clutter the nest. And their taste
in music! You know what this teenager likes? Madrigals!" The
Griffin groaned in agony. "Give me a good old Gregorian chant
any day!"

The Griffin walked over to the shoe and stared straight
into a buttonhole. "But let's put that aside. We all want to work
together. Let me show you our list of seventy-three proposals.
Of special interest is our suggestion for a joint wizard and
mythological beast steering committee. Of course, we'll need to
receive some modest funds to get it going. Think of it as an act
of good faith on the part of wizards everywhere."

The Griffin paused and looked out to the crowd. There was
quite a commotion in the middle of the audience. I made out an
occasional "Doom!" amid the hubbub.

"Look here!" called a voice so grating that it only could be
Snarks. "No one's eating anybody else here. And no animal
with the head of a chicken is going to tell me anything!"

The noise rose considerably. I thought I heard sounds of
genuine conflict.

"Indeed," said the wizard within his shoe. "Do you think
your fellow creatures could stop molesting the newcomers? I
would like to see those two up here with us." A hand emerged
casually from the shoe, as if to test the temperature of the air.

"Most certainly!" The Griffin laughed its barking laugh, as
if this were all great fun among old cronies, then turned and
gave instructions to the crowd to let the strangers pass.

"Doom," Hendrek said when he arrived on the stage. "We
have come to save you."

Snarks peered at the Griffin. "Look here! Another creature
with a chicken head!"

The Griffin was speechless. Its tail whipped about as if it
were looking for something to strangle. Snarks, for the moment
at least, was standing out of reach.

"You know," Snarks went on, "I've noticed that a lot of the
creatures around here have an attitude problem." He paused to
survey the crowd. "Well, I suppose when you look like you've
been put together from spare parts in somebody's tool shed,

there's bound to be difficulty. Still, if I had a brief talk with them, I'm sure I could straighten them out. I have Netherhells experience, you know!"

"If you were not under the protection of a wizard—" The Griffin became too choked with emotion to continue.

"And the wizard's under my protection as well," Snarks added happily. "For I can see the truth, wherever it may hide. There seems to be little enough of it around here at the moment."

"Doom." Hendrek moved to Snarks's side. Headbasher swung free in the large warrior's hand.

The truth-telling demon waved at the warrior. "Never fear, friend Hendrek. We have the upper hand here. Compared to all these creatures, you look positively normal!"

"So what do we do now?" Hendrek turned to me. "We have come to rescue you from fiends unknown."

"Wait a sec," the Hippogriff cut in. "Rescue him from what? I'll have you know that this is the first annual meeting of a very important new bestiary interest group!"

"Like the man said," Snarks chimed in, "we've come to rescue you from fiends unknown." The demon looked down at the crowd of mythological animals, who seemed to be growing more and more restive as the drama played itself out onstage. "And not a moment too soon, either!"

"Excuse me," the wizard intoned from his leathery depths. "While I am sure we could go on exchanging pleasantries all day, there are matters we must attend to. Let us finish our business here quickly and be on our way."

"Certainly." The Griffin ruffled its feathers in an attempt to regain composure. "We mythological animals don't ask for much. We only want to gain the stature in society that rightfully belongs to us. It will be so easy! We've made up some tapestry design guidelines that will revolutionize the industry. And I think we've been more than reasonable in our maiden-allotment quotas."

"Indeed," the wizard said. "And exactly what is it that you want wizards to do?"

"Why, the same things wizards always do! Make things happen." The Griffin sidled even closer to the shoe. "Listen, we're not fooled by traditional power structures. After all, we're mythological. That, to say the least, gives one a unique perspective. We know, with all the kings and mayors and knights and town councilmen around, things only get done when a wizard steps in. In fact, the higher the king/mayor/knight/town councilman to wizard ratio in a certain area, the longer it takes anyone to do anything!" The beast's voice dropped to a whisper. "Besides that, there also seems to be a lot of money around wizards."

The Griffin paused, but the shoe made no reply.

"All right. So we want to talk business. It is not enough that all but a few haughty mythological beasts have joined together to make a statement of purpose. We need wizards to spread the word. Other humans listen to wizards. They know that if they don't, bad things just might happen to them. And that's just the kind of spokespeople my organization needs!"

"Then you're speaking of a cooperative agreement?" I thought I noted some interest in Ebenezum's muffled voice.

"Well, eventually, there will be money involved," the Griffin continued. "It's all part of our seventy-two demands, which I'm sure you'll enjoy reading when you have the time. Why, I imagine the tapestry royalties alone will net us a small fortune—"

"Indeed. You used the word 'eventually.' Say wizards do spread the word? What is the working wizard to do for ready cash until that 'eventually' comes about?"

"An old, established order such as the wizards—" The Griffin paused ominously, doing its best to glare at the shoe. I saw for the first time how my master's leather covering might enhance his bargaining power. The Griffin took a deep breath. "The least wizards can do is make a voluntary contribution as a sign of good will!"

"No," Ebenezum said slowly. "I think not."

The Griffin roared. "No one ever says no to us! We are fearsome mythological beasts!"

"That is true," Ebenezum replied. "And I am a wizard."

My chest swelled with pride at my master's bargaining skill. The beasts were no match for him, even while he was trapped in a shoe. As his apprentice, I knew that there were many truths about my master, but one was truer than all the rest:

No one fights Ebenezum over money matters and wins.

"What say, guys?" Snarks's voice filled the ominous silence. "Let's blow this zoo and get back on our way to Vushta. If we stick around here much longer, we're bound to get fleas!"

The Griffin screamed in rage. The Hippogriff, somewhat more mildly, remarked: "Mythological animals never have fleas."

"Not even mythological fleas?" Snarks rejoined. "What's the matter, you not good enough for them? Come to think of it, from the way you look, I'd hate to imagine how you taste. Ugh. It's enough to put a demon off his lunch. And you should see what demons eat!"

"Friend Snarks," I cut in, "perhaps it is time to resume our journey as you—"

The Griffin leapt to where Snarks had been standing only seconds before. The beast's claws shredded the floorboards.

"Not only ugly, but slow," Snarks added. "If you're going to leap after me, you should lean back more on your haunches, you know. It'll give you more spring. And if you'd extend your claws the teeniest bit—"

The Griffin lunged again, overshooting the demon and flying completely off the stage.

I turned to the wizard. "Master? What are we going to do?"

"Hey, is it time for another Brownie wish?"

The little fellow stood by my foot. In all the excitement, I had completely forgotten him.

"Yeah, you'll have to excuse me," the Brownie continued. "I've just been standing here, admiring my handiwork. Here before us, the living embodiment of Brownie Power, and the first of what I am sure will be several successful wishes in my career. My only problem now is how do I top this?"

"Perhaps," the wizard said from deep within the shoe, "you can find some way to get this shoe and the rest of us out of this place." The wizard's sneeze was muffled by the shoe as well.

"No problem at all!" the Brownie said as Snarks went sailing by, the Griffin in pursuit. "Give me a moment to get my wits about me. I'm still new at this, only one wish under my belt. And, incidentally, I won't be offended at all if anyone has any suggestions!"

He tapped on the shoe. "I did need some help before from His Brownieship to move this thing around. Maybe we could all get together and carry you? Of course, you and the shoe would be pretty heavy. We might need you to come out, too, to help support the load. Well, that wouldn't do, though, in the midst of all this magic, would it?" The Brownie fell to silent musing.

"You really shouldn't take offense at what I say!" Snarks panted, obviously out of breath. "I am but voicing my humble opinion on the appearance of your following. I'm sure they're dressed at the height of fashion for things made out of spare animal parts. And who are we to dictate fashion? Why, look at the warrior Hendrek, here. Did you ever see a more ugly belt than that checkered thing he's wearing?"

All the color drained from Hendrek's ruddy face.

"I have never worn a belt!" The warrior looked to his waist. "Doom!"

The belt slithered away from Hendrek's waist and assumed standard demon form. It was Brax, in its demonic checkered suit.

The warrior swung Headbasher far over his helmeted head.

"Fiend!" he intoned. "Must you forever plague me?"

"Oh, come on now, Hendy baby." The demon smiled broadly as it dodged the warrior's wild swing. "What did I tell you about protecting my investment?"

The demon turned and looked out over the audience. "Hey there! I haven't seen such a large group of potential customers in my entire career. What, you think being uniquely magical creatures will be enough to see you through the coming conflict? Don't you believe it! You're going to need all the help you can get."

"Wait a moment!" the Griffin shouted. "Coming conflict? What coming conflict? We have an agreement with the Netherhells!"

"So you haven't heard!" the smiling demon chortled as it ducked another blow from the warclub. "On the day of the Forxnagel, all contracts are null and void!"

"The Forxnagel!" Ebenezum cried from within his shoe.

That's right! With all the excitement here, I had forgotten to tell my master what I had learned during my grackle spell.

"Wuntvor!" the wizard called.

I ran to his side and told him that Norei had confirmed this news.

"Indeed," Ebenezum murmured. "And me trapped within a shoe! We will have to find a way to convey my new home from place to place, even if we must carry it all the way to Vushta! Ask if they have any carts about."

"Carts?" the Hippogriff snorted. "What use have mythological beasts for carts when we have the wings of eagles and the hooves of stallions? Besides, I'm afraid we've never been very good at building wheels. It's the lack of thumbs, you know." The beast nodded toward its wings. "Guess you're out of luck."

"Yes, you're all out of luck!" Brax the salesdemon cried. "But you might be able to extend your freedom, and perhaps even your miserable lives, for hours or perhaps even days if you own one of my enchanted weapons!"

"Doom," Hendrek muttered in my ear. "Extend our miserable lives? This new twist to the demon's sales talk does not bode well."

Brax indicated the larger warrior with a wave and a hop. "Just look at this satisfied customer! Why, if he does not fulfill his contract with the Netherhells now, he will complete it gladly, after we have won!"

"Doom!"

Headbasher went crashing through the stage.

"What a weapon!" Brax shook its head in admiration.

"It can't be," the Griffin repeated. "We have an understanding with the Netherhells."

"Griffins sometimes get set in their ways," the Hippogriff confided.

"Understandable," Snarks cried as he ran past. "It takes the beast so long to keep its body parts straight, it doesn't have time to think of anything else."

Snarks ran. The Griffin roared. Brax sold. Headbasher

crashed. And my master sneezed again.

The situation had been merely out of hand before. Now it had degenerated into something completely beyond human comprehension. The shoe had seemed to shield my master up to a point. However, there was such a sorcerous overload hereabouts that even the Brownie's protection could not hold it back for long.

The world was falling apart around us. We had to escape. I only prayed we could reach Vushta in time.

But how could we carry my master?

My eyes wandered to the pen at the side of the stage. The pen that contained the unicorn. That overmuscled beast had helped to get us into this situation. Perhaps it could help us out of it as well.

"What a mess!" the unicorn cried as I approached. In all the tumult, no one had even noticed my leaving the stage. "What do they want me here for? I'm supposed to be out frolicking through verdant fields!"

I knew exactly what they wanted the unicorn for. One look at this creature, and the mythological beasts' demands began to make sense. Even I had had enough of his frolicking speeches.

"Listen," I said bluntly. "How'd you like to get out of here?"

The unicorn blinked its large brown eyes. "At last! The voice of reason! It is painful how few virgins there are around this place! Although—" The unicorn looked at me significantly. "I can sniff one out if I have to."

"Never mind that now!" I said, exasperated. "If you want to get away, there's a job you're going to have to do!"

"No need to get rough!" the unicorn exclaimed. "You know, I don't go in for any of that kinky stuff."

"No! No! I need you to carry my master away!" "Your master? Do you mean—" The beast shook its splendid golden horn. "I do not carry shoes."

"Well, then we'll make a litter, and you can drag the shoe!" I paused. I should not let my frustration with this beast's attitude get the better of me. How would my master handle this?

"Indeed," I added. "It should be no problem for a beast as magnificent as you."

The unicorn hesitated. "Well—"

Brax suddenly appeared between us. "How about an enchanted dagger to put on the end of that horn? I tell you, I have accessories to improve even your best mythological features. The dagger's chrome-plated, too!"

"Doom!" Headbasher came crashing down, narrowly missing the demon.

"Easy terms!" Brax called as it leapt back on stage. "A lifetime to pay!" The warrior's huge bulk lumbered after it.

"Oh, for the verdant fields," the unicorn whispered. It turned to regard me solemnly. "Perhaps we could work something out."

I regained the stage to tell my master.

The two demons were circling the Griffin. Nothing much had changed; everyone was still shouting or running or bellowing or bashing.

"I might be able to sell you a weapon," Brax added hot on Snarks's heels, "guaranteed to do away with pesky demons."

"Excellent idea," the Griffin rumbled in response. "And then I could do away with both of you."

"Wait a moment!" Brax cried. "Do not dare for an instant to compare us! I am but a poor salesdemon, trying to eke out an existence during one of the most turbulent and potentially lucrative times in the history of the world."

"Notice," Snarks retorted, "when he describes himself, he does not resort to the word 'honest.' "

"Why don't you come back to the Netherhells and say that, traitor? Just wait until—urk!"

Headbasher connected with Brax's forehead. There was a dull thud.

"Where was I?" the demon said weakly. "Who was I? What was I?" It disappeared in a cloud of sickly yellow smoke.

"Ah." Snarks smiled. "Teamwork."

"Doom," Hendrek replied.

From within his shoe, my master sneezed mightily.

"Enough!" I shouted, seeing my opening. "The great wizard and his entourage must proceed to Vushta!"

"I think not," the Griffin rumbled, emphatically.

"But what of the demon's warning?" I insisted. "The foul

creature implied that the Netherhells has a plan that will destroy us all!"

"A mere charade," the Griffin said, "once you consider it in the pure light of reason. We are familiar with demonic sales practices."

The great winged creature turned to the crowd. "Think upon it, my fellow beasts. Better yet, let me ask the wizard a question. One wonders why he has not used the lightning trick again."

The Griffin strolled over to the shoe and raked it gently with its claws.

"It seems to me that you have some weakness, and must hide within this shoe for a reason. Besides which, it restricts your mobility. Maybe we could learn to dodge lightning, and keep you around for a while. I'm sure, given sufficient time, you could see the mythological point of view—"

"Urk!" the Griffin cried suddenly. "Then again, there are always two sides—"

The Griffin collapsed in a heap of feathers and claws. Headbasher had done its hellish work again.

"Doom," Hendrek intoned.

The crowd of mythological beasts roared as one and surged for the stage.

"I think this might be a good moment to leave," I suggested.

"Uh-oh. It's time for Brownie Power!" The little fellow was once again at my side. "Why don't we wish us out of here?"

The Brownie paused expectantly.

"Oh," I said after a moment. "I wish we were out of here."

"That's more like it! We have to observe the conventions you know. Now, how to do it? A distraction of some sort?" The Brownie glanced at my master.

"The very thing!" He leaned close to me and whispered. "A rain of shoes!"

The Brownie began to dance a merry jig.

There was a rumble in the distance. The crowd paused, startled by the noise. The Hippogriff looked up with some trepidation, anticipating lightning.

From high up in the sky fell a single pair of sandals, tied

together by their ankle straps. They bounced off the stage with a muted thump.

"Oh dear," the Brownie fretted. "Not quite what I expected. Well, let's not count that as a wish after all, shall we? Remember, I'm still learning."

The crowd once again approached the stage.

"I wonder how Brownies taste?" something cried.

"Yeah!" something else answered. "Waste not, want not!"

"Wait a moment!" the Brownie cried. "Maybe if I did the tango!"

Both my master's arms emerged from the shoe.

"Doom," Hendrek whispered.

I wished I had my stout oak staff. We would not go down without a fight!

Suddenly, the world went dark. I looked aloft. Something very large plummeted from the sky, blotting out the sun.

"No!" the Hippogriff cried. "Not that!"

But it was. Why hadn't I recognized it? It was, I knew, what I had seen before.

CHAPTER NINE

There comes a time when a wizard must put his fate totally in the hands of another. This takes great courage, and great faith in the ability of others to perform some function that is beyond you. But there are benefits to this course of action as well. Should this task reach a successful conclusion, it will show you the worthiness of your fellow beings, and lead you to trust in the providence of the universe. And, of course, should the task not be successful, there is always someone else to blame.

—from The Teachings of Ebenezum, Volume XXVII

The crowd dispersed rapidly to make way for the dragon. The giant reptile landed with a resounding thud.

"Excuse me, my dear," the dragon said. "Not the most graceful of landings, I'm afraid. Do you have my hat?" The reptile turned to the crowd, most of which was cowering around the edges of the clearing.

"Pardon me," the dragon enunciated. "Did I arrive at an inauspicious moment?"

"Pop! Wake up!" the Hippogriff cried. The Griffin snored, still under Headbasher's awesome power.

The blond woman sitting on the dragon's back reached into a satchel in front of her and extracted a large top hat. She handed it to the dragon.

"Thank you," the giant reptile said as it placed the hat atop its head.

I had thought I knew this dragon! Now, I was sure. "Hubert!" I cried.

"Good heavens!" The dragon blew a smoke ring of surprise. "Could it be a fan?"

" 'Tis Wuntvor!" I called. "You remember—the Western Kingdoms, and that business with the duke?" Hubert nodded. "I never forget an engagement. You should see my scrapbook on that one."

"You remember Ebenezum, too?" I pointed across the stage. "Well, at the moment, he's inside that shoe."

"Oh, does he do escapes, too? We had a fellow like that on our bill when we played the Palace. Used to get out of locked trunks and iron maidens, that sort of thing. Never a shoe, though. Rather a unique touch." Hubert nodded his head approvingly.

I wondered if I should correct his line of conjecture. Then again, perhaps it was best if we did not discuss my master's malady in too great detail at present. The crowd seemed to be getting over their shock at the dragon's sudden entrance, and were slowly moving closer to both Hubert and the maiden on his back.

"Hello, Wuntie."

My heart stood still in my chest. Only one woman had ever called me Wuntie, and then only in our most intimate moments. Could it be?

It was! Alea waved from her perch atop the dragon.

It was little wonder I hadn't recognized her. She had changed in the weeks we had been apart. No longer was she but a duke's daughter, forced to while away her hours in a drafty keep deep within the Western Kingdoms. Her hair, once straight, was curled, and seemed a lighter shade than I remembered, probably bleached from hours of flying through sunny skies on a dragon's back. She wore a gown of lightest blue, no doubt all the rage in Vushta. Vushta, the city of a thousand forbidden delights, what a magical place! For when Alea had left on a dragon's back a scant two months before, she had been little more than a girl. Now though, in dress, in manner, in bearing, she seemed a woman of experience, an actress who had taken Vushta by storm, and therefore could do whatever she pleased.

Once, she had been fond of me. And she remembered, for she called me Wuntie!

"Indeed!" my master called from deep within his shoe. Apparently, after everyone had ceased to run madly about, he had gotten an opportunity to regain his breath. "So nice of you to drop by and give us an escort, Hubert!"

"Why, yes! Of course! My pleasure!" The dragon leaned close to me with a chuckle. "I can ad-lib with the best of them," he whispered. He turned to the audience, and spoke with the full power of his dragon lungs.

"Ladies and gentlemen—and assorted beasts—in but a moment from now, you are about to witness a feat designed for the crowned heads of the Continent, yet performed for the first time anywhere on this stage before you. Yes, it's Ebenezum and the Amazing Shoe Escape!"

No! No! This was all wrong! I pulled urgently on the dragon's tail.

"Pop! Wake up!" The Hippogriff nudged its sleeping father with equal urgency.

"Excuse me," Hubert intoned. "I must have a brief conversation with the magician's assistant."

I explained, as briefly as possible, that, rather than have Ebenezum escape from the shoe, the five of us, Hendrek, Snarks and the Brownie included, were attempting to escape from here entirely. If not, I concluded, we were in danger of being eaten.

"Ah," the dragon nodded his head knowingly. "A rough audience, huh? Say no more."

Hubert glanced briefly at Alea, then resumed.

"Actually, it is not mere coincidence that brings me here. We were flying through the air, between engagements, when I spied you in the midst of these monsters. I spoke briefly with Alea, and she agreed, that if we but had the time, we would like to drop in and say hello. And, with such a large crowd, there was always the possibility of staging a show. As itinerant theater people, you know, we must earn our bread wherever we can. But, a previous engagement called."

"But I thought you had gone to Vushta!" I cried. "Didn't they care for your act?"

"Oh, on the contrary, we were quite a hit. Especially our novelty numbers!"

"Yes!" Alea rejoined enthusiastically. "You should have seen the reaction to the 'Maiden and the Rings of Fire' routine!"

"That's right!" Hubert continued. "But that was nothing compared to the big finish, when Alea would play my scales! We'll show you our whole act if we have a chance! We were even offered extended contracts in some of Vushta's choicest nightspots. But I did not want the crowd to become overfamiliar with our act. Always leave them wanting more, that's this dragon's motto!

"In short, you can only play in Vushta for so long. We are on a tour of the provinces, playing the smaller halls, and in some cases," the dragon sighed, "the larger barns. Still, that's show business!"

"Yes," Alea added indignantly. "And they cancelled our last show right out from under us!"

"Something about fire laws!" Hubert snorted a puff of smoke. "What can you expect from farmers!"

"Pop! Wake up!" the Hippogriff wailed. "It's time for leadership!" I looked up to see the crowd of monsters considerably closer to the stage.

"Would you please be quiet?" Hubert roared. "How do you expect artists to prepare?" The dragon raised his snout and sent a column of fire into the air. The crowd decided that some distance was a good idea after all.

"Fine," Hubert puffed contentedly. "Now we must come up with an escape worthy of my talents." "Couldn't we just run away?" I suggested.

"No, I'm sorry, that just doesn't have the right—dramatic unity! I have an image, you know. My fans expect a certain special flare in all my actions. Now that I'm on the verge of becoming one of the true stars of the Vushta stage, it's the least I can do."

"What?" I cried, exasperated. This was all too much! "Do you want our escape accompanied by music?"

"What a wonderful idea!" Hubert blew three perfect smoke rings. "A big song and dance, with Damsel and Dragon, those two toe-tappers all Vushta is talking about, in the foreground, of course. And then we escape! What a finale!"

"Hey, this is the perfect diversion! Talk about Brownie Power!"

I glanced at the little fellow. Now what was he talking about?

"Those sandals that fell from the sky, I just had the steps wrong! I knew I should have done the tango ail along!"

"Oh," Hubert remarked. "A Brownie."

"At last!" the Brownie cried. "A true creature of the world! A fellow who knows quality when he sees it. You'd be surprised, my good dragon, how often we wee folk are confused with Fairies!"

" 'Tis the confusion of the uninformed," the dragon chortled. "You're much too lively to be a Fairy. It's a shame. If Brownies weren't so short, they could have a real future on the stage."

"Short?" The little fellow stamped his tiny feet. "Brownie stereotyping! I'll have you know Brownies are the perfect height! The rest of you creatures are far too tall!"

The Griffin groaned.

"Pop?" the Hippogriff asked hopefully.

"Perhaps we should get under way," I urged.

"Just what should we do?" the dragon asked in a low voice. "As I recall, when I get too close to your master, he begins to sneeze."

"That was before Brownie magic came along—"

"Yes," I cut the little fellow off short, "that shoe somehow protects him from sorcerous influences."

"Excellent!" the dragon cried. "That means the wizard can stay and catch our act!" Hubert tipped his top hat towards the shoe, then turned back to me. "How's this for a plan? At a prearranged signal, the damsel and I will cause a distraction upon the stage. The rest of you will bolt for the forest during the confusion. I'll shoot a little flame around to liven things up a bit more, then join you presently in the forest."

I mentioned that there was only one problem with Hubert's plan. The wizard, trapped in a shoe, was unable to run.

"A small problem, at best," Hubert rejoined. "As long as Ebenezum is in his protective shoe, I should be able to scoop him up and carry him at the end of our performance."

It sounded as if it actually might work. I quickly introduced the dragon to the others in our party.

"Doom," Hendrek remarked.

"A dragon with a top hat?" Snarks peered up at Hubert. "Tell me, why do you feel you need these affectations? Some trouble at home?"

Hubert looked at Snarks with some disdain. "You want me to rescue this?"

"You know," Snarks added, "if you stood up straighter, you'd be much more fearsome. Nobody's really scared of a dragon who slouches."

"Did you see the pretty birdy?" the Griffin intoned. "I saw the pretty birdy!"

"What is this?" Hubert remarked.

"The leader of the group here," I replied, "still somewhat undone by a bash on the head from Hendrek's magic warclub."

"Pop!" the Hippogriff cried. "Pull yourself together! I know I haven't always been the perfect son—"

The Griffin blinked. "Does the birdy have any gold?"

"Wuntvor!" Ebenezum hissed from within his shoe. "I fear the beast is regaining its senses!"

The Griffin staggered to the front of the stage. "Fellow creatures!" It stopped and shook its head. "Ladies, gentlemen, and birdies!" It paused and blinked again.

"Pop! You can do it! I tell you what! No more old-age jokes! That's a promise!"

"Old age?" The Griffin came to its senses with a roar. "Whosoever has done this to me will feel the wrath of—urk!"

"Thank you, Hendrek," my master remarked.

"Doom," the warrior replied.

There were shouts out in the crowd. They began to move closer to the stage again. If they had started out as a rough audience, I feared they would soon get far rougher.

The dragon cleared his throat. Small flames lapped around his teeth.

"Listen, creatures," he said. "Let's get something straight here. I am a dragon."

"Sure, you can talk!" something shouted. "You've already got your maiden!"

"Yeah!" came another voice. "I wonder how she'd taste with salt?"

The dragon roared, sending a shaft of fire thirty feet into the air.

It seemed to quiet the conversationalists in the crowd.

"As I was saying," Hubert continued, "I am the dragon. You are not the dragon. Are there any questions?"

"Yeah!" something replied. "You are the dragon, but you are only one dragon. We here at AFTAOMAIBAC are many!"

"You here at what?" the dragon said. "Oh, never mind. Look here, fellows, do we really want bloodshed, sizzled flesh, the whole rotten mess? Or would we rather see a show?"

"A show?" the Hippogriff asked.

"Yes!" the dragon cried. "The music, the lights, the laughter! Not only will you see Ebenezum and the amazing shoe trick! As an introduction, you will get to see one of the premier song-and-dance duos of all time!"

"A show?" the Hippogriff repeated.

"Yes!" the dragon reiterated. "For what is a gathering of this size without entertainment? Now, if you will but give us a mere moment to prepare—"

Hubert let the words hang in the air as he turned to our party.

"The element of surprise is on our side, but we will still have to make this quick. We'll do a couple of songs, a little patter, something to put the crowd at their ease. Then, when we get into our big finish, 'Flames of Love,' you folks will have to make a run for it!"

"Flames of love?" Snarks interjected.

"Yes," the dragon nodded. "It is rather poetic, isn't it? So, when the damsel here cries 'Burn me dragon, with the fire of desire,' that's when you should make your exit." The dragon blew a contemplative smoke ring. "It's a shame you won't be able to stick around and see it. Talk about great theater!"

I assured Hubert that we would be glad to witness his performance in its entirety at some other time. Behind us, though, the crowd was busy getting restless again.

"Okay!" Hubert said. "It's time for the big build-up. Are you ready, damsel?"

"Ready, dragon!" Alea called.

"Good enough! Showtime in three minutes!"

The dragon strode out to center stage, careful not to tread on the sleeping Griffin.

Hubert breathed a sheet of flame over the heads of the audience. "And now, to begin the entertainment! A smoke ring demonstration!"

I leaned close to Alea. "What's Hubert doing?"

"Oh, don't mind him." Alea put a reassuring hand on my shoulder. "He's just warming up the crowd."

I felt a little warm myself. I had forgotten what it was like to have someone as wonderful as Alea so close by my side. And she was no longer the girl of the forest whom I had known. Now, she was a woman of Vushta!

I looked deep into her eyes. "Tell me about Vushta," I whispered.

"Vushta?" She laughed, the sound of dew falling on a summer's eve. "Why, it is a magical place, but treacherous as well. One must be careful, or a maiden's honor, yea her very life, may be forfeit!"

"Yes, Alea?" I said, entranced. I wanted to hear it all!

Her blue eyes looked deep into my own. "Yes, Wuntie, Vushta is almost like a different world. It makes one think about where one has been, and sometimes—" Her hand moved down my shoulder, running gently along my arm. "Sometimes it makes one realize how much one misses what one has left behind."

I swallowed. "Yes, Alea?"

"Yes, Wuntvor, when you are an actress on the Vushta stage, whole new worlds open up to you. Many men would like to court you; worldly men, versed in magic and every other art. But, with their worldly ways comes a cynicism, a shell they keep around themselves so they cannot truly touch others, or be touched in return." Her nails stroked my knuckles just before her fingers intertwined with mine. "Wuntie, it makes one long for a simple, homespun boy like you."

"Yes, Alea," I whispered, barely able to get the words out. My throat had suddenly become very dry. It had something to do with how warm the world had become in the last few minutes. A late summer heat spell, perhaps, or the warm spring glow that came from Alea's eyes.

She turned toward the stage for an instant, her blond curls shining in the sun. Hubert was stomping back and forth on the worn floorboards, breathing rings of fire. The crowd seemed uncertain how to respond. Isolated cheers came when Hubert breathed a fire pretzel. However, I thought I heard low grumbling out there as well.

I looked back at the woman who once had been mine. Simple? Homespun? Alea's words began to sink into my overheated consciousness. How strange were the fates! When we had first known each other, back in Wizard's Woods, she had wanted me for my worldliness. Now, she wanted me because I reminded her of home.

Alea turned back to me, her eyes full of excitement, and kissed me full on the lips.

"Do I look all right?" she asked brightly. "Everything in place? It's almost time for my entrance!"

I was having some difficulty breathing. "Yes, Alea," I managed at last.

She stood up. "Okay, Hubert!" she spoke in a hoarse whisper. "Let's break a wing!"

I shook my head in an attempt to clear it. Alea's attentions were all very nice, but somehow, all wrong. There was someone else.

"Norei!" I cried aloud.

I swallowed hard. I realized then that I must stop thinking thoughts of Alea. I was promised to another!

The audience was getting rougher. Cries of "AFTAOMAIBAC!" and "Let's fire the dragon!" wafted my way.

Hubert paused in his demonstration. "All right, fellow creatures!" he called out. "You want change?"

A ragged cheer rose from the crowd.

"You want excitement?" the dragon cried.

The answering cheer was stronger this time.

"Then how about this? Take it, damsel!"

Alea ran up to the dragon's side. They broke into song:

We do the dragon walk, from town to town.
We do the dragon walk, we really get around.
When we go steppin', people get kinda shy,
'Cause when you're stepped on by a dragon, goodbye!

Alea proceeded to perform an elaborate tap dance between the dragon's toes. Hubert hummed to give her musical accompaniment.

"Doom!" Hendrek said. "So now we prepare ourselves." He nervously shifted his grip on Headbasher as he watched the audience through half-closed eyes. "This plan strikes me as difficult, at best."

Snarks nodded his head in agreement. "I never knew I would end like this, a victim of musical comedy."

"Come on, guys!" a small voice piped. "Don't be so glum! You've got a Brownie on your side!" The Brownie did a little dance in time with Hubert's humming. "There's more than a dragon here to depend on. I've got another wish or two up my sleeve, let me tell you!"

"Wuntvor?" my master's voice called from his shoe. "Exactly what is happening?"

I realized then that my master, in his shoe, sitting on the far side of the stage, would have been unable to hear our whispers and thus knew nothing of our plan. I ran quickly to his side. Too quickly, for I did not watch my feet.

I tripped over the Griffin.

"What? Where?" the beast mumbled, still half-asleep. "Look at the two birdies!"

I explained the situation as briefly as I could.

"Indeed," Ebenezum replied. "You show great initiative, Wuntvor. Should you grow out of your clumsiness, you will make a great wizard." My master again poked his hands into the outside air. "I have managed to recover quite a bit. This shoe, silly looking as it is, offers a great deal of protection. Alas, we have learned that the protection is not total, but it should be more than enough to suit our purposes."

Ebenezum waved his hands about. There was the sound of

distant thunder. "Yes," the wizard said. "Quite fully recovered. While the dragon's plan might have been somewhat problematic with me in my sneezing state, I can now lend a hand with a well-placed spell or two. We should be on our way to Vushta in no time."

I ran back to the others. I felt as though I might leap with joy! With Ebenezum once again able to perform magic, we could not fail!

"Hello, birdy," the Griffin mumbled as I passed. "Yummy, yummy birdy."

Still, I reflected as I reached the others, the sooner we were out of here, the better I would feel.

The assembled beasts seemed to have stopped shouting. I glanced at Damsel and Dragon's performance. If they had not quieted the crowd, at least they had them reasonably stunned. Hubert had now taken center stage, and was singing a sensitive ballad:

> *My flame's gone out,*
> *I don't feel bold.*
> *My legs don't work,*
> *And my wings don't fold.*
> *When I sun myself*
> *My blood's still cold.*
> *I'm just a lizard in love.*

Snarks sidled over to me. He jabbed a thumb at the singing dragon. "Couldn't we escape a few minutes early?"

"No, no," I whispered back. "Everything is set. The wizard even has a spell or two up his sleeve."

"Doom," Hendrek said, a hopeful note in his voice.

"Wow!" a small voice piped. "A dragon, a wizard, and a Brownie! Talk about your triple threats!"

The Griffin raised its head.

"Birdies. Birdies everywhere."

I turned toward Hubert and Alea, silently hoping they would speed up their act. I did not wish to end up as a birdy.

Alea finished a song about being just a maiden in a dragon tower that seemed to remind some members of the audience why they were here in the first place. She and Hubert ignored the shouts and began their snappy patter.

"Get ready!" I whispered to the others. "It's going to come at any time now!"

"Say, dragon?"

"Yes, damsel?"

"How do you pick up lady dragons?"

Hubert breathed a ball of flame. "I say 'Hey, baby, want to have a hot time?' "

Alea and Hubert began a dance number.

"I knew there was a catch to this plan!" Snarks muttered. "In order to hear the escape line, we have to listen to their act!"

I looked sharply at the demon. We had to suffer through this together. The rest of our party listened in grim silence.

"Help! I'm a damsel in distress!"

"Really? I didn't know!"

"Oh, sure! But as soon as the show is over, I'm going back stage to change into dat dress!"

Their dance number grew faster.

"Maybe we should let the monsters eat us," Snarks suggested. "It would be a kinder end."

"Birdies." The Griffin was on its feet. "Pretty, pretty birdies." The beast staggered toward us.

"Doom!" Hendrek raised Headbasher aloft once again.

"Oh, no, you don't!" The Hippogriff reared up before us. "You've bopped my pop once too often! Make one more move, you get a hoof in the head!"

"Birdies." The Griffin made smacking sounds with its beak. "Yummy, yummy, pretty birdies."

"But what if he eats one of us?" I pointed out.

The Hippogriff shook its head. "That's the least you should let him do after the way you've treated him. What kind of guests are you, anyway?"

I felt the floorboard shake ever so slightly by my feet. The Brownie was doing a dance. Hendrek grumbled deep in his throat, both hands on Headbasher. And both my master's arms were free of the shoe, ready to conjure.

"Are we hot, damsel?"

"We're hot, dragon, and we're getting hotter!"

The audience did not seem to agree. I heard a dozen angry shouts. The crowd began to surge forward.

"But we can get hotter, can't we, damsel?"

"Yes, we can make it hot! So hot!"

This must be the build-up to their last big number. The signal to escape was coming at last!

"Yummy birdy." I felt something grab my shirt. I looked down, and saw that I was held by a Griffin claw.

"Tell me, damsel!" Hubert screamed. "How hot do you want it?"

"Burn me, dragon, with the fire—" Alea's voice died away as she watched a huge bird descend from the sky.

"Hey! Cool it! Stop everything!" the great bird cried. It landed on the edge of the stage, in front of the dragon.

The crowd paused in its surge. Hubert stopped his patter. Everyone froze where they stood, eyes on the Rok.

"Man, you know I don't shake easy." The Rok pointed its beak to the sky. "But just feast your eyes on that!"

My mouth opened when I looked up. Now we were in real trouble!

CHAPTER TEN

It is of tremendous importance, when a wizard enters a battle, that he should have prepared sufficient spells beforehand to meet anything he might face during the coming fight. It is even more important that the wizard act bravely during the course of the fight, so that he might do credit to the names of wizards everywhere. And what happens should the magician's army lose the fray? Of the greatest importance of all, therefore, is the wizard's insistence that, before the battle, he be paid in full.

—from The Teachings of Ebenezum, Volume III

"Look at all the pretty birdies!"

The Griffin's claw dropped from my shirt as it turned to stare.

Hundreds of dark shapes filled the sky.

" 'Tis the Netherhells!" I heard Ebenezum shout.

"Doom!" Hendrek cried.

Was this, then, the Forxnagel? Was everything we had worked on for so long truly over? Would I never see Vushta, city of a thousand forbidden delights?

Alea ran across the stage and threw herself into my arms. She kissed me passionately.

"If this is the end, Wuntie," she breathed in my ear, "I want to die held by a simple, country boy."

The warmth of her kiss almost made me forget what I had seen. But the sight had been too chilling for even Alea's passion to erase. I turned away from the woman to look at the sky again.

They were closer now, hundreds upon hundreds of demons with wings. At a distance, I thought many of them seemed to have two heads, but I saw now that some of the winged creatures held two-footed demon riders. Then again, others in that flying congregation did have two heads. It was a truly fearsome sight.

"Wuntvor!" my master called. "Gather our party together! We face great odds, but we are not without our resources. We must fight them together!"

I turned to the others. "Hendrek! Hubert! Snarks! Brownie! We rally around the shoe!"

There was a sharp banging behind me. I turned to see the unicorn, beating its golden horn on the edge of the stage.

"Wait a moment!" the splendid beast cried. "I am not with these creatures! I thought we had a bargain!"

In the heat of events, I had completely forgotten the silly creature. The heavens knew we could use all the help we could get. Still, would a beast that spent all its time standing around looking fantastically beautiful really be all that handy?

"Um," I answered indecisively. "What would you like to do?"

"Why, fight magnificently for freedom, of course." The unicorn snorted and pawed the soft earth. "I have been imprisoned. If I escaped, they would only bring me back here again. Now, though, I see a chance to roam the verdant hills again. How much better your party will fight, with a noble unicorn to guide them on!"

The beast reared upon its hind legs. "Unicorns also make a very attractive centerpiece if you're contemplating painting the scene of battle." It raised its golden horn toward the sun. "See?"

"Wuntvor!" my master called.

The demons were almost upon us!

"Pop!" the Hippogriff cried nervously.

"What?" The Griffin shook itself and blinked. "Those aren't birdies. Those are demons! What is going on here?"

A voice called down from on high:

"Guxx and his demons have come today,
And soon will hold the world in sway!"

"Join us, then!" I called to the unicorn. " 'Tis the dread, rhyming demon, Guxx Unfufadoo!" We would need all the help we could get to defeat this fiend quickly, for, with every rhyme the demon made, its power grew!

The unicorn leapt upon the stage with a movement so graceful that it took my breath away.

The great beast's nostrils flared. "Then let them fight a unicorn!"

"Wait a second here!" the Griffin shouted to the sky. "Do you have an invitation?"

The demons appeared to be tightening into battle formation.

"Doom!" Hendrek was at my side. "Come. We will form a circle around the shoe. That way we can defend ourselves, until Hubert and the wizard find an opening."

So Ebenezum was well enough to guide us into battle. Somehow, despite the hopeless odds, I began to think we might see Vushta after all.

But oh, for my stout oak staff! I looked over at the corner of the stage where the Griffin had done much of its wood shredding. Well, if I had no staff, a plank would have to do. I quickly found a loose board of sufficient size.

Alea was waiting for me in the battle circle. "Oh, Wuntie," she cried. "Our last moments—together!"

I wished she wouldn't kiss me that way. It disturbed my concentration. Still, if you were going to your death, I imagined there was worse preparation.

"You'll be able to fight better if you start breathing again," Snarks suggested. "And you'd probably get better leverage if you held that board a little lower. Well, I don't need to mention your posture again, but you could have a more efficient stance if you—"

"You shouldn't be doing this!" the Griffin bellowed aloft, causing Snarks to pause midsentence. "We have an agreement with the Netherhells!"

The rider on the first flying demon replied:

"Your claims to my ears sound absurd,
For soon demons will rule the world."

"It is Guxx all right," I muttered. The talent behind that particular poem wiped all doubt from my mind.

Snarks nodded grimly. "For rhymes that bad, his power should decrease."

The unicorn snorted, and looked at me with its large, soulful eyes. "I would probably be much more effective if I had a rider."

I hefted my new-found plank experimentally. "A rider?" I asked.

"Yes!" the unicorn replied with half-closed eyes. "Someone to ride with me, nobly into battle." The beast sighed. "I tell you, it's been so long since I've had a virgin by my side."

"Oh, Wuntvor!" Alea whispered. "Look at the creature! How beautiful!"

I breathed a sigh of relief. Apparently, Alea had not quite caught what the beautiful beast implied. But Alea! Now that was an idea! I turned back to the unicorn. "Why not let the woman ride you?"

The unicorn glanced briefly at Alea. "Sorry. Not interested." The beast lowered its horn. "Oh, but my head is so heavy! Oh, for a virgin lap before battle!"

I decided this might be a good time to confer with Ebenezum on battle strategy.

"All right," the Griffin was saying a little uncertainly. "Well, perhaps you weren't invited. But there's always room for a few more. Why don't you just land your troops in that field over there, and we mythological beasts can get on with our meeting. You wouldn't happen to have brought any gold? No, no, silly of me to assume— Well, we're all friends here. Why don't you land? We'll even let you bring up points of business."

Guxx pointed at the shoe.

"You harbor my enemy!
You are no friend of me!"

The rhymes were getting worse. I began to wish the demons would attack.

I looked up at Guxx. He was close enough now so that I could make out what would, for want of better words, be called facial features. If anything, the demon was more hideous than I remembered. His skin was still a sickly, dark green, and his evil smile betrayed a mouth that was far too wide, with far too many teeth. Now, though, the demon sported something new—a mane of what looked like bright red hair.

" 'Tis much worse than I thought!" Snarks shuddered. "Guxx has made himself the Grand Hoohah!"

"The Grand Hoohah?" I asked, taken aback. "What is the Grand Hoohah?"

Snarks turned to me, his face a mixture of fear and pity. "Trust me!" he whispered. "You don't want to know!"

My eyes slid from Guxx, who was shouting order poems to his lieutenants, to the demon beast that he rode. I wished I hadn't looked. The thing was the color of yellow clay after a rainstorm, except for its eyes, which seemed to glow green from within. It had the requisite fangs and claws that seemed to be standard equipment for all creatures of the Netherhells. It nodded at me and licked its lips.

"Dinner," it said.

Moments before, I had anticipated being eaten by some of the less ethical members of the mythological community. Somehow, that now appeared greatly preferable to the option currently before me.

"Much worse," Snarks muttered. "The Grand Hoohah? Much worse. Oh, why did I have to leave the Netherhells? Oh, why did I have to turn honest?" The demon nervously chewed upon his stubby fingers.

For an instant, the world was still. I knew then that the battle was about to begin.

"Boy!" The Brownie began to dance furiously. "Is it time for Brownie Power!"

"For a change," Snarks whispered, "I wish the Brownie was right. What can he do? Give everybody a hot foot?"

"Why don't you go suggest it?" I asked.

But there was no time. Guxx lifted both his demonic arms and mussed up his flaming red badge of office. A hundred hideous things began their descent from the sky.

Guxx screamed:

"Now our foes will get their due!
Minutes from now we'll have wizard stew!"

"Wait a second!" the Griffin was shouting. "You know that mythological beasts should be strictly neutral in arguments of this sort! What about the Camelot Convention?"

"Drive our enemies to the ground!
First demonic horde, go down!"

The wizard's hands shot up in the air. I could hear my master's muffled voice shout a quick string of mystic words.

The first group of demons plummeted toward earth.

Until they suddenly slowed down, then stopped, then started plummeting up. Their alarmed cries faded into the upper air.

"Simple gravity reversal spell," my master explained. He sneezed once. "Pardon me," he intoned. His hands disappeared within the shoe to seek out his handkerchief.

"Think twice about what you are doing here!" the Griffin called upward. "If you want us to get out of your way, just let us know. Don't be hasty! Remember the Mabinogion Accord!"

Guxx roared at his first setback. He tore furiously at his red headdress:

"Now it's time we start to fight,
Second demon horde, take flight!"

Ebenezum was still busy blowing his nose!

"Hubert!" I called. "It's up to you!"

"A command performance!" the dragon yelled back. He took a deep breath and shot out a ball of flame half his size. The second horde dispersed in panic. The fireball consumed all but the quickest. The few survivors fell fighting among the crowd.

"Hold it a second here!" the Griffin called. "Now, if we all keep cool heads, we can avoid bloodshed! We're really just one big happy family after all, aren't we? Remember the Grendel Non-Aggression Pact?"

Guxx was enraged. Handfuls of his red crown fell to earth.

"Attack, third horde! Give them a lickin'!
Don't forget their leader with the head of a chicken!"

"What?" the Griffin roared. "AFTAOMAIBAC! Let's wipe these vermin from the face of the earth!"

The Griffin took flight, followed by the Rok and the Hippogriff. The dragon took another deep breath.

"Stay, friend Hubert!" Ebenezum called. "Now that there are other than demons on the field of battle, we will have to be more selective in our attack."

"Well, if you say so," Hubert said reluctantly. "They weren't a very good audience."

"Make way! Make way!" cried a small voice, barely audible in the melee. "It's Brownie time!"

There was a crash of thunder twice as loud as anything Ebenezum had produced.

Cries of alarm came from the demons overhead, followed by a great banging, as if someone were beating upon the Netherhells horde with drumsticks.

"Cover your heads! Cover your heads! In a moment, we'll be getting the fallout." The Brownie laughed delightedly. "I knew I should have used the tango!"

Shoes fell everywhere. Boots, slippers, sandals, those funny things with the curved toes that you found in the Eastern Kingdoms; if it could be called a shoe, it fell. So did demons. Hundreds of them scattered on the stage and through the crowd.

Now the battle began in earnest.

I moved close by my master's shoe, my new-found plank held high. The wizard Ebenezum was the key to this battle. I would protect his shoe to my last ounce of strength, so that he might concentrate upon his spells. Come, demons, I thought! But for some reason, the fiends of the Netherhells were keeping their distance.

I looked around to see my compatriots in the midst of the fray. Headbasher whirled about Hendrek's head, leading the immense man in a complex dance, thrashing and clubbing his way through the throng. Hendrek moved in an entirely different way when he held his weapon, leaping and pirouetting with a grace that seemed highly improbable in one of his bulk. It was almost as if the enchanted club controlled the warrior, not the other way around. Cries of "Doom!" and "Urk!" filled the air.

Snarks had managed to find a staff of some sort, and was playing a complicated game with a whole force from the Netherhells. The truth-telling demon would shout something out to one of his opponents that seemed to outrage the Netherhells denizen so that it would rush at Snarks in a blind anger. Snarks would then render the demon foe unconscious with a sharp rap from his staff, and confront the next enemy in line.

Why weren't they attacking my master? For a second, I felt

as if I should leave the wizard's side and wade out into the midst of things, dealing destruction with my sturdy plank. But perhaps the demons were not attacking for fear of the combined might of a wizard's magic and an apprentice's muscle. Maybe they wished to distract me, and attack Ebenezum when his guard was gone.

My master's hands once again emerged from their protective shoe. Now we would show them a thing or two! His hands made a complex series of mystic passes in the air. A close-packed group of demons howled hideously as they began to sink into the earth, accompanied by a loud sucking sound. Soon, they had disappeared altogether, leaving nothing but a muddy expanse of ground. There was a final loud rumble, as if some underground gases had escaped from a hidden fissure. That corner of the battleground fell silent.

"Simple mud activation spell," Ebenezum remarked. This time, though, he sneezed deeply a half-dozen times.

A great deal of noise still came from overhead. I looked up to see the Griffin, the Hippogriff and the Rok surrounding the still-airborne Guxx.

"I'll teach you not to bring any gold!" the Griffin shouted.

"Careful, Pop!" the Hippogriff warned. "He's a magic demon, after all. We need to employ some strategy!"

"I can dig it," the Rok remarked. "Why don't you two cats grab his arms while I rip off his head?"

Guxx tossed handfuls of red hair at his attackers.

"Rip his head, they say with glee
Fourth demon horde, attack these three!"

A horrible cry arose as a hundred more demons came screaming through a bank of clouds. Rok, Griffin and Hippogriff flew in different directions.

"There're too many of them!" screamed a panicked mythological creature. "We'll never defeat them!"

"On the contrary," a deep voice rumbled. "They have already lost the battle."

A dozen creatures turned to face the large gray shape.

"What do you mean?" one of them said.

"Simple," the gray shape replied. "They have never faced wombling!"

With that, the Bog Wombler began to roll and shake simultaneously. The demons in the vicinity didn't have a chance.

But there was a host of demons above us as well! Hubert lessened their numbers with well-placed spears of flame, while Alea held tight to the dragon's tail.

"Now!" she cried.

The tail crashed down on three demons who had wandered too close.

"What an act!" Alea cried as she examined the squashed remains. "If only the critics could see us now!"

"It takes two to tango!" a small voice cried.

"I've got you!" a demon yelled as it leapt for the Brownie. "Mzzmflx! Grzzllbllg!" The demon fell from the stage, its mouth full of shoes.

The unicorn leapt upon the stage, impaling demons upon its razor-sharp horn, then tossing them jauntily aside with but a flick of its well-muscled neck. The gorgeously sweating beast paused before me.

"Ride with me!" the unicorn cried. "How magnificent I look destroying demons. How attractive their blood appears, set off by my shining, golden horn."

The beautiful beast sighed, a single tear forming in one dark eye. "Yet I am incomplete. Oh, with the proper rider, how even more magnificent I would be!"

I mentioned that I was certain it had a point, but this was not the best time to discuss it.

"Wuntvor?"

Thankfully, my master interrupted.

The wizard blew his nose. "If you would move a bit? I need a better view aloft."

As I hastily scrambled to the side of the shoe, Ebenezum's hands once again emerged. Magic words and motions came in quick succession.

The cloud the demons had passed through grew hands. Dozens of hands. They began slapping any demons near enough to reach. Confusion reigned in the sky.

The wizard blew his nose again. "That should give our side a little time."

"I thought we would lose the battle for sure," I admitted.

"Indeed. Yet I was prepared. Demon hordes always come in fours. Twas nothing more than a simple cloud-hand formation—"

Suddenly, the wizard began to sneeze as though the shoe weren't even there.

The wizard gasped for air. "I've done too much... need to rest... keep the others away, for but a moment." The sneezing resumed.

My master had overextended himself! Well, I had stayed by his side in case he needed me. Now, I was his sole protection. I gripped my plank with a new ferocity.

I heard a great scream overhead. Despite the rain of shoes and slapping hands, Guxx had somehow managed to stay aloft. He stared at my master's shoe with naked hatred.

"The wizard spoils my every plan!
But now I'll go end his lifespan!"

That was why no one had attacked. The other demons had saved the shoe for Guxx! He would have to get through me before he could assault my master! I would beat away the demon Guxx with my plank!

Guxx landed on the stage with a mighty thump. I found myself face to face with Guxx's demon mount.

"Dinner."

"Eat wood, foul fiend!" I cried, swinging my plank.

To my surprise, the demon took a large bite out of my plank with razor teeth. It chewed thoughtfully. "Not bad," it remarked, "but I much prefer human flesh."

"Indeed." Ebenezum blew his nose behind me. "Haven't we met somewhere before?"

The demon Guxx ripped off his red headdress and threw it on the floor before the wizard.

"You've forgotten Guxx, you wizard upstart,
But you'll remember me when I tear you apart!"

"Let me think," Ebenezum replied. "I do feel that I know you from somewhere. One meets so many demons, you know, that they all run together after a while."

Guxx screamed:

"I'm one demon you can't mistake,
For I'll have your head upon a plate!"

"Indeed," Ebenezum remarked. "For a while, I thought you were attempting poetry. I used to know a demon who always attempted poetry. Unpleasant fellow. Never bathed, either. Luckily though, you don't seem to be saying anything that could even be considered a rhyme."

Guxx jumped up and down and shook his fists.

"I'll teach you to mock my poetry!
Now Guxx will go and kill his foe—et—
Er, that doesn't work."

The demon cleared his throat.

"So you criticize my poems!
But soon you'll be nothing but broken bo—"

The demon stomped his clawed foot in frustration.

"Your pardon," the wizard said. "If you'll excuse me for a moment while I free my hands?"

"Enough of this little drama!" The demon mount facing me swallowed the remains of my plank in a single gulp. "We have our own destinies to decide. And yours, good fellow, rests within my stomach. Glmmphmtt zzzznrrbbtt!"

The demon's mouth was full of shoes.

"Brownie Power to the rescue!" a small voice piped.

The demon mount swallowed all the shoes in one gulp. "Trying to fill me up won't do. Flying is hard work. Airborne demons are insatiable!" It paused in its pursuit for an instant to look down. "And Brownies make an excellent dessert!"

"No, you don't!" a magnificently modulated voice cried. "A unicorn will save you!"

The flying demon belched. "It's much too crowded and noisy down here. Wreaks havoc on one's digestion." The creature flew straight up in the air, barely missing a death blow from a golden horn as the unicorn came galloping across the stage.

My master had begun another series of mystic passes. Guxx, momentarily preoccupied with determining a proper rhyme, screamed in anger.

"No more spells, don't even start,

For now I'll tear your shoe apart!"

Guxx launched himself straight for the wizard. The shoe rocked with the force of his landing as Guxx grabbed both of my master's gesticulating hands. The air was filled with shouts of both demon and wizard, Ebenezum attempting desperately to complete a spell, Guxx madly trying to devise poems to increase his power.

The flying demon had settled back upon the stage. "There, now that the horse with the horn is gone. I hate to eat and run, but sometimes—urk!"

"Doom. Headbasher does its hellish work again."

Hendrek turned toward the furiously struggling Guxx and Ebenezum. The giant shoe seemed to be leaping across the stage of its own accord.

"Demon!" I heard Ebenezum gasp. "If you do not release me... there will be..."

"Stop your threats, my enemy!" Guxx replied. "For I shall soon rend—uh—thee. No, that doesn't work, either!"

My master's criticism had totally undermined the demon's poetic confidence. Perhaps this battle could be won!

My master gasped again. "...trouble."

Ebenezum then sneezed one of the world's great sneezes.

The shoe exploded outward, taking Guxx with it to some distant place. Only Hendrek's intervening bulk saved me from being blown off the stage. Even the mighty warrior, thick and heavy as he was, staggered back from the ferocity of the blast.

The warrior's great size blocked my view of the rest of the stage. What had happened to my master?

Hendrek turned to me.

"Doom," he said.

CHAPTER ELEVEN

Perhaps I have given you the wrong impression. A wizard's life is not all fame, fortune and frivolity. There must be periods of rest as well, when a wizard should find a safe retreat where he can seclude himself from sorcery and restore his health and vitality in the proper ascetic atmosphere. While lengthy retreats can deplete a wizard's fortunes, I have always preferred the ascetic atmosphere present in the pleasure gardens of Vushta, where a dozen handmaidens can attend to your every need. And the budget-conscious sorcerer should be sure to ask about their special midweek retreat package plans.

—from The Teachings of Ebenezum, Volume XCV (SPECIAL ANNUAL SUPPLEMENT)

"Demons are no match for mythology!"

The Griffin landed on the edge of what was left of the stage. "Let us crush our few remaining foes! Shout out our victory! AFTAOMAIBAC! AFTAOMAIBAC! AFTAOMAIBAC!"

The cheers grew stronger as the remaining demons took hasty flight or were soundly thrashed.

I quickly stepped to Hendrek's side, and looked to where my master had sat within his shoe. There was nothing left but a gaping hole.

I felt a sudden chill. Had the great sneeze exploded not only the shoe, but Ebenezum as well?

Something sneezed beneath my feet.

Joy buoyed my sinking heart. My master had managed to sneeze himself into the crawl space beneath the stage!

"Master!" I cried, and was rewarded with a muffled "Indeed."

A moment's pause, and the wizard spoke again. "Wuntvor?

If you might assist me for an instant?"

I clambered into the hole. It was dark down here after the brilliant sunshine above. I blinked in an attempt to orient myself.

My master's sneeze told me the way.

Dim light filtered through from where the Griffin had torn up a corner of the stage. I crawled a few feet to find the wizard tangled in a mass of robes and leather.

I asked my master if he had hurt anything.

"Nothing but what few shreds of dignity I had remaining," the wizard replied. "But there is no time for dignity now. There is only time for Vushta."

The wizard shifted and groaned. "Now, Wuntvor, if you might help disentangle me?" He grunted as I pulled away the bottom of the shoe. "Thank the stars for that cushioned insole. If the shoe had not been so well made, I might have been more seriously hurt."

Ebenezum withdrew his arm as I tried to disengage cloth from leather. His sorcerous robes appeared to be more shredded than before.

"Five demon hordes!" Ebenezum shook his head. "Not four, but five! Trust the Netherhells to devise fiendish innovations." He replaced his arm in what remained of his sleeve. "How fares the battle above?"

I told him that it was all but done, with the beasts dealing with a remaining demon here and there.

"We have been fortunate there," the wizard agreed. "As powerful as Guxx is, it appears that his strategy is as poor as his poetry."

The wizard was free at last. Ebenezum stretched and sneezed.

"We must be away from here, and hurriedly. Beneath the stage, I am somewhat protected, but once I reach the open air, my malady will return full force." The wizard chewed on his moustache for a moment, considering his options. "Wuntvor, I need you to speak with the dragon. When I emerge, I will need Hubert to carry me immediately out into the forest, while I hold my breath as best I can. Once I am out of range of these mythological creatures, I will have a chance to recover. And that will give you and the rest of the party time to join me on foot, so that we may be on our way to Vushta!"

Vushta! I jumped up to do my master's bidding.

"Wuntvor! Watch your head! It would be best to get to Vushta in one piece."

Rubbing my head where it had smacked the underside of the stage, I crawled back through the hole into sunlight.

"I will call you as soon as things are ready!" I said to my master as I left.

The flying demon that had been Guxx's mount lay on the stage. It must have recovered from Headbasher's blow, for green blood was flowing freely from half a dozen new wounds, including one about the right shape for a unicorn horn. It looked up at me and groaned.

"I guess you won't be my dinner now," it whispered.

"No," I murmured back. "I guess not." There was a roughness in my throat. It was sad to watch even a demon die. "Then Guxx left you behind?"

"Yes," the demon said. "Even after he became Grand Hoohah."

"Grand Hoohah?"

"Don't ask!" the creature gibbered. "You don't want to know!" The demon licked dry lips. "It's not fair! You look so tasty. Just the right fat-to-muscle ratio. Maybe—" The creature winced. "—as a favor to a dying demon—you'd let me nibble a finger or two?"

I stepped hastily away as the thing made one last pitiful attempt to chew.

Hubert was deep in discussion with the Griffin.

"Well, of course!" the Griffin was saying. "No hard feelings! Without your considerable help, we would never have defeated the demons!"

"Pop!" the Hippogriff put in. "If they hadn't been here, we wouldn't have had to fight any demons at all!" The Griffin turned on the boy. "A fight with a demon is a fight with a demon! What's the matter with you kids today?" The creature turned back to the dragon, shaking its head. "That's the trouble with these youngsters—no perspective. You know, when my son meets strangers, he hardly ever thinks to demand their gold. I mean, we raise them from infants, and this is the thanks we get—"

"Excuse me," I said somewhat timidly. But, as afraid as I was of interrupting this imposing creature, I was even more afraid that the Griffin would never stop talking. "May I have a word with Hubert?"

"What did I tell you?" the Griffin began, but he quieted when the dragon turned to me. I quickly told Hubert of the wizard's request.

"Well," the dragon said reluctantly, "I was hoping for an encore." He looked wistfully out to the audience, who seemed too preoccupied with dragging away the dead and wounded to be in the mood for light entertainment. "Still, no one has asked. I shall have a short talk with Alea, then I shall be ready. When one thinks of it, it is a very dramatic exit."

"We'll be ready in just a moment, master!" I called. As the dragon had moved away, I looked up with some trepidation to see if the Griffin was still annoyed, but the leader of the conference was now in deep discussion with the unicorn.

The beast shook its mane. Long, white hair flared wonderfully in the wind.

"Let bygones be bygones," the unicorn intoned. "These are perilous times, which call for noble and magnificent measures. And who better to suggest such measures than myself?" The beast paused and struck a pose that took my breath away. "The fight with the Netherhells is not yet over. We need to join together to weather this crisis. You have had a fine idea, but it has not been taken far enough! What is needed is a true alliance of all mythical creatures, Griffin and unicorn, Hippogriff and dragon!"

"Maybe," the Griffin replied dubiously. "I'll have to check the bylaws. Might there be any gold in it?"

"What need have we for gold, when a unicorn leads the way?" The grand creature snorted a fine mist from its nostrils. "I will, of course, be first on your new membership list."

"What?" The Griffin flapped its wings furiously. "I'll rip off your horn, you conceited beast! It's probably the only part of you worth anything!"

Alea bounded across the stage and into my arms, causing me to lose interest in the argument.

"Oh, Wuntie!" she breathed. "Hubert tells me he's going to fly the wizard out of here, and I'm to walk overland with you!" She hugged me tightly. "Oh, it all sounds so adventurous!"

"Yes, Alea," I said through the mass of blond curls that covered my face. I turned my head. "Hendrek! Snarks! Brownie! Get your gear together! We must be off for Vushta!"

The Griffin looked up sharply from listening to the Hippogriff talk about how the unicorn might not have such a bad idea.

"You know, Pop," the Hippogriff said, "that unicorn is really kind of cute. I've been thinking, maybe ocelots are not for me. Give me a chance to get to know that big, beautiful horse a little better—"

"What?" the Griffin cried in my direction. "You can't leave now. We have treaties to sign! Accords to iron out! Amounts of gold must be exchanged!"

Hubert shook his large, befanged dragon head. "No. We must go. There will be other demon attacks. The fate of Vushta, indeed, the fate of the world, depends on us now. Were we to hold back another day, there might be no tomorrow."

"Oh," the Griffin said. "Well, if you put it that way."

I, too, was impressed. Listening to Hubert describe our actions in his stentorian tones made them sound desperately vital. I began to see advantages in having an actor deal with matters of diplomacy.

I knelt at the edge of the hole and exchanged a few words with my master.

"Fellow creatures!" the Griffin spoke to the assemblage. "Our friends must leave, on matters so urgent that all our lives may depend on their actions. We have fought beside them, and, though we have only known them a few hours, have grown to accept them as comrades. We will miss them! We wish them good weather and good speed!"

With that, the wizard emerged from the hole and, holding his nose, sat quickly upon Hubert's back. The dragon gave a brief wave to the crowd. "Until next time!" he cried. "We love you all! Up, up, and away!"

Dragon and rider were soon lost among the clouds.

"You have witnessed Brownie Power today!" a small voice shouted to the audience. "May you be blessed with the luck of the Brownies!"

Snarks added: "And after the two minutes it takes to use that up, I hope you have other luck as well."

"Then again," the Griffin said, "we may not miss all of you."

"Doom!" Hendrek remarked, and we were on our way.

We made our way rapidly through the Enchanted Forest. According to my last-minute conference with the wizard, we were to meet him at the first river crossing of the eastern path. It seemed the best possible landmark in an unfamiliar terrain, but I had no idea how far away that first river might be. So, while I felt it was imperative that we reach Vushta with all speed, I realized that we must pace ourselves at no more than a steady march so that we might have strength for the rest of our journey.

As a result, my compatriots had some opportunity to talk.

"Doom," Hendrek said. "We fight greater and greater battles with the Netherhells. Every fight, I fear, shall be our last. Still, we survive."

"My truth-telling instincts say that there must be a reason for this." Snarks's bright green demon face was set in a ponderous frown. "I knew Guxx before I was banished from the Netherhells. We are vaguely related, you see. He is a fifth cousin on my grandmother's side, and we used to meet at these ceremonies called 'Family Picnics.' Auggh! What ghastly affairs! They gave a new definition to boredom. Be thankful you have not yet devised such tortures here on the surface world!"

"Doom," Hendrek murmured in sympathy.

"So, as I said," Snarks continued, "I am somewhat familiar with Guxx Unfufadoo. He is evil, underhanded, dishonest, cruel, ruthless—in short, perfect leadership material for the Netherhells. Why, then, when he fights us, does he keep losing?"

"Simple!" a small voice chimed. "That's because he never had to fight Brownies before!"

"And, if I had my way, he'd never fight Brownies again!" Snarks snapped. "No, that is not fair. Your shoe trick was rather good. Short as you are, you did play a part in this battle." The demon rubbed thoughtfully at one of its small horns. "And I think you have given me a clue to Guxx's defeat."

"Yeah! Like the positive force of Brownie Power!"

Snarks chose to ignore the tiny voice.

"Guxx seems intent on attacking us with as large a force as he can muster at any one time. But why attack us when we were in a large group, instead of waiting until we were more isolated? The answer lies with Ebenezum."

I paused, letting the beautiful Alea go a few paces ahead. It sounded as if Snarks's Netherhells training might be strategically important after all.

"The Forxnagel is imminent," the demon continued. "The first encounter the Grand Hoohah had with the wizard Ebenezum was decisive in more ways than one. Not only did it cause your master's malady, and thus bring about this journey, but it affected Guxx as well. I believe the wizard's resilience in facing Guxx's demonic hordes has actually made the demon lord afraid. He attacks blindly, without reason, whenever he has the opportunity. Even though he has attained the Grand Hoohah, I feel that Guxx fears, as long as the wizard Ebenezum is alive, that his Forxnagel spell will never succeed!"

"Doom! So he will attack again and again?"

"Wow! It sounds like you're going to need Brownie Power even more!"

"Doom!" Hendrek repeated. "An amazing piece of conjecture. And yet, in a fiendish way, it makes sense."

"As does everything I say," Snarks readily agreed. "Now perhaps you'll listen to those diet plans I've laid out for you. Not to mention a few technical pointers I can give you on handling your warclub!"

"Doom!"

"Oh, Wuntie!" Alea rubbed my shoulder gently. "Do you think we might stop and rest for a little while?"

Uncertainty stabbed me as I glanced at the young woman. Had I been driving them too hard? I asked Alea if she was tired.

"Well, of walking, yes. I'm always a little jumpy after a performance. Wuntie? I was wondering if, when we stopped, we might be able to rest a bit farther down the path from the others?"

Alea was right. We had not really had time for a serious talk since she and Hubert had dropped in among the mythological beasts. I looked at her bouncing blond curls, dark gold in the forest shadows.

Still, I pondered Snarks's words. If he was correct, the demons would not leave Ebenezum alone. What if they attacked my master and Hubert as they awaited us?

"Alas," I said reluctantly. "Alea, we have no time for that now. Our purpose is to travel as far and fast as we can. We must succeed, for Vushta, and my master!"

"Oh, Wuntie!" Alea sighed. "I love a simple man of principle!"

"Indeed," came a voice from just up the path.

With my concern over Alea's welfare, I had failed to notice that we had entered a small clearing. Some fifty feet before us was a nearly dry riverbed. And sitting on a rock at the river's edge was the wizard Ebenezum.

"Wuntvor," my master said. "If you can ask the others to wait there, I think now would be a good time to have a conference." He nodded to Alea. "Hubert is up in the air. Said he wanted to stretch his wings."

I told my master briefly about Snarks's conjectures.

"Interesting," my master replied, "and very possibly true. I knew Snarks could be a valuable addition to our party. And, if he is correct, there is even more reason for us to hurry. For, Wuntvor, we are getting close to our destination."

"Vushta?"

The wizard nodded. "I believe we have nearly traversed the entirety of this so-called Enchanted Forest. There is but one final obstacle to overcome. If my calculations are correct, this path should lead us to a fishing village on the edge of the Inland Sea. Once we are there, it should be a simple matter to book passage on a boat, and sail across the sea to Vushta!"

Vushta! I swallowed hard. With the labors of recent weeks, the word had almost lost its meaning, and I had sometimes felt it might be an unattainable dream. Now, though, I might walk in that dream, and pass down streets where, were a man not careful, he could be cursed for all eternity. It was almost beyond imagining! Would I really get to see the thousand forbidden delights for myself?

"Hey!" a small voice called from the other side of the clearing. "Isn't it about time for another Brownie wish?"

"Indeed?" Ebenezum queried. "Are you eager for us to use them up?"

The little fellow shook his tiny head. "I just want to show you what a Brownie can do! I mean, we got one good wish going awhile ago. Since then, though, my track record hasn't been so terrific!"

I thought I detected a look of panic deep within the wizard's eyes. Perhaps the thought struck him, as it did me, that we might have a wish-attempting Brownie as a constant companion for the rest of our lives.

"Wait a moment!" I exclaimed. "What about that rain of shoes? That was a wish if I ever saw one!"

"Hey!" The Brownie brightened perceptibly. "Those shoes were a first-class wish! Okay, if you insist. Two down and one to go. But that means I have to make the last one a whopper!"

"Good work, Wuntvor," Ebenezum whispered. "I am glad the Brownie wishes are nearly over. I fear we could not survive too many more."

Someone seemed to be humming a fanfare overhead. I looked up to see Hubert rapidly descending.

"Hello, fun seekers!" the dragon called out. "Ah, I see I didn't have to go flying to find our friends. They got here quite nicely by themselves." Hubert tipped his hat at the wizard. "Oh, I did get a look at the Inland Sea. Flying as much as I do, I'm not that good at judging walking distances. Still, I don't think that village can be much more than half a day's journey away."

Only half a day? I had to restrain myself from shouting with joy. We were virtually in Vushta already!

"Indeed," Ebenezum said, and paused a minute to blow his nose. "Well, you and Alea will be on to Vushta, then."

"Exactly!" The dragon turned to the damsel. "Sorry to thrust this engagement upon you so suddenly, sweets, but I think the wizard here has a point. We're to go ahead and inform the powers that be in Vushta about Ebenezum's findings. Then, when the rest of our party reaches the city, we'll be that much further ahead of the Netherhells' plans!"

Hubert swept his top hat in a wide arc. "Just think of the kind of entrance we can make! The publicity value of this is staggering!"

Alea looked wistfully in my direction. "Oh, there was so much I meant to say to you! So much I wanted to do!" She gave me a final, tearful kiss and then ran to the dragon. "Still, when the theater calls, one must be ready. Look me up when you arrive in Vushta!"

And with that, the two of them took to the air. Ebenezum was on his feet. "We must get to Vushta as well. Even now, I fear we may be too late."

He straightened his robes and walked eastward on the path.

CHAPTER TWELVE

A wizard must always know how to use words. Practice smiling as you recite the following simple exercise. First: "The spell has not worked. It is best that you get out of your house before it explodes." Second: "The spell has not worked. It is best I get out of here before you explode." And third: "The spell has not worked. Will you please pay me the rest of my retainer before your money explodes with you?" Delivering lines like these with conviction is the sign of a professional sorcerer.

—THE WIZARD FINALS: A STUDY GUIDE EBENEZUM, GREATEST MAGICIAN IN THE WESTERN KINGDOMS (THIRD EDITION)

"I have something for you."

Snarks held up a length of wood. It was my stout oak staff!

"Where did you get this?" I asked incredulously.

"We found it on our way to rescue you from those creatures. It was easy to follow. There was stuff littered all over the ground."

"Yeah!" a small voice piped from the rear. "But you needed a Brownie to point it out."

I swung the staff experimentally. Its familiar weight felt good in my hands. "Wait a second. Did you use my staff in that battle?

The demon shrugged. "Well, I needed something. It would have been difficult to push my way through that bunch of animals, just to say, 'Oh, by the way, here's your staff.' Besides, I saw you'd gotten yourself a plank!"

I glanced at the patterns the sun made through the trees

high overhead. I decided I would rather not think about the plank.

"Besides, I'm pretty handy with a staff myself. Got a lot of training at Heemat's place. In fact, I could give you one or two pointers—"

"Doom," Hendrek interjected. "We found this as well."

The warrior drew a crumpled pack from out of Headbasher's sack. It took me a moment to realize that it was the wizard's— the same pack that I had carried on my back for most of our journey!

"I fear most of the contents have been lost," Hendrek intoned as I opened the thing. "We picked up what was nearby, but we felt coming to your rescue was more important than a concentrated search."

It was true. Almost all the arcane paraphernalia was gone. Nothing remained but a few books and one rumpled piece of cloth.

I pulled what at first looked like a rag from the pack. It was the same dark fabric as the magician's robes, tastefully inlaid with silver moons and stars. I hastily shook it out. Yes! It was the wizard's cap!

"Master!" I called.

Ebenezum turned from where he walked, some twenty paces ahead of the rest of the party. I held up my discovery.

"Indeed?" the wizard said with one raised eyebrow.

"They found it on the way to rescue us! " I explained.

"That's right!" the Brownie cried. "The things you lost led us right to you! Brownies are very good at following trails. It comes from being compact and close to the ground! Talk about Brownie Power!"

"I'd rather not," Snarks murmured.

"You'd better watch out, or the next Brownie wish will center on you!"

"Gentlemen, please," Ebenezum called. "We can argue once we get to Vushta. Would you bring that cap to me, Wunt?"

The wizard fit the somewhat rumpled cap on top of his head. He allowed himself a smile. "Indeed, a wizard is never complete without his cap. Did our party rescue anything else?"

I told him about the pack and the stout oak staff.

"Nought but a few books?" The wizard sighed. "Well, let us hope that, if we encounter any difficulties, those worthy tomes will suffice. We are close enough to Vushta that, should luck be with us, we shall not need any of them."

He scratched at the hair beneath his hat. "I am glad for the return of the cap, nonetheless. The more you look like a wizard, Wuntvor, the more people treat you like a wizard."

The mage shifted his shoulders beneath his robes and began to walk once again toward Vushta.

"And speaking of magic," Ebenezum said, "were you ever able to reestablish contact with that young witch?"

Norei! With all the recent excitement, I'd barely had time to think about her. I shivered when I remembered her scream, and Guxx's demonic face reciting deadly poetry. Briefly, I told Ebenezum what had happened.

"So the demon is aware of the grackle spell?" the wizard mused. "Pity. Then we can no longer use it. Let us pray that the young lady has not been harmed."

Norei? Harmed? A cold chill shot from my hairline to my shoes. She wasn't like me, a bumbling apprentice who, with luck, could manage an extremely simple spell. She was a qualified young witch! I was so sure of her abilities that I never doubted she would be safe.

But I had not really considered who she was fighting. Guxx was no ordinary demon. He had almost defeated my master, the greatest wizard in all the Western Kingdoms! What hope would a mere young witch have against something as strong as that?

"Indeed," Ebenezum said, as if he could read my thoughts. "We can help her best by getting to Vushta as quickly as possible."

Yes, my master was right. It would do me no good to recriminate myself for walking with Alea when I should have been thinking of Norei. We were all due to fight in a drama much larger than our petty, everyday concerns. There was no time for grief. Action was all that mattered now.

The trees had been thinning for some time, so that we could see regular patches of sunlight here and there. The leaves whispered overhead as the wind picked up. The air smelled moist and tangy.

"Doom!" Hendrek called from behind. " 'Tis the smell of the sea!" The trees ended abruptly, and we found ourselves on a cliff. Below us was a small village, built entirely from stone. Beyond the two dozen houses was the largest body of water I had ever seen.

"Indeed," Ebenezum said. "The Inland Sea." He looked over the cliff edge. "There must be some way down from here."

"How about Brownie Power?"

"No, I think unless you can make a flying shoe—" The wizard hesitated. "Let me rephrase that. Unless you can make a flying shoe that you have tested before, I think we would be better off finding another way."

"Well, all right," the Brownie said reluctantly, "if that's the way you feel about it. Gee, a flying shoe? What a nifty idea! You sure you don't want to try it? I mean, my wishes have been pretty good about coming true." The Brownie tried on a winning smile. "Well, at least two of them have."

"Indeed." Ebenezum nodded at the others. "Hendrek, Snarks, see if you can possibly find a path, would you?"

"What about a bouncing shoe?" the Brownie asked. "If I made it big enough, we could all bounce down together!"

Snarks and Hendrek went quickly about their business.

"Doom!" Hendrek called. "There are some stairs here, cut into the rock. They curve around the edge of the cliff, but they appear to descend toward the village."

"Oh," the Brownie said, rather disappointed. "Then I don't suppose you want a climbing shoe, either. I mean, I could make one with really strong laces, which you could tie around trees and outcroppings of rock. What do you say?"

"Indeed," the wizard replied. "I feel the stairs might be faster." He walked over to the cliff edge where the large warrior stood. "Hendrek and Wuntvor will come with me. I fear that you other two must wait here for the nonce. We need to secure the use of a boat from the village below, and I suspect that, should the villagers see a demon and a Brownie in their midst, it might somewhat hamper our negotiations."

"I have to stay up here?" Snarks asked, a look of horror on his face. He pointed at the Brownie. "With him?"

"I think it would be for the best," Ebenezum asserted.

"Don't worry," the little fellow said cheerfully. "I can relate some fascinating anecdotes from Brownie history to help pass the time. By the time the others return, you'll know just how Brownie Power came to be!"

"Doom," Snarks remarked.

"We must be off!" the wizard called. "Hendrek, lead the way. And keep your warclub at the ready, in case we encounter demonic intervention during our descent."

Hendrek nodded grimly, and led the way.

I heard the Brownie laugh as we carefully took the steps down.

"It won't be so bad! I'll tell you all about how Brownies got into the shoe business in the first place. You know, originally, we were going to make magic socks—"

Mercifully, the cliff face cut off any further noise from above.

The descent was not as bad as I had first imagined. What began as a cliff face soon became little more than a steep hill, and the steps carved from stone became a rocky path. We reached the village quickly, without a single sign of demonic intervention.

An old man sat on a stump at the edge of the village, smoking reflectively on a long, clay pipe. He nodded at us as we approached. Ebenezum took the lead.

"A good day to you, good sir," the wizard began.

The old man smiled. "Ah, it is a fine day, isn't it? I sometimes think late summer afternoons like this are a gift from the gods. It gives an old man like myself a chance to smoke quietly and contemplate the glory of the world around me. But I always talk too much. What brings fine people like yourselves to Glenfrizzle?"

"That's the name of your town then?" Ebenezum asked.

The old man nodded.

"Actually, we've come seeking advice."

The old man laughed. "Lucky for you, advice is my specialty. People come to me all the time to ask questions about farming and fishing." He puffed once on his pipe. "I've become an expert. That's what happens when you get too old to do anything else."

"Ah," the wizard said. "Then you're just the man we want to see. We are traveling to Vushta, and seek passage across the Inland Sea. Would you know where we might be able to hire a boat?"

"Well let's—" The man's face suddenly contorted. His eyes crossed and he blew smoke through his nose. "Passage? Vushta? Hire a boat?" He swallowed. His eyes uncrossed. He smiled at my master. "I have a pipe. It is fun to smoke my pipe."

The wizard frowned. "Indeed, but can you tell us where to find a boat?"

The old man waved his pipe in circles. His eyes followed the movement of the bowl. He giggled in delight.

"Boat?" he said at last. "What is a boat?"

"Indeed." Ebenezum stepped away from the old man. He glanced at me. "Perhaps we have some trouble with the local dialect." He turned back to the old gentleman and spoke slowly and distinctly. "Sir, we seek a ship to take us across the Inland Sea."

"Ship." The old man rolled the word around on his tongue, as if trying it out. "Shipship shipship. What is a ship?"

"We need a vessel to take us to Vushta!" Ebenezum stepped away and took a deep breath. He had been shouting.

"Oh," the old man said. "What is a vushta? I have a pipe. It is a very nice pipe."

Ebenezum sneezed.

"Sorcery!" he cried. "I should have suspected. Quickly, men, we must get into the village before this foul spell spreads!"

Ebenezum took off at a run. Hendrek and I did our best to keep up with him.

We ran past a young woman carrying a small child. Ebenezum stopped abruptly. Hendrek and I stopped as soon as we could.

"Quick, woman!" the wizard said. "We desperately need your help."

The woman was quite taken aback. "Well, sir," she said after a moment's pause. "I will do what I can."

"Good," Ebenezum replied. "We must go to sea."

The woman nodded.

"Do you know," the wizard asked, "where we might hire a boat to take us to Vushta?"

" 'Tis child's play," the woman began. "Just—" Her head jerked back for a second. Her eyes crossed. "Boat? Hire? Vushta?" Her eyes uncrossed. She smiled sweetly and bit her lip. "Have you come out to play?"

"No!" Ebenezum insisted. "We must book passage to Vushta."

"Oh," the woman said. "I can't read books. What's a vushta?"

"The spell is spreading too fast!" the wizard cried. "We must hurry!"

We ran down the street until we reached the docks. A stocky fisherman sat on the edge of his boat, mending a net.

"Quick, man!" Ebenezum cried. "We need your help!"

"A wizard needs my help?" the man said. "And what can I do for you?"

"Perhaps the spell will not work if we are away from land. May we come aboard?"

"Sure, if you don't mind the company of a few fish."

The wizard stepped hastily onto the boat.

"Now, answer at once, for we must be away. We will pay you well if you take us to Vushta."

"Vushta?" the man grinned. "Well, as I said, if you don't mind—" His eyes crossed. His grin grew wider. "I have lots of fish."

"I don't care about your fish!" Ebenezum shouted. "Will you take us in your boat?"

"Sure," the fisherman said. "What's a boat?"

"It's what we're standing in," the wizard replied. "We need you to take us across the Inland Sea."

"Sure," the fisherman said. "What's a sea?"

Ebenezum shook his head. "We are too late again."

"Doom," Hendrek intoned.

The fisherman held up his net. "Look at the pretty string. I have lots of pretty string."

My master scrutinized the large warrior.

"Hendrek, have you ever piloted a boat?"

"Wait!" I interjected. "Be careful what you say." My master's last few words had given me an idea.

"Doom!" The warrior looked about warily. "What have you learned?"

"Don't you see?" I turned to Hendrek. "The spell only works when we turn to someone and ask, 'Can we hire a boat to go to Vushta?' "

"Doom," the large warrior said. "Then we shall never—" Hendrek paused. His head shook and his eyes crossed. "Boat? Vushta? Hire?" His eyes uncrossed. He smiled broadly. "Doom."

"Hendrek? Are you all right?" For a moment, I was afraid that I had inadvertently used the spell on him.

"Doom," he said again.

He sounded like his old self. Perhaps it hadn't really affected him after all.

"Doom," Hendrek repeated. "Doom de doom de doom de doom. I like to sing. Doom doom de doom."

"Indeed!" the wizard cried. "Wuntvor, speak no more! You have hit on the very thing. If I wasn't so preoccupied, I would have thought of it before! It is a variation on Gorgelhumm's Spell of Universal Stupidity!"

"Doom," Hendrek said. "Doom de doom doom."

Ebenezum pulled thoughtfully at his beard. "We will cure Hendrek in Vushta. From this point on, Wuntvor, we must choose our words carefully."

Another boat bumped against the nearby dock. "Quickly, Wunt!" Ebenezum urged. "But cautiously as well!" He ran toward the docked boat. I followed close behind. Hendrek meandered after us as well, playfully bashing in portions of the dock with his warclub. "Excuse us, sir," the wizard called.

The boatman looked at us dubiously. "Is something wrong?"

Ebenezum stopped running and tried his best to appear casual. I attempted to imitate my master. Hendrek doom-de-doomed behind us.

"Actually, nothing is wrong, save that my two companions and I are stuck here on land, and we wish to—uh—" My master paused and smiled. "We wish to not be on land."

"What?" the boatman asked. "Where would you be if you weren't on land? Do you want to walk around on the air?"

"No, no!" Ebenezum said, still smiling. "You don't understand! You see, uh, we need to get to different land!"

"Really?" The boatman began to unfurl his sail. "Well, I hope you enjoy the walk."

"No!" Ebenezum cried. He made shooing motions toward the ocean. "Can you go out?"

"Go out? I just came in."

"No, no!" Ebenezum waved frantically in an attempt to keep the man's attention. "Can we go out?"

"Out where?" The man's eyes narrowed. "A tavern someplace, I suppose. You're not trying to get me drunk to steal my boat, are you? Those wizard's robes look pretty old and torn to me. They don't fool this old boatman for a minute. Where did you dig them up?"

"I beg your pardon!" Ebenezum stiffened, the smile gone from his face. "I am a true wizard! These are my real wizard's robes! I have been through great hardship and adventure to reach this point. It is not my fault if you do not feel you have time to listen to a reasonable request!"

"Reasonable request?" The boatman threw up his hands. "I haven't even heard anything that could be considered a civil question. Until you got angry, I wasn't even sure you were conversant in the common tongue! What are you, some sort of religious fanatics?"

"I beg your—" Ebenezum paused and pulled on his beard. "That it is. We are simple pilgrims, unable to use certain words for religious reasons." He drew a sack of gold from inside his robes. "Fortunately, we are rich religious pilgrims, and will pay you well for your services."

"Oh," the boatman smiled. "Why didn't you say so? Where would you like to go?"

"Well, I need you to take my two companions and me from this land to—uh—another land."

"Yes, yes?" the boatman urged. "Come on, my good man, I can't take you there if I don't know where I'm going. What land do you want to go to?"

"Indeed," Ebenezum mused. "Well, we need to go to a big city, on the other side of the—uh—water. A magic city!"

"Aha!" the boatman cried. "You want to hire my boat so I can take you across the Inland Sea to Vushta! Why, that's simple—"

The man paused and shook. His eyes crossed. "Hire? Sea? Vushta?" His eyes uncrossed. He laughed. "I like to laugh."

"Doom de doom de doom," Hendrek sang behind me.

"Doom de doom de doom," the boatman replied.

"Oh no!" I moaned. "We can't even imply that we wish to hire a boat for Vushta, can we?"

"Indeed not," Ebenezum replied. "Apparently, this spell—" The wizard paused and shivered. His eyes crossed. "Vushta? Hire? Boat?" The mage sneezed.

"Master?" I whispered.

Ebenezum turned to me, his face lit by a beatific smile.

"I am a good wizard. I have pretty robes. Indeedy!"

The wizard sneezed.

"Master!" I cried. What had I done?

"Doom de doom," Hendrek hummed. "Doom de doom."

CHAPTER THIRTEEN

Some people think of wizards as nothing more than men in pointy hats who like to go around turning people into toads. Nothing could be farther from the truth. Perhaps wizards should come together and agree on a saying or two to better humanize their profession; for instance, "Wizards are wonderful!" or "Take a wizard to lunch!" Yet I doubt this will ever occur, for wizards are by and large a solitary breed. Still, this should not stop you from trying to understand my profession. If you should offer, for example, to take a wizard to lunch, I imagine he would go gladly. And if you were to tell a wizard he wasn't wonderful, I'm sure he would be quite happy to turn you into a toad.

—from The Teachings of Ebenezum, Volume I

"**W**untvor!"

A woman's voice called to me. I turned in haste, almost losing my balance on the edge of the dock.

It was Norei.

"Beloved!" I cried, running back up the dock and onto the cobblestone street on which she stood. "I'm so glad to see you! Ebenezum, Hendrek, all the townspeople—"

"Oh, dear," she said. "You've been trying to hire a boat for Vushta, haven't you?"

"Then you know! It was—" I began to shake. I could no longer speak. What was a boat? What was a vushta? What was a hire?

"Oh, I'm sorry," Norei said. She recited a quick string of magic words. I blinked.

"—terrible." I finished my sentence and rushed into her arms.

"I had no choice! I realize it was a little severe, but I had to do some— Wuntvor, please!" she said as she disentangled herself from my embrace. "I know you're happy to see me, and I'm glad to see you, too, but, frankly, when I kiss you, all I can think about is a grackle!"

I stepped away from her, startled. What was she saying?

"That's much better. I'm afraid we have far too much to do right now to think of ourselves, anyway. Wait for this crisis to be over, Wuntvor. Then we can become reacquainted."

Yes, she was right! This was no time to think of ourselves! What about my master, and Hendrek, and the townspeople caught by the stupidity spell?

"So," the boatman asked, "just how much gold would you be willing to offer me?"

"Wait a moment!" called the stout fisherman. "The wizard has already asked me to ferry him across."

"Indeed," the wizard said levelly. "Apparently, we can now discuss this at our leisure. If the two of you would care to quote me rates?"

"Doom," Hendrek intoned.

"Norei!" I cried happily. "You've removed the spell!"

"And why wouldn't I?" A playful smile touched her perfect lips. "It was my spell in the first place. I'm sorry I had to use such a strong one, but the demon Guxx would have blocked anything gentler. And I had to keep you from leaving without me, at any cost."

"Indeed?" the wizard said. "Would you care to tell us why?"

"I have been sent by my family to—" She paused, glancing at the two boatmen, "—to discuss certain matters of the strictest confidence. When you are finished with your negotiations, we should find a private place to talk."

"Agreed," the wizard replied, then returned to his haggling. In a few moments we had secured the services of the larger boat for half what the smaller would have cost us. The boatman, who believed he had struck an excellent bargain, smiled and said we would leave at dawn tomorrow. When the wizard began to protest the delay, the boatman threw up his hands and said he had to wait for the morning winds. If the wizard could produce the winds sooner, they could leave sooner.

Ebenezum turned to Norei. "No," he said, after a moment's pause. "I don't think my malady could abide it. Besides, we require some rest. And we have things to discuss."

Ebenezum gave the boatman a piece of gold to seal the bargain. Then Norei, Ebenezum, Hendrek and myself retired to the town's only inn.

"Doom," Hendrek said as he walked beside me.

"Doom de doom doom doom."

"Norei!" I cried. "Hendrek still feels some ill effects from your spell!"

"On the contrary," the large warrior shook his enormous, bearded head. "The spell has benefited me. I have discovered that I like to hum. Doom. Doom de doom doom."

I wondered what Snarks would think of the warrior's new hobby.

"Master?" I asked, reminded of the demon. "What should we do about the rest of our party?"

"A good question," the mage replied. "We will have Norei contact them, and tell them to meet us on the docks tomorrow morning. They may both be of use during the trials ahead. Tonight, however, I think we may need the quiet only their absence can bring."

With that, the wizard led the way into the tiny inn.

The room we entered was pleasantly dark and cool after the late summer's heat outside. Cooking smells wafted in through a door on the far side that apparently led into the kitchen. My mouth watered. I'd forgotten how much I liked good, inn-cooked food. I thought fondly of plates piled high with pork and mutton, perhaps a fresh-caught fish from the Inland Sea, even a roast fowl or two, washed down by a good, strong ale. Life at its fullest!

The innkeeper greeted us cheerfully, his hands wringing his apron. "Strangers in town? Of course. You would like dinner? Of course. Would you step this way please? We will give you our best table, of course. We treat strangers well here. My wife sometimes asks me, can you be sure with strangers? 'Of course!' I cry. Who are strangers but people just like us, only from a different place. Lania! Mugs and settings for this fine company!"

A serving wench appeared, laden with plates and cutlery. She smiled as she passed me. Quite a nice smile, actually. If I was not promised to Norei—but, there was no time for foolish thoughts. We must prepare for the last leg of our journey.

"And what would the party care for?" The innkeeper spoke to all of us, but his eyes rested on the warrior Hendrek.

"Doom," the huge fellow replied. "I need to keep up my strength. One of everything."

"Of course! Lania, help me in the kitchen!"

"Indeed," Ebenezum said once the innkeeper had disappeared. "Now that we are alone, Norei, I must know what your message is."

"Oh, yes," Norei answered quickly. "It is something my mother, grandmother and I discerned during one of our sessions of group magic. We tried to contact you immediately, but the demon Guxx had already blocked the way. Since I was youngest and could move the fastest, I was sent to tell you in person."

She sipped her ale. Her neck looked very attractive as she swallowed. How I wished I could kiss that neck! But no, for now I must abstain. There were more important things to attend to. Besides, I reasoned, perhaps it was best if I simply spent some time around her as an obviously human apprentice, as opposed to the grackle she seemed to remember all too well.

"I trust Wuntvor told you most of what we learned." She glanced at me for but an instant with her pale green eyes. I looked away, lest the fire building inside me consume me whole.

"But there was one thing I did not impart to our bravely flying grackle," Norei continued. "The Netherhells had prepared a truly devastating fate for Ebenezum, once he had set out to sea!"

At that point, the kitchen door banged open. The innkeeper walked to our table, bearing a large platter. Lying upon that platter, and sagging slightly over the edges, was an even larger fish.

"For our honored guests, nothing but the best!" the innkeeper exclaimed. "Of course, we begin with a specialty of my humble establishment, the great rainbow fish of the Inland Sea!"

Cooked, the fish's scales gleamed a dozen pale pastels, gray to blue, pink to purple. The colors were set off even more by the orange-and-green checkered vest the fish appeared to be wearing.

"Odd," the innkeeper said, staring at the vest. "That isn't usually a part of the preparation. Lania, what did you put on this fish?"

Hendrek reached quickly for the platter. "Doom!" he exclaimed.

The vest was quicker than Hendrek's hands. It slipped from the platter as Hendrek grabbed, and fell to the floor, where it solidified into Brax the salesdemon.

"Boy, are you guys in for it this time!" Brax cackled as it puffed on its cigar. "I don't know why I even bothered showing up. Well, you might just have the slightest chance of survival if you stock up heavily right now. And lucky for you, I'm still overstocked on some very attractive enchantments!"

Hendrek swung Headbasher out of its protective sack and across the table towards the demon. All four mugs of ale went flying.

"Doom!" Hendrek cried as Headbasher hit the floor where Brax had stood but a moment before. The warclub left a sizable crack in the flagstone.

"See here!" the innkeeper protested. "I'm always glad to welcome strangers into my inn. I feel as if I am fairly open to differences in foreign customs. Still, there are limits—"

Brax ran behind the innkeeper. "Listen, I could sell you a little something that would rid you of unwanted guests instantly. It's a small, enchanted bog, completely portable. Simply place it underneath unwanted company, and they're sucked into the mire! And it's hardly used at all, comes with a few bones of extinct creatures—"

"Doom!" Hendrek pushed the innkeeper out of the way to get closer to the salesdemon. Brax scooted beneath the table.

The displaced innkeeper pointed at Brax with a quivering finger. "If this creature is going to stay for dinner, you'll have to pay for an extra place setting."

"How about it, Hendrek?" the salesdemon shouted as it

somersaulted gracefully over the swinging warclub. "You're way behind in your payments. Now, with what's going to happen, you'll probably never be able to pay anything, ever again, if you catch my drift. How about using that fine, almost-new warclub to knock over what's available around here, say, a young witch or a magician's apprentice—"

"Doom!" Hendrek screamed. He leapt for the demon and landed on the table, and the fish. The fish and the table collapsed beneath his enormous weight.

The demon was panting as it ran to the other side of the room. "Really, I'm not doing this for my health. By this time tomorrow, you folks won't have any health to worry about. You don't stand a chance unless you stock up with my weapons, and I mean stock up heavily!"

Hendrek picked himself up from where the tabletop had met the floor. The innkeeper looked on in silent horror.

"C'mon guys, I've got an investment here, you know. It gets harder every day for a salesdemon to make a dishonest living!"

Hendrek threw the fish at Brax.

"No, no, I'm sorry," the demon said. "It's too late to make things better by giving me little gifts. Hmm. It is tasty though. Urk!"

Distracted by the fish, Brax had not seen the flying Headbasher until the enchanted club had found its hellish mark.

"Easy terms!" The demon wobbled. "Years to pay!" The demon gasped. "Except, perhaps, in your case—" The demon popped out of existence.

"Doom!" Hendrek intoned.

"Is this what passes for table manners wherever you come from?" the innkeeper shrieked. "Of course! I let strangers into my inn, and this is the thanks I get. No, no, my wife tells me, what are strangers but people just like us, from another land. Hah! A land where people fall atop their food! Where people appear out of nowhere and offer to sell you swampland! I am never having strangers in my establishment again!"

"Indeed, my good fellow." Ebenezum pulled out his small sack of gold.

"Of course!" the innkeeper shouted. "You offer me gold!

Another time, perhaps! But now, I will not be silenced! Out in the street! Strangers! Just wait until I talk to my wife!"

We left with whatever speed we could muster.

"Well," Ebenezum said as the door to the inn slammed shut behind us. "Perhaps we can sleep on the boat."

We walked back down toward the docks.

Ebenezum moved between Norei and myself. "You were saying that you had a warning for me?"

"Yes, Guxx is very worried about your reaching Vushta. In fact, he seems to be petrified by the idea."

"Indeed?"

"Yes." Norei frowned. "Guxx feels you must be put out of the way at any cost. They have planned something at sea which you cannot possibly survive."

"I see." The wizard stroked his mustache in thought. "But if what you say is true, why then did they attack us in the forest?"

"Oh dear," Norei said with a sigh. "I'm afraid I'm to blame for that. It happened when Guxx discovered that Wuntvor and I had been talking, after the demon was sure he had effectively stopped all magical communications from reaching you. I might have been in trouble then, if the demon had not been so hysterical. As it was, though, the spells Guxx threw at me unraveled when he began to scream incoherently about conspiracies against him. I think he felt then that your sea death, sure though it would be, was not soon enough. So he mustered whatever demons he could find and attacked you immediately."

"Doom!" Hendrek said. "Snarks was right!"

"Indeed," Ebenezum said, pulling reflectively on his beard. "Still, I wonder if perhaps it would be best not to congratulate him, at least until this campaign is over?"

Hendrek nodded his head in agreement. "Doom."

The wizard turned back to Norei. "You still haven't told me; exactly what is this sure death I am supposed to meet at sea?"

"That's the problem!" Norei said, throwing out her hands in a gesture of helplessness. They were very beautiful hands. "I don't know. We couldn't find that out. Guxx discovered our spying, and the magical link vanished. But our eavesdropping did reveal one important fact! We learned the spell that would defeat whatever it was they sent against you!"

"Indeed?"

"Yes! All we know beyond that is the bringer of your death is very swift and sure, so we must use the spell the moment we see it, whatever it is."

"And what is the spell?" Ebenezum asked.

Norei paused for a second to concentrate.

"It is a poem of sorts," she began.

"Go, you creatures! Back down in the blue!
Go, you demons! Wakka doo wakka doo!"

"Indeed," the wizard agreed. "It is fiendish enough to come from Guxx. And bound to be powerful. The rhyme scheme is better than most."

"Doom," Hendrek murmured.

"No, I don't think so," Ebenezum replied. "With the information Norei brought us, I think our mission has a chance."

"Hi, there!" a small voice piped. "Rise and shine! The Brownie has arrived!"

"Doom," Hendrek mumbled, half-asleep.

"My thoughts exactly!" Snarks cut in. "But all is not lost. I am here as well!"

"Indeed." Ebenezum looked out from where he was using a sail as a blanket. "Could you get on the boat discreetly? I'm afraid the owner has not been completely informed as to the true nature of his passengers."

"Don't worry," Snarks said. "I've come prepared." Once again in close proximity to the wizard, the demon was heavily cloaked. He lifted his hood over his head. "Brrffll gllmlcch!" he exclaimed.

"Fine," Ebenezum said. "Now Brownie, if you will hide in Snarks's pocket?"

"A Brownie? Hide?" The little fellow placed his hands defiantly on his tiny hips. "No sir! Those days are over! Brownies hold their heads up high!" He looked angrily at Snarks, who had said something indecipherable. "Well, maybe not that far aloft, but plenty high for our size!"

The wizard sighed. "I'll make it the third wish."

"But you can't! A pitiful wish like that? I'm sorry, the last wish has to be a whopper! I mean, we're making Brownie history here!"

"Indeed," the wizard said. "I wish the Brownie—"

"Stop where you are! I'm going!" The Brownie jumped into the pocket of Snarks's cloak.

"Good day, sir!" the boatman called from the shore. "I see you are here promptly, and you have brought your party. Excellent. We will be off. And I see you'll give me a hand with the sail?"

The rest of us stretched and stood. As stiff as I was from a night attempting sleep on this boat, I did not care. In another day or two, I would see Vushta!

My eyes were drawn to Norei, who had risen from where she had slept at the other end of the boat. There she was at the first light of dawn, her lovely hair in her eyes, yawning magnificently! Oh, what a lucky fellow I was to be in love with someone as fine as that!

The boatman stepped on board. "We are in luck. The weather is with us! We should make Vushta by nightfall tomorrow." He brushed past Snarks. "If you will excuse me?"

"Bllflldmmp!" Snarks answered.

"Beg pardon?" the boatman said. "Say, you're not a member of the original party, are you? You must be that fifth person the wizard said he was going to bring aboard. I don't believe we've been properly introduced."

"Indeed," the wizard interrupted. "That is the last member of the party, a religious zealot, who must, to fulfill his vows, always keep himself heavily cloaked. In addition, we all attempt not to speak with him."

"He hasn't taken a vow of silence, has he?" the boatman asked. "I mean, I just heard him talk."

"Indeed," the wizard replied. "In his sect, the vow of silence is not severe enough. He has therefore taken the ultimate oath of his religious order, the vow of incoherence."

"Kllfvrmmll!" Snarks complained.

"See what I mean?" the wizard added.

The boatman nodded, momentarily awestruck. Ebenezum instructed me to lend a hand in casting off from the dock. In situations of this sort, the wizard always said, it is better to act quickly, rather than to give anyone time to think.

In a matter of moments, we set sail. It was the first time I had ever been in a boat large enough for me and five others to stand in. And it was the first time I had ever been on an expanse of water larger than a small lake.

It was quite beautiful, watching the sun rise over the water, turning the sea pink, then red, then burnished gold. The gentle waves that broke across the ship's bow, at first disconcerting to someone new to sea travel, soon became comforting in their regularity, and the way they gently rocked our craft. It was a very pleasurable experience, actually, being out on that inland ocean at the first light of morning. Much of the comfort was taken away, however, by the grim fact that the Netherhells' fatal plan would attack us here, on this calm Inland Sea, and, indeed, that the attack might come at any moment.

CHAPTER FOURTEEN

Some mages balk at performing spells during an ocean voyage, preferring instead to dabble in sorcery in tiny rooms, precariously perched high atop the aerie towers that this sort of magician always seems to favor. The logic of this preference has always eluded me. After all, should something go amiss with either your spell or your relationship with your employer, just think how much easier it is to swim than it is to fly.

—from The Teachings of Ebenezum, Volume XXXVIII

Ebenezum turned to Norei and spoke in a low voice.
"Perhaps you could conjure a small wind spell? Nothing too big, something perhaps that would only slightly irritate my nose."

Norei frowned. "Well, I might be able to do something. I see problems, though. What if I'm busy with the wind spell when the Netherhells attack? It might take me awhile to disengage. And what if, by bringing about a wind, I rush us into the Netherhells' trap too fast for us to counteract it?"

"Indeed," the wizard replied. "I am so anxious to get to Vushta, I am not giving proper consideration to the consequences. Now it might be that, by producing a wind, we could outrun whatever the Netherhells will send against us. But there is no way of knowing. I think we need you, alert and about the deck, more than we need a breeze."

"What is this talk of spells?" the boatman called from his place at the tiller. "I am always glad to take a wizard on as a passenger. I do not discriminate in those areas as others do. But I draw the line at magic on my boat! I mean, this craft is almost paid for! I don't want anything to happen to it now!"

"You have nothing to fear on that account," Ebenezum called from the bow. "For the time being, we would like to stay as far away from magic as yourself!"

"Doom," Hendrek spoke to my master in a low voice. "Look at the way the seagulls gather on the horizon. Could that be part of the Netherhells' plot?"

I looked where the warrior pointed. Dozens of seagulls whirled in the distance.

"Indeed," the wizard mused. "Either that, or they're above a large school of fish. What would the Netherhells attempt? A seagull suicide spell? Too risky; you can never trust seagulls to do as instructed. They're always off looking for fish. Still, they may bear watching."

Hendrek nodded, his eyes fixed upon the whirling birds. "Doom," he murmured.

"Pardon," the boatman called. "Are you sure this is but a regular pleasure trip?"

"Certainly," Ebenezum replied. "What makes you ask that question?"

"Well, you folks act very odd for a group on a pleasure cruise. Every time I turn around, you're having a conference. Now look here, I would have to charge more if this were a business venture."

"Indeed." The mage stretched out upon his wooden seat, and scratched beneath his beard. "Oh, no, we intend nothing more than pleasure to come from our actions. After all, what else is Vushta for?"

"Quite right," the boatman replied. "Sorry to question you. The renter is always right, as they say."

"Indeed." Ebenezum turned out to look at the ocean.

"Brwnnmmpwrr!" came a muffled shout. The voice, somehow, sounded much too high to be Snarks's.

"Llgvvbrwrph!" Ah, now that was Snarks. I looked over to the middle of the deck, where the well-cloaked demon seemed to be doing an elaborate dance.

"Is something wrong?" the boatman called.

"Not at all!" Ebenezum said reassuringly. " 'Tis nothing more than a complex religious ritual. Wuntvor, could you go over to our friend and make sure his ablutions do not tangle his robes?"

I did as my master asked. As I approached the demon, I could see that most of the movement was in Snarks's pocket, the very place we had stashed the Brownie! What was happening?

I spoke quietly, through clenched teeth, to a point in the demon's robes where I imagined an ear would be: "Don't you think you should quiet down?"

"Snnrfhm!" Snarks replied.

"Brwnprrfrffrr!" the Brownie yelled back.

"Will you control yourselves?" I whispered. "You two can argue when we get to Vushta."

"Up with—" the Brownie cried before I could stuff his head back into the pocket.

"I can take it no longer!" Snarks shouted, flinging off his hood. "I have suffered enough! I will not have a little person inhabiting my clothes!"

"What is going on here?" the boatman demanded.

I turned around, trying to shield the struggling demon and Brownie with my body. "Please try to ignore it. Tis nothing but the latter stages of the religious ritual. It gets rather hectic, I'm afraid."

"It will get much more hectic if this Brownie doesn't get out of my robes and off this boat immediately!"

The little fellow popped his head out of the pocket. "Brownies come and go as they please. Let's see how Brownie Power does at making shoes out of demon leather!"

"Wait a second!" the boatman cried. "That fellow having the religious experience isn't human! And I think he has two heads!"

"Indeed," Ebenezum said. "That is very observant."

"Observant, nothing! If it's not human, it doesn't stay on my boat!"

"A moment, my good man." Ebenezum stood, fixing the owner with his best wizard's stare. "You were contracted to take the five of us to Vushta."

"Wait a moment!" The boatman shook his head violently. "You contracted for five persons! Human persons!"

"I'm afraid, my good man, I did not. I simply asked you if you could take five on a boat. Species was never discussed."

The boatman fumed. "I should have listened to my grandmother!"

"Indeed," the wizard replied. "We would probably all be far better off if we had listened to everybody."

The boatman continued as if he had not heard my master. "My aged grandmother was a wise woman. She used to say, always make your contracts in writing. She used to say, never trust a wizard until you have his gold. She used to say—"

"Indeed," Ebenezum interrupted the other's meanderings. "You know, there are certain rules that my aged grandmother told me as well. I believe one of those is apt in this situation."

The boatman blinked unhappily. "Which is?"

Ebenezum pulled back his sleeves, exposing his hands in prime conjuring position. "Never argue with a wizard."

"Oh. Yes, well, I guess you have a point. Sounds like your grandmother was every bit as wise as mine. Actually, come to think of it, mine liked to talk a bit too much. Never would shut up—"

The boatman returned to his tiller. Snarks and the Brownie seemed to have quieted as well. The prospect of being thrown bodily into the ocean had temporarily calmed their anger. I placed Snarks's hood back on his head.

"Thmmnnllf!" Snarks said.

"Doom!" Hendrek called.

The sky above us was filled with seagulls.

"Quickly, Norei!" the wizard said. "Everyone, cover your heads!"

In a high, lilting voice, the young witch cried:

"Go, you creatures! Back down in the blue!

Go, you demons! Wakka doo wakka doo!"

The seagulls continued to circle, as the boat slowly moved away from them.

"I don't think that was the Netherhells' curse," Norei remarked.

"Indeed," the wizard replied.

"What was that all about?" the boatman called.

Ebenezum rolled up his sleeves. "Do you wish to argue with a wizard?"

"Hold on, now!" the boatman said, pushing as far back against the tiller as he could manage. "It's one thing to argue with a wizard. It's another thing to send your boat, your sole means of livelihood, to sure destruction."

"In truth." The wizard paused, pulling at his beard. "We have not been totally fair with you, my good man. Our trip is serious business, and we will pay you accordingly. We will even pay for the sixth person, short though he is, who resides in the cloaked one's pocket." Ebenezum pulled forth his bag of gold and rested it upon his palm. "You must excuse me. Sometimes my wizard's frugality gets the better of me. But we no longer have time for such petty concerns as money. I will give you a fair share of this purse, once our job is done. We must get to Vushta as soon as possible. There are demons who are trying to stop us, for they have a plan whereby the Netherhells will control the surface world. Because of this, your ship may be attacked during this crossing, although we have developed countermeasures that should be more than sufficient to protect us. I hope you understand the importance of our mission. The fate of Vushta, and the whole world, hangs in the balance."

"Oh." The boatman smiled. "Is that all? The fate of Vushta hangs upon our actions? We might be attacked by demons at any moment? Why don't I just jump off my boat now, and be done with it?"

"Doom!" Hendrek contributed. "Heed the wizard. Even I don't think our situation is that hopeless."

"I should have listened to my grandmother! She was always talking. Threw peach pits at me if I didn't listen. She was always talking, and eating peaches. Had a deadly aim with those pits, let me tell you. It's why I went to sea in the first place." The boatman shuddered. "I'll end up as dinner for some demon! And my grandmother said I'd never amount to anything!"

"Indeed," the wizard replied. "Fear not, friend Hendrek. The good boatman is already beginning to accept the situation. In the meantime, mayhaps there is something we can do beyond mere waiting. Wuntvor, you said there were still some books in the pack?"

I nodded, pulling the pack from where I had stashed it beneath my seat. I took out the three remaining books, reading the embossed letters on their spines aloud.

"Um," I said. "Here's Aunt Maggie's Book of Home Remedies?"

Ebenezum nodded. "Gift from my old mentor. We met her on our travels through a haunted valley. We helped her get rid of some ghosts and she gave me the book. Knowing her, she probably put a spell on it so I wouldn't lose it. What else have you got, Wunt?"

I looked at the two other books in my hands: Vushta on Two Pieces of Gold a Day and a well-worn copy of How to Speak Dragon. My master frowned as I told him.

Ebenezum chewed his lip. "Disappointing, although we may be able to use the Vushta book, should we reach our destination. Who knows? Maybe Aunt Maggie's book has a recipe for seaweed tea? I fear that wits, not spells, will have to see us through the coming test."

The wind picked up suddenly. It started to rain.

Ebenezum huddled in his tattered robes. "Does the weather always change so quickly?"

A streak of lightning relit the darkening sky.

"Aye," the boatman said. "We're subject to squalls out here on the water." He stared up into what was fast becoming a downpour. "Usually, though, there's more warning than this."

"Doom," Hendrek muttered. "Could it be—"

"Only one way to find out," Norei replied, and began to recite:

"Go, you creatures! Back down in the blue!
Go, you demons! Wakka doo wakka doo!"

The rain got heavier.

"On my grandmother's grave!" the boatman shouted over the gathering storm. "Not only do I have to navigate this boat, I have to listen to your poetry. Before, I was not sure. Now, you will have to pay me double!"

"Indeed," the wizard said. "We will pay you well enough."

He stared up into the stormy sky. "Apparently, the poem wasn't appropriate."

"Doom," Hendrek said. "Will we have to use the poem on everything out here?"

"More poetry?" the boatman cried. "The fight with the Netherhells was one thing. That I can accept. But you should have warned me about the poetry. I may have to charge you triple!"

"Hey, guys!" A small form jumped out of the pocket in Snarks's robe. "You have forgotten the obvious solution. Brownie Power!"

The rain lessened overhead. The sun peaked through the clouds. There was a rainbow.

Snarks tossed his hood away from his face. "Mere coincidence." The demon sneered. "It has to be!"

"Who are these passengers?" the boatman complained. "The price of rental is going up by the minute!"

"You've laughed at Brownies for the last time!" the little fellow shouted at the demon. "We'll show you what Brownies are made of! Remember the Brownie Creed: We may be tiny, but we're terrific!" He began an elaborate dance.

Snarks placed a restraining hand on the Brownie's cap. "Are you sure you should do this? If something goes wrong, we'll all drown."

"There have always been naysayers who have sneered at greatness!" the Brownie cried. "Big ideas don't happen without taking big risks! I must do it, for the glory of Browniedom everywhere!"

"What is he doing?" the boatman demanded.

"I think it's called the Lindy Hop," the Brownie explained obligingly. "And boy, wait 'til you see what happens when I'm done!"

"I think it's going to happen almost immediately," Snarks retorted, looking about him for something to throw. "No Brownie's going to dump me into the ocean!" He picked up an oddly-colored oar.

"Where did that come from?" The boatman pointed at the orange-and-green checkerboard piece of wood.

"Doom!" Hendrek intoned, reaching for Headbasher.

"That's right!" The oar began speaking even before it had completely metamorphosed into Brax the salesdemon. "It is your doom, unless you act now!"

"Hendrek!" I warned. "Be careful of the bottom of the boat!" But the large warrior's club was swinging mightily, heedless of anything in its path. Wood splintered as Headbasher took a chunk out of the mast.

"This is the end!" the boatman shouted. "Why didn't I listen to my grandmother and become a tinker?"

"Wait a moment!" Brax ducked under the warclub. "I have something that just may save all of you! Then again, it may not. And heaven knows, it will cost a lot. But, let's face it, you're going to need something really big-"

The salesdemon paused and blinked. It swallowed, hard.

"Oh no, not that," he whispered. "I have to be going. Sorry to have bothered you."

The demon blinked out of existence. Headbasher wisked through empty air. The large warrior sat down, hard.

"Doo-oof!"

"No!" Snarks cried in horror. "Not that! Even I don't deserve that!"

A hundred voices cried as one:

"It's Brownie Power!"

I looked up to see that our boat was filled, from stem to stern, with Brownies.

CHAPTER FIFTEEN

In a world that was totally objective and fair, size should make no difference in the worth of any individual or creature. But, then again, wizards should not have to work for a living, either.

—from The Teachings of Ebenezum, Volume XXIX

One of the small multitude jumped down from atop the tiller. The boatman stared after him, obviously in a state of shock. While most of the others were dressed more or less like our own Brownie, this one wore a cap and cloak of dark brown fur.

"You called, Tap?"

"Yes sir, Your Brownieship!" our Brownie responded.

"I don't believe it," Snarks muttered. "Tap?"

"I understand," His Brownieship intoned, "that some of this company have been giving you trouble, even, perhaps, implying things that might be detrimental to Browniekind?"

"Well, sir," Tap replied, "it's really only one of them, and I think he's only trying to be friendly."

"Now, now," His Brownieship chided, "that's just the positive side of your essentially optimistic Brownie nature talking. From what I've heard, things are far worse than that! We Brownies have been belittled far too long! Remember the Brownie Creed: We may be short, but we stand tall!"

Snarks looked longingly over the side of the boat. "Maybe I could learn to swim."

"Ah," His Brownieship said. "So this is the perpetrator."

Snarks edged toward the bow. "Maybe I could learn to breathe underwater."

"Now, now," His Brownieship urged. "My good fellow, we

don't want to hurt you. We just want to show you the positive nature of Brownie Power!"

"Maybe I should just jump," Snarks muttered. "I could always come up with a plan later."

"Come, fellows, let us entertain this newcomer with one of our inspirational cheers! What can you always use?"

"Brownie Power!" came the chorus.

"What always pays those dues?" His Brownieship continued.

"Brownie Power!" the chorus responded.

"What keeps away the blues?" His Brownieship was jumping up and down with excitement.

"Brownie Power!" The chorus was jumping as well. The boat began to rock.

"What should you always choose? No, no, fellow Brownies! Pull him back in the boat! You don't need to jump, friend demon! You'll grow to like this! That's what Brownie Power is all about!"

"Wuntvor?" Norei's hand gently touched my elbow. I turned to her, and found her face full of concern.

"I worry for your master."

I looked behind the young witch. Ebenezum sat at the farthestmost point of the bow, with his head over the side of the boat.

Of course! The sudden appearance of all these Brownies must be playing havoc with my master's malady. What kind of an apprentice was I to be watching some silly little drama when the wizard was in dire straits?

I moved quickly to my master. Kneeling by his side, I stuck my head, too, over the edge of the boat.

"Indeed," my master said as my head approached his. He appeared to be breathing quite normally. "One must be prepared for any eventuality, Wuntvor. When one has a malady such as mine, instant measures are often called for."

I asked the wizard if I should tell the Brownies to leave.

"On the contrary," Ebenezum replied. The end of his beard sent ripples through the water. "For the moment, I seem to be functioning quite well. And it occurs to me that, every time we have fought Guxx Unfufadoo and his demonic hordes, we have won because we had access to resources he could not foresee.

Thus, when we fought together in the Western Woods, the demon did not take into account my sorcerous skills. In our first big battle at Heemat's Hovel, we were aided by hordes of religious seekers and a minor demigod. In our second battle, we were joined by a legion of mythological beasts. No, Wuntvor, I think the Brownies should stay around. They might be Guxx's undoing."

"See?" a small voice said in my ear. "What did I say?"

I turned to see Tap, sitting on the edge of the boat, grinning at me.

"This third Brownie wish is going to be a big one!"

Ebenezum sneezed briefly. "Wunt," the wizard said. "While I am thus indisposed, I trust you to manage the business on board. If you need me, you know where I'll be."

I nodded briefly and stood, surveying the once again clear blue sky. I looked back over to the other end of the boat. The Brownies continued their ragged cheers. Snarks was pleading with Hendrek to bash him unconscious with Headbasher. "Have you no mercy?" the demon cried.

I turned and waved our Brownie back into the boat.

"So your name is Tap?" I asked, doing my best to distract the small fellow from talking to Ebenezum.

"Yes!" Tap exclaimed cheerfully. "All Brownies are named after shoemaking noises. You know—Tip, Tap, Hammer, Buckle. We take pride in our work!"

"Wuntvor?"

I turned at the sound of my beloved's voice. She smiled in a way I hadn't seen in far too long. I forgot Tap's enthusiasm, I forgot about the boat, I forgot the impending demon attack. The world fell away, lost in Norei's eyes.

"Wuntvor?" her perfect lips said. "In all this madness, we really haven't had time to say hello. I'm afraid I've been ignoring you. We've been away from each other for so long. Our relationship before was new; we still don't know each other all that well. Yet, on my journey here, I found myself thinking about you, over and over again. Now here we are, on a ship together, awaiting imminent death. These may be our last moments together!"

"Norei," I whispered. "There's never been anyone but you."
We kissed.

Norei broke it off abruptly. "If only I could get the image of a grackle out of my head! But, Wuntvor, you really meant—"

"By my grandmother's bones!" the boatman shouted. "Something else is coming!"

I looked aloft to see what had stirred the boatman from his state of shock. Something very large was flying our way. Something very large, with a human rider and a top hat.

It was Hubert.

He landed with a gentle splash to the starboard of the boat, and tipped his hat in our direction. "Don't worry," he said. "I can float. Dragons have a lot of hot air. But, if you don't mind, Alea would like to come on board and stretch her legs."

Alea jumped nimbly from the dragon's back onto the boat.

"Doom," Hendrek inquired. "Why are you returned already from Vushta?"

"Because, alas, we never made it there," Hubert replied. "It seems that Vushta is encircled with an impenetrable fog. I had to turn back. I couldn't see to land."

"Doom," Hendrek nodded grimly. "We will have to sail into it, then."

"We will have to sail where?" the boatman cried. "Not on this boat! First, you sneak aboard nonhuman passengers! Then, we are set upon by a plague of Brownies! Next, a dragon lands next to my boat. No thank you! I'm turning around! Not on my boat, you don't."

"But we have to!" I insisted. "The fate of the world may depend upon our reaching Vushta!"

"No!" The boatman shook his head. "I hear my home port calling."

"Let me handle this," Hubert remarked. "Did you ever consider how you would feel charbroiled?"

"Char-what?" the boatman asked. "Then again, my home port isn't calling all that loudly. You have to have some adventures in your life. That's what my aged grandmother used to say."

"Be of good cheer, boatman!" His Brownieship called. "You

have nothing to fear! You have Brownie Power on your side. Tell me Brownies: What's too good to ever refuse?"

"Brownie Power!"

"And what's one way you can never lose?"

"Brownie Power!"

"And what's better than eating—"

"Oh no you don't!" Snarks screamed, startling His Brownieship midcheer. "I've had enough of this Brownie business!"

The Brownies, who had been jumping about with their Brownie Power cheers, continued leaping and shouting. But there now seemed to be an angry edge to their voices.

"Fellow Brownies!" His Brownieship called out, quieting the multitude. "We have tried Positive Brownie Action on this lost soul. But, occasionally, some of the uninformed have too many barriers to accept the simple truths that we embody as very special magical creatures. It is time, therefore, to have a reasoned dialogue! Come, sir demon! Say what you will!"

Snarks was taken aback. "You want me to talk back to you?"

"Certainly, sir!" His Brownieship replied. "Whatever you want! It's your turn now!"

"Well," the demon said tentatively, "you are rather short."

"Yes, that is undeniably true," His Brownieship stated. "On the whole, we are much shorter than demons. An important point, well worth making."

"You're not going to disagree?" Snarks replied.

"No, no, it was a valid point."

"Well—-of course it was. All my points are valid."

"Even those two at the top of your head? Sorry, just a little Brownie humor, there. I'm sure you believe in everything you say. Are there any more points you would like to make?"

"Well, maybe not." Snarks seemed rather unnerved. I had a feeling this was the first time in his demonic existence that anyone had totally agreed with him. It was a strategy diabolic enough for the Netherhells!

"See how much better things are when you have a reasoned Brownie dialogue? That's what we call Brownie Power!" His Brownieship shouted. The rest of the Brownies cheered.

Snarks retreated within his hood.

"Wuntvor?" Norei whispered. I turned to look at her large green eyes, flecked with little bits of brown. "You were saying something, before the dragon came."

"Yes, my beloved?" I replied. Was this the moment I had been hoping for, when Norei would tell me she was mine?

"Oh!" another voice called. "There you are, Wuntie!"

"Wuntie?" Norei cried in a voice much louder than a whisper.

I shook my head to try and stop the ringing in my ear. Alea stood before me.

"Uh," I began. My mind raced, trying to think of something appropriate to say.

"Hello," I managed after a minute.

"Since we had to turn back from Vushta, I thought we could finally spend that time together—" Alea paused when she saw Norei's hand touching mine. "And who is this creature?"

I turned to Norei. She was staring at me with a look more severe than anything I had ever gotten from Ebenezum. I swallowed.

"Wuntvor?" Norei's words were clipped, as if they had been cut from her breath with knives. "Why is this woman calling you—" She paused to increase the intensity of her stare. "—Wuntie?"

"Well, um, er," I began.

Alea snorted derisively. "Wuntie, why don't you tell this newcomer what we meant to each other, back in Wizard's Woods?"

Norei gasped. "Wuntvor!" she cried. Her voice had heated considerably. "Is this true?"

"Well, er, um," I tried to explain.

"You let me waste all this time, thinking of you, building an image of the two of us together!" Norei recoiled from me in horror. "And to think I let you nuzzle me when you were a grackle!"

"A grackle?" Alea asked. "Oh, I knew a relationship with a wizard would be different! Oh, Wuntie, we could have had such fun! If only you hadn't started up with another woman the minute my back was turned!"

I had to stop this! "Well, um, that's not exactly—" I interjected.

"The minute your back was turned?" Norei repeated. "Wuntvor, you claimed but a moment ago that I was the only woman you had ever loved!"

"Wuntie!" Alea demanded. "Is this true?"

I had to say something! "Well, it is, well, I mean, but-"

How could this get any worse?

There was a noise like an earthquake beneath the boat.

No! It wasn't an earthquake. It was two hundred dancing Brownie feet!

Then there was an explosion. The boat seemed to have moved some distance.

Something huge reared its head at that spot in the ocean where we had been mere seconds before. This was the Netherhells' attack!

"Krrraakennn!" a mouth in a head the size of your average palace howled.

"Wow!" Hubert replied from above. "What an entrance!" He seemed to have taken flight about the time of the explosion.

The monster turned to regard us. It was a deep green color, close to the shade of the sea at twilight. At the moment, it pretty much took up most of the sea, anyway. Its giant, reptilian coils surrounded the boat, sending displaced water cascading across our decks.

"Yoouu moovvedd!" the huge head remarked. "Iii willl havvve tooo trryyy aaggaainnn!"

"Excuse me, you very large fellow?" The dragon shot out a spurt of flame to try to draw the monster's attention. "You are a Kraken, aren't you? Do you think we could have a little talk, reptile to reptile?"

The huge head glanced slowly up to regard the dragon. "Noooo!" it said at last. "Tiime tooo eeeeattt!"

"Come on, Brownies!" His Brownieship cried. "Time to do your stuff!"

The two hundred sets of tapping toes were at it again!

"Quick now, for Brownie Power! Let's try Plan B!"

I imagined the "B" stood for Brownie. While most of the little fellows maintained their relentless dancing rhythm, about a dozen or so split off to do some sort of alternate dance all their own.

The wizard sneezed mightily. "Norei!" he gasped. "Your counter spell!"

"Heavens, yes!" The young witch shook herself out of her shocked stupor. "Wuntvor! Join with me. We must be heard over the dancing!"

As one, we began the rhyme:

"Go, you creatures! Back down in the blue!
Go, you demons! Wakka doo wakka doo!"

"Hhuuhh?" the Kraken responded. "Wwellll, allll rriighttt!"

"No, you don't, you're all at sea!
The Kraken stays right here with me!"

It was only then that I saw the Kraken had a rider, a green hairy fellow wearing a helmet. The fellow pulled his helmet off. It was Guxx Unfufadoo!

"Geeee," the Kraken said. "Mmmaake uupp yoouuurrr mmindddss."

Guxx cried:

"Don't worry, that spell is obsolete!
All you should do now is eat!"

"Oooohhh," the Kraken remarked with a smile the length of your average river. "Goooddd. Mmmmrrrrfffllllxxxppttt."

An incredibly giant shoe had appeared to cover the Kraken's head.

The Kraken ate it.

"That's always been the problem, using that spell on omnivores," His Brownieship admitted. "Tap! Are you ready?"

"You've got it, Your Brownieship!" The smaller group of Brownies danced with redoubled fury.

Guxx jumped up and down on the Kraken's enormous coil and screamed in our direction:

"I've got you now, you wizardly pest!
In a Kraken's stomach you will rest!"

The wizard, for his part, seemed to be sneezing his life away in the bow of the boat.

Norei and Alea stood to either side of me, transfixed with terror.

"Wuntvor!" Norei shouted over the furious dancing. "I don't know any spells big enough to stop that thing!"

"Wuntie!" Alea sobbed. "What can we do?"

"Well, um, er," I replied.

There was another sizable explosion.

"What's going on here?" an authoritatively grating voice shouted. "I hope whoever brought us here has some gold!"

"Pop? Look down there! I don't think we should worry about gold at a time like this!"

It was the mythological creatures! Flying above us were the Rok, the Griffin, the Hippogriff, and half a dozen more. The Brownies had brought reinforcements!

"Waaiittt aa minnuute! Arrre theeessse creeeatuurress onnn thheee ootheerrr ssiide?"

Guxx screamed:

"What does it matter? Big or small?

Open your mouth and eat them all!"

The Kraken looked down at the demon. "Nnnnoooo. Iii knooowww theeeesse beeeaassstss offf aairrr annnd sseeea! Annnd mmyyy taaaiilll isss beeeinnggg wommbleddd! Theeyyy arrrre mmyyyy uuuunnionnn bbrrroothherrs! Iii hhaavvee aaa carrrdd ffoorr AFTAOMAIBAC!"

"Afteromay what?" Guxx shrieked as the Kraken's scales began to resubmerge.

"Yoouuu dooo nnott eeeatt youuuurrr uunnionn brrotherrs!" the Kraken stated as it settled into the sea.

"Oh, no!" Guxx cried. "Wait a minute while I—" The demon paused, its skin a pale green. There was a note of panic in its voice. "What rhymes with helmet?" Guxx was swallowed by the ocean depths.

The Brownies cheered as one.

"Now that—" Tap shouted, "that's what I call a wish!"

The Griffin landed on a bare spot on the deck. "So we meet again. We seem to have been displaced rather abruptly from the conclusion of our meeting. We had only managed to ratify the first fifty-seven of our demands. All I can say is, for your sake, I hope there's money in this!"

Hubert belly-flopped into the water. Distracted, the Griffin turned its head.

"Now, now!" the dragon exclaimed. "Let's look at what you've done here. Your intervention helped to prevent this very important party from getting eaten. Thus they can now travel to Vushta and save us all! What need have you of monetary reward? Soon, you'll have the thanks of a grateful world."

"Oh. That's true, isn't it?" the Griffin ruminated. "I still wouldn't mind some gold."

"We apologize for the abruptness of our spell," His Brownieship interjected. "That's just the way we are, I'm afraid. We Brownies like to make bold strokes, and stay right there in the center of the action. That's what we call Brownie Power!"

"Still," the Griffin mused, "this trip might not be a total waste. Tell me, friend Brownie, have you and your virtually limitless group of brothers considered the benefits of joining a union of mythological beasts?"

His Brownieship tapped his tiny foot. "We might indeed be interested, if we got the recognition we deserved. We were about to return you to your meeting. If you don't mind adding a hundred Brownies to your gathering, we'll be glad to talk!"

The Brownie's small hand briefly shook the Griffin's wing. His Brownieship turned to the others on the boat. "Tap's final wish is done. So we will say good-bye, with a final rousing cheer!"

"What small folks are making news?" His Brownieship cried.

"Brownie Power!" the others shouted back.

His Brownieship waved his tiny fists aloft. "Who's so cute you can't refuse?"

"Brownie Power!" the others cried, raising their tiny fists as well.

His Brownieship paused dramatically, took a deep breath, and shouted even louder than before:

"And who's the best at making shoes?"

"Brownie Power!"

The response was deafening.

"Next time you need to save the world, don't hesitate to call!" Tap called to us.

And the Brownies and mythological beasts were gone.

CHAPTER SIXTEEN

The sages put great stock in saying that every ending is truly a beginning, or every beginning an ending, or insisting that there are no endings or beginnings, or remarking that there is nothing new, and we are doomed to endlessly repeat ourselves. Or have I said all this before?

—from The Teachings of Ebenezum, Volume LXXXVII

"At last!" the wizard sighed. "I can breathe again!" He blew his nose profusely on the remains of his sleeve. When he was done there was nothing but quiet. The world seemed perfectly still.

"By my grandmother's beard," the boatman swore, "the wind has died completely."

"Doom," Hendrek remarked, rebagging his enchanted warclub. "Don't you mean your grandfather?" The boatman shook his head. "You don't know my grandmother. If there were beards to be grown in my family, she would have been the one to do it."

I looked out over the ocean. It was as if it had seen too much action with the Kraken and the others and now needed time to rest. We were totally becalmed.

"Indeed," the wizard remarked, much recovered. "Do you have any idea how long this lack of wind will last?"

The boatman frowned. "After what has happened here today, I refuse to predict anything."

The wizard nodded. "Too true. With what has happened here today, we may have turned nature completely around." He pulled on his beard reflectively. "But we must get to Vushta at once! Norei, can you help?"

The young witch bit her lip. "I fear I lack the experience. I can think of a wind increase spell that I might be able to recite from memory. But how can I increase a wind that isn't even there?"

"Hubert!" Alea called. "You remember the big finish we used to do at the Middle Kingdoms' Summer Fair, where you would drag the house across the courtyard? Could you tow the ship as well?"

The dragon sighed deeply. "Alas! On a better day, I would give it a try. But this day has taxed all my strength and cunning. You saw my last landing. Terrible! I am deeply in need of sustenance!"

The boatman looked alarmed. I hastily assured him that the dragon would eat no one with whom he was personally acquainted.

"Doom." Hendrek pointed beyond our bow. "The fog is coming."

The large warrior was right. A cloud seemed to skim silently across the ocean, headed in our direction. It was still some distance away, but the gray tendrils looked as if they were closing upon us rapidly.

Ebenezum picked up his pack. "If only I had not lost my library when we were captured by the Rok. When I left the Western Kingdoms, I brought a spell for every occasion." He pulled the three remaining books forth. "Now all that is left is a travel guide, a dictionary in case we wish to speak with Hubert in his native tongue, and this slim volume of household spells from my old mentor."

I thought back on our visit to Aunt Maggie, and how she had given Ebenezum a spell to sneeze his way free of death and his legion of ghosts. I remarked upon it to the wizard.

"It's too bad we don't have Aunt Maggie here to help us all over again," I added.

"Wuntvor!" The wizard jumped up so quickly that he almost fell out of the boat. "That's it!" He pounded the book in his hand. "We do have Aunt Maggie here! We adapted one of her crop increase spells to my needs, so that, instead of sneezing like a normal human being in dire distress, I would produce a superhuman sneeze! Such a sneeze is needed again!"

Quickly, the wizard told me what to look for in the book, and the slight adjustments that needed to be made. He removed his hat and placed it in his pack. He turned to the others.

"Snarks, take off your hood! Hendrek, wave that warclub about! Hubert, breathe what flame you can muster! Norei, ready your spell! And boatman, steer true, for all our lives depend on it!"

My master took a deep breath. "I must be careful to face the stern. Wuntvor! Repeat the spell of increase!" We all did as we were told. And my master reacted magnificently.

Thus did we sneeze our way to Vushta.

Or so we thought. The fog thinned as we approached land, and enough of a natural breeze arose to allow Ebenezum a rest.

But Vushta was not before us. I strained to see the city of a thousand forbidden delights, but all I could discern was a series of low, brown hills.

"Indeed." Ebenezum propped himself up on his elbows from his position at the bottom of the boat. "Perhaps I have blown us off course."

"Not according to my calculations, you haven't," the boatman replied. "On my grandmother's grave, as hard as you blew, I steered this boat straight. We should see the city at any moment. That is, of course, unless Vushta has moved." The boatman laughed at his own witticism.

The fog was clearing as we approached the shore. The low, brown hills were getting clearer. And there was something behind them, something darker. Perhaps I would be able to see the towers at any second, maybe even glimpse a forbidden desire or two taking place high atop some minaret.

"Oh, Wuntie!" Alea said close to my left ear. "It is such a wonderful city. You must let me show you the sights!"

I was aware of Norei, close by my right ear. "Alas, if only you had the time, Wuntvor. I fear we will all be much too busy defeating the Netherhells. But I guess that's something actors don't have to think about!"

"They couldn't have!" Snarks cried sharply, stopping any further exchange from the women at my sides.

The fog lifted entirely, and we all saw what Snarks's sharp demon eyes had discerned a moment before.

Behind the low hills of the shoreline was a black, gaping hole.

"It's gone!" Hubert, who had done his best to swim behind us, cried.

"Indeed." Ebenezum sat up entirely. "Are you sure?"

"Of course!" the dragon cried. "It was here two weeks ago when I left! But now Vushta is gone!"

"What does this mean?" Norei asked.

"It can mean but one thing." Ebenezum pulled grimly at his beard. "The Netherhells could not prevent us from getting to Vushta. Instead, they have prevented Vushta from coming to us."

The true horror of it overwhelmed me. "You mean," I whispered, "the Netherhells have stolen Vushta?"

The wizard nodded grimly. "It is their master stroke. They have pulled the sorcerous resources of Vushta beyond our grasp." He frowned and pulled upon his beard. "Now, I fear that nothing can stop the Forxnagel!"

"Doom!" Hendrek intoned.

For once, we all feared he might be right.

THE END

(or is it?)

A NIGHT IN THE NETHERHELLS

Book Three of the Ebenezum Series

Introduction

Idecided I wanted to be a science fiction writer in the fifth grade, at the Hoover Drive Elementary School in Greece, NY. My teacher, Mr. Fabry, would read to us at the end of the every day; lots of Mark Twain, as I recall, but a smattering of other writers, including, for a couple of glorious weeks somewhere in winter, THE INVISIBLE MAN by H.G. Wells. Whoo, doggies! First off, you have a guy who figures out how to become invisible (neat, huh?) and then he goes crazy (which, to my ten-year-old brain, was even neater.)

I immediately sought out SEVEN SCIENCE FICTION NOVELS OF H.G. WELLS, and read the first five of the seven. WAR OF THE WORLDS! THE TIME MACHINE! FIRST MEN IN THE MOON! THE INVISIBLE MAN (one more time!) And, best of all, THE ISLAND OF DR. MOREAU! Creepy beast men were even neater than being invisible. (The last two in that volume, FOOD OF THE GODS and IN THE DAYS OF THE COMET seemed a bit too dense for me at the time.) I was hooked. I read everything in the school library; the Heinlein "juveniles", and the "Paul French" (Isaac Asimov, actually) books, and bugged my parents to buy me every volume of TOM CORBETT, SPACE CADET. The town of Greece finally built a standing library (before that, we had only had a Bookmobile), and I quickly devoured their collection of sf books as well. In addition, some kind soul had donated all their old science fiction magazines to the library, so I'd bring home half a dozen issues of AMAZING, GALAXY, ANALOG and all the others and read them cover to cover. I moved on to the larger library in downtown Rochester NY. Ace and Ballantine and half a dozen other publishers put out new paperbacks every month. I ended up getting a paper route to support my habit.

So, I got the reading part of it down. But I wanted to write the stuff, too.

Back in the fifth grade, my teacher had the students put out their own mimeographed newspaper. It contained my first published story. "Frankenstein Meets Juliet." In junior high school, I wrote parodies of the stuff that me and my buddies read ("Doc Cabbage, the Man of Chartreuse") and eventually went on to make a couple of silent films, a pair of Tarzan takeoffs starring my best buddy, Glenn Garman, called "Garman of the Grapes" and "Garman Baby."

High school ended. College came and went. I'd write a short story now and then, send it out to the markets I'd find in Writer's Digest, and get rejected. Getting rejected is never any fun. But I realized, some six years out of college, that I wasn't really writing enough (a couple of stories a year) to say I was serious about breaking into publishing.

I attended a couple of science fiction workshops, including one run by Hal Clement, which bolstered my confidence to actually become a writer. As a result of the Clement workshop, I posted a notice posted at the Science Fantasy Bookstore in Cambridge, which led to the first meeting of a writers' group that would get together every couple weeks. Suddenly, I had deadlines and structure.

The second story I wrote in our new workshop was called "A Malady of Magicks." The basic idea came from "What if a wizard became allergic to magic?" But I didn't think the wizard should tell the tale. Instead, I invented a young apprentice, who would tell the great man's story, much like Dr. Watson does for Sherlock Holmes. I submitted the story to all the major markets, from highest paying down to the lowest. And the last, poorest paying market actually bought it – FANTASTIC, edited at the time by Ted White, who would go on to helm HEAVY METAL.

Six months later, the story saw print, and got picked by Lin Carter to appear in THE YEAR'S BEST FANTASY collection. More people read it, and I got requests to submit further Ebenezum stories to a pair of anthologies. Pretty soon I had a bunch of stories, all gently lampooning the fantasy novels I had grown up with. In those days, there were regular science fiction

conventions all year round up and down the east coast. These were great places to get known and to talk to real live science fiction editors. Which I did. It was at one of these conventions (at Disklave, I believe, held outside Washington D.C.) that Ginjer Buchanan, newly hired as an editor for Ace Books, asked me if I had anything she might be interested in. I suggested an Ebenezum trilogy. She liked the idea, and the books ended up selling quite well, going through multiple printings and really launching my funny fantasy career.

Someday, I hope to collect all the other Ebenezum stories that aren't in the original six-book series into a collection of their own. If these books do well in their new e-format, that just might happen.

But, in the meantime, this series, which started with *A Malady of Magicks*, is where it all began. I hope you enjoy it.

Craig Shaw Gardner
May 2013

ACKNOWLEDGMENTS

The wizard and I go back a long way. I started writing about Ebenezum "way back" in 1977. (In fact, my first major published story was "A Malady of Magicks" in the October 1978 issue of Fantastic.) Now, almost ten years later, the Ebenezum Trilogy is finished and in your hands. I couldn't have done it without the help, encouragement, and general all-around browbeating of a lot of people, including Ted White, Orson Scott Card, Marvin Kaye, Lin Carter and Jim Frenkel, who bought the original short stories; my ever-encouraging agent Merrilee Heifetz; and my editor with the great sense of humor (i.e., she likes my stuff), Ginjer Buchanan—along with the rest of the incredibly helpful editorial staff at Ace/Berkley. Thanks, and a tip of Hubert's top hat, are also due to Mary Aldridge, Michael Barton, Stephanie Bendell, Victoria Bolles, Richard Bowker, Jeffrey A. Carver, Amy Sue Chase, Caryl Fox, Charles L. Grant, Heather Heitkamp, Maggie Ittelson, Spike MacPhee, Jonathan Ostrowsky, Alan Ryan, Charlotte Young and Tina Zannieri, for services above and beyond the call of duty.

And then there's my dedication:
This one's for Elisabeth
especially without whom...

CHAPTER ONE

Contrary to rumor, working side by side with a group of fellow wizards is not the most unpleasant task in which a magician might participate. In fact, I can think of numerous other experiences, such as breaking both arms and legs while being pursued by a ravenous demon, which, under certain conditions, could conceivably be even worse.

—from The Teachings of Ebenezum, Volume XXII

Vushta was gone.

We stood on the rocky shore of the Inland Sea and stared at the spot where once the greatest city in all the world had reached its towers to touch the sky. How could an entire city simply vanish? I had looked forward all my short life to visiting Vushta, city of a thousand forbidden delights, where great knowledge and great temptation go hand in hand. How I had longed to see the great University of Wizards, and walk the whole length of the Grand Bazaar, and, just perhaps, skirt a corner of the Pleasure District, where, it is whispered, brave men had yielded to their baser drives and had never been seen again. But no, the university, the bazaar, even, yes, the Pleasure District, were beyond me now. Of all the cities in the world, why was Vushta the one to go?

The boatman had left the seven of us here, on the shore which once led to the city that was the goal of our quest. Each of us had had a reason to come on this perilous journey, to come at last to Vushta, a place where we might realize our hopes and cure our ills. Now we were all silent, staring at the empty sky, waiting, perhaps, for the wind to tell us what to do.

"Doom," intoned Hendrek, the large warrior at my side. His great bronze breastplate, which housed a girth fully as wide as he was tall, glinted blindingly in the midday sun. All shade had gone with the city and the wind brought nothing but choking dust.

Hendrek nervously stroked the bag that held his weapon, the cursed war club Headbasher, which no man could own, but only rent. His mood, I could tell, fit the rest of our small party. The wizard Ebenezum, once the greatest mage in all the Western Kingdoms, and the leader of our quest, stroked his long, white beard reflectively, the tattered remains of his once tasteful robes flapping in the unnatural breeze. The others in our party watched his grim countenance—the demon Snarks, Hubert the dragon and his beautiful companion, Alea, and Norei, the wondrous young witch—all looked at my master, waiting for a decision, or a sneeze.

But the sorcerer breathed deeply, his malady unaffected. If magic had taken Vushta away, it had gone with the city.

The warrior Hendrek took a deep breath in turn. Once again his great voice reverberated across the wasteland.

"Doom!"

"I beg your pardon?" answered a voice from somewhere.

My master waved us all to silence. I held my breath, anxious to hear other words rise from the dust. But the mysterious voice said no more.

"Hendrek," my master said after a moment. "Repeat your curse."

The warrior did as the wizard instructed.

"Doom!"

"Oh!" called the mysterious speaker. "Doom! You see, I thought you were saying 'dune'! Well, there certainly are a lot of them around now, nothing but sand. You'd hardly believe there was a city here only the other day. Still, I didn't know if I wanted to start a conversation with someone who pointed at piles of sand and said 'dune'! But 'doom'? Well, that's another matter. Doom implies angst. I'll always talk to somebody about angst!"

The demon Snarks muttered darkly from deep within his robes. The stranger's monologue had returned the rest of us to shocked silence.

"There!" Ebenezum pointed. From out of the dust before us a figure emerged, clad all in robes as red as blood.

Hendrek pulled his enchanted weapon from his sack. Ebenezum rapidly retreated and held his nose.

"Doom!" Hendrek repeated.

"Yes, isn't it?" the approaching man replied. "Or at least it was the doom of Vushta. I assume that's what you folks came for, to visit Vushta. It's a pity you weren't informed that it was no longer here. But then again, none of us were informed that it was going. One minute there it was, just over the hill, and the next..." The newcomer waved a bony hand.

Ebenezum gestured at Hendrek to rebag his club. The wizard stepped forward as the warrior complied.

"Indeed," Ebenezum said. "Have we not met before?"

The newcomer paused a few paces before us. He was a gaunt man, well on in years, his weathered skin pressed tight against skull and finger bones. His whole body—face, hands, and clothes—was covered by a fine layer of dust, which made him appear more ancient still.

"It is possible." The newcomer nodded. "For have we all not met, if not in this life, then on some other plane, or in some prior existence, or perhaps even in the future? For what is time, but an arbitrary structure we mortals—"

"Yes, of course we have met!" Ebenezum cut the other's rambling short. "Are you not an instructor at the Greater Vushta Academy of Magic and Sorcery?"

"Instructor?" The man frowned. "I am a full professor in the college of wizards!"

"Ah, yes." Ebenezum scratched his mustache in thought. "Pardon my oversight. I had forgotten your eminence."

"Quite all right." The old professor smiled again. "Oversight, unfortunately, is common to us all. Reaching for the stars, we lost sight of what is within our grasp. Did I mention that I might have been able to save Vushta? As you see, even a full professor is capable of occasional error. What matters, though, is how we cope with our shortcomings once we discover—"

"Indeed," Ebenezum said with somewhat more force than usual. "And is your name Snorphosio?"

"Why, yes," the elder replied in surprise. "Although what is truly in a name? Is it but a label we hang upon our souls, or do those few syllables somehow imbue us with their essence, in order that we—"

"Indeed!" Ebenezum cried, clasping his hands together so that they might not accidentally do some damage to the old gentleman "And is not your field of expertise theoretical magic?"

"Why, yes." Snorphosio's smile grew even broader. "I like to look at magic in the broadest possible sense. Just what is magic? How does it differ from real life? Or is magic just real life under another name? Or are we just imagining that magic exists? Or are we imagining that real life—"

"I was a student of yours," Ebenezum cut in this time.

"Really!" Snorphosio was delighted. "Did you take 'Basic Theory' or 'Conjuring the Unconjurable'? Do you remember my famous lecture: 'If a Magician Pulls a Rabbit From a Hat, But There Is No Hat, Is There Then No Rabbit?' Oh, I tell you, I always was one for catchy titles."

"Perhaps," my master remarked, "you can tell us what happened to Vushta."

"Vushta?" The professor coughed. "Oh dear, it's gone. The entire city, buildings, streets, people, animals, every single one of the forbidden delights, sucked into the earth. I could hear their screams when it happened. Horrible!"

"Indeed." My master fixed the professor with his best interrogatory stare. "How did you manage to escape?"

"Easy enough." Snorphosio's smile returned. "I wasn't there. I was visiting East Vushta. Charming little town." The old man peered at Ebenezum. "Hmm. You're getting on in years. Probably a senior wizard by now? East Vushta hadn't really grown up yet when you were in school, had it? Lovely place. Many people have been building small castles there to get out of the rush of the city. That was always a problem with Vushta, you know. It's not easy living in the middle of a thousand forbidden delights, let me tell you!"

"If you could," Ebenezum suggested, "perhaps go into the details of the city's disappearance?"

The frown reappeared on Snorphosio's face. "I'll tell you what little I know. I was sitting in a tavern at the time, in East Vushta, that is. Of course, what I know about this situation is probably more than most other people know. Degrees of knowledge are always relative, aren't they? It reminds me of the parable about the blind men and the dragon—"

Hubert snorted from where he stood some distance down the beach. "Must we?" the dragon remarked. "I really detest those old stories. Talk about species stereotyping!"

The professor waved cheerfully at the dragon. "Sorry. Didn't see you there. My eyes, you know, are not as strong... Still, I suppose that's no excuse for spreading ancient tales." Snorphosio sighed. "The world has changed so much in my day. Once dragons did nothing but hide in caves and collect maidens. Now"—the old man wheezed with laughter—"can you imagine, I actually saw one of the big lizards try to sing in a vaudeville act?"

"Big lizards?" Hubert rumbled. "Alea, if you would hand me the satchel?"

The dragon's beautiful assistant bounced over to him, her blond curls dazzling in the sun. Hubert rummaged quickly through his case, extracting a top hat with one purple claw. He placed the hat atop his head and snorted a cloud of smoke.

"Does this look familiar?" Hubert remarked dryly. Snorphosio scratched at his chin in consternation. "Damsel and Dragon?" He cleared his throat and looked about as if he might disappear back into the dust. "Oh dear. Well, perhaps I didn't catch you on one of your best nights. All criticism is subjective, as you know. One man's opinion—"

"Indeed!" Ebenezum broke in again. The wizard had backed off for a moment when Hubert stepped in. Because of the nature of his malady, he had to keep his distance from the dragon. Still, this was an emergency. If the old man got off on enough of a tangent, we'd never find out what happened to Vushta.

"I'm sure you can both discuss the merits of the Vushta stage with more enlightenment once we have discovered what happened to Vushta!" the wizard continued. "Snorphosio, if you would be so kind?"

"Of course!" The professor self-consciously brushed the dust from his all-too-red robes. "I did not mean to offend. Still, those in the performing arts must remember that the audience views them subjectively, and inasmuch—"

"Subjectively!" Hubert roared. "That's the problem with you intellectuals. Great art appeals directly to the emotions! Listen to this! Number seven, damsel!"

Alea began to sing in a high, clear soprano as Hubert beat time with his tail.

"Oh, there might be a thousand forbidden delights, but my favorite delight is you—"

"Enough!" Ebenezum cried as he ran between professor and dragon. "Can't you see—can't you—"

My master, the great wizard Ebenezum, fell to the ground in a sneezing fit.

Snarks had his hood off in an instant. "This is impossible! I've known both humans and demons to be longwinded, but this fellow has the lungs of an elephant! And talk about bad taste in clothes!"

My beloved Norei touched my left shoulder. My heartbeat raced.

"Wuntvor!" she cried in a voice more musical than the Vushta stage might ever produce. "We have to do something!"

"A demon's work is never done." Snarks pushed back his sleeves to reveal thin green arms. "Let's drag the wizard out of there."

As briefly as possible, I pointed out to Snarks why this might not be such a good idea. Some weeks past, in the Western Kingdoms where my master maintained his practice, he had accidentally loosed a particularly fierce demon by the name of Guxx Unfufadoo. My master had managed to send that foul fiend back to the Netherhells from whence he had come, but it had cost the wizard dearly. Now, whenever he encountered anything demonic or magical in nature, he would break out in a fit of uncontrollable sneezing. Thus had his current situation been brought about by his proximity to a dragon. If the wizard's proximity to magic ailed him, it did not make sense to have another magical creature come to his aid.

Snarks rolled his sleeves back down. "A demon's work is never appreciated. 'Twas ever thus. Why do you think they kicked me out of the Netherhells in the first place?"

I knew the answer to that, but my master was sneezing far too much for me to reply. I turned to Hendrek for aid. The large warrior and I dragged Ebenezum to a safe distance.

Both Snorphosio and Hubert looked temporarily abashed at what they had caused to happen to my master. Now, I thought, it was time to get to the bottom of all this. And since my master was indisposed, I would have to act in his stead.

"Indeed," I began. "And just what has happened to Vushta?"

"In a physical, or in a metaphorical, sense?" Snorphosio inquired. "Inexact questions, I am afraid, are one of the pitfalls of modern civilization. How many wars could be avoided if we might only learn—"

"Indeed!" I said, rather more loudly. I feared that, should the professor go on at much greater length, I would not be able to match my master's restraint. I glanced meaningfully at Hendrek. The warrior pulled the doomed club Headbasher from its restraining sack.

"Where did Vushta go?" I asked.

Snorphosio looked at the war club with some alarm. "Now see here, you wouldn't think of using—"

"Doom!" Hendrek remarked. He let the tip of Headbasher fall to the ground. The earth shook.

"Oh," Snorphosio intoned. "Vushta went down."

"Doom!" Hendrek reiterated. "Down?"

"Yes, down. Beneath the earth." The professor's voice dropped to a whisper. "I fear it has been taken by the Netherhells."

Snarks gave a muted cheer. The rest of our company glared at him.

"Sorry," the demon said, embarrassed. "Old habits."

"Oh, Wuntie!" Alea ran up to me breathlessly. "What a diplomat!"

I smiled somewhat foolishly. Alea was an attractive young woman, and, as a professional vaudeville entertainer from Vushta, much more worldly than myself. And yet, long ago, when I was first apprenticed to Ebenezum, Alea and I had shared an innocent young love. Even now, gazing deep into her blue eyes—

"Wuntvor!" Norei was at my side again. "We must have a plan. What shall we do?"

"Yes, Wuntie!" Alea chimed in. "You've gotten us this far. What next?"

I cleared my throat. The young women pressed on either side of me, both far too close. Norei sometimes had trouble with Alea's pet names for me, or the way Alea would refer to things the two of us had done long ago, or the way Alea occasionally treated me as her own personal property. It didn't matter how often I explained that everything that had happened with Alea occurred before I had even met Norei. Well, almost everything. Could I help it if Alea was an attractive and enthusiastic woman? According to Norei, I certainly could.

Norei pinched the flesh of my upper arm in a manner almost too hard to be playful. But I knew that the events around us here had taken a great toll on the young witch, as surely as I knew that she was my own true love. And, unlike my childish infatuation with Alea, what I felt for Norei was a truly mature love, for in the weeks we had been on our quest I had gained experience, responsibility, and insight.

"Doom!" Hendrek said to the three of us. "What shall we do now?"

I had no idea.

"Indeed," I said, stalling for time.

There was a honking sound behind me. I spun about, my stout oak walking staff ready to be used as a weapon if need be. Ebenezum blew mightily into his robes.

"Indeed," the wizard remarked, looking past our party to the somewhat befuddled Snorphosio. "So, if I heard you correctly, the Netherhells have captured Vushta?"

The aged professor nodded rapidly. "That is my surmise. Of course, I am basing this theory upon incomplete evidence. Perhaps my fears are ungrounded. Perhaps something less dreadful has happened to my city than I suspect, some other rationale may be divined from the evidence at hand. For you see"—Snorphosio paused, his voice dropping to a conspiratorial whisper—"there is one final event that has not yet occurred, one last bit of evidence that, were it to be untrue, would show me for the pessimist that I am. Without this last event, there is still hope. Perhaps Vushta can still be saved. Perhaps all of the city's inhabitants will not be cursed to eternal, unspeakable damnation, the true extent of which is probably beyond human imagining. If this final catastrophe does not occur, we can still hold onto a thin ray of hope that perhaps the great city, with all its learning, its diverse people, its thousand forbidden delights, might yet be rescued. But, should this event occur..." Snorphosio's voice dropped away, as if the final consequences might be too horrible to even say aloud.

The silence that followed was shattered by a great rumble beneath our feet. We had been through Netherhells-inspired earthquakes before. I looked for something to hold onto, but there was nothing around us but piles of sand.

The quake ended before I could even lose my footing. As I turned to the others, another loud noise erupted from beyond the dunes, a great, belching roar, as if the earth itself had swallowed something and found that it disagreed with its digestion.

Snorphosio had fallen to the dirt. Although the quake had passed, he was still trembling violently.

"That was the event I was waiting for," the old man managed after a moment.

"Doom," Hendrek replied.

Snorphosio pushed his hands against the sand to stop his spasms. He nodded at last.

"All is lost. Vushta is gone forever."

CHAPTER TWO

Why don't you conjure a legendary city, full of magic spells and mystic beasts, out of thin air?" the uninformed client asks. "Well, where would you put it?" the wise wizard replies. "Have you seen the price of real estate?

—from Ebenezum the Wizard's Handy Guide to Better Wizard/Client Relationships, fourth edition

Vushta was gone forever.

"Indeed," my master said to the cowering Snorphosio. "Are we then the only wizards left in all of Vushta?"

"In all of Vushta, yes, we are the only wizards that remain." The old professor regained his feet somewhat unsteadily. He dusted at his sleeves halfheartedly. "Of course, there are also wizards in East Vushta, some two hills over, but whether East Vushta is part of the greater metropolis has always been open to debate. At the moment, I would imagine that East Vushta is quite separate from the rest of the city." He paused to stare off into the dust. "Yes. Quite separate indeed."

Ebenezum nodded and scratched beneath his wizard's cap. "Wuntvor, shoulder your pack. We all need a place to spend the night. I think East Vushta shall do nicely."

I did as my master bade. The pack, which had once bulged with a large number of sorcerous tomes and arcane paraphernalia, was now much lighter due to the loss of almost the entire contents when I was carried off by a large, mythological bird in one of our more recent adventures. Ebenezum had hoped to replace what he had lost once we reached the fabled centers of learning in Vushta. But that, along with most of the rest of our plans, now seemed futile.

I looked to my master, once the greatest mage in all the Western Kingdoms, as he led our party in a march across the sand. Even though his clothes were torn, his beard matted, his skin burned red by the sun, still he looked every inch the master magician. The casual observer would never have guessed the sorcerer suffered from a malady so great that he must shun all magic; indeed, that the malady affected him to such an extent that he had embarked on a long and arduous journey to seek a cure, even if he had to travel to far, fabled Vushta before he found the knowledge he sought.

And now that there was no more far, fabled Vushta? You would never know it in the way he strode across the dunes, trailed by Snorphosio, who continued to discuss various fine points of sorcery as if some of the others in our party could understand him. Hendrek came next, ever wary, his hand constantly on the sack that carried his enchanted club, a weapon that saw him forever plagued by demons demanding rental payments. He had sought Vushta as well, to free him from Headbasher's dire curse.

All of us had had similar hopes and plans embodied in Vushta. But there had been a further bond holding us together, for, as we won our way closer to Vushta, we discovered an insidious plot on the part of the Netherhells. No longer were these demons satisfied with ruling the world below the earth. No, now they plotted to conquer the surface world as well and subject us all to their fiendish tyranny. Our only hope to stop them was to reach Vushta and alert the Greater Vushta Academy of Magic and Sorcery of the danger. Only with the massed might of the greatest wizards in all the world could we hope to defeat the Netherhells.

A chill ran through my sundrenched frame. Until now, I had not realized the true enormity of our catastrophe. Vushta was no more. Was there no hope? Had the Netherhells won?

Then we climbed to the top of the second hill and I saw the most magnificent city in the world.

"East Vushta," Snorphosio remarked. "I never realized how small it was until Vushta disappeared."

Small? I might call the vista before us many things, but

"small" was not among them. The city seemed to take up the whole valley. Graceful towers of a dozen different colors rose a full three stories above the earth. Furthermore, these great structures were interspersed among literally hundreds of smaller dwellings. There might be a thousand people living here, maybe more. It was enough to take your breath away.

Still, I felt a pang of loss through my sense of wonder. If this vast expanse was only East Vushta, what had the greater city looked like? I felt a prickling sensation at the back of my neck, as if I were being tickled by the ghost of the last, lingering forbidden delight. I was so close! Now, perhaps, Vushta was gone forever!

So intent was I on the sight before me that I did not watch my feet. It was perfectly natural, then, that I should bump into Hendrek's massive bulk, the same bulk that prevented both of us from losing our balance and tumbling down the hill.

"Doom," Hendrek remarked dourly, not noticeably fazed by my abrupt arrival. "Now I will never be free of my cursed war club."

Snarks walked up and removed his hood. "Don't fret there, Hendy. My demon-trained senses tell me we have not yet found out all we need to know about Vushta's disappearance."

Hope suddenly returned to my despairing frame. I turned to Snarks. "You have discerned some clue as to the Netherhells' plans?"

The demon shook his bright green head. "I just know the way the folks down below work." He pointed forward to Snorphosio. "My theory is that the Netherhells rejected this guy on purpose. Why else would they steal the city only when he was out of town?"

I nodded slowly, not absolutely convinced. Still, Snarks's surmise did have a certain fiendish logic behind it. Snarks was certainly familiar with the ways of the Netherhells. After all, he had been raised there, though he was different from other demons. Snarks's mother had been badly frightened by demon politicians shortly before he was born. The traumatic experience caused Snarks to develop an overwhelming need to tell the truth, something that can be quite crippling when you're a professional demon. Eventually, it led to Snarks's banishment from the Netherhells, a move which, after hearing some of the demon's choicer remarks, even I could sympathize with.

"Excellent!" my master's voice cried from far up the path we had walked since coming to the valley. He pounded Snorphosio heartily upon the back. Snorphosio almost fell down the hill.

"Wuntvor!" the wizard called to me. "Hurry the others! We must enter East Vushta with all haste! There is still hope!"

I knew my master would think of something! We had come too far on our journey, overcome too many perils. A simple vanished city was not enough to stop someone of Ebenezum's skill and resourcefulness. I ran down the hill to join the mage. So the Netherhells had swallowed Vushta! We would reach down and pull it back to its rightful place, out there amidst the sand.

"Do you have a plan, master?" I cried breathlessly as I slid on a patch of loose earth, tumbling past both wizard and professor.

"Indeed," Ebenezum replied as he walked down to the point where I once again picked up myself and my pack. "As you heard, Wunt, the Greater Vushta Academy of Magic and Sorcery has gone with the rest of the city. The demons apparently wished to imprison all the great mages of this sprawling metropolis, probably to counter any resistance to their fiendish plans for dominance of the surface world. Fortunately for us, demons tend to be very shortsighted. It probably has something to do with living your whole life underground."

"Demonic thought processes?" Snorphosio contributed as my master paused to take a breath. "Do demons really think? It's a thorny issue. Did you know their brains are generally green in color? This whole Netherhells thing may not be their fault, after all. How would we think with a green—"

"Indeed!" Ebenezum broke in. "Snorphosio was good enough to inform me as to a point on which I had been ignorant. While the demons have taken the Greater Vushta Academy of Magic and Sorcery to no one knows where, they have completely ignored East Vushta. And, by doing so, they have completely ignored the Greater Vushta Academy of Magic and Sorcery Extension Program at East Vushta!"

"Extension program?" I replied, quite confused by my master's rush of words.

"Why, yes," Snorphosio beamed. "We teach courses there mostly at night, for part-time wizards. Still, we pride ourselves on maintaining the same strict standards for graduating mages that we observe at the day school. Of course, our facilities are somewhat limited at the East Vushta location—"

"That may be," Ebenezum broke in, "but there are facilities! And there are wizards, both instructors and students, who have come far enough along with their studies. I tell you, Wunt, it might be possible to save Vushta after all!"

"Might it?" Snorphosio mused. "Well, I suppose anything might be possible. That's a problem with theory, you know—the possibilities are endless. Still, when you deal with the fine line between possibility and probability—"

"Indeed!" my master cried. "Lead us to the extension program!"

Snorphosio cheerfully walked to the head of our party, remarking at some length on the responsibilities of leadership, and the nature of responsibility, and the responsibility we all have to nature, and how leadership within nature makes animals responsible. As he began a discourse on whether or not animals were responsible to nature within their leadership capacity, we came to a building even more imposing than any we had already seen.

East Vushta was far different from any city I had ever visited. In fact, I realized it was the first group of buildings I had walked through that could truly be called "a city." House followed house, each one made of some colorful stone or preheated brick. There was none of the mud or straw so prevalent in the Western Kingdoms, and none of the one-room hovels that I had lived in most of my life. Dwellings here were built to sprawl and impress. I gazed about me in fascination as we walked to the center of the city. It was almost enough to make Snorphosio's monologue sound interesting.

And now we had come to a large bright red structure, the same color as the old professor's robes.

Snorphosio turned to the rest of our group.

"Gentlemen!" he began. "Um, gentlemen and ladies—um—that is, gentlemen and ladies and assorted nonhumans! Welcome to the Greater Vushta Academy of Magic and Sorcery. Or at least the East Vushta division of the Greater Vushta Academy—no, come to think of it, this is now the entire Greater Vushta—"

"Well?" my master interrupted. "Are you going to invite us in?"

"Why, certainly," Snorphosio replied. "Actually, there isn't all that much to see. Well, the dragon may have to wait outside. Low ceilings, you know. But he can follow our progress if he cares to look through the upper-story windows—"

"Indeed," Ebenezum remarked, knocking on the structure's great oak door.

There was no immediate answer, so Ebenezum knocked again. This time he was rewarded by a great deal of creaking and banging from somewhere within.

A small window opened in the middle of the door.

"Go away!" cried a heavily mustached face. The window shutter slammed shut.

"Hmmm." My master tugged at his beard. "Snorphosio. If you would be so kind?" He indicated the door.

"Certainly." Snorphosio knocked in turn. There was no answer.

My master stepped away from the door. "Hendrek," he called to the large warrior by my side. "I believe this is a job for you."

"Doom," Hendrek murmured as he loosed Headbasher from its sack. He bumped it lightly against the door three times. The door shook. And the small window opened again.

"We don't want any!" the face screamed.

"Doom!" Hendrek replied as he brandished his club.

"Oh," the face remarked. "Well, then again, perhaps we do."

There was a great deal more banging from within. Then the door swung open. The man inside cowered in a corner.

"Spare me!" he cried. "For some reason, they left me in charge. And I'm not even a wizard! They're cowards, every sorcerous one of them! I'll be good, I promise. Demon kind forever!"

"Indeed," Ebenezum said, stepping within. "You say that all the wizards have left?"

"Yes!" the other man cried. "And a good thing, too, for what is the pitiful might of wizards compared to the overwhelming strength of demons like... The man's voice faded as he peered at Ebenezum through the gloom. "Wait a second! You're not demons!"

"Well." Ebenezum stroked his mustache. "At least some of us are not."

"Why do you let me go on and on, making a fool of myself? Some people! It's no wonder they left me in charge here, for they knew of my keen wit and my ability to make instant decisions."

The fellow peered more closely at my master's soiled robes. He paused to clear his throat. "Don't get me wrong! Wizards are truly wonderful people. I've worked side by side with them all my life. I respect them even more since they left me in charge. They obviously realize that I'm the only one with the foresight to deal with a situation like this."

"Indeed," Ebenezum replied. "And could you tell me where the other wizards have gone?"

"Gone?" He made an all-encompassing wave with his hands. "Why, home, of course. As I would have done, had not my home been swallowed by the Netherhells!" The mustached man shivered.

"I see. And do you have a list of their whereabouts?" "Why, certainly. You are a wizard yourself, aren't you, sir? I pride myself on always being able to spot a wizard. Of course, with your proud bearing and magnificent speaking voice, you were all too easy to spot." The mustached man reached within his tunic. "Here. This parchment should give you everything you need. I would stay and chat with you further, but, now that you have come to take possession of the college, I have important business elsewhere. Should you desire any more, don't hesitate to ask next time you see me. Klothus is the name, service is my game."

Klothus nodded, smiled, and walked rapidly toward the door.

Snarks removed his hood to look around. "So this is what

a wizards' college looks like. Well, I certainly hope the fellows who built this place know more about magic than they do about decorating."

Klothus gave a small cry when he spotted Snarks's shiny green head, complete with horns.

"Oh, no!" he gasped. "Why, you are demons after all! And here you have, by trickery, gained information about the remaining wizards' whereabouts! Well, I never would have given it to you voluntarily, let me tell you!" Klothus looked around surreptitiously. "Now that it's out, though, it's probably just as well you have it. You'll get the mess over with right away, won't you? I'm sorry I don't have any other worthwhile information. No information at all. So I guess I'll just be running along, and let you demons take over. I tell you, in a way I'm really looking forward to a change in government. The way the wizards ran this city was laughable." But Klothus was not laughing as he shuffled through the doorway.

"I don't think you should leave just yet," said a voice from on high.

Klothus looked up at Hubert. "They've enlisted dragons, too? I had no idea this thing was so large. I admire your planning. I really do. But I must be off—oh—someplace else. Anyplace else…" Klothus's voice died in his throat as he watched thick smoke trickle from Hubert's nostrils.

"I think the most important place is right here," the dragon rumbled.

"You may be right," Klothus remarked, backing into the college. "I'm sure whatever you have to say is quite correct." He turned to the rest of us. "This fellow doesn't breathe fire indoors, does he?"

"Indeed!" Ebenezum, carefully keeping his distance from Snarks and Hubert, called from across the room. "However, since you are happy to cooperate with us, I'm sure the dragon's fire will not be necessary."

"So glad to hear that," Klothus responded. "And how may I serve you?"

"As you have discerned," Ebenezum replied, "most of us are new to the city. Therefore, a list of the remaining wizards' whereabouts does us little good without either a map or someone with a good knowledge of the surroundings. We shall need you to go and personally summon the wizards."

"Oh, is that all?" Klothus smiled craftily. "I shall go right away. If you gentle demons will excuse me."

"Doom!" the large warrior grumbled. "We are not—"

"Wait!" Ebenezum cried. "To lighten your burden of responsibility, Hendrek will accompany you."

Klothus's smile vanished. "Why, of course, show someone else the city while I'm at it. Always glad to oblige!"

"Hubert!" my master called to the dragon. "While they are about their business, I think you would do well to circle East Vushta for signs of further demonic activity. Simply because the Netherhells have spared this location so far does not mean that they will continue to do so."

Hubert tipped his hat to the wizard, then handed it to Alea. He turned and launched himself aloft.

Alea waved at the retreating dragon. "Look at that, Wuntie! What dramatic style!"

"Indeed," Ebenezum continued. "And while the rest of you are busy on your various errands, Snorphosio and I will quickly search this place to see what magical materials are still at hand. Go now, Klothus! Tell the wizards to meet us here within the hour."

"Snorphosio?" Klothus exclaimed. "I did not realize Snorphosio was among your number. You could not possibly be in league with demons! Snorphosio is not the type. How do you expect me to draw the proper conclusions if you do not give me all the information?"

"Doom," Hendrek remarked as he approached the gray clad Klothus. The other man turned and hurried through the door.

"Wuntvor?" Norei was at my side. I felt her hand brush against my hip. It was good, I thought, to have my young witch near in this time of trial.

"Oh, Wuntie!" Alea was at my other side. Her blond hair shone even in the filtered sunlight here in the hall. The room had become uncomfortably warm for so late in the year.

"I shall need all of you as well," the wizard called. "We

must search as much of the college as we can before I meet with the other wizards. Wuntvor will take the left corridor, Norei the right, Alea will search the grounds, Snarks the guardhouse, and Snorphosio will see what implements are left in the basement vaults."

"How did you know?" Snorphosio asked. "I must say, you are very perceptive for a younger wizard. I am quite astounded that you discerned that even a college this humble would have an underground vault. Did you see some secret panel, or perhaps some mud of a different color, that led you to suspect some underground—"

"Indeed," Ebenezum interrupted with a wave of his hand. "There are always basement vaults. It is how wizards think. Now go, and report back to me with whatever you find."

"Wizards' thought processes," Snorphosio mused as he walked toward a flight of stairs that led downwards at the rear of the hall. "Now that is grounds for conjecture. How does magic affect thought? How does thought affect magic? How does thinking about magic affect magical thought? How does magical thought affect..." His voice was lost as he descended the stairs.

"Indeed," Ebenezum remarked dourly. "Hurry with your search, Wuntvor. I may need you to fetch the professor from down below."

There was one thing I had to know before I left.

"Do you have a plan?" I asked.

Ebenezum pulled reflectively at his beard. "I will by the time the other wizards arrive. The Netherhells have already done their worst. In an hour, Wuntvor, we begin the counterattack!"

CHAPTER THREE

The professional wizard, it is said, should always watch his hands. Actually, the truly professional wizard should watch a great many other things as well, including the reactions of his audience, the door or window that constitutes the nearest exit, and, perhaps most important, the constantly fluctuating interest rates on his retirement account in the First Bank of Vushta.

—from The Teachings of Ebenezum, Volume VI

I walked quickly through the wizards' college, passing from the entranceway into a grand hall high enough to accommodate even Hubert. The whole place was made of stone. Huge blocks had been piled atop one another to make vaulting hallways and even larger rooms. As I walked, I wondered if this whole place might have been built by magic; that perhaps some sorcerer as great as Ebenezum had waved his hands over a patch of ground, and the stones before him had rearranged themselves into this magnificent structure.

It certainly seemed possible. No matter how this place had come to be, it gave one pause for thought. This college of wizards was a place of magic, and within its walls, all things were possible. What wonders had been conjured in this great room through which I now passed? Perhaps, on this pink-and-white marble dais before me, a mage produced strange flowers and stranger birds, never before seen by man. Perhaps the audience in this amphitheater had been shown visions of civilizations at the bottom of the sea, or looked above the clouds at cities made all of silk and glass. Or perhaps the scholars at the long table by the door had contented themselves with visits from demons and demigods so they might chat over tea about the meaning of all existence.

I walked from the great hall into a smaller room, a library of some sort, filled with perhaps a thousand books, twice as many tomes as even my master had possessed. My heart raced. Surely we could find something here that might help us to save Vushta!

My eyes eagerly scanned the shelves. There had to be something! Surprisingly, the first book I saw I had used before: How to Speak Dragon. My hopes rose. While not perhaps relevant to our current predicament, it certainly was a standard tome for communication between species. I eagerly turned to the next volume on the shelf. It was also How to Speak Dragon, as was the one after that. I frowned. Perhaps there was somewhat less variety here than I had first imagined. The same book lined the entire shelf. In all, I counted twenty-six copies.

Still, that left over nine hundred other tomes that might be helpful. I searched about at random through the other books. Sixty-three Easy Herbal Remedies for Tired Feet didn't seem to be of any immediate use either, but at least the library carried only four copies of that volume.

I concentrated my search on the lower shelves. Here now were things of more interest: some dozens of copies of Lives of the Great Magicians, Volume VI: The Clerics. Any work about magicians should contain some useful spells. I eagerly pulled the book from the shelves. Other volumes were listed on the cover: The Innovators, The Daredevils, The Pragmatic Geniuses, The Demonologists, The Champions. This was more like it!

I opened the book at random and quickly read the chapter heading: "Duckwort, the All-Purpose Herb."

All-purpose? Perhaps there was some spell herein for vanquishing demons or retrieving lost cities. How proud Ebenezum would be when I brought him the solution to his problems!

My hopes died as I scanned the pages. The author went on about how early magicians evolved the proper notation for the storage of duckwort in all its forms, from Highland Golden Duckwort to Eastern Spotted Duckwort, with a special section on how to dry duckwort leaves, duckwort flowers, and duckwort stems. By the time, some twenty-six pages later, I had

gotten to the next chapter, "Eye of Newt, the Wizard's Friend,"
I feared that this book, though certainly thorough, could
contribute nothing of any value to our current problem. Still,
some other book in the series, say The Demonologists, or even
The Champions, would probably go into exactly the detail we
needed.

I ran my finger down the row of identical volumes, for that
was what I found—some forty-one copies of The Clerics in all.
What kind of a library was this, anyway?

I had spent far too long in this small room. I was but a
magician's apprentice. Full-fledged mages could probably enter
this room and within seconds find the very information they
required. I would tell Ebenezum about this place, but for now
it was more important that I continue my search. The solution
to all our problems might wait just beyond the next door, or
beyond the door after that. I had to explore the rest of this wing,
and quickly!

The next room was even smaller than the library. It was
filled with four long benches, all of which faced another dais,
although this one was smaller than the one in the great hall,
and fashioned of wood rather than marble. But what interested
me most was a chart on the wall, labeled "Simple Magic
Production." Here, at last, was something I might be able to use!

The chart showed three objects surrounded by a great deal
of script. On closer examination, I realized the pictures were
three different styles of hats currently favored by wizards. I
assumed this was some sort of hat magic. Ebenezum had never
shown me any sorcery of this type, but then my master had had
little occasion to show me much of any kind of magic before his
affliction overcame him. Perhaps this chart might be of some
value.

My foot hit something as I walked over to the diagrams. It
was a hat, probably used for practical demonstrations. I looked
back at the chart. How easy was this magic to do? Maybe I could
return to the others with something far more practical than
books.

The script work around the pictures seemed to be a series of
instructions for the production of flowers, scarves, and certain

small animals. Again, there didn't seem to be anything of value here to our immediate problem. But, as long as I had the hat in my hand, what harm would it do to give the spells a try?

I held the hat, a traditional magician's skullcap, about a foot away from my chest and made the four mystic passes called for in the directions. From a quick reading of the chart, scarves seemed to be the easiest thing to produce. I said the three words clearly and reached within the cap.

My fingers grasped something soft. I pulled forth a scarf of midnight blue!

Excitement almost overwhelmed me. Although I was a full-fledged magician's apprentice, circumstances had prevented me from practicing all but the most rudimentary of spells. In addition, due somewhat to haste and inexperience, many of my earliest conjurations had not been as successful as I might have hoped. Ah, but this cap spell was different; the ideal learning tool for the young magician! I repeated the mystic passes and the three words. This time I pulled forth a pair of scarves, one the color of spring leaves, the other the shade of the sky at dawn. Oh, if only I had had equipment like this in the Western Kingdoms, by now I might be a full-fledged wizard!

I turned back to the chart, eager to discern what other secrets the text might reveal.

It was even simpler than I had imagined. According to the remainder of the scrollwork, you could simplify the magic even further, so that each of the three basic conjures could be produced with but a single word. The scroll suggested you start with simple words, such as "yes," "no," and "perhaps," assigning one to scarves, one to flowers, and the third to small animals. I did the necessary secondary conjurations. Wouldn't my master be proud of me when he saw how easily I had acquired a new skill!

"Yes!" I cried with a brief wave of my hand. I reached into the cap and brought forth four scarves tied end to end, red to blue to green to gold.

I laughed and flung the scarves about my neck. "No!" I cried and reached into the cap to pull forth a bunch of daisies.

"Wuntvor?" a soft voice called.

I looked up to see the beautiful Alea watching me through a window.

"Alea!" I cried. She smiled her brilliant smile. Her hair, as always, shone magnificently in the sun. I was holding flowers in my hand. What could be more natural after this than I should give her a gift? True, now that I had Norei, Alea and I were a thing of the past. But it was a fondly remembered past, and Alea's eyes were the blue of summer skies.

"Wuntie?" Alea replied.

"Here," I said, offering the daisies. "It's a gift for you."

"Oh, Wuntie!" Alea squealed. "I'll be right in!"

Right in? I began to object, but thought better of it. How could she have known that I was simply going to hand the flowers to her through the window and then get on with my work? Oh well. I supposed it was a little more romantic this way, and I really owed it to Alea, for what we had once meant to each other. It would only take me a minute to hand her the flowers before continuing my search.

She entered through the far door of the room. She had been running and her chest heaved with the exertion. I marveled at how lovely she looked, even when she was winded.

"Are those flowers for me?" she managed after a moment.

"Yes!" I replied, holding the daisies out to her with my free hand. "I thought it would be nice to give you a little gift, for all that we once meant to each other."

"How sweet!" she exclaimed, taking the bouquet. A beatific smile spread across her face as she smelled the flowers. I noticed that the daisies went quite nicely with her hair.

The hat in my hand suddenly felt heavier. Puzzled, I reached inside and pulled out a large string of scarves.

Alea clapped her hands. "Oh, how clever! Can you do that again?"

"No," I frowned. The number of scarves seemed to be multiplying with every repetition of the key word. "I had better not. I don't want this place to become overrun with scarves."

The hat was heavy in my hand once again. I tipped it over. A much larger bunch of daisies scattered to the floor.

"Oh, how pretty! Are these for me as well?"

I stared at these newly produced flowers with some distress. What had I said to conjure these?

"Wuntie?" Alea prompted.

"Are the flowers for you?" I repeated. "They may as well be, now that they are here."

"Wuntie!" Alea pouted. "That's no way to give a present!"

She was right. Just because the magic had gotten a little out of hand was no reason to be rude. I stammered an apology.

"Don't worry," Alea replied as she picked daisies from the floor. "I know you've been under a lot of pressure lately, what with the disappearance of Vushta and everything." She smiled impishly. "I know of a good way to distract you!"

"Alea?" I said in alarm. I was somewhat disconcerted by her rapid approach.

Her face was incredibly close to mine. Her lips were closer still.

"Anyone"—she was speaking in a whisper both slow and deep—"anyone who gives a woman so many flowers deserves a reward."

And then she kissed me.

"No!" I cried. Didn't Alea know I was promised to Norei? An exchange of gifts was one thing, but kissing...

I paused in my thoughts. I had forgotten how well Alea could kiss.

The hat in my hand felt heavier than ever. I tipped it over. An enormous number of flowers fell out.

"Oh, Wuntie!" Alea said with delight. "If that's the reaction I'm going to get, I'll kiss you all day!"

"N—" I began, then thought better of it. I realized now that if I said "no" the hat I held would produce flowers and if I said "yes" it would produce scarves. With the help of the nearby chart, I had made a simple conjuration far too simple. I wondered how I might reverse the process.

Alea used my hesitation to kiss me again.

After a moment, I managed to break free. I shook my head in an attempt to clear it and regain my breath.

"Perhaps," I began, "this could best be saved until another time."

Alea's face was still far too close to mine.

"If you think so, Wuntie," she breathed.

Suddenly, the hat in my hand became so heavy that I almost lost my grip upon it.

"Eep, eep!" said the hat.

"Oh!" Alea cried. "Do you have a bunny rabbit now?"

Bunny rabbit? I had said "perhaps!" I had forgotten about the small animal part of the spell.

"Eep, eep!" the hat repeated. Two dark eyes blinked at me from the cap's dim interior. A long, reddish-brown snout popped out of the cap.

"That's no bunny rabbit!" Alea wrinkled her nose in disgust.

"No," I agreed. "Actually, it looks more like a ferret."

"A ferret?" Alea watched the small, reddish-brown creature as the small, reddish-brown creature watched Alea.

"My father used to keep them," I replied. "The farm where I grew up had moles."

"A ferret?" Alea repeated. She backed away, all thoughts of romance fled.

"Eep, eep!"

The ferret scrambled out of the cap, which was now filled with flowers.

"Wuntvor?" Alea asked uneasily. "Don't you think it's time you stopped making things appear in the hat?"

"Yes, I do!" I agreed, shaking the flowers free. "I just have to figure out how to do it."

Scarves began to boil out of the hat at an alarming rate.

"No!" I cried without thinking, and watched flowers displace the scarves. I let the hat drop. The flowers kept coming.

I pushed past Alea to get a better view of the chart.

"Wuntie! What shall we do?"

"I have to read this," I explained. There had to be some way out of this mess. Everything would be fine if I could only stop this hat producing things before anyone else arrived.

"Oh dear! Is there anything I can do?" Alea asked.

"Yes!" I called back. My voice was somewhat louder and more agitated than it should have been. "Help me read this char—" The hat was producing scarves again.

"No!" I jumped for the hat, trying to push the scarves back inside.

The hat began to produce both flowers and scarves simultaneously.

"Oh, Wuntie!"

I jumped back to her side. "Read!" I insisted. And I did the same.

There didn't seem to be any notation about stopping the simple spell. How could the chart makers be so shortsighted? Didn't they expect people to practice with their merchandise?

"Wuntie! I can't move!"

Alea was right. The scarves and flowers were so deep around our feet that it was getting difficult to walk. I pulled Alea free of a nasty knot of scarves.

"Perhaps," Alea suggested somewhat hysterically, "if you said the spell backwards?"

"Perhaps you're right!" I replied. It was certainly worth a try. "Sey! On! Spahrep!"

"Eep eep! Eep eep!"

A pair of ferrets leaped from the hat. Apparently, out of everything I'd said, only the "perhaps" had worked. But maybe, just maybe, if I said the complete spells in reverse, I might be able to stop this madness.

"Oh, Wuntie!" Alea grabbed me tight.

"No," I cried. "I have to conjure!"

But Alea held me in a death grip. "At least we will be trapped together," she said, her voice tinged with panic. It was touching, at that moment, that she still cared for me.

Alea sighed, calmer now that she was in my arms. "Still, I had hoped to die with a much wealthier man. Sorry, Wuntie!"

I assured her it was all right as I pushed her delicately away. Perhaps I still could reverse the spell and undo the damage before my master wondered where I had gone.

"I beg your pardon!"

"Someone's here!" Alea regrabbed my neck.

"What is the meaning of this?"

I turned around. Norei stood in the doorway.

I smiled weakly. "It's not what you think. Things have gotten a little out of hand!"

"I should say so!" Norei placed her hands on her hips. "Perhaps the two of you would like to be alone!"

"No!" Alea cried, still keeping me in her stranglehold. "We need your help!"

I tried to explain, as briefly as possible, about the hat, and the spells, and the innocent gift of flowers to Alea.

Norei nodded when I was through. "So you want to clean up this mess before Ebenezum gets wind of it? It's quite true that he might misunderstand, and get angry with your simple experiments. He probably simply wouldn't comprehend your intense need to play with hats with the situation so serious and all." She bit her lip. "Well, I might be able to do it. Give me a minute to think."

I breathed a long sigh of relief. Ebenezum was a truly mighty wizard, but when he became upset, his anger could be more mighty still. Now he would never have to know. Norei was the savior of us all!

And then a great roar filled the room. It took me but a moment to recognize the sound for what it was: a tremendous sneeze.

CHAPTER FOUR

Magicians must exercise caution in all things. Each of you has heard the story of the mage who perfected the gold producing spell, only to be crushed by his newfound wealth. Less well known is the story of the sorcerer who turned everyone he didn't like into a toad, until the day he exercised the spell on an entire unfriendly village and was found the next morning hopped to death. Then, of course, there is the extremely unpleasant story of the wizard who doubled as a gentleman farmer, and his perfection of a manure abundance spell. Whether this latter mage is still alive or not is open to debate, for no one has ever had the wherewithal to visit the scene of his accident to find out.

—from The Teachings of Ebenezum, Volume XII

"Master!" I cried. "Back away quickly. There is too much magic here!"

The sneezing retreated.

Alea clutched me harder than ever. I was finding it difficult to breathe.

"Quickly now!" Norei demanded. "How did this spell begin?"

I paused in my attempt to disengage Alea's grip long enough to point at the chart, now half covered by flowers and scarves.

"Oh," Norei ruminated. "This should be easy enough. But for the spell to really work, Wuntvor, you should repeat my words and gestures."

"Alea!" I insisted. "I need my hands free!"

The woman at last backed away, an odd expression on her face.

"I love a man who speaks with force," she whispered.

I had trouble looking into Norei's eyes. The temperature of

her gaze seemed slightly below that of a winter gale.

Norei began to speak, her words as cold as her gaze. Still, I repeated those words and the movements of her hands.

The hat stopped producing things.

"Yes," I said experimentally.

Nothing.

"No," I added. "Perhaps."

Still nothing, not even an eep. I let out a great gasp of relief.

Norei was still frowning. "I am glad we were able to cure your problem. I hope you have more success when it comes time for us to rescue Vushta."

"Norei!" I moaned. I wanted to run to her, to try somehow to explain, but Alea was in my way, watching me through half-closed eyelids.

"Oh." Norei turned back to me as she was about to pass out the door. "One more thing. The spell outlined on that chart is almost too simple. Be careful, Wuntvor, to steer clear of the gestures and words you used before, or you might find the hat producing all over again."

All over again? I had a sudden picture of a peaceful afternoon with Norei suddenly overflowing with flowers, scarves, and ferrets.

Norei had disappeared from the room. I grabbed the hat and tore it into little pieces.

"Wuntvor!" It was my master's voice, calling from another room. I hastily tucked the pieces of what was once the magic hat inside my shirt. At the first opportunity, I would toss them down some local well.

"Eep eep! Eep eep! Eep eep!"

Three reddish-brown heads had emerged from the sea of scarves and flowers around my feet.

Alea gave a little cry as she backed away. The three heads nuzzled at my legs.

"Wuntie?" Alea said with wonder. "I never knew ferrets could be so affectionate."

"Eep eep!" said one.

"Eep!" another replied.

"Actually, they're sort of cute this way. They almost act as if you were their mother." Alea giggled. "I suppose in a way you are their mother."

The third ferret looked at me with its big brown eyes. "Eep, eep!" it piped happily.

I had to get out of here. My master needed me. Even now, I could not think of ferrets as cute.

"You know," Alea said slowly, that dreamy look back in her eyes, "maybe I should reconsider marrying a wealthy man. Being a good parent can be so important!" She stroked my shoulder meaningfully.

I gave Alea a final smile as I dodged her grasp.

"Watch the ferrets for me, will you?" I called as I leaped free of the scarves and ran from the room, leaving a cry of "Wuntie?" and a chorus of "Eeps!" behind me.

"Wuntvor!" the wizard called again. If anything, he sounded more agitated than before.

"Yes, master?" I replied. If I had to face Ebenezum's wrath, I might as well get it over with. I ran back through the library into the large hall, where my master waited for me with a dozen others.

"So good of you to free yourself," my master said upon my arrival. He smiled coolly in my direction. I tried to smile back. Apparently, Ebenezum did not feel it seemly to show his anger in front of so many others. Somehow, the smile he showed me was almost worse.

"This is my apprentice," the wizard remarked to the others. "Now that he is here, I think we should all take a moment to become acquainted. I am Ebenezum, a wizard of some repute from the Western Kingdoms, here in Vushta as the result of a personal quest. Some of you I already know."

He nodded at Alea as she entered the room at my heels. My master quickly introduced Snarks, Hendrek, Alea, and Norei, and alluded to Hubert as "that dragon out in the courtyard."

"Two others here I think we all know: Snorphosio, a professor of some repute here at the university; and Klothus..." My master hesitated. "Indeed. In my haste, I neglected to ask Klothus just what function he did perform." He nodded at the man in gray. "If you would be so kind?"

Klothus took a deep breath and tilted his head upward, as if he might look down his nose at my master. Since Ebenezum was considerably taller than the man in gray, this gesture was not as successful as it might have been.

"I," Klothus stated, "am the assistant royal costumer for all of Greater Vushta!"

"Indeed?" My master smiled. "An honorable profession, and one that is of great service to all other professions."

Klothus nodded soberly. "I am glad you understand me."

"Indeed." My master tugged at the remnants of his robes. "By the way, do you think you might find the time to get me a new set of these?"

Klothus nodded. " 'Tis the very reason I am here, to refit all the wizards of the extension program with new robes befitting their station."

"Excellent!" Ebenezum clapped his hands together in approval. "Then I should tell you that the robes I always wear—"

Klothus stamped his foot in agitation. "No, no, don't say another word! I know at a glance what you need! It was no accident that Klothus has risen to the top of his profession!"

"Just so." My master scratched absently at his left eyebrow. "Now, if those here whom I have not yet met might do me the honor of introducing themselves?"

The half dozen newcomers each said a few words. Four of them were part-time students, not far along the way with their studies. The fifth was a professor, also dressed in red. However, it was there that his similarity to Snorphosio ceased. His name was Zimplitz. He was stocky where Snorphosio was thin and shouted when the other professor muttered.

"I am in charge of all the practical field magic," he concluded. "You know, directed studies." He pounded the table before him for emphasis. "Places where wizards can get their hands dirty!"

Snorphosio sniffed at the other professor's enthusiasm. "Alas, that most wizards choose to ground themselves in something so common. If more mages were to think on the theory behind their craft, imagine what heights we might have—"

"Yeah, yeah," Zimplitz interrupted. "I know all about your lectures on imaginary rabbits and imaginary hats. Well, let me tell you all something. When we find a hat in Field Magic, we darn well use it!"

I glanced at my feet and quietly wished the talk would move away from hats. It occurred to me that the pieces of one such magic cap were still tucked within my shirt. I really would have to get rid of them at the first convenient opportunity.

"I-Imaginary rabbits?" Snorphosio sputtered. "Imaginary hats? I'll have you know that my students can pull—"

"Indeed!" Ebenezum cried. "And I'm sure both of you are perfectly correct. But there is still one gentleman here yet we have to meet."

The last of the newcomers nodded at my master and smiled uncertainly. The fellow was every bit as tall as me, and probably better muscled. He doffed his hat before he spoke.

"My name is Tomm," he said in a voice barely audible. "And I am but three credits short of my wizard's degree. I would have had it already but that I have to pursue my humble craft to pay my tuition."

"Excellent!" my master said. "And what craft do you pursue?"

Tomm hesitated, looking at the floor much as I had but a moment before. "You see, good sir," he began, "I have attended wizard school to improve myself, to change my lot in life. I..." He paused, as if he might choke on the words. "I am a tinker." He raised his hands to stay any comments from the rest of us. "Some of you may wonder what troubles me so. Surely, you will say, it is an honorable trade. But how many of you, day in and day out, when asked about your occupation, must say 'I tink'?"

Tomm paused and let out a long sigh. His eyes rose to meet my master's gaze. "But I have nearly finished my wizard training. Soon tinking will be a thing of the past. But I have another shame that may be more difficult to live down."

We all stared at the tinker in silence. He swallowed hard and continued to speak in a voice barely above a whisper.

"I might have been able to save Vushta, but I ran away instead."

"Aren't you," Ebenezum replied, "being a bit hard on yourself? The power to make a city the size of Vushta disappear is great indeed. Can you berate yourself for being only one man, facing all the might of demon kind?"

"Yes, I can!" Tomm shouted with surprising force. "I was near the center of it all! I could have stopped it, I know. I was in Vushta mere moments before it disappeared!"

Tomm shuddered. "Let me tell you my story, and you will know my shame."

Quickly, the young wizard-to-be told his story. He had been on his way to his weekly visit with his aged mother when he noticed things were changing. Great black clouds covered the sky to turn it dark as night, brightened suddenly by jets of flame, appearing with blinding suddenness high in the heavens.

"Doom," Hendrek remarked.

Tomm nodded. "I thought so as well. I hurried into the dwelling where my mother had a room on the very top floor, taking the steps two, even three at a time. I prayed nothing was wrong. I knew if anything happened to my mother, I would never forgive myself!"

Tomm paused again to take a ragged breath.

"And?" Zimplitz prompted. All of us had gathered close to the overwrought tinker.

"I knocked upon the door." Tomm's lower lip began to tremble.

"And?" Alea whispered. The look of concern upon her face seemed to light her blond curls from within.

Tomm's voice was nothing more than a croaking whisper. "And my aged mother answered it."

I noticed my master pulling his beard with some agitation. "Indeed?" he said. "Then what was the problem?"

The tinker looked to my master and Ebenezum's authoritative gaze seemed to calm him.

"She told me to be quiet," he said in a voice both louder and calmer than before. "She had some sort of pest in her apartment. I noticed then that she was holding her umbrella. A pest, I thought? Surely it was only a mouse or some large insect I could easily catch and remove. My mother's eyesight is not what it once was, so it could not have been something really small. But when I saw the pest she spoke of..." His voice died again.

"And?" Norei urged, her hands before her as if she might pull the words from his lips. The tinker had gone too far to stop now. Like me, I was sure she wanted to shake the young man until his entire story came spilling out.

"First, I heard the voice," Tomm continued, his own voice not so calm and not so loud. "If you could call it a voice. I knew from the first words that the speaker was not human! It sounded like the deep groan of an unoiled gate, crossed with the noise of a giant crushing rocks beneath his feet. And the words this inhuman voice spoke!

"Come my demons, now arise,
For Vushta is our greatest prize!"

"Guxx!" I cried. The tinker had encountered the dreaded rhyming demon!

My master waved me to silence and bade Tomm to continue.

"You know of this fearsome creature?" Tomm said, awestruck. "Well then, perhaps you will understand my weakness. I strode forward as if in a dream to confront whatever inhuman force had invaded my mother's dwelling place. After all, was I not a wizard, only three credits shy of my diploma? Thus it was that I stepped boldly out on the balcony and confronted the largest demon I had ever seen!

"Some of you have already seen Guxx. I do not need to tell you about his bright blue scales, or the size of his teeth and claws. Perhaps, if I had had but a moment to collect myself after our first confrontation, I might have discovered some way to deal with this fearsome apparition before me. But, you see, there was my aged mother..."

Tomm's voice once again caught in his throat, but he cleared it and went on before any of us could prompt him further.

" 'Where is that pest?' she shouted. 'I'll show you what happens to things that materialize on my balcony!' And she swung her umbrella high above her head.

"The demon snarled at her:
"Begone old woman, do get back,
Or Guxx shall eat you for a snack!"

"Well, what was a son to do?" Tomm sighed. "My mother was always a woman of spirit!"

"Amf?" Snarks cried from deep within his hood. Would this tinker never finish his story?

Tomm shook his head. "I didn't even think of spells, only of protecting my dear old mother, who was busily beating her umbrella against the monster's head. And how did the demon react to my attack?"

Tomm laughed. "The demon took me in one large clawed hand and tossed me from the balcony as he shouted out another rhyme:

"No more worry, no more fuss!
Vushta now belongs to us!"

"There was a great crashing roar, and I was sure it was my death. But, a moment later, I found I had landed safely in a pile of sand. And, once I had regained my breath and the dust had cleared, I discovered Vushta had disappeared!"

"Indeed," Ebenezum said when it became apparent that Tomm was done with his tale. "I know far more of Guxx than you can imagine. You should not berate yourself, for you had no chance of success. The foul demon's power grows with every rhyme he makes, and it sounds as if Guxx was in prime rhyming form. Amazingly, even his meter was more or less correct. Against odds like that, even the greatest magicians in Vushta would have little hope."

"Doom," Hendrek added.

"Most interesting," Snorphosio commented. "Guxx is involved, then? That does change our perspective on the seriousness of the situation. As all good theoretical magicians know, Guxx Unfufadoo is the sort of demon that must be faced directly if one is to have any hope whatsoever of success. As the sages say, the only way to defeat a rhyming demon is to defuse his rhyme scheme. That was one thing about the sages, they always had a way with words. But then again, I suppose a rhyming demon needs a way with words as well. Thus do both sages and demons come under the scope of our discussion. Opposites attract, they say, and who could be more opposite than—"

"Fine!" Zimplitz broke in. "Your meaning is simple enough! We need a champion, to snatch Vushta back from the grasp of Guxx and the Netherhells!"

"Simple?" Snorphosio sniffed. "Nothing I ever say is ever simple, my good Zimplitz. You perhaps have not yet studied the ramifications of my ideas. That is the problem with you practical magicians, always leaping in before you fully weigh all the alternatives and—"

"Problem?" Zimplitz shrieked. "The only problem we have in this academy is those theoretical magicians who are so busy talking that they never get around to making any decisions, much less acting on them!"

There was a rumble in the distance, like thunder.

"Is it the Netherhells?" Zimplitz asked.

"Nonsense!" Snorphosio replied. "If it was, there would be a quake beneath our feet. Besides, this college is surrounded by a protective shell to ward off all demonic assaults. As all good theoretical magicians know—"

"Your pardon," Ebenezum interrupted, intent on defusing this argument before it got totally out of control. "If I might speak to you two gentlemen in private for a moment?"

My master would have this whole difficulty cleared up in a matter of minutes. But this exchange reminded me that I had a misunderstanding of my own that I had to straighten out. I turned to Norei, my beloved.

"Dearest," I whispered in her ear. "Might we also speak for a bit?"

She looked at me sternly. "Dearest?" she said rather more loudly than I might deem appropriate for a private conversation. "Aren't you getting the young women of your acquaintance confused? I would have thought, from your recent demonstration, that there is someone else who is the object of your affections!"

"Norei!" I cried. A number of others in the room had turned to stare at me. I lowered my voice to an urgent whisper. "Please! She was but a summer romance, long before we had met. We were trapped by the magic from the hat, and she panicked. Beyond that, she means little to me, and I mean nothing to her!"

"Wuntie?"

I jumped. Alea had walked up behind me as I had earnestly engaged Norei in conversation. She wrapped both of her arms around one of mine. She frowned at Norei.

"Wuntie, dearest, is this young witch giving you trouble?"

"Wuntvor?" Norei stared dourly at Alea. "Are you telling me the truth about all this?"

"Yes!" I insisted. Wait a moment! Who was I answering?

"Uh, no!" I stammered. What was I saying? Why was Norei's breath so hot against my neck? Why did Alea have to stand so close? "Uh, I don't know!"

Both women looked at me wide-eyed, their faces a mixture of shock and anger. Both turned to leave.

"Wait..." I called. How could I get Norei to turn around? She shot me the slightest withering glance.

"Yes—I mean, uh..." I had trouble finding the exact words I needed. And Alea had turned around. She was walking back to me! Why did her blond curls have to shine so, even in this enclosed space?

"No, wait..." I began again.

Now Norei paused. She frowned in my direction.

"I mean..." My voice died out completely.

"Indeed," my master interrupted. "While I hate to intrude upon your good time, Wuntvor, we must get on with things. My fellow wizards have come to a decision. Zimplitz?"

"We have agreed," the other wizard began. "Rescuing Vushta is more important than our differences of approach to magic. Ebenezum is correct. We will do our best not to argue until our city is saved."

Zimplitz stepped back, yielding the floor to Snorphosio.

"Although my learned colleague and myself have some differences of opinion over the proper ordering of magic, we shall put our differences aside. While I am sure all the students and true magicians here realize that theoretical magic is the basis of all sorcerous thought, and without the development of theory there would be no advancement within the field and we should soon slip back to some dark age where we would forget all but the simplest spells, still, despite these many obvious and overwhelmingly far-reaching disadvantages..." Snorphosio's voice died in his throat as he saw the way my master was looking at him. The elder wizard coughed. "Rescuing Vushta is more important!"

"And"—Ebenezum's stern expression turned to a benevolent smile—"what else have we decided?"

Zimplitz once again stepped forward. "Both Snorphosio and myself have massive libraries of magical craft. We have yet to agree on what series of spells would be best to assure our victory over the Netherhells. However, we have agreed on one thing. What spells we use cannot be performed totally from a distance. One of our party must travel through the Netherhells until he finds whatever horrendous spot wherein the demons have hidden our beloved city. Once that person stands in the remains of Vushta, our spells will be complete."

Zimplitz took a deep breath. "In short, for our plans to succeed, we need a champion."

"Doom," Hendrek remarked.

"Oh, Wuntie!" Alea shivered at my side. "Into the Netherhells! How horrible!"

Norei allowed me an icy stare from where she stood some distance away.

"The Netherhells!" Snarks had sidled close to me. He pulled back enough of his voluminous hood to be understood. "I've always wanted to visit my homeland again. The sulfur pools! The boiling oil! The cries of the damned!" The demon used one edge of the hood to dab at the corners of his eyes. "I'm just a sentimental old fool!"

"And now," my master said, "we must choose our champion."

"It will not take long," Zimplitz added. "I sense that there is a bearer of great magic in our midst. Magic always lingers in the halls of this academy, but my years of training tell me there was an extraordinary burst of sorcery within these walls mere moments ago. And we will need an extraordinary man or woman as our champion. He or she must be brave and true, for, should he make a single false step in the Netherhells, he may be damned for all eternity."

Zimplitz lifted both hands high in the air. "The champion is among us! We have but to wait and we will be shown the way!"

The room was silent. I stared about the great hall of the academy, a bit in awe of all that must have happened here before, as well as what occurred now around me. Perhaps Zimplitz was right, and magic at this moment did fill the air. Who would be our champion? One of the professors? Tomm, or one of the other students? Or could it even be one of the band with which I had traveled from the Western Kingdoms?

I heard a rustling in the far distance. The hairs on the back of my neck tingled with anticipation. There was magic near!

The rustling grew louder, like a dozen tiny feet scrabbling on stone. It was coming from the direction of the library. All of us turned to see what magic might be revealed.

"Eep eep! Eep eep! Eep eep!" The three ferrets burst into the room as one, their red-brown forms streaking straight toward me.

"Our champion!" Zimplitz cried. "It is a sign!"

The three ferrets nuzzled against my legs.

"Ferrets?" Snarks murmured.

"Indeed. This is our champion." Ebenezum pulled at his beard. "Forgive me, Wuntvor, if I remark that you are not exactly what we originally had in mind."

"Agreed." Zimplitz nodded silently. "But you cannot deny that the magic was there. I think you sell your own apprentice short. With Vushta gone, we are woefully low on champions. He will have to do."

"Oh, Wuntie!" Alea exclaimed. "To the Netherhells?"

CHAPTER FIVE

Heroics can be costly and involve some degree of personal danger for the participating wizard. But for the truly resourceful magician, this does not have to be! Consider the advantages of long-distance magic, by which you may gain all the publicity value and save all the expense. But, you say, don't heroes have to be present at the battle? For the properly prepared mage, nothing could be more heroic than a well-timed combination of printed handbills, subtly placed rumor, and perhaps a brief personal appearance tour. Still expensive? Nonsense! Do you know how much a heroic wizard can charge for personal appearances?

—from Ebenezum the Wizard's Handy Pocket Guide to Everyday Wizardry, fourth edition

I was going to the Netherhells.

I looked down at the ferrets rubbing my legs. It all seemed a bit unreal, as if I were taking part in some midsummer pageant and looked up to see snow on the trees.

In a way, I had been given a great honor. After all, somebody had to do it. It would be better if I looked on the bright side. Perhaps I would finally see the thousand forbidden delights!

Snorphosio cleared his throat. "We probably have not made all the ramifications of this choice clear, either to the rest of our party here, or to our—er—champion." The aged professor waved vaguely in my direction. "You will not have to go alone on your quest, and neither will you have to go unarmed. We will pick a suitable companion or two from amidst our group to accompany you in your peril. All champions, of course, need companions. It states so clearly in the Hero's Guide to Weapons and Etiquette. Page forty-three, I believe."

Zimplitz seemed about to say something, but Snorphosio continued his speech rapidly, refusing to be interrupted. "You will also be provided with weapons, magical weapons, the very best that can be found in the whole of"—Snorphosio paused again—"er—well, let's see what we have left in the basement, shall we?"

I had the feeling Snorphosio was speaking to instill confidence in me. For the moment, it did not seem to be working.

"Very good—" Zimplitz began.

"And one more thing!" Snorphosio shouted to override his fellow magician. "We will of course provide you with certain spells and duties to perform once you have reached your goal, so that we can defeat the Netherhells forever. You will be informed as to the exact nature of these duties—er—once we ourselves determine what they are."

"Indeed," Ebenezum said. "I believe we all need to prepare. What say we gather together in this hall at sunset?"

All agreed to my master's plans and the various parties began to leave the hall, many with specific duties assigned by one or another of the three wizards.

For the first time I grew afraid. Would I be left all alone here on my last day on the surface?

One thing I determined: If I was going to go underground in a few brief hours, perhaps never to see the sun again, I wasn't going to spend the rest of my afternoon standing about inside the wizards' college. I strode briskly outside into the sunlight.

"Oh, Wuntie!" Alea cried, her blond curls truly brilliant in the late summer sun. "To the Netherhells?"

I silently wished she would stop saying that. It was bad enough that I had to go and be a hero. It would be infinitely worse if my last few hours on the surface were spent with people constantly reminding me of my heroism.

Hubert waved his top hat in my direction. " 'Tis a noble thing you do for us all," the dragon intoned. "We thought later this afternoon we might do a little something in your honor."

Alea jumped with glee. "That's right, Wuntie! A real send-off!"

A sudden chill ran down my spine. I whispered my reply:

"You're not thinking of having another show, are you?"

"The very thing!" Hubert confirmed. "Alea, didn't I tell you this apprentice was a perceptive lad?"

"Oh, yes, Hubert." Alea was once again looking at me through half-closed lids. "And he's very good with animals, too."

Alea stepped close to me. "Oh, Wuntie!" she said, taking my hand. "Maybe we can sing a song just for you!"

"Yes!" the dragon cried. "A brilliant idea! We could call it 'The Ballad of Wuntvor'!"

Hubert sang the first few notes tentatively:

Wuntvor the hero sure is swell,

Went for us all down to the Netherhells...

Alea frowned. "That's not quite it. I think we need to develop his character a little at the beginning, and let the audience know exactly what kind of human being would go on such a hopeless quest. You know, like..." She began to sing in her clear, high soprano:

Wuntvor was honest, couldn't be bought,

Though he sometimes acted before he thought...

"Well, the pathos is nice," Hubert agreed, "but it's the blood and guts that always gets the audience!"

The dragon sang again:

Wuntvor strode boldly, no fear in him,

though the demons might tear him

limb from limb...

I decided it was time to excuse myself. Although I was sure the two vaudevillians meant well, their attempts to honor me felt as reassuring as lying down for a nap and thereupon hearing someone read your eulogy. Perhaps I could find some quiet place in the sun where I might meditate.

"Wuntvor? May I talk to you?"

There, at the edge of a copse of trees, stood Norei.

I ran quickly across the intervening field. Had my beloved forgiven me at last? I took her hand and kissed her chastely upon the cheek.

Norei frowned. "Not in front of everyone, Wuntvor! I only

wanted to talk to you for a moment!"

Norei looked at me with eyes the color of a forest glade, her perfect lips pressed into a perfect frown. Oh, how could I make her see that, compared to her, Alea was a rapidly fading memory!

"Norei—" I began.

"I don't want any excuses, Wuntvor." Her voice was grim. "I want the truth."

"The truth?" What was my beloved saying? "But I always tell—"

"Oh, yes, I know." Norei grimaced. Did I detect the slightest beginnings of a smile? "But you do sometimes tend to embellish here and there. It is part of your nature, I know, and I don't think you mean badly by it for the most part..."

I stepped closer to her, but she backed away.

"Now I'm trying to talk!" she exclaimed, her voice stern again. "After the things you've said to me, your recent actions with that—blond person—are very—unethical." She spoke haltingly, each word louder than the one before it, as if she could barely contain her anger.

She paused to stare at me. She bit her lip. When she spoke again, the words came quickly.

"Well, it's just that I may never see you again, so I thought I'd give you a chance to explain."

My heart leaped in my chest. So my beloved might forgive me after all! Quickly, but rationally, I tried to explain how I had discovered the chart, and the hat, and the flowers in my hand, and how, just at that moment, Alea had been passing by, and I had had a generous impulse, but had not made myself clear enough, so that Alea had come into the room instead of allowing me to give her the flowers through the window, and then the true nature of the hat had become apparent, and I, gentleman that I was, could not bring myself to remove Alea's hands from about my protective neck, even though she was strangling me, which was approximately the moment that Norei had chosen to enter the room.

I stopped, totally out of breath, and looked into her eyes.

"I understand," she said at last. "Well, actually, I don't

understand, but the whole thing is so complex that I'm willing to give you the benefit of the doubt." She looked toward the wizards' college. "It's a bit too public out here, isn't it? Let's take a walk, back among the trees."

I did as Norei asked. Maybe there were some advantages to this hero business after all.

"Wuntvor?"

It was my master's voice! I took a sharp breath.

"Ebenezum is calling!" I whispered.

"Wuntvor?" His voice was much closer now.

"Perhaps you had better go," Norei whispered back.

"Wuntvor?" He was at the edge of the trees now.

"Perhaps I should," I replied. We did our best to rapidly disentangle ourselves. There seemed to be a problem. Somehow our shirts had gotten buttoned together.

"I shall remember this moment always," I said as I hastily attempted to unbutton and rebutton our respective shirts.

Norei glanced down at my handiwork. "At the rate you're going, this moment will never end. Here, let me do that." Her sure fingers had us free in no time.

I turned to go, but Norei's hand was on my neck. I glanced back at her, and her lips were touching mine. We kissed a final time.

"Wuntvor!" my beloved whispered. "Good luck!"

I managed somehow to crash my way out of the thicket and reach the spot where Ebenezum stood, calling my name.

There was a look of concern on the wizard's face. "Do you feel well, 'prentice? You appear somewhat dazed."

I assured him it was only a bit too much of the summer sun.

My master nodded soberly. "I can understand your need of it, going so soon to face the underworld. 'Tis a thing both noble and dangerous you are about to attempt, Wuntvor. And I am glad that you are the one who is going to attempt it."

Ebenezum paused a moment to stroke his beard, then spoke again. "I, who know you best of all our assembled company, believe that we have made the proper choice for our champion. We have been through a great deal together, Wuntvor, and, no matter what perils we have encountered, either singly or together, we have prevailed. You have a way, 'prentice, of seeming to invite disaster, and then at the last moment averting it. There are those in our company who might call it dumb luck, but I believe you have a unique magical gift!"

Ebenezum chuckled softly. "Anyone else playing with that hat would have produced rabbits. Only you, Wuntvor, could bring forth ferrets!"

I smiled along with my master. I had never quite thought about my production of the ferrets in that way. Perhaps I did have a unique magical gift. I would march down into the Netherhells and bring Vushta back straightaway! With my master's faith behind me, how could I possibly fail?

"I have been talking with the other mages," Ebenezum continued, "and I think we have decided upon a very positive course of action. The other two are ironing out the fine points while I keep my distance." Ebenezum sniffed delicately. "I have not yet had time to discuss my malady in any great detail with either of these learned men. But, from what little discourse we have had, I believe there is hope of at least a temporary cure! Therefore, while the uncertainty of my condition prevents me from personally entering the Netherhells, I should be able to magically assist you on a regular basis from our temporary headquarters here at the wizards' college."

This was even better news. What could possibly go wrong now?

"Learned sirs!" someone called to us from the entranceway to the college. I turned to see Klothus waving in our direction. "Your wizardship! I have your new robes!"

"Ah, very good." Ebenezum patted at his mustache. "I have not felt very wizardly of late. At least now I can look the part."

I accompanied my master as we walked rapidly over to the royal costumer. How fine Ebenezum would look in brand-new robes of royal blue, tastefully inlaid with silver.

But my master's smile vanished as he approached. He grabbed the fabric in one trembling hand.

"What is the meaning of this?" he rumbled.

"What is the meaning of what?" Klothus replied. "I got what

you needed, a new set of four-nineteens."

I looked carefully at the bit of cloth Ebenezum held in his trembling hands. It was midnight blue, but the tastefully inlaid silver pattern was not of moons and stars. It was, rather, tastefully inlaid with ducks and bunnies.

"Ducks and bunnies?" My master was truly enraged.

"Of course!" Klothus retorted. He squinted at the remnants of robe still on Ebenezum's body. "Oh dear, those are moons and stars, aren't they? That would be a four-seventeen, wouldn't it?" The costumer cleared his throat. "Well, it's a natural mistake."

"Natural?" My master sounded like there might be an earthquake beginning in his throat.

"Well," Klothus frowned, "is it my fault that you can't keep your clothes clean? I've been under a lot of stress, what with Vushta vanishing and all."

Ebenezum's shaking became more violent as he turned a very unattractive shade of white.

"You—" the wizard began.

"I see," Klothus remarked, somewhat taken aback. He continued rapidly. "It's an awfully popular number—"

"—call yourself—" The wizard's voice was rising. It seemed to hold a hint of winter storm.

"—and the costume shop here is not as well stocked as the main branch—well, what used to be the main branch." Klothus had begun to edge away from my master.

"A costumer?" Ebenezum's voice was approaching full gale.

"Still," Klothus called over his shoulder as he ran away, "I'll see what I can do."

My master shuddered and took a deep breath. "Yes," Ebenezum said slowly. "Indeed. See what you can do."

But by then Klothus was lost in the distance.

Ebenezum turned back to me. "Sometimes it is the day-to-day problems that wear you down the most. Still, when you return, all this should be behind us. If I have not found a permanent cure already, one will surely be forthcoming with all the might of Vushta returned to us. And, once I am able to again use magic to my fullest powers, we will begin your wizardly training in earnest!"

Ebenezum looked at the sky. "There are still a few more minutes before sunset. I must return inside and consult with my fellow mages. I shall see you there soon enough." With that, the sorcerer spun about and walked rapidly back into the college.

So I was alone again, to silently witness the last few minutes of a late summer's afternoon. The wind shifted, carrying the singing voices of Hubert and Alea.

"No, no!" Alea cried. "We still need to personalize the danger!" She sang again:

Wuntvor was young and not too discreet,

And when he walked he had two left feet!

"No, you are wrong!" Hubert retorted. "We must stress the danger of his mission if we are to keep audiences interested!" The dragon's voice boomed:

Wuntvor the hero can't be a dud,

For the demons will then drink his blood.

They'll tear him apart with hideous groans,

And pick bits of him from their teeth with his bones!

"Hey," Alea admitted grudgingly, "that's pretty good. Yes, we'll put that in for sure!"

Pick their teeth with my bones? I tried to swallow, but my mouth was suddenly far too dry. I decided that I should walk in some direction where the wind could not possibly carry Alea's and Hubert's voices to me.

I made my way back through the copse of trees. Snarks and Hendrek stood in the shade at the far side.

"Wuntvor," Snarks remarked. "You appear a little green. Still, you're going to have to do better than that if you really want to imitate demonic coloration."

I smiled halfheartedly at Snark's comment. My mind was elsewhere. With my bones?

"Doom," Hendrek added.

No, I thought to myself, not if I could help it. I took a deep breath. Ebenezum had often told me that the difference between a good magician and a bad one was the magician's attitude. Well, I was determined to have the best attitude possible under the circumstances.

I thought for a moment about Snarks's remark.

"Should I attempt to imitate demonic coloration?"

"Actually, I don't think that is at all necessary," Snarks replied. "Things are changing in the Netherhells these days, you know. It is not the barbaric place it once was."

"Really?" I said. Hearing Snarks speak reasonably about the place of his birth reassured me tremendously. Perhaps, I thought, I should find out a little more. "Is it safe then for humans to walk among demon kind?" "Oh, without a doubt!" Snarks chuckled. "Provided, of course, you have a reasonable story for being in the Netherhells. In the last couple years I was there, they were establishing regular human-demon trade routes. I imagine by now that that commerce is even more highly developed."

"Then," I asked hopefully, "demons don't really eat humans?"

Snarks chuckled at my naiveté. "On the contrary, demons eat humans all the time! But don't worry, you are perfectly safe as long as you can show the demons you have a reason not to be eaten!"

"Oh," I replied. This was not as reassuring as I had hoped. Still, there was one more question I had to ask. "Then do demons really rip you apart and drink your blood?"

Snarks shook his head sadly. "Another example of negative demonic stereotyping! True, human ripping and blood drinking used to be big problems in the past. But now"—Snarks gave a dismissive wave of his hand—"in the course of regular human-demon encounters, I don't imagine that sort of thing happens more than once out of every five meetings."

"Once in five?" I asked.

Snarks nodded. "Of course, the statistics are a little higher in summer or around festival time. But what are a couple of humans more or less to the Netherhells? So, as you see, you can come and go as you please!"

"Oh," I answered. I decided not to ask him how demons picked their teeth. I sighed at some length and sat down beside them.

Snarks looked at me with some consternation. "That's the problem with humans," he began. "They really never plan anything out in demonic detail. It's really too bad I can't go with you to show you the place. But I have been banished. If I were to return..." The demon shuddered. "Well, what they would do to me would make this college look tasteful!"

"Doom," Hendrek agreed. "I have much the same problem. If I were to go to the Netherhells, I should be beset by demons demanding hellish payment for my weapon. We would be stopped before we had even begun."

I nodded glumly. There seemed to be no escaping it. Whatever terrors I would have to face in the Netherhells, I would have to face them alone.

"Doom," Hendrek commented. "The sunset is the color of blood."

I turned to see where the warrior pointed his doomed club. He was right. The sky at the edge of the valley was a brilliant crimson tinged with orange. It was quite beautiful, really.

I also realized it might be the last sunset I would ever see.

CHAPTER SIX

Q: And how do professional wizards cope with stress?
A: Stress? The real wizard doesn't even recognize the meaning of the word. Why are you still asking me questions? Can't you see I'm busy? This spell is two days overdue! You 're sitting on my reference books!

—from "A Conversation with Ebenezum, Greatest Wizard in the Western Kingdoms," Wizard's Quarterly, Vol. 4, No. 4 (Spring)

The sky was rapidly darkening. The time had come to go inside and face the collective wisdom of the three mages.

I must admit that there was a part of me that did not want to go, what with the demons that made odd use of your bones and all. But the fate, not only of Vushta and my master, but of the entire world, depended on the success of my mission. And that was an even more sobering thought. All in all, I was probably much better off worrying about demonic dental habits.

Still, I thought of Ebenezum's words as I approached the Great Hall of the wizards' college. He had thought I had some extra quality that always let me succeed, no matter what the odds. It made me feel proud to know that my master had such faith in me. And I knew I would do everything possible to justify that faith.

Snarks and Hendrek walked close behind me and I saw the others of our party also gathering about the college. I knew all would be present for the final moment of decision.

The wizard students had placed large torches on either side of the foyer and around the perimeter of the Great Hall. They also had opened a window at hall's end large enough for Hubert to put his head through and watch the proceedings. This extra opening seemed to have made the large room particularly drafty, for the torches flared and guttered and gave everyone in the room a dozen dancing shadows.

A cheer went up as I entered the room. I couldn't help but smile. If fame was so wonderful now, how magnificent it would be when I was a full-fledged wizard!

"Welcome!" Zimplitz cried from where he stood on the marble dais. "Now that the most important member of our little band is here, we can make our final plans!"

There was some polite applause, led by Zimplitz along with Ebenezum and Snorphosio, who stood slightly behind the other wizards on the raised platform.

"Indeed." Ebenezum stepped forward. "The three of us have conferred at some length as to the best plan to follow for the rescue of Vushta. However, our discussions are not so final that we do not still solicit your help. If any of you assembled here find that you have any questions or comments about any of our plans, we will be glad to give you the floor for as long as you feel necessary." My master looked at me. "And that applies doubly to our young champion, Wuntvor the Apprentice!"

There was another brief cheer. Perhaps I was expected to say something now. To all these people, at the same time? For the first time since I was given this honor, I began to sweat. It seemed only natural that, if I was about to go off and face the Netherhells, I should be able to gather enough courage to address this assembly. Yes, now was the time. My master had given me an opportunity to reply, and I was their champion, after all. I took a deep breath and swallowed.

"Well—" I began.

"Of course," Snorphosio said over my hesitant voice, "we do not have time for too much discussion. As my colleagues have impressed upon me, now is the time for action! Of course, action without proper discussion is often meaningless, as discussion without action sometimes lacks meaning as well, especially for those acting, not to mention those acted upon. But what happens when meaningless action is discussed—"

"Indeed!" Ebenezum interrupted. "I believe it is time we

began our business. We must discuss three things this evening: the nature of your quest, your companions, and your magic weapons." He motioned to Zimplitz. "First, the weapons!"

Zimplitz pulled a sack from the back of the dais. "Come forward, Wuntvor," he called, "and I shall explain the nature of each of these three magic charms!"

As I approached, he reached into the sack and pulled forth a golden horn.

"This," Zimplitz intoned, "is Wonk, the Horn of Persuasion." He handed the golden instrument to me. "One blast upon this mighty horn and even the foulest demon will do your will."

The horn was cool in my hands. I held it up closer to the torchlight to examine the fine scrollwork etched into its handle.

"There is but one precaution I would ask of you," Zimplitz continued. "Whatever you do—"

I took a deep breath and blew.

Every man, woman, and mythological beast screamed and covered their ears as one.

"All right!" Zimplitz cried. "All right! You can do whatever you want!" His hands shook as he removed them from his ears. "But please don't blow it again!" The audience before me murmured in all too ready agreement. I gingerly laid the horn on the edge of the platform before me.

"Next," Zimplitz continued, doing his best to regain his composure, "we have a very special sword."

He reached into the bag and pulled forth a silver sword in a scabbard of midnight blue, close in color to my master's robes when they were still clean and whole.

I took the weapon in both my hands. I touched the ornate silver hilt tentatively.

"May I?" I asked.

"Why of course!" Zimplitz replied. "There's no problem at all—uh—with taking out the sword."

Gently, I drew forth a length of highly polished steel.

"Hello," the sword said.

I almost dropped it. No one had told me this sword was going to talk!

"I hate to ask this," the sword continued, "but are you

drawing me out of my scabbard for any particular reason?"

I shrugged. "At the moment, no," I replied, doing my best to keep up my end of the conversation. "Just wanted to get introduced."

The sword emitted a low whistle. "That's a relief, may I tell you! Very pleased to meet you! My name is Cuthbert!"

I introduced myself in turn, and told the sword we were going to go on an adventure together.

"Oh," Cuthbert replied with very little enthusiasm. "I don't—ahem—have to kill anybody, do I?"

I was rather taken aback. I told Cuthbert I really didn't know.

"Drat!" the sword cursed. "I just hate drawing blood. It gets me all splattered, and it's even worse if the mess dries. And let me tell you what happens if I hit bone! I mean, it can dull my blade in no time. And the noise people make! All that shrieking and grunting and crying. I tell you, it's enough to make me want to go into another line of work!"

"Excuse me," Zimplitz said, "but I think it's time for Cuthbert to go back into his scabbard."

I slid the sword back into its midnight-blue casing.

"Cuthbert is a bit of a coward, I'm afraid," Zimplitz remarked. "Luckily, we have no such problem with the third charm." Zimplitz put the bag down and reached into his pocket. He pulled out a small, red card and handed it to me, saying, "You never know when this will come in handy."

I stepped back a few feet to better read the card in the torchlight. There, printed in block letters, were the words GET OUT OF JAIL FREE.

I looked questioningly at the wizard.

"Put it in a pocket where it will be safe," was all Zimplitz said. "And now on to the choice of companions!"

This seemed to rouse the crowd again, which had been a little subdued ever since my experiment with Wonk.

"We considered a number of different methods of choosing suitable companions: a contest of valor; whoever picked the short straw; a study of possible royal blood in someone's lineage; one potato, two potato; but none of them suited all our needs until Ebenezum hit upon the scheme of complementary companions."

"Indeed." My master stepped forward again. "In order that we might best choose companions, I need to speak with certain of our number. Hendrek, step forth!"

"Doom!" The large warrior shuffled out of the crowd.

"We all have reasons for being here tonight. All of us, of course, wish to rescue Vushta and defeat the Netherhells! But some of us have more personal and more urgent reasons for coming here."

"Doom!" Hendrek agreed.

"Hendrek, unsheathe your club from its restraining sack," my master instructed.

The large warrior looked questioningly at my master for an instant. Ebenezum nodded and Hendrek brought forth Headbasher.

"As you see, much of my malady has been brought under control," my master proclaimed. "Thanks to a series of simple remedial spells that Zimplitz located in one of his tomes, I am able to remain in the presence of modest magic with naught but a slight nasal drip." He paused to blow his nose. "Snorphosio has studied the spells already worked upon me and believes they have theoretical possibilities that may eventually lead to a total cure. Therefore, although I am still incapable of setting foot in the Netherhells, I should be able to fully participate in the above-ground operations."

So my master was on the way to a complete cure! I found my face had broken out into a smile. For the moment, I didn't even care that I faced imminent death.

"But, if I supervise the operations above ground," my master continued, "who will accompany Wuntvor to protect him from the dangers down below? It is a thorny problem."

"Doom," Hendrek concurred. He tentatively swung Headbasher above his head. The torchlight sputtered in the sudden breeze.

"It is especially difficult for you, for should the demons take over the surface world, they would demand payment for your cursed club and you would be forced to do their fiendish bidding."

"Doom," Hendrek remarked once again.

"Unless, of course," my master continued, "the spell we three wizards have been working on can sufficiently mask the true nature of your weapon from demon kind!"

"Doom?" Hendrek inquired.

"Then you could join Wuntvor on his trip to the Netherhells and add your might to our quest to save the surface world. It is your only chance, for, should the demons take the surface world, all wizards would be surely killed and any spell we concocted for you would quickly become null and void!"

Hendrek stared at his war club for a long moment as if deep in thought, then, with a grunt, smashed Headbasher to the floor.

"Doom!" the large warrior cried.

"Good!" Ebenezum replied. "We have our first volunteer!"

Snarks was at my side. "I never cease to marvel at how good your master is at talking, especially for a human being. Of course, being raised with demons, I am immune to most forms of verbal persuasion."

"Now," Ebenezum called. "I must talk to the demon Snarks. No, no, don't replace your hood. I am quite capable of talking with you now." My master blew his nose again.

Snarks strode up to the edge of the dais. "So at last we can talk face to face? What a relief. You can't believe how many things I've been meaning to tell you. About your costume—"

"That is being attended to." Ebenezum pulled at his beard. "I'm afraid I have some questions to ask you as well. You are a demon and thus have not formed the fears the rest of us have concerning the Netherhells."

"Perfectly true. Now I wanted to mention a little something about the way you sneeze—"

"That is being attended to as well," Ebenezum replied. "And yet you were banished from the Netherhells. What do you think will happen when the Netherhells take over the surface world?"

Snarks hesitated for a moment. "Well, demon kind doesn't bear me any great ill will, as long as I keep completely out of their sight. The way I figure it, if they didn't kill me before, I see no reason for them to kill me now. They will simply kick me out of the surface world."

"And where will you go?"

Snarks was temporarily speechless.

"Therefore," my master added quickly, "you must accompany Wuntvor and provide him with the necessary knowledge of the Netherhells."

"I must." Snarks nodded slowly. "Now let me give you a little advice about your hand gestures—"

"We have our second volunteer!" Ebenezum cried.

"Doom," Hendrek put in for emphasis.

"Now," my master added, "we must talk about our plan."

"A moment!" my beloved Norei interrupted. "Are there to be no more volunteers?"

"Indeed," my master replied. "I am afraid not. Two is all we can afford."

"But shouldn't an experienced magician accompany them?"

"Ideally, yes. Unfortunately, there are too few of us here to make use of any ideal plans. Wuntvor has performed magic before. He will be given a basic spell to help him complete his quest. That, plus his weapons and companions, must be enough to see him through."

Norei glanced at me, her deep green eyes filled with concern. She turned back to my master. "Why can't I go?"

Ebenezum again pulled at his beard. "Because we need you here. We have scoured the countryside and been unable to find even a dozen wizards. Now my companions here believe that there are still another half dozen mages hiding in the vicinity who may reveal themselves once our sorcery becomes evident. In addition, we will place a magical call to bring what rural wizards we can to join us, but our time is limited. The Netherhells have already struck once. We have no idea when they will strike again."

Norei still looked doubtful.

"You must join us!" Tomm the former tinker cried. "We will need your woods-trained senses in the battle to come. I look forward to working side by side with you, and trading bits of magic lore."

Trading bits of magic lore? Who was this big ox kidding? How dare he smile at my beloved that way? I knew the sort of things a lummox like that wanted to trade, and I didn't like it one bit!

"I am afraid," Ebenezum interjected before Norei could speak again, "that you will have to stay and give your fellow magicians a hand. We have no time to make any other changes in our plans."

There was a tremendous crash. The room shook once, tossing all those standing to the floor. It was as if the earth heard my master's remark and felt the need to reinforce it.

"Is it the Netherhells?" Ebenezum asked the others.

"The possibility exists," Snorphosio agreed. "Although this college is surrounded by a protective shell that is meant to ensure it against demonic assault. Although, come to think of it, the entire metropolis of Vushta was surrounded by a protective shell as well—"

"We may have taken too long with our plans!" my master cried. "Hubert! Quickly! Go and scout the area!"

"What?" Alea cried as the dragon departed. "Does this mean we don't get to do our song?"

Ebenezum shook his head. "Indeed. There is no time."

"And we worked so long on it!" Alea sighed. "We decided at last on a traditional ballad about the death of heroes. It had such a wonderfully mournful quality."

"Indeed." My master had already turned his attention to me. "Listen carefully, for any word I say might be my last. You have seen how the horn works. The sword not only talks, but is capable of communication with us at the college. That is, if the college still exists. As to the card, well, Zimplitz thought it might be of some use."

"It was the best we could do on short notice!" Zimplitz interjected. "Our magical weapons storeroom is almost as bad as our library."

"Be that as it may," Ebenezum continued, "I have written down on this scrap of paper the one spell you need. Memorize it at your first convenience. Now you must go to the very heart of the Netherhells, for that is where they have hidden Vushta. And it is in Vushta that you will find the only one who can effect a cure: Guxx Unfufadoo!"

"Guxx?" I whispered. I would have to face the dreaded rhyming demon.

Ebenezum nodded grimly. "The other wizards have determined that all we have experienced is somehow intertwined: my malady, the overabundance of magic in the land, and the disappearance of Vushta. To cure all three, and to stop the Netherhells from making any further gains, you must enter Vushta and get one thing, and one thing only, from the demon Guxx."

Only one!? I tried to find hope within my breast. I had been given weapons, companions, and a special spell. With luck, and the proper strategy, it might be possible. Snarks and Hendrek pressed close to me on either side. I looked up to my master.

"What," I whispered, "do I need to take from the demon Guxx?"

Ebenezum stared deep within my eyes. "A single nose hair," was his reply.

"Doom," Hendrek observed.

And then the earth really began to shake.

CHAPTER SEVEN

Wizards are constantly subject to negative publicity. A case in point: One elderly wizard of my acquaintance, whenever he was bothered by unexpected guests, would immediately cast one of three spells upon them, either turning them to stone, transforming them into segmented worms, or blasting them entirely out of the kingdom. Now, some wrong-headed do-gooders, hearing about the aged mage's predilections, formed an angry torch-bearing mob, forcing the now wronged wizard to flee to a distant kingdom altogether. How much better it would have been if the aged wizard had thought to inform the populace of the true benefits of the spells he used on those who came to bother him! For example, those people who have experienced it will tell you that nothing is more restful than being turned to stone, while transformation into a worm brings you closer to the earth. As to being totally blasted from the wizard's domain, I challenge you: Can you think of any other way you can travel such a great distance for free?

—from The Teachings of Ebenezum, Volume XVI

It happened in an instant. Where once there was a floor of solid stone, now there was a gaping hole. Something small and sickly yellow in color leaped from the hole into the great hall. And that something was wearing a loud blue-and-orange checked suit.

"Greetings from the Netherhells!" Brax the Salesdemon cried.

"Doom!" The mighty Hendrek was the first into the fray, moving with amazing speed for one so large. But then Brax was his personal demon.

"How you doing, Hendy baby!" the salesdemon said. "I have just a minute here before the battle really gets under way, and

I want to make a request. As you no doubt realize, you're way behind on your rental payments for the cursed club Headbasher. I've done what I can to keep the powers that be from demanding the final payment, but Fin afraid your credit rating is not very pretty. Still, I've been authorized to give you one more chance. All you have to do is make one large payment right now and the contract will be considered paid to date!" The demon nimbly dodged the war club's swing. "That's right! All you have to do to return to the good graces of the most fearsome creditors in the Netherhells is to hand over Ebenezum the Wizard!"

"Doom!" Hendrek swung his club again.

"My good warrior!" There seemed to be an edge in the demon's voice. "Be reasonable here! How can we strike fear into the masses, not to mention damning souls for all eternity, if our customers won't cooperate? Surely you can see my point of view!"

"Doom!" Headbasher crashed into the stones where Brax had stood but a second before.

Brax waved both hands in the air. "Well, what can I do? My hands are tied. We will simply have to take Ebenezum anyway, with no credit to your account!" The demon whistled. "Bring on the Dread Collectors!"

I felt as if my veins had turned to ice. We had only seen the Dread Collectors once before, but I remembered them all too well. I especially remembered their many claws, their even greater number of teeth, and the relentless ferocity with which they attacked.

This time they seemed even more horrible than before.

They burst from the hole in the floor.

It is difficult to describe the Collectors, for they move so fast you can never quite make out their exact shape. There appeared to be three of them, and all they did was slash and bite and try to rip out your neck. They moved as fast as Hendrek under the enchantment of his club. Whenever you turned around, they were there.

The last time we had seen these fiends, it was but for an instant. This time, it would be far worse. As they approached, I realized there was a pattern to their growling, mewling, squealing voices. After a fashion, they actually spoke!

The three things swept across the floor in our direction and all three spoke as one.

"We come for payment!" the Collectors growled.

All around me, I saw my companions readying for battle. I vowed that I would do the best I could as well, though I had but a stout oak staff to protect myself.

But wait! No longer did I have to defend myself with only my stout oak staff. I had been given weapons—magic weapons! Quickly, I reached for the midnight-blue scabbard. I leaped toward the nearest Collector. With a blood cry on my lips, I drew forth Cuthbert, the enchanted sword.

"Wait a minute!" the sword cried.

I stumbled mid-lunge. It was somewhat disconcerting to be in battle and have your weapon talk to you. I lost my balance and fell by the feet of the nearest fiend. The Collector's claws raked the air above my head.

The sword screeched against stone as I fell. The Collector reared back at the noise. I scrambled quickly to my feet.

"Really!" the sword continued. "Do you think this is such a good idea?"

I swung the sword toward a rapidly retreating Collector. "I do not think"—I managed between lunges—"that this is the best time—for a conversation."

"I could not disagree more!" the sword retorted. "I mean, have you exhausted all the other possibilities? You'd be surprised how many times a conversation between adversaries, even a very short one, can prevent a—yelp!"

The sword connected with the Collector as the fearsome beast spun away. I pulled the blade free of the matted mass. The shining steel was covered by an ichorous green.

"Do you see what happens when you start fighting?" the sword complained. "I mean, green ichor! Do you know how long it takes to clean off green ichor?"

The Dread Collectors had once again retreated to their fearsome formation. So we had somehow repulsed the first attack. But then they growled and came for us twice as fast.

"We come for blood!" the Collectors snarled as one.

One of the things was heading straight for me.

"See what you've gotten us into?" the sword remarked.

I ignored the weapon's prattle and quickly stepped aside. But I had expected to find a bare spot on the floor on which to stand. Instead, I encountered all-too-solid flesh.

"Doo-oof!" Hendrek cried as we collided. Both of us lost our footing simultaneously.

Two sets of Dread Collectors' claws raked the air above our heads, digging deep into each other's pelts. Their screams were deafening. There was green ichor everywhere.

I rolled away from the still interlocked Collectors and regained my feet in front of the dais. I took a moment to catch my breath and see where next I could use my sword.

The student wizards and Hubert seemed to have joined together to keep the third collector at bay with a combination of well hurled paving stones and dragon fire. Snorphosio and Zimplitz had used the extra moments during which the rest of us had been fighting the Collectors to each develop a counter spell. Zimplitz's enchantment was a bright red hammer that smashed to the floor whenever a Collector was near, while Snorphosio had devised a delicate web like thing that didn't quite seem to work as of yet. Snorphosio cursed as a second Collector passed through the device without apparent harm, then shouted another quick spell, which apparently had no further effect whatsoever.

And what of my beloved? Norei was at the other end of the dais, using her spells to fight off Brax the Salesdemon, who appeared to be brandishing one of his enchanted daggers.

"No!" I cried. I rushed forward, intent on rescuing her from her peril.

I felt something strange brush against my chest. Was this some other insidious form of demon magic? I quickly reached inside my shirt and pulled forth a single flower. The delicate stem felt cold between my fingers. I remembered Norei's warning about excess magic bringing back the spells! I tossed the flower away as I ran for my beloved. I definitely would have to get rid of the pieces of that hat at the first opportunity!

And then I heard the sound which I had dreaded most. My master had begun to sneeze.

Even with Zimplitz's cure, then, the magic here was too much for him. Little wonder, with a pair of spells and half a dozen fantastic creatures in the room. But that meant that he was totally defenseless!

I then made one of the most difficult decisions of my young life. Norei was capable of holding her own. I must protect my master! I leaped to the top of the dais and turned toward the battle on the floor, sword at the ready.

I had acted none too soon. All three Collectors, sensing my master's weakness, had disengaged from their other battles to attack him as one!

"We want the wizard!" the Collectors roared together.

But there was another noise as well, like the scrambling of many tiny feet across a floor of stone. An instant before I saw them, I heard their familiar cry:

"Eep eep!/Eep eep! Eep eep!"

And the three ferrets jumped upon the lead Collector.

It was an unequal fight at best, but it made me proud to see those ferrets attempt the impossible; boldly giving their lives to protect me, no doubt, the person who gave them life upon this earth.

"Violence always ends this way," the sword muttered. "Mark my words. If you play around, you're going to get hurt!"

I ignored the whining weapon and shifted my position, sword forward, back to the wall. Thanks to the ferrets, I was as prepared as I could be for the Collectors' worst assault. They would surely kill me, but maybe I could take one of the fiends along.

"We will not be stopped!"

The lead monster shook my tiny allies across the room.

The ferrets dispensed with, the Collectors continued their headlong charge. I braced myself, knowing that in a moment it would all be done.

Ebenezum sneezed.

Thankfully, I had repositioned myself slightly to one side of the great wizard and thus was spared the main force of the blow. The Dread Collectors were not so lucky. The full extent of my master's nasal effluvium sprayed mightily upon them.

The dread fiends stopped dead in their tracks.

"We don't like getting wet!" the Collectors yelped as one.

"Now we will take the upper hand!" I cried.

"Are you so su—" my weapon began. But I sheathed the offending sword before it could complete its sentence. I had more than one enchantment up my sleeve. I knelt quickly and reached into the sack on the dais's edge.

"Hurry, Collectors!" Brax called from where he still dealt with Norei. "Guxx is expecting us!"

It was Guxx then, behind the attack? I could no longer hesitate. I drew forth the horn of persuasion.

I took a deep breath.

And I blew.

I blew mightily upon Wonk. Everyone screamed and covered their ears.

"Must you?" Brax said with some irritation. "Oh, very well. We'll take this one instead."

The salesdemon nodded once and a pair of Dread Collectors grasped Norei's arms. They rushed away, back to the hole from which they had erupted.

"Wuntvor!" Norei screamed as she was lost from sight.

Brax shrugged. "I can't go back empty-handed." And he jumped in the hole after the others.

I stared for a moment, stunned, at the last place I had seen my beloved.

"Doom," Hendrek commented as he appeared at my side.

"I must go after her," was all I could say.

"She is a qualified witch!" Snorphosio reminded me. "With luck she will survive. You need to know more about your weapons, and the spell we will use—"

"I must rescue her," I cut in. I had no more time for theory.

"But Wuntie!" Alea called from where she had cowered in the corner of the room. "You look as if the battle has exhausted you! You must rest first! I can help you relax!"

I shook my head. "I must follow her." I swallowed, but my throat was still far too dry. "Now."

Ebenezum blew his nose mightily.

"Indeed! Let the lad go! But remember, Wuntvor, you must

rescue Vushta as well. Until the kingdom is once again whole, they may come and snatch any one of us, at any time!"

"I'll remember, master!" I gathered up my magical weapons. I wore Cuthbert at my belt and carried a sack filled with Wonk over my shoulder.

"Hendrek!" I called. "Snarks! Are you coming?"

"Doom!" Hendrek said at my side. The cursed club Headbasher quivered in his enormous hand.

"I'm coming! I'm coming!" Snarks cried, tying his monastic robes tight about his small form. "That's the problem with humans. All these last-minute decisions!"

I waved a final time to my master. With Snarks and Hendrek behind me, I began my descent into the Netherhells.

CHAPTER EIGHT

And what do you do if you come upon a dark cave? Then the knowledgeable wizard would say: Into darkness, let there be light." And the truly knowledgeable wizard would add: "Let there also be cheese, bread, fresh vegetables, plenteous members of the opposite sex, and enough mead to make it a thoroughly enjoyable weekend!"

—from Thirty Days to Better Wizardry by Ebenezum, Greatest Wizard in the Western Kingdoms, fourth edition.

There was nothing but darkness.

Something bumped into me.

"Doom," came a voice behind me.

"Hey, watch your feet! Just like humans! Didn't anybody think enough to bring a light?" a second voice complained.

"Zrrrmmmnn," a third voice mumbled. For a minute, I thought Snarks had hidden himself again beneath his hood. But then I realized I had just heard him speak.

Who else was here with us?

"Hendrek?" I called. "Snarks? Is there anyone else around?"

"How could you tell?" Snarks retorted.

"Doom," Hendrek added.

"Ouch!" Snarks cried. "Watch where you swing that club, will you?"

"If we don't stay together, we're going to get lost," Hendrek stated.

"Hey," Snarks replied. "I'm never going to get lost here. The Netherhells is my home turf!"

"Grrffmmm!" the other voice mumbled with some urgency.

"Wait!" I insisted. "Don't you two hear something?"

"Only the labored breathing of this out-of-condition warrior.

And after all the diet plans I've suggested!"

"Doom! It was lucky for all of us that I thought to bring food with us. The wizards, you know, had put some provisions in a second sack."

"Wait a second," Snarks interjected. "You didn't need to bring any food! Demons have to eat, too, you know. It would probably do both of you some good to sample some Netherhells delicacies. Like sweet demon pie! Ah, there's a dish! Of course, you have to be careful! Those brambles can really stick to your gums!"

I felt something banging at my hip.

"Crffllvvmm!" the muffled voice cried with frustration.

"No!" I repeated. "Wait! I'm sure there's another sentient being here!"

"I'm not all that sure how many sentient beings are here already," Snarks added.

"Doom." I felt Hendrek's great bulk bump against my back.

"Would you keep off my feet!" Snarks screamed. "I should be leading the way, anyways. I'm the demon here!"

"Grrjjfflblltmm!" the voice mumbled in earnest.

"There!" I said in triumph. "Didn't you hear that?"

"Oh, that!" Snarks replied. "I just thought Hendrek had indigestion."

The beating on my leg redoubled.

"It's the sword!" I exclaimed as I suddenly realized the source of the sound.

"What's the sword?" Snarks began. But he fell silent when I drew my weapon from its scabbard.

Cuthbert glowed with a blinding light.

"Well, it's about time," the sword said haughtily. "Here I am, shouting my head off, and no one's paying the slightest bit of attention to me!"

"We didn't know," I answered, shielding my eyes from the sword's blinding intensity. "We could hardly hear you at all."

"Oh, it's that nasty scabbard again!" Cuthbert complained. "It's so dark and close in there. No ventilation whatsoever! But it's what I have to call home now, isn't it?"

"Still," I remarked, doing my best to change the subject, "I'm glad I pulled you out so you can glow. I never imagined you could do that!"

"Well, that's what I was trying to tell you all along. Of course I can glow! I'm a magic sword, aren't I?"

"Up until now," Snarks interjected, "all your magic has been in your mouth." The demon looked away from Cuthbert's blinding light. "Say, couldn't you tone down your brightness a little bit?"

"I'm doing my best," the sword huffed. "Still, my light would be much better if I wasn't coated with green ichor."

"Doom," Hendrek responded. "It is a weapon's lot to be coated with the results of battle."

"And that's the problem, isn't it?" Cuthbert said. "I didn't ask to be a sword, now did I? Why couldn't I have been a magic mirror? I would have been perfectly happy, lying to people about who was the fairest in the land. But no, those magicians needed a sword, so—"

"Excuse me," I interrupted, "but hadn't we better be getting on with our quest? I mean, the woman we're trying to rescue may have been dragged halfway through the Netherhells by now."

"Doom." Hendrek nodded grimly.

"You know, folks, we could go back up to the surface. Then I wouldn't have to glow at all. We could just sit around and talk in natural light!"

"Let's get this over with," Snarks agreed. "I don't mind this sword giving us light, but does it have to talk, too?"

"Oh, dear," Cuthbert said. "You really don't want to listen, do you?"

"Let's look at it this way," Snarks replied. "Who wants to take advice from a sword?"

"My point exactly!" Cuthbert exclaimed. "But now, what if I was a magic mirror? You'd certainly take advice from a magic mirror!"

I lifted Cuthbert before me and led the way down the tunnel to the Netherhells.

"Does any of this look familiar yet?" I asked Snarks. "Nothing I recognize," the demon answered. "I believe we're still in the access tunnel. They build these things all the time to perform some bit of mischief or other on the surface. I'm surprised sometimes, with all this tunneling going on, that bits of the surface world don't come crashing in on top of the demons' heads."

"Doom," Hendrek said. "Perhaps it has."

I was struck by the warrior's thought. "Do you mean Vushta might have fallen through by accident?"

"Where would demons be more likely to perform mischief than in the city of a thousand forbidden delights? Doom!"

"Hmmm," Snarks mused. "There is truth in what you say. Still, I prefer to think the demons built their tunnels to sink Vushta by design rather than accident. It's that old Netherhells pride, you know."

"Doom!" Hendrek responded.

My eyes were at last adjusting to the light from the magic sword. The tunnel we traversed seemed to be carved out of solid rock. I did my best not to think of how much power it would take to make a tunnel like this. Or how much magic.

Cuthbert whistled. "This place does go on, doesn't it? That's one thing about being a magic sword. You sure get out a lot. I've seen places I would never have imagined when I was but a small spell on some magician's lips. I should look on the bright side more often. Magic mirrors get stuck in one spot, you know. All they ever get to do is hang around all day long."

Cuthbert sighed. "If only I didn't have to kill people. It's almost always a mess, let me tell you. And their death screams get on my nerves!"

"Could you shut up for a minute and turn your glow down?" Snarks asked. "I think I see some faint light up ahead."

"I do all this work for you, and this is the thanks I get!" Cuthbert complained. "Well, if that's all the use you have for me, why don't you just put me back in the scabbard, then?"

I did as the sword suggested. The weapon's complaints were muffled by its midnight-blue sheath.

Snarks had been right. There was a light ahead, faint compared to the blinding glow of the sword, and a little greenish in color.

"Now!" Snarks said with some satisfaction. "We are approaching the real Netherhells!"

I let my hand rest on my sword hilt. Somehow, descending through the tunnel, we had seemed distanced from both the surface and the hells below, somehow separated from our quest. Soon we would see the real Netherhells, filled with the real demons. The question was: Would the real demons let us pass?

"Snarks?" I asked. "Should we be prepared for trouble?"

"Not necessarily," the demon reassured me. "It depends in what sector of the Netherhells we find ourselves at tunnel's end. Once I see the vista before me, I shall know in an instant what to do."

"Doom," Hendrek remarked. "Then do you know the whole kingdom under the earth?"

"Virtually like no other," Snarks admitted. "As a truth-telling demon, it behooved me to move quickly and often through the Netherhells. In my formative youth, I therefore roamed the world underground from end to end. I would venture that I know as much about this place as any demon, for I have seen every nook and cranny along my kingdom's edge, and I have visited most of them. In a way, I feel it is fate that has brought us together, for in this quest, you could have no better guide than Snarks!"

His speech had been awfully reassuring. I just hoped Snarks was telling the truth. And then I realized that he had to be.

The light was growing brighter and the tunnel wider as we continued our descent. I noticed as I turned to glance at my companions that the light gave Hendrek's complexion a greenish glow not too far different from Snarks's natural shade. I wondered, if we resided down below for great enough a time, if we would not all begin to resemble denizens of the Netherhells. It was not a pleasant thought to contemplate.

"I feel some trepidation," Snarks remarked. "It has been so long since I have seen my home. And yet will I be welcome there?" He sighed. "A demon without a country!"

We rounded another corner in the snaking tunnel. It was bright enough here to look for signs of some sort. A scrap of witch's clothing, perhaps, or a tumble of loose rocks where Norei had struggled with her captors. Might she have had time to etch some message into the dirt walls when the Dread Collectors paused to rest? But there was nothing beyond the constantly brightening rock about us.

"Are you sure they would have taken Norei this way?" I asked Snarks.

"No, the Dread Collectors would have taken her down some entirely different tunnel, then they'd come back and build this one just to fool us!" Snarks regarded me with demonic ire. "Sometimes I wonder about you humans! Of course they went this way! Quite some time ago by now. The Dread Collectors aren't too bright, but they're awfully fast. Don't worry. Even if we have to search the length and breadth of the Netherhells, we'll find her."

The demon pushed in front of me. "Oh, we're getting close now. I can already smell the sulfur!" Snarks emitted a high, raucous giggle.

"Doom!" Hendrek commented from the rear.

"My small green heart is palpitating!" Snarks cried as he ran ahead. "What part of the Netherhells will we see first? Maybe we are near the acid lakes. Then again, I think that Vushta was located above the East Netherhells Slime Pits!"

"Don't go too far!" I called to the rapidly advancing demon. "We don't want to get separated!" But Snarks was already out of sight.

"What is this?" his voice cried from some distance away. I thought I detected a note of panic.

"Doom!" Hendrek replied. The two of us rushed to help our comrade. We rounded one final corner and found Snarks at tunnel's end, staring out into a world of green light.

"Snarks!" I called. "Are you all right?"

The demon nodded dumbly.

Hendrek stepped to our compatriot's side, war club at the ready. "Doom. Where are we, then? The acid lakes? The sulfur pools? The slime pits?"

"Oh, no!" Snarks whispered, gazing in horror at the vista before him. "I don't remember this at all!"

I looked out on truly the strangest sight I had ever seen. The scene before us was lit with signs that seemed to glow from within. They began at the tunnel mouth where we stood, and stretched in either direction for as far as the eye can see. Beneath each sign was a great window. Some windows were also lit from the inside, while others had great torches burning in front of their establishments. And the torches were also exceedingly strange, for they burned not only yellow and red, but blue and green as well.

Snarks swallowed grimly. "Well, you had best follow me anyway. There apparently have been some small changes in this neighborhood. I'm sure, once we start to walk, I'll recognize it immediately. We just have to move quickly and try not to attract attention."

We stepped from the tunnel mouth onto the green, glowing ground.

"Hey, you!" a voice called. "Yes, you! At the tunnel mouth! You looking for something?"

"Doom," Hendrek mumbled.

"Not necessarily," Snarks said. "Let me do the talking."

With some trepidation, Hendrek and I let the demon lead us away from the tunnel, our only means of escape. Snarks was walking straight for a short figure who waved at us in the distance. I told myself that we had to face up to the denizens of the Netherhells at some point. I had hoped, however, our first conversation would have been at a much later date.

"Hello!" Snarks called ahead. "Can you tell us exactly where we happen to be? I seem to be a bit lost."

The other demon hobbled in our direction. He appeared to be quite aged. "Little wonder, sonny," the old fellow wheezed. "Things have changed here a lot lately. You're out in the country now, halfway between the cities of Blecchh and Yurrghh."

"Between Blecchh and Yurrghh!" Snarks cried. "But that's unspoiled Netherhells countryside! Where is the brilliantly flowing magma? What happened to the pool of molten sulfur that I loved so much as a child?"

"Gone," the old fellow whined. "Covered over with what you see here, the Blecchh to Yurrghh Intercity Mall! Say, aren't those humans with you?"

"Yes, of course," Snarks said dismissively. "You mean the bramble fields are gone? And the poison berry groves? How could they do something like that?"

"It's called progress," the old demon replied. "Time was, you knew where you stood in the Netherhells. Now, if you stand too long in one place, they build a mall around you!"

"Doom." Hendrek looked darkly about him. "Then we are trapped in a—what was the word—mall?"

"So those are humans!" the old fellow exclaimed. "Say, sonny, just what are you folks doing here?"

"Oh, we are just here to rescue Vushta from the hands—"

Snarks yelped as I grabbed him and threw his hood over his face. "Mmmnffggllkfftt!"

It was only then that I realized the true nature of our peril. Snarks always had to tell the truth! If anyone were to ask him a direct question about our quest, he would answer it. And, should a demon in any authority ask, we were surely doomed.

"I am afraid what you ask is secret information!" I cried, trying to think fast. What would my master do in a situation like this? "We are here on a special human and demon cooperative mission, to—uh—deal with certain situations that affect both humans and demons!"

The old fellow smiled slyly. "So it does have something to do with that city they dragged through here a few days ago! Netherhells know where they're going to put it! Somebody mentioned they were going to stick it right smack in the middle of Upper Retch! Can you imagine what that will do to property values?"

"Doom," Hendrek said. "Upper Retch?"

Snarks tossed his hood away from his face. "The capital of all the Netherhells! Very interesting indeed!"

The old demon nodded. "It's been real interesting out here the past few days. Why, just a short while ago some Collectors ran on by here, toting a human female. Let me tell you, was that woman carrying on!"

"Oh, no! Was she screaming?" I asked before I could help myself.

"Nope." The old fellow shook his head. "Mostly she was

yelling and beating the Collectors over the head with her fists. Let me tell you, she called those Collectors a few things we don't even say down in the Netherhells!"

I breathed a quiet sigh of relief. At least Norei was still alive, and she appeared to be as spirited as ever. Perhaps we could still rescue her before it was too late!

"Well, we had best be going," I said, anxious to be off.

"Doom," Hendrek added. "Nice meeting you."

"Demon and human relations, do you say?" the old fellow mused. "I think I might just come along."

Snarks frowned. "But you can't!"

"Oh?" The old fellow scratched his wrinkled green pate. "And why is that?"

"Oh," Snarks answered. "Because we have to go down and rescue mllffttgghhnnttrr!"

Once again, I had been forced to cover the demon's face with his hood. I realized I would have to say something as well to keep the old fellow from getting suspicious.

"This is dangerous work!" I insisted. "Of the greatest secrecy!"

"Oh, that's all right," the old-timer drawled. "I don't need to know all the fine points. Give me a moment to get my things. It really seems like a nice time to travel!"

"But this is your home!" I objected.

"Well, it was my home at one point, before it got 'revitalized.' That's what they say to you when they tear down your home to build a mall, you know. You're being 'revitalized'!"

Wouldn't this old fellow listen? "But we can't have too many people! We have to remain inconspicuous!"

The elder chuckled. "Two humans traveling with a demon who keeps hiding under a hood? I thought you were trying to draw attention to yourselves! I tell you what. If the demon here wants to take off his hood and give me one good reason not to come, I'll stay here in the mall."

We stood there for a moment in strained silence. At last, Snarks took off his hood.

"You'll have to bring something to eat," he advised. "All we have is human food."

"It's probably better than what they sell around here these days." The old fellow made a face. "The pies are full of artificial brambles!"

He bent over to reach behind a large circular container that bore the words DON'T BE A LITTER DEMON— HELP KEEP YOUR NETHERHELLS CLEAN! He pulled out a small sack and slung it over his shoulder.

"I'm as ready as I'll ever be," the elder said. "Who knows? Maybe on our travels I can revitalize a thing or two myself!"

"Doom," Hendrek replied.

"That your name?" the oldster asked. "Has a nice ring to it. Folks call me Zzzzz."

"Doom," Hendrek repeated. "Zzzz?"

"No, no, Doom," the elder corrected. "Not four 'z's. Five. Zzzzz."

"Doom. My name is Hendrek."

"Hendrek?" Zzzzz scratched his wrinkled forehead. "Oh, so sorry. Doesn't have quite the same ring as Doom, though, does it?"

Hendrek opened his mouth to speak, but though better of it. Snarks and I each introduced ourselves.

"Well, now that we know each other," Zzzzz remarked, "what say we get started? I guess you've got a job to do."

I tried to make one final objection to the old demon accompanying us, but Snarks cut me off.

"No, Zzzzz is right in this," Snarks said. "Two demons and two humans is a much less conspicuous way to travel. After all, you could be our slaves."

"Slaves?" Hendrek commented. "Doom!"

"There's the word again!" Zzzzz interjected. "See how catchy that is? Maybe you should think about changing it."

"Whatever we do," Snarks insisted, "we must avoid detection."

So we began to walk down the long, green-glowing corridor, between two rows of buildings all too brightly lit. I heard faint music coming from somewhere.

A yellow demon clad in a loud orange-and-green-checked sport coat sauntered out of a storefront before us. He waved an unlit cigar in our direction.

"Excuse me, gents," he said behind a smile that was far too wide. "Anybody got a light?"

It was Brax the Salesdemon.

CHAPTER NINE

Being trapped in the Netherhells is not the most fearsome thing that can happen to you. It is, in fact, probably no worse than being trapped in a cave for a weekend with all your spouse's relatives, and, in most cases, will not lead to total drooling, gibbering madness, as is the popular misconception. If, on the other hand, you find yourself trapped in the Netherhells for a weekend with all your spouse's relatives, well, sometimes drooling and gibbering can be fun.

—from The Teachings of Ebenezum, Volume XXXIII

"Doom!" Hendrek cried. He hoisted his war club as I went for my sword. This foul demon would tell me what had happened to Norei!

Brax stepped back quickly. "Hendy baby! You and your friends misunderstand me completely! I am here to welcome you to the Netherhells!"

"You know these characters?" Zzzzz asked.

"I most certainly do!" Brax beamed. "One of them is a customer!"

"Oh, what a shame," Zzzzz frowned. "That must mean they're legitimate. It's really too bad. I had so much wanted to go and revitalize something before I died!"

"Well," Brax confided in a low tone, "they're not that legitimate!"

For some reason, Brax was not going to reveal our identities. What did this mean? And what had he done with Norei?

Snarks was gazing at the newcomer with barely controlled fury. "Fiend!" he shouted. "What have you and your kind done to my Netherhells?"

"I beg your pardon?" Brax replied mildly. "As far as I know, the Netherhells is right where it always was."

"That's beside the point!" Snarks insisted. "It's what has happened to the Netherhells. It's been—it's been..." Words seemed to fail him.

"Revitalized," Zzzzz suggested.

"Well, whatever!" Snarks continued. "What have you done to the countryside? Where are the acid lakes? Where are the sulfurous pools? Where are the slime pits?"

"Why," Brax said, a bit surprised, "they're still here. They've just been improved a bit."

"Improved?" Snarks challenged.

Brax waved his cigar aloft. "Surely. Just read the signs."

I looked up at the row of glowing signs that lined the top of the never-ending parade of buildings we had walked along. I hummed along with that quiet, ceaseless music as I read the placards. Brax was right. Directly before us was a place called "Acid City." A few doors beyond was another called "Sulfur Universe." And we stood before a door marked "Slime-O-Rama, Home of the Famous Slime Burger!"

"It's no use!" Snarks wailed. "Your kind will never understand!"

"Maybe we can revitalize him!" Zzzzz suggested hopefully.

"Hold it, hold it!" Brax snapped two fingers together to produce a flame. He puffed his cigar alight. "As I said before, you guys have got me all wrong. Believe it or not, I'm on your side."

"Doom!" Hendrek lifted Headbasher aloft.

"Hear me out! Hear me out!" The salesdemon danced away. "After all, now you're in my neck of the woods."

I placed my hand on the warrior's shoulder. "He's right, Hendrek. We should listen to him. After he tells us what he has done with Norei!"

"At last. Someone with some common sense." Brax smiled in my direction. "Maybe I could sell you a good used weapon some day. But that's not the reason I'm here. At least not directly."

"Does it have to do with Norei?" I demanded. "Where is she?"

Brax blew a smoke ring in my direction. "The Collectors

have taken her. Just as well. I never knew a human could be so much trouble. Not even Hendrek!"

"Doom!"

"But that's my whole point!" The demon jabbed his cigar toward Hendrek for emphasis. "Humans were meant to give demons problems, as demons were meant to bedevil humanity. Guxx Unfufadoo is a big thinker, perhaps too big. He wants to take over the surface world and run everything! But, if demons control both above and below ground, who do I have left to sell used weapons to? It's that simple, gentle beings. If the Netherhells take over the surface world, I'm out of a job!"

Take over the surface?" Zzzzz marveled. "This is bigger than I thought! Oh, there's going to be some revitalization for sure!"

"Perhaps you have a point, friend Snarks," Brax continued. "We have made all the progress we see around us, but is demon kind happy? Why do the Netherhells want to take over the surface, anyway? It's negative feelings about their own kingdom, that's why! I say, rather than disrupt the order of things, let's develop a more positive image of our own home caves! Up with the Netherhells!"

Brax paused as if he expected the rest of us to echo the cheer.

"Doom," Hendrek said to fill the silence.

"Indeed," I added a moment later. I had to be careful. The logic of a fiend like Brax could be very slippery. "You say you are against the Netherhells taking over the surface world. Then why did you assist Guxx by abducting Norei?"

"Oh, I knew that would come up!" Cigar smoke wafted from Borax's nostrils as he sighed. "Yes, I was working for Guxx there, wasn't I? Well, there were two reasons. The first is you do not say no to Guxx Unfufadoo. You may have noticed that as well. The slightest misstep and he throws one of his rhymes at you!" The demon shivered.

"But it was working for Guxx that made me decide on this course of action. I realized that if he got what he wanted, all of humankind and all of demon kind would be changed forever!"

"Indeed," I replied. "And how can we believe you?" "Not believe honest Brax?" The demon blew another smoke ring. "I

have already made a gesture of good faith. I only took the young
witch, Norei. I had been sent to capture the wizard Ebenezum!"

The demon did have a point. I paused a moment to consider.

"But why are we all so glum?" Brax continued. "Now, now,
you just haven't gotten into the spirit of this yet! The underworld
can still be a fun place. If you listen carefully, and the wind is
right, you can still sometimes hear the screams of the damned!
The Netherhells forever!"

"Now wait a minute," Snarks interjected. "I was the one who
was nostalgic for the Netherhells countryside—the magma, the
brambles, the slime pools. I was banished to the surface world!
You don't know how much I longed to come back!"

"Exactly! That's the attitude I want to see! More loyalty to
the Netherhells' grand traditions! In fact, I've come up with a
whole series of jingles and clever sayings for that very purpose.
Listen to this." Brax cleared his throat and sang in a gravelly
tenor.

If we don't have it, it can't be got!
The Netherhells is hot, hot, hot!

"I don't think I want to come back anymore," Snarks
muttered.

Well, no matter what Snarks said, it was sort of catchy.
"Indeed," I remarked in my best wizard tone. "And what do
you want from us?"

"Why, to work side by side." Brax opened his arms to include
us all. "The Netherhells should be for demon kind! I think we
should put Vushta back where it belongs!"

I frowned at Brax. If we were to work together, we would
have to strike a bargain. "Will you help us to find Norei?"

"And have her hit me over the head again?" The demon
sighed. "Very well. If I must."

I looked to Snarks and Hendrek. "What do you think?"

"Doom," Hendrek replied.

"We need to speak alone," was Snarks's answer.

The truth-telling demon and I moved a few stores away
from the others. Snarks spoke to me in a low voice.

"Trust me," Snarks said. "You never want to trust a demon."

"Indeed," I replied. "Still, he knows of our whereabouts,

and he knows of our purpose. Isn't it better that we keep him with us, rather than rejecting him and not knowing what he is up to?"

"You have a point!" Snarks admitted. "I tell you. What you can learn about people in times of peril! You were always good with that staff of yours. I never knew you could think, too!"

"Indeed," I agreed. "Still, I wish there was some way I could have my master's counsel in this."

Snarks slapped me on the back. "But there is a way to talk to your master! That's why he gave you a magic sword!" The demon shook his head. "Isn't that just like a human! Do I have to tell you everything?"

Of course! Ebenezum had told me that we could communicate through the sword! There was no time to lose! I pulled Cuthbert swiftly from its scabbard.

"What do you want?" the sword shrieked.

"We must use your magic to talk with my master," I replied.

"Oh, thank goodness," the sword said in a relieved tone. "I thought you expected me to kill someone or something! It's all this dried ichor on me. It's very disorienting!"

Perhaps the sword was right. I untucked my shirt and did my best to rub the ichor off.

"Ah, that brightens my outlook on life, let me tell you!" the sword remarked. "Remember, a clean sword is a happy sword! Now, who is it that you want to contact?"

"You must contact Ebenezum!" I insisted.

"Who?" the sword queried.

"Ebenezum," Snarks interjected. "He's a wizard back in East Vushta. Is there anything else you need to know? Perhaps we should contact Ebenezum ourselves and bring him to you!"

"Please!" Cuthbert cried, deeply offended. "We swords may look like simple tools of power and mayhem, but we harbor sensitive souls within." The weapon paused for a moment, as if gathering its reserves. "You. The fellow who is holding me. What is your name?"

"W-wuntvor," I stammered in surprise.

"Wuntvor!" Cuthbert repeated with satisfaction. "Very pleased to meet you. No one ever thinks to introduce anybody to a magic sword. It's just pull you out, hack, slice, hack, and back in the scabbard again. I mean, what's the use of being magic?"

"Indeed," I replied. "So could we contact Ebenezum now?"

"Oh, certainly," the sword responded. "It's so difficult being stuck in the scabbard all day. I mean, if you can never talk about it, what's the use of being magic? Oh, the contact! Now, lift me over your head and swing me around three times. I'll do the rest!"

I did as the sword instructed. The first time I swung the sword, a small light appeared before me. The second swing, and the light grew to the size of an apple. On the third swing, the light exploded outward, until it appeared we were looking through a window right onto the lawn at the Academy of Magic and Sorcery Extension Program campus!

"Your wizardship!" Klothus called across the greensward. "I have your robes for you at last!"

"Indeed?" came a voice from outside the picture. "Bring them here quickly! There is work to be done." Klothus moved across the lawn. The image in the window blurred and shifted. When it cleared again, Klothus stood before my master!

"Here they are," the costumer said with some pride. "Just as you specified, model four-seventeen!"

And yes, they were just what my master ordered. The magical window was clear enough so even I could see the delicately embroidered silver moons and stars.

"Excellent!" Ebenezum cried. "Now I can once again truly feel the part of the wizard!" He eagerly unfolded the robes that Klothus had given him. But then he paused and frowned, lifting a short piece of cloth that was sewn to the main body of the garment.

"Indeed," my master inquired. "And what is this?"

"Oh?" Klothus replied dismissively. "What else would that be? It's a short sleeve."

"Short sleeves?" My master's voice trembled. I could see his anger grow as he rapidly unfolded the rest of the garment.

"Well," Klothus said rapidly as he sensed my master's growing displeasure, "I told you the resources of the college here are somewhat limited. That robe is a four-seventeen. It's the summer model. I did not think you would mind. While it is no longer high summer, it is still somewhat warm. Well, at least warmish..."

Klothus's voice died as Ebenezum stared at him, the robes held at arm's length from the wizard's body. From the look on my master's face, you could tell he was not pleased.

Klothus seemed to evaporate from the window. I guessed he had made a silent retreat. Looking at the costume he held, I could see Ebenezum's point. In an emergency, perhaps, my master might have been capable of wearing the upper part of the modified summer tunic, but I could never have seen him wearing the shorts.

"It's probably none of my business," Cuthbert remarked from above my head, "but now that I've gone to all the trouble of making magical contact, don't you think you should say something?"

The sword was right! I had come upon this quest half certain that I would never see the surface world again. I had been so overwhelmed to see my master once more, in obviously good spirits, that I had temporarily forgotten my purpose!

But what should I say?

I cleared my throat.

"Excuse me?" I began.

My master started violently. He turned to look into the magic window.

"Indeed!" he cried. "Wuntvor!"

"Indeed!" I replied. "Master!"

"So that sword is working after all!" Ebenezum tugged reflectively at his beard. "Frankly, Wunt, after seeing the condition of this place's underground storage vaults, I had my doubts."

"Not that it's any of my business," Cuthbert interjected, "but don't you think you should ask him your question? I mean, I can't keep up this magic window business all day!"

The sword was right again. Quickly, I filled my master in with regards to Brax.

"I believe," my master said when I was done, "your decision

was the best for the moment, Wunt. Still, I am glad you called me. This way, in case Brax is involved in some secondary Netherhells scheme, we will be ready for it. There's no way they can surprise us now."

I smiled at that. I, too, was glad I called my master! But was there anything else I should discuss with him while we still maintained magical contact?

"Excuse us, Ebenezum," a deep voice said from somewhere. Hubert stuck his dragon head into the magic picture. "If we might just have a moment—why, look who's out there! Alea!"

Alea's blond curls danced brilliantly into the frame. "Wuntie! How good to see you! We've been working on that heroic song about you, Wuntie, ever since you left! I think we're really getting it nearly right now, something that combines your vulnerability with a real sense of danger."

"Yeah!" Hubert added. "It's bound to be a hit!" Alea and Hubert glanced at each other for the merest of moments.

"Look, Wuntvor," Alea began. "We know you don't have much time—"

"Yeah!" Hubert interrupted. "But maybe if we sing a couple bars, it'll spur you on your way! Hit it, damsel!"

Wuntvor was a youth who had nothing to hide
Went on a mission that was suicide—
The picture vanished.

"I'm sorry." There was a note of condescension in Cuthbert's tone. "I don't use my magic window for projecting vaudeville!"

"Indeed," I replied. I lowered the sword and turned it about to slide it back into its sheath.

"Must we be so hasty!?" Cuthbert blurted. "Magic swords can be a lot of fun, you know. Can't I stay out just a little while longer and ta—"

Sword back in place, I nodded to Snarks. I had spoken with Ebenezum. It was time to continue our quest.

"Well," Brax said when we rejoined the salesdemon, "what are we waiting for?"

"Revitalization, here we come!" Zzzzz cheered.

"Doom," Hendrek added as he took up the rear.

On we walked, down the never-ending row of brightly lit

establishments, any one of which would put the gaudiest inn on the surface world to shame. I had been afraid to look within these strange structures, fearful that I might be enticed inside by some Netherhells trick. But now that we walked mere feet away from the gaudily painted windows and doors, some even surrounded by multicolored torches, I found my eyes wandering repeatedly toward whatever might lay inside. Smiling demons waved as we passed, holding aloft arcane and complicated contraptions that I was happy I did not yet know the use for.

I hummed along with the ever-present, faint music. Actually, it seemed louder here. Wait a moment. Why was I walking so quickly by these charming storefronts? I thought again on the contraption I had seen the demon show me one window back. Actually, that thing had been rather novel, in its way. Now that I thought of it, I really had to go back to that window and look at it once again! Yes! It was the very thing I needed! I would go in there and get it right now. Wait! I didn't have any money! Oh, no matter. I was sure they would take a magic sword in barter. I could not live without it! There was the perfect place for it in my den.

"Hendrek!" I heard Snarks cry. "Grab him quickly!"

"Doom!" The large warrior wrapped his arms around me and pulled me away from the door.

"But I have to!" I shouted. "I need it for my den!"

Hendrek shook me roughly. What was I saying? I must have been under some sort of spell. I didn't even have a den. I didn't even know what a den was!

Snarks confirmed my suspicion. "Netherhells Buying Fever," he said grimly. "Lucky we got you before it was too late. Once you begin to shop..." The demon shivered.

Somewhat shakily, I resumed the march. At Snarks's suggestion, we moved more quickly than before.

Brax sidled up to me as we walked. "By the way," he remarked, his voice barely above a whisper, "I've been meaning to talk to you."

"Indeed?" I responded. I would have to do my best not to let Brax see how shaken I still was. Maybe now I could learn the demon's true purpose.

"Well, I tell you," he continued, "I couldn't help but notice that you have a magic sword."

A chill went down my spine. What was he getting at?

"Indeed?" I said after a moment. "What do you mean?"

"Oh, don't act coy with me. I have an eye for this sort of thing. It's something you develop in the used-weapon business."

Brax paused dramatically before he spoke again.

"Listen. Do you know how much money there is in magic swords?"

I told Brax that I did not.

"I didn't think so. You may be sitting on a gold mine there!" The demon smiled convivially. "Or at least you have one hitched to your belt!"

"Indeed?" That was it! Only moments ago, the deadly sales forces of the Netherhells almost had me in their grasp. Now this demon wanted to take my only weapon and leave me defenseless! But I had discerned his insidious plan. Somehow I would have to outsmart this foul fiend!

"I could offer you a pretty price for it," Brax added when it became clear that I would say no more.

"Indeed," I said reflectively.

"That's all?" Brax complained. "Just 'indeed'? Here I am, offering you riches untold for one measly little sword and you won't even give me a simple yes or no? Ah, say no more, human. You are a shrewd bargainer. I can foresee a whole new career for you." The demon's voice lowered to a more confidential tone. "Listen, after this is all over, I was thinking about setting up some franchise operations above ground. You might be exactly the sort of fellow—"

"Doom!" The bold Hendrek interrupted the sales demon's spiel.

I looked up to see what had caused the large warrior's outburst. A whole section of the Netherhells mall seemed to have been totally destroyed. After seeing nothing but one establishment after another with names like "Pitchfork Paradise" and "Lost Soul City," we had come to a stretch where there was nothing but debris.

"Revitalization," Zzzzz whispered in wonder.

"I think not," Snarks replied grimly. He picked up a sign that read MAX'S BLASTER FURNACE! and then in smaller letters below: Hot enough for you? It will be inside!

"This does not seem to fit in with the Netherhells idea of progress," Snarks continued. "I smell human intervention here. This is part of the counterattack!"

So Ebenezum and the other wizards were already making themselves known! I stepped carefully through torn bits of wood and broken glass. The carnage here certainly was impressive. Perhaps we could defeat the Netherhells after all!

"Doom," Hendrek repeated.

And he was right. I felt it, too. It was odd, in a way, how quickly one became used to the nature of something. We had been walking through this strange mall for mere moments, yet I had already grown used to the never-ending rows of strangely named buildings with their bright displays and demonically smiling shopkeepers. While I knew that with every step through the Netherhells we were in danger, somehow that parade of shops had made it a controllable danger.

Now, though, we had stepped into chaos. Debris was scattered everywhere, pieces of displays, parts of goods, decimated building materials, perhaps even pieces of demons. The detritus covered virtually every inch of the green glowing ground, plunging the whole region into a darkness far more profound than any I had ever seen on the surface.

"Mmmmmmm!" came the cry from my belt.

Of course! I drew forth Cuthbert, the enchanted sword.

"That's more like it," the sword sighed as it burst into light. "I don't have to kill anybody, do I?"

"No, no," I quickly reassured the sword. "It just got a little dark down here."

"And you need a little light?" Cuthbert chortled. "That's the kind of job I was made for!"

We walked in silence for a moment.

"Why do you think it's so dark?" the sword added with some trepidation.

"Indeed," I mused. "There are signs here of a recent battle." I kicked the remains of a placard out of my path. The battle seemed to have been of some proportion. Had Ebenezum and his fellows at the college conjured up a magical army to come to our aid?

"Battle?" the sword shrilled. "Oh, I knew this whole thing would come to no good. Perhaps you should place me back in my scabbard. I mean, do you need me around that desperately? It isn't that dark now, is it?"

Actually the sword was right. It was getting lighter as we walked. We seemed to be reaching the end of whatever great struggle had taken place. In the distance, I could see where the row of stores resumed, all of them still brightly lit.

Brax was at my side again. "You've been holding out on me! You didn't tell me that the sword could talk!"

"Indeed," I replied, intent on looking ahead to where the stores resumed. "You did not ask!"

Was it my imagination, or did I hear the faint sound of battle?

"Wait a moment!" Cuthbert cried. "Do I hear someone appreciating me? Yes, I certainly do talk! And how about this light!" The sword glowed even more fiercely.

"Actually, glowing magic swords are fairly common," Brax remarked. "Intelligent conversation, on the other hand, is much more unusual."

"Conversation, perhaps," Snarks put in. "I don't think anyone here ever mentioned the word intelligent."

"You," Cuthbert whined. "Are you the one who called me measly?"

Snarks threw his hands forward protectively. "No, I would never say anything like that. I, for one, know your true worth." He pointed at Brax. "It was the other demon!"

"The other demon?" Cuthbert shrieked. "You mean the one admiring me? You two-faced denizen of the Netherhells! You play with fire when you toy with a magic sword!"

"Who, me?" Brax smiled endearingly behind his cigar. "I am but a poor salesdemon, trying to eke out a living. What did I say?"

"I heard you distinctly. You referred to me as 'one measly little sword'! I know! That's what people think of you when all you can do is hack and slash! I tell you, I wouldn't have this problem if I were a magic mirror!"

"Doom," said Hendrek close to my ear. "I thought that the

sword could not hear when it was placed inside the scabbard."

Hendrek was right. I had been under the same impression. I pulled the sword down in front of my eyes and inquired as to the discrepancy.

"Oh. Only a little white lie," Cuthbert admitted. "You don't know how boring owners can be. Whenever they pull me out, they always go on and on about honor and valor and stuff like that. Ah, but when they put me away, it's a different matter! I tell you, I hear some of the best bits when I'm not supposed to be able to hear at all!"

For my part, I heard a great crash before us. We had come quite close to the other end of the debris-laden no-demon's-land. In fact, that crash had come from the mall.

"Doom," Hendrek said.

I thought about returning Cuthbert to his scabbard to put an end to his arguing. But I might have quick need of a sword, and anyone standing within a mile or so of our present location had surely heard us by now. Still, perhaps whatever small army was fighting within would be too busy to bother with us and let us continue on our way.

The mall road curved ahead so we could not see more than a half dozen buildings before us. We did, however, hear the three voices call in unison from somewhere far ahead.

"We will catch the intruders."

"Doom!" Hendrek voiced what I thought. " 'Tis the Dread Collectors!"

"We will throw them in prison!" the voices, now closer, cried as one.

Another loud crash came from the shop to our left. Perhaps we could hide in one of the buildings! But the storefronts here were dark and the doors bolted against catastrophe.

"We will trap them there forever!" the voices, now quite distinct, chanted in unison.

"Quick!" Snarks urged. "We have to do something!"

A foot flew through the window of the building to our left, right through the painted sign that read "Snurff's House of Degradation." The foot withdrew within the building, followed by a chorus of screams.

CHAPTER TEN

Magic weapons can, on occasion, be of great use, yet one more part of the truly rounded wizard's arsenal of tricks, spells, and remarks for all occasions. However, the thoroughly prepared mage will find certain spells of even more importance than these, especially those enchantments which produce magic wings, magic carpets, and magic running boots, for those times when the rest of your arsenal fails you completely

—from The Teachings of Ebenezum, Volume LVII

As bad as it sounded outside of Snurff's House of Degradation, it was much worse inside. Whatever the original purpose of the shop had been, it now looked like its sole purpose was to sell debris. The air was full of dust and the ground crunched and snapped beneath our feet. I drew Cuthbert again from its midnight-blue scabbard, but even the sword's magic light was lost in this gloom. I instructed Snarks to grab hold of my belt, and Hendrek to grasp Snarks's hood, and so on down the line. With the atmosphere this murky, the only way we might stay together was to form a living chain.

"Do I have to be out here?" Cuthbert whined. "I warn you, I tarnish very easily!"

I told the sword to be still. There were other voices up ahead.

"You!" a particularly nasty voice screamed. "You really disgust me!"

"Glurph!" a second, equally nasty voice cried in panic. "I don't think he came here for that!"

"Remember the really bad things your mother used to call you when she was mad at you?" the first nasty voice continued. "Well, she was right! Except she was your mother, so she was being too kind!"

"Glurph!" the second voice screamed. "You'll only make him angrier!"

"You remember when you failed that examination? When you forgot your beloved's birthday? You thought you were unworthy! You called yourself a miserable worm, unfit to do anything but crawl through the earth on your belly! Well, youwere being too kind! Even the ground under your feet is too good—"

"Glurph! Are you crazy? You keep this up and we're both dead demons!"

"No!" the first nasty voice shouted in triumph. "I know precisely what I'm saying to this miserable piece of slime! I was born a degrader. I lived as a degrader. Now let me die as a degrader! Urrracchhtt!"

There was a thump, as if something heavy had fallen to the floor.

"Glurph?" the other voice said tentatively. "Oh, I see. Look, I can be much more pleasant than that dead fellow over there. Really! For example, I'm sure your mother didn't really mean all those terrible things she said about you. Oh, surely, there must have been some truth in—urracchhtt!"

There was another heavy thump and a large, black-clothed, extremely well muscled shape loomed before me.

"Not satisfying," the shape said. "Not satisfying at all."

With a sudden shock, I realized that I recognized that shape and the voice behind it.

"You!" I exclaimed.

The shape turned around, a man dressed all in black, a symphony of perfectly tuned muscles in motion.

"Oh, excuse me," a mild voice said. "I haven't seen you in quite some time."

I was right! It was the Dealer of Death!

I held Cuthbert before me. "Come!" I shouted. "Try to take me, if you must!"

"Wait a second!" the sword cried. "Is this a fight? Don't I get to say anything about this?"

"A talking sword?" The Dealer's well-muscled face smiled. "Now that is interesting. Very little has been of any interest whatsoever, you know, since my descent into the Netherhells."

"That's right! I'm a talking sword! And I really want to ask you two fellows to talk things over! It's amazing how often bloodshed may be avoided with a little reasoned discussion--"

"I beg your pardon?" the Dealer inquired. "Who said anything about bloodshed?"

"Oh, well," Cuthbert coughed. "I just assumed, being a drawn sword and all--"

"On the contrary, Wuntvor and I here--I did recall your name right, did I not?--anyway Wuntvor and I have nothing at all to fight about. Oh, it is true that I had a contract to kill him and his two companions, one Ebenezum and one Hendrek, I believe, but that was back on the surface world. Besides, as you may recall, the king who gave me the contract was being a little stingy and perhaps more than a little underhanded in his terms. I've had a lot of chance to think since I've come to the Netherhells, and I've come up with a great many questions about that contract's legality. Therefore, if I'm going to kill Wuntvor, I can't do so until I renegotiate the contract in question." The Dealer smiled with muscular lips. "So there's nothing to fight about whatsoever!"

"Thank goodness!" Cuthbert cried. "See what a little talking can do?"

"Excuse me," I said to the Dealer as a pointed the sword toward its scabbard.

"Where are you putting me?" Cuthbert complained. "I was getting interested! You can't--"

"There," I said with some satisfaction. The scabbard allowed us to hrear only the most muted of overwrought mumblings. "Indeed," I said to the Dealer. "I believe you had your hand in all the destruction we saw on our way here?"

The Dealer smiled again. "In all humility, I must say I did have something to do with it." He flexed his great muscles absently. "It all has to do with frustration, really. I've strangled thousands of demons. I'm afraid the fun's going out of it. Ah, sometimes I long for the simple pleasures of the surface world. I say, one of you wouldn't happen to have a wild pig handy?"

A quick conference revealed that no one had stashed a pig.

"A pity." The Dealer tried to smile through his disappointment. "Oh, well, it was an insane hope. I so enjoy strangling pigs. It's a real hands-on experience! You can't get that kind of grip on a demon, you know." The Dealer made a particularly muscular frown. "Demons tend to squish."

"Indeed," I replied, sensing that it was time to change the subject. "We are on our way to rescue Vushta. Would you like to come along?"

"Rescue Vushta?" the Dealer asked. "Where has it gotten itself to?"

I explained briefly about the dastardly attack of the Netherhells.

"Oh, that does sound rather more interesting than what I've been doing of late." The Dealer cracked his large and impressive knuckles. "I'll still be squishing demons, I suppose, but now I'll be doing it for a cause! You don't suppose there'd be a wild pig or two left in Vushta, do you?"

"Anything is possible," I suggested.

"One can still dream." The Dealer sighed wistfully. His breath cleared the dust from half the room. "But there are more demons here!"

I hastily explained that Snarks, Brax, and Zzzzz had joined us on our quest.

"It is a strange land here, with strange customs." The muscles in the Dealer's neck rippled as he nodded his head. "I will abide by your guidance. My skills have become dulled down here. I think rescuing the largest city in the known world from hordes of demonic fiends is exactly the sort of thing I need to hone my reflexes. It sounds like it will be extremely difficult and very, very bloody!" The Dealer laughed with delight at the thought.

"Good," I replied. "Then we should be on our way. Is there a back way out of here?"

Before the Dealer could respond, I heard three other voices cry as one: "We have found you!"

"Doom!" Hendrek moaned, Headbasher at the ready.

The shapes moved toward us through the dust-laden store.

"The Dread Collectors!" cried Snarks.

"Revitalization at last!" cried Zzzzz.

"Hey, fellows?" cried Brax. "We used to work together! Remember me?"

"Collectors?" the Dealer inquired. "Perhaps they have stronger necks than demons! Perhaps it will feel much like strangling a wild pig!"

"We have come to take you prisoner," the three voices proclaimed as one. And then the claws and teeth came for us.

Hendrek's war club somehow deflected one tearing, howling mass of death. I pulled Cuthbert free of its sheath.

"What?" the sword screamed. "What are you doing now? Let's run away! I don't want to get involved in this again!"

"It will be easier if you do not resist us!" the three voices exhorted as they slashed and bit.

Brax danced away from the triple engine of mayhem, waving his cigar. Snarks and Zzzzz rooted through the debris of the shop for something they might use as a weapon.

"We do not plan to kill you yet!" the three horrible voices chanted.

Snarks came up with some sort of long metal bar, which he expertly twirled around to keep a Collector's claws at bay. Zzzzz threw bits of broken glass and pottery as he shouted "Revitalization! Revitalization!" in a high and eerie tone.

"We must deliver you to the demon Guxx Unfufadoo!" the Collectors all cried. "Before you die, Guxx must torture the truth from you!"

I felt a sudden moment of fear. What if that was what the Collectors had done with Norei? Had my beloved perished some horrible way at the hands of that foul fiend, Guxx Unfufadoo? If so, then all the Netherhells would pay!

"Easy there!" Cuthbert screamed as I slashed at the nearest Collector. "Watch out! Coming through!" My sword grazed the thing's dark and oily pelt. Green ichor once again stained the blade.

"Now see what you've made me do?" Cuthbert squealed, absolutely beside itself. "Oh, I can't tell you how much I hate ichor!"

I barely dodged a set of raging Collector's claws as I watched the Dealer launch himself onto the thing's back.

"Where's the neck?" the Dealer bellowed as he felt rapidly beneath the thing's pelt. "Hold still for a moment so I can find your neck!"

"Doom!" Hendrek cried as he smashed Headbasher into a Collector whose claws were perilously close to my head.

"We can defeat these things!" the large warrior called to me. "Let us stand back to back. I will have at the fiends with my club while you stab away with your sword!"

"Must we?" Cuthbert wailed.

And then I realized that I did not have to wield my sword! The last time, I had defeated these foul things through the use of another of my magical weapons—Wonk, the horn of persuasion! But Wonk was in a sack which I had set aside when I began the fight. Where had I put it?

"Look out!" Cuthbert screamed in a voice much higher than usual. I was looking straight down a black hole bordered all around with sharp Collector fangs!

Blue sparks flew as Cuthbert bounced off the thing's razor teeth. I leaped sideways. The jaws snapped shut inches from my face. And the thing kept on going, toward the back of the large warrior who was fighting behind me!

"Hendrek!" I cried as the slavering creature descended upon him, jaws open so wide that it made the huge warrior seem no more than a child.

"Doom!" Hendrek's voice echoed in the vast cavern of the Collector's mouth as the warrior spun about to face it. His war club came down full force upon the foul thing's nose.

The Collector staggered back.

"Urk!" all three Collectors howled as one.

"Doom!" the large warrior intoned. He swung his war club in ever-widening arcs above his head. "We have them now! Doom! Doom! Doom!"

Snarks appeared at Hendrek's side, twirling his iron pipe. Zzzzz had found a long jagged plank, which he wielded much as I used to handle my stout oak staff. He stepped to Hendrek's other side. The Dealer still rode one of the Collectors somewhere out in the vast dust-filled shop, crying, "The neck! Where's the neck?"

We did seem to have the upper hand. But it was all too easy. Where was the third Collector?

My eyes swept that part of the room I could see through the dust, searching for the third fearsome monster. It had seemed too easy to defeat the fiends this time. Were the three Collectors luring us into some sort of trap?

And then my gaze fell on the sack that contained Wonk, the horn of persuasion. If I could reach that fearsome instrument and blow but a single note, whatever trap the Collectors were planning would evaporate as fast as the quick-moving fiends could disappear.

"Listen." Brax's voice came from somewhere. "There must be some way we can compromise!"

I moved, rapidly but carefully, toward the sack. Brax ran from the dust-laden darkness, his lit cigar like a beacon before him.

"Well, you can't say I didn't try—oof!" he grunted as he ran into my quickly moving legs.

I yelled as I fell. My sword yelled as it was flung from my grasp.

I felt a weight upon my back. A sharp point pricked at my skin. I feared it was a Collector's claw.

I could still see Hendrek from where I lay. He swung once again for the Collector's nose. But this time the thing's claws, moving even faster than the warrior's enchanted weapon, lifted both club and man aloft. The Collector casually tossed Hendrek over its shoulder.

"Dooooooo—" And then his voice was lost in the dust and the distance. The Dealer was similarly tossed away, as a horse might remove a fly.

"We will take you to Guxx now," three voices said in unison. The claw at my back grasped my shirt and lifted me aloft.

"Wait a minute!" Snarks protested as a Collector bent to pick him up. "I'm a demon!"

"So we noticed." The Collector who held me shook me in Snarks's direction. "Is this then a demon in disguise?"

"No," Snarks admitted. "Actually, that's a young wizard intent on rescuing Vushta from the clutches of the Netherhells."

"So we thought," the Collectors intoned. "We will take him to be tortured by Guxx."

The three Collectors turned and marched from the store, one by one. The one that carried me moved after the other two. It slung me over its shoulder. I stared in horror at Snarks, rapidly shrinking in the distance.

Snarks shrugged. "I cannot tell a lie."

CHAPTER ELEVEN

*"What?" you cry. "Wizards sometimes must endure torture?"
And it is true, for being a wizard does not exempt you from any of the
trials and tribulations experienced by other humans.*

*But I would ask you to consider just what you mean by "torture."
What of those occasions when you save a kingdom and then are forced
to sit there and listen for hours to endless numbers of boring elected
officials extolling your praises while the kingdom's tax collectors
repossess nine-tenths of what you gainfully earned at your task? Is
this not torture? What about the times when you are on the verge of
creating a spell that will give you inner peace at last and your spouse
bursts into your study and tells you to clean up the mess because all of
your in-laws are coming to stay for three weeks, and we will have to set
up a bed in here because Aunt Sadie needs a place to sleep? Is this not
torture? And say you are attending a wizard's convention and are sure
that your gold production spell will win first prize in the competition,
and then they give the award to the animal husbandry spell of some
part-time wizard because the judge has a particular fondness for pigs?
Is this not—but why belabor the obvious? By now you surely see my
point. Laugh in the face of torture! It is, after all, no worse than what
they do to you every other day of the week.*

—from Ask Ebenezum: The Greatest Wizard in the Western
Kingdoms Answers the Four Hundred Most Asked Questions
about Wizardry, fourth edition

So now I would be tortured by Guxx. I would perish in some
horribly complicated, painful way, far from my homeland, I
having failed both my master and the entire surface world. I
tried to think of some positive aspect of my situation. So far, I
could not come up with one.

"We will take you to the dungeon," all three Collectors said.

"Indeed!" I cried, eager to keep these creatures talking. Perhaps I could get them to reveal some secret of the Netherhells that I could somehow use to my advantage. "Will I meet Guxx there?"

"We will leave you at the dungeon until Guxx is ready!" the three monstrosities answered. "He will torture you at his leisure!"

So Guxx wouldn't get me immediately! In an odd way, it was almost heartening. I would find some way yet to escape from these fiends and continue with my quest! They had not heard the last from Wuntvor the apprentice!

"Indeed," I continued. "And what will you do?"

"We?" the Collectors chorused. "We must collect!"

These creatures were still not telling me anything I did not already know. I would have to question them more closely.

"And do you always take what you collect to the dungeons?" I asked tentatively.

"No, we do not!" The Collectors turned as one, moving down a passageway that cut away at right angles from the constant row of stores.

My heart leaped. I remembered, long ago, my master telling me about magical creatures sometimes having hidden weaknesses. Perhaps there was some secret code or special bit of magic that would force these demonic monsters to free me!

"Indeed!" I remarked. Perhaps, if I was clever, I could discover the weakness that would allow me to escape from the Collectors before I ever saw the dungeon!

"And what happens to those you do not take to jail?" I asked craftily.

"Oh!" the creatures replied calmly. "We rip them into tiny shreds!"

"Indeed," I replied with somewhat less enthusiasm. Then again, perhaps this was not the proper line of questioning after all. What should I try next? Perhaps I should quiz them on their home lives.

"We are here!" The Collectors stated proudly.

"Here?" I said. "Where?"

I was unceremoniously dropped in the dirt.

"Your home," the Collectors added, "for the rest of your life!"

I looked up beyond the three fanged horrors. There before me was a great wall of greenish gray, topped with a row of daggers. Beyond the daggers stood a dozen blood-red hounds who snarled down at whatever had the misfortune to lurk on the wall's other side. Directly before me was a gate that seemed somehow to be composed completely of sharpened spikes. Above the gate was a great sign, carved in stone ten feet high:

NETHERHELLS MOST HORRENDOUS

DUNGEON NUMBER FOUR

JUNIOR DIVISION

And below that, in words two feet high:

LOSE VIRTUALLY ALL HOPE YE WHO ENTER HERE

"For the rest of my life?" I whispered.

The gate of spikes opened seemingly of its own accord and the fattest demon I had ever seen waddled forth. Bright purple in color, he reminded me of nothing so much as a grape with legs.

"Don't worry," the bloated demon remarked. "Your life won't be all that long." The fiend waved at the Collectors. "You have done your job well. The doomed soul is mine now. You may go."

"We go to collect!" The three massive monsters turned in unison and ambled back up the passageway.

"I am called Urrpphh!" The bloated demon grinned fiendishly. "And I am your master, at least for what little time you have left!" Urrpphh laughed hideously, as if he had said something funny.

"But I must introduce you to my minions," the demon continued. "Come to me, my lovelies!"

"Slobber!" they cried as they poured from the gates. "Slobber! Slobber!"

I knew what they were in an instant. I had seen trolls before; tall, dark, muscular, but mostly mouth, rather like a walking set of very sharp teeth.

One of them tentatively put its mouth around my head.

"No! No!" Urrpphh shouted. "Not to eat! To torture!"

"No slobber?" the troll whined, genuinely disappointed.

"Come," the demon said graciously. "Allow my minions and me to escort you around the grounds."

We entered a large enclosure full of the green glowing moss I had seen elsewhere in my travels underground. It almost looked like an open field. It might even have been pleasant were it not for the screams I heard in the distance.

"Oh, those?" Urrpphh said as I winced. "Yes, you will become more familiar with those as time progresses."

Urrpphh and his trolls led me to the first of a series of low buildings built in a circle around the edge of the field. A heavily spiked door swung open as we approached.

"My office." Urrpphh waved me in before him. "You are welcome to visit at any time. Number Four, you see, is a merciful dungeon. When your torture has become truly unbearable, you may come here to grovel on your hands and knees, perhaps even on your belly, and beg for mercy. Not, of course, that it will do any good."

I looked about the virtually featureless room. Everything seemed to be made of stone. Walls, floor, and ceiling were all built of great gray blocks. Even the desk looked as if it had been carved from a boulder.

"Yes, I see you've noticed!" Urrpphh exclaimed with some pride. "I've done the entire place in Modern Rock!"

The demon rested easily on a corner of his great stone desk. "I take great pride in this dungeon. I've built this place up from almost nothing! You saw those words, etched in stone at the entranceway? 'Lose virtually all hope...' well, you know the ones. You don't know how much I struggled to get those words. And still they call this dungeon a junior division! I push forward a mile and they give me an inch!"

The demon pointed to one wall of his cavernous office. "Look at the signs I've managed to take down over the years! I keep them all as a measure of my achievement!"

I looked to where he pointed. There were three more of those two-foot-high sentences etched in rock. I quickly scanned the one on top:

LOSE A GREAT DEAL OF YOUR HOPE YE WHO ENTER HERE

The one immediately below it read:

LOSE SOME OF YOUR HOPE YE WHO ENTER...

I didn't even bother to finish the sentence, instead glancing down at the lowest inscription of the three:

YOU MIGHT LOSE A LITTLE BIT OF YOUR HOPE IF YOU'RE THAT TYPE YE...

I looked back up at Urrpphh. I could see his point.

"Yes!" The demon nodded. "And every upgrading was a struggle, let me tell you. You have to keep your thumbscrews perpetually tight, your iron maiden polished, your oil just about to boil! Real estate! That's all the Netherhells cares about these days! You have to fight or they'll take away your pretty jail and put a Slime-O-Rama in its place. Think about it! Here you are, a hard-working demon devoting all your life to the furtherance of pain and suffering. Then one false move and it's goodbye dungeon, hello Slime Burgers!"

"Indeed," I said when I perceived it was my turn to speak. "I suppose that's what they call progress?"

"Progress?" Urrpphh grimaced. "Have you ever tried a Slime Burger? But I forget." He laughed diabolically. "You are a guest here. Soon they will be your total diet!"

Slime Burgers my total diet? I was beginning to like this demon's laugh even less. Perhaps he had brought me here to taunt me, to extend my suffering as long as possible. Well, I would show him that Wuntvor the apprentice was made of sterner stuff!

"Torture me, then," I cried. "Do your worst! It will be over soon enough!"

"Oh, no!" The demon's laugh was even more hideous than before. "We don't torture you yet! First it is time for your agonies!"

Agonies? I didn't like the sound of that at all. Could there be something worse than torture?

"Come," Urrpphh said solicitously. "We will show you to your cell."

"Slobber, slobber," the trolls added.

I was once again surrounded by the ill-smelling creatures. There seemed to be no chance of escape. What had I to look forward to? Torture? Agony? Perhaps, I wondered, it would be better if I were to provoke one of these trolls and end it all?

And then I thought of Norei. Where had they taken her in this vast, strange kingdom? She might even, I realized, be trapped in this very dungeon. I had come down into this place where danger lurked at every turn more to save her than to rescue Vushta. I could admit that to myself now that I was so close to death. Letting the trolls eat me was the coward's way out. If there was one chance in a hundred that I might escape, even one chance in a thousand, I owed it to Norei. I was not fighting for only myself now. I was fighting for my beloved!

I gritted my teeth as we entered another low building. "Do your worst," I murmured.

"Oh, don't worry," Urrpphh replied. "We intend to."

The trolls grabbed my arms and dragged me rapidly down a long, circular stone stairway.

"No!" a voice screamed from down below. "Not again! Have you no mercy?"

"Halt, minions!" Urrpphh instructed the bustling trolls. "I want our new guest to see this. It is most instructive as to our methods."

"Slobber!" The trolls pushed me forward so that my face was pressed against the iron bars of a window that looked into a large, well-lit room. The room seemed to be used for purposes of public assembly, for it was filled with rows of benches. At the moment, however, only one man sat in this hall, his form secured to a bench by a dozen thick chains encircling his body. His once fine clothes were torn and caked with blood and his scholarly face was surrounded by a crown of wildly matted hair. He faced a long stage, occupied now by no more than a large yellow sign with ornate, red letters which spelled: "Showtime in two minutes."

"No!" he shrieked. "I can't stand it again!"

"The man you see before you," Urrpphh whispered in my ear, "was once a famed dramatist upon the surface world, producing both wondrous comedy and dire tragedy. Due to a slight error on his part, he signed an agreement with certain demons down below. And we have him now!"

"And you force him to watch plays?" I replied with some relief. "That doesn't sound so bad."

"Bah! There are no plays performed on that stage!" Urrpphh laughed again. "We force him to watch vaudeville! And it is the worst vaudeville imaginable!"

I blinked.*** There was a new sign on the stage, larger than the one before, yellow letters on a royal blue background. This one read: "Showtime in one minute!" "No!" the playwright pleaded. "Please. Please! I cannot take any more!"

"This is a particularly successful agony," Urrpphh said with smug satisfaction. "Few individuals realize the great care we take in producing our agonies, you know. It takes great skill to do it just right. Why, until recently, we not only employed demonic actors and stage technicians, but a full staff of demonic writers to concoct the most horrendous vaudeville routines imaginable!"

"Until recently?" I inquired.

"Yes!" The demon chuckled evilly. "As you may know, we in the Netherhells dungeon business are always on the lookout for efficient cost-cutting measures. Our scouts have located a vaudeville act on the surface world far worse than anything our former writing team could ever come up with! We simply steal this act verbatim, and our guest the dramatist goes through far worse agonies than any he had ever experienced." Urrpphh laughed again even more horribly than before, a sound halfway between that of some large animal retching and water gurgling down a drain.

Perhaps the most bloodcurdling scream I have ever heard issued from the dramatist's throat. He thrashed about wildly in a vain attempt to rearrange his chains so that his bench no longer faced the stage. There was an even larger sign there now, pale green in color with huge, black letters: IT'S SHOWTIME!

"This is so bad!" Urrpphh chortled.

A pair of demons trotted out onto the stage. One wore a dress while the other appeared to be garbed in the skin of some large lizard. The two began to sing together:

Wuntvor wasn't much of a wizard,
No ifs, no ands, no buts!
Surely demons drink his blood,
And they've ripped out all his—
"But you have seen enough!" Urrpphh interrupted. "Now it
is time for an agony of your very own!"

The dramatist's incoherent screams faded in the distance as
the trolls dragged me down the corridor.

"Slobber!" the trolls cried as they opened the cell door at
corridor's end.

"Slobber!" they shrieked as they threw me inside."Slobber!"
they called as they slammed the door behind me and shuffled
away.

"Enjoy your suffering!" Urrpphh exclaimed, and then the
demon was gone as well.

It was soft where I had landed. I looked up with some
trepidation to discern the true nature of my prison. But what
was this? It looked as if I were sitting in the midst of a forest
glade upon the surface world, the bright midday sun filtered by
a roof of green leaves.

I forced my heart to slow, my breathing to become regular. So
far this wasn't at all terrible. Perhaps Urrpphh and his minions
had made some mistake.

"Wuntvor?" a woman's voice called to me.

My hopes suddenly took wing. Could it be?

A woman appeared between the trees, but it was not Norei.
The newcomer was comely enough, with raven tresses and
piercing black eyes, but I could not hide my disappointment.
Somewhere in the distance I heard faint music play.

"Wuntvor!" the woman pouted. "At last you have come.
Why aren't you happy to see me?"

"Excuse me," I replied, still somewhat distracted. "Have we
met?"

She laughed, a sound usually reserved for bells of finest
silver. "Oh, that is it! You toy with your beloved!" She walked
toward me over the soft earth that was strewn with pine needles.
"Still, you have met me at our favorite spot, here by our forest
bed."

Forest bed? What was she talking about? Had this woman been sent here to entice me? Well, she was certainly beautiful. But no! I was true to Norei. I would not fall victim to some Netherhells trick! I noticed that strange music again. It seemed to have grown louder.

"Oh, Wuntvor!" the woman cooed as she reached my side. "You are so tense. Here. Allow me to relax you." She stood before me and placed one long-fingered hand on each of my shoulders, then gazed deep into my eyes. I did not find it relaxing. Why was my mouth so dry? Wasn't that music getting louder?

"Wuntvor," the raven-haired woman whispered. "You don't know how long I've waited, nay, how long I've dreamed about this moment. Oh, how I burn for your kiss!"

Yes, I was sure the music was louder now. It surrounded us both and made it difficult to think. What was happening? Was it the Netherhells Buying Fever again? But there was nothing here to buy. My, but this woman's eyes were awfully large. I hadn't really noticed how attractive her lips were, either. I was finding it difficult to breathe, also.

"Oh, Wuntvor," the woman sighed, and my name on her lips was the most wonderful sound in the world. "Oh," she moaned, "Wuntvor! Take me!"

Yes, I would! Yes! Anything she wanted! Yes! Her hands moved across my shoulder blades to draw me near to her. Yes! Our faces grew close, our lips closer still. Yes! Yes! Yes!

"Daughter?" cried a voice gruffer than that of the trolls.

I kissed empty air. My raven-haired beauty had pulled away.

"Oh, woe!" she moaned. "It is my father, who is sworn to kill any man who might love me. You are so brave, Wuntvor, to love me as you do, knowing that my father is the greatest swordsman in all of the kingdom. But hark! He comes through the trees!"

There was a great rustling just out of sight, as if not one swordsman, but an entire army, approached.

"Run, my beloved, run, or he shall skewer your liver!" My raven-haired beauty leaned over to kiss me, but then thought better of it. She pushed me into the trees opposite the approaching sounds of her father.

I ran until I reached another clearing. I paused to gain my breath as best I could, to run farther if need be, but I heard no sounds of pursuit.

It was only then that I had time to think about what had happened to me.

Who was that raven-haired beauty? What had she wanted from me? Even though we had only just met, my lips still ached for her kiss and my arms still yearned for her embrace.

I shook myself. Why wasn't I thinking of Norei? I remembered the music then, swelling all about me, carrying both me and my new lover to heights of anticipation. It had to be another Netherhells trick! Well, whatever they were doing to me, I knew of their foul plans now. I would not let it happen again!

Something warm covered my eyes.

"Guess who, Wuntvor?" a woman's voice said. She removed her hands from my face and I turned to see a woman with hair blonder than Alea's.

"Do I know you?" I asked. Did I hear that music again in the distance?

"Oh, so you are playing games with me as well!" The woman laughed. "I know a game we can play!"

So the Netherhells would try the same trick! No, this time I knew! Somehow I had to get out of this trap and find Norei, my true beloved! I began to turn away.

"Why do you not answer me, sweet one?" the blond woman pouted. She grabbed hold of my arm with surprising strength. I looked back into the deepest blue eyes I had ever seen.

No! I would remember Norei! The blond woman took my chin between her thumb and forefinger. Yes, the music was definitely there! I could almost make out the melody!

"Ah, that is more like it," the beautiful woman said. She was using her other hand to stroke the back of my neck at the bottom of my hair line. It made chills pass through my whole being. I was supposed to remember somebody, wasn't I? Or something? Oh, who cared! All I needed to remember were my beloved's eyes, my beloved's lips, and my beloved's hair.

I leaned forward to kiss her.

"Where are you, wife?"

"Oh, no!" the blond cried, leaping away from me. "We are discovered! I knew we should stop meeting like this! But you were so insistent, even though my husband is the greatest archer in the kingdom! Oh, how could I resist!"

An arrow embedded itself in a tree by my left ear.

"He has seen us!" The blond shuddered. "Oh, Wuntvor, my husband is such a vengeful man! After he shoots you, he will have you drawn and quartered! Oh, run, Wuntvor! Run for your life!"

Another arrow whizzed close by my right ear. I turned and took my beloved's advice, although it meant we could never fulfill our love.

I stopped running after a moment. What was I thinking of? What love? Norei! That was who I was supposed to remember. It was so hard to think with that music playing!

"Wuntvor!" a woman's voice called from the woods before me. "What a surprise!"

Oh, no. I wouldn't let this happen to me again! I would turn and run, somewhere where there were not all these women constantly hounding me.

And then the third woman stepped out from between the trees. She had red hair, just as Norei had red hair. But Norei's hair was dull by comparison. This woman's hair was the color of flame!

"Wuntvor!" she cried. "Do not reject me!"

I could hear the music building behind me. If I did not escape now, I knew it would be too late! "Excuse me," I said without conviction. "I have something I have to do—er—in another part of the forest."

The beautiful red-headed woman walked quickly up to me and threw me to the ground. "Wuntvor!" she repeated. "Do not reject me!"

And seeing her this close, how could I? Those perfect lips, those eyes the color of the sea. Why had I wanted to run away from her? I let her pull me up to her by my shirt front, let the music swell around us, binding us together. We would be as one forever! I needed to take her to my den!

"Lunch time!" came a voice from behind me.

I heard a door slam against a wall. They had opened my cell! I had quite forgotten I was in a cell.

"Beloved!" I murmured to the beautiful red-headed woman. Her lips were so close to mine!

There was a roar in the distance.

"Oh, no!" she said. "It is my intended, who through enchantment has been turned into the most fearsome fire-breathing dragon in all the kingdom! He swore, if ever I was to even kiss a man before—"

"Slobber!" A troll grabbed my arm and pulled me away from my rapidly-speaking love.

"W-what?" I stammered as Urrpphh's face suddenly loomed before me. "Who?" I shook my head, but it was as if I could not awaken. Why didn't they stop that too-loud music? "Where?"

"Sorry you got pulled away mid-embrace, huh?" the demon smirked. "Pardon me. It was really almost mid-embrace, wasn't it? Well, you'll have plenty more of the same opportunities, believe me. But for now, you have to eat. You need to keep up your strength, you know!"

The troll dragged me toward a table set for one. On the place before me was a sea of gray muck surrounding two slices of soggy bread.

"This is a real occasion," Urrpphh chortled. "You're about to eat your very first Slime Burger!"

Slime Burger? They expected me to eat Slime Burgers? This, at last, was too much. Even the Netherhells could only push Wuntvor the apprentice so far. I struggled mightily in the troll's grasp.

The troll calmly flipped me over its shoulder and began to carry me toward the offending meal. Two things fell from my pocket: a piece of parchment and a small, red card.

The troll picked up the card.

"No slobber!" it squealed in terror.

"Let me see that!" Urrpphh demanded. The troll got rid of the card as if it burned its fingers.

"Why, you..." Urrpphh began, almost beside himself with rage. "How did you get—" He stopped with visible effort, staring at the card, and then turned his hate-filled gaze straight at me.

"Get out of here!"

Yes! It was so obvious! Why hadn't I thought of it! There were the words of the card, in bold, block letters: GET OUT OF JAIL FREE!

The door to my cell opened of its own accord. They were letting me go! I would not question my good fortune. I moved rapidly out the door and down the corridor.

"No!" the dramatist screamed as I passed. "Not an encore! Anything but an encore!"

But I could spare nothing but a moment's pity for the poor, doomed soul. Through a stroke of either luck or my master's foresight I had been spared from almost certain madness. And I had been given another chance to find my beloved Norei and save Vushta in the bargain!

"Slobber!" the trolls yelled behind me. "Slobber!"

They sounded close behind me. Too close. Were they following me?

"Of course, once you are beyond the dungeon walls," Urrpphh called after me, "there is nothing to keep us from taking you prisoner again." He laughed demonically. "But this time you will no longer have the card!"

I distinctly heard a rip. The rip of a small, red card, without doubt.

Huge hounds barked down at me from the parapets. The main gate opened before me barely wide enough to let me pass between its crimson spikes.

"Slobber!" the trolls chorused, even closer now than before. "Slobber!"

I stepped beyond the spiked gate to freedom. I thought I felt hot troll breath upon my neck. I began to run through the spongy glowing moss with every ounce of strength I had remaining.

"Slobber!" a troll sounded in my ear.

How long could I stay free? I had to escape, for my master, for Vushta, and my beloved.

"Norei!" I cried as I ran.

And someone answered me.

CHAPTER TWELVE

Reunions can be a wonderful thing, especially when neither of the reunited parties manage to recall what separated them in the first place.

—from The Teachings of Ebenezum, Wizard's Digest Condensed edition

"Slobber!"

"Slobber! Slobber!"

There were trolls on either side of me!

"Wuntvor!" the voice called to me again from up ahead. It couldn't be! And yet it was!

"Norei!" I shouted with every bit of breath left in my lungs. And then the trolls grabbed me.

"Slobber! Slobber! Slobber!"

They surrounded me. There must have been a dozen or more of them! Large, hairy hands grabbed my arms and legs and hair. The trolls began to drag me back toward the dungeon.

I felt a cold wind blow all about me. The trolls stopped in their tracks.

"Slobber!" the trolls cried in confusion. "No slobber!"

I looked up as the trolls loosened their grip upon my body. Where were we? I couldn't tell in what direction the trolls had been dragging me, nor could I tell quite where I had been.

Then it occurred to me. Norei must be using a misdirection spell! Maybe this would give me a chance to escape. Summoning my remaining strength, I jerked free of the last troll's grasp. I would run to my beloved witch! Together we would turn back the trolls and rescue Vushta in the bargain.

But which way was Norei? I could barely distinguish between up and down, let alone right, left, forward, and back!

"Norei!" I cried out to the chaos.

"Wuntvor!" she called back and the spell was broken for me. My beloved stood a mere fifty paces farther down the corridor! I ran, calling her name again.

"Slobber!"

I was seized again by hairy hands. Unfortunately, when the spell broke for me, it also broke for the trolls as well. I felt myself being pulled back toward the dungeon.

"Norei!" I shouted, more than a tinge of panic in my voice.

A warm wind blew by us all.

"Slobber!" the confused trolls cried again. "No slobber!" The ground seemed to have turned to mud, sucking their feet within so they could not move. But how could I escape? My feet were disappearing into the mud as well!

"Wuntvor!" Norei called as she ran up to the edge of the muddy morass. " 'Tis but a temporary hindrance spell. There are too many trolls here. I will need to think of something really powerful to set you free!"

"Norei!" I responded. "I have faith in you!"

"Good. I believe we can use all the faith we have." My beloved frowned, as if concentrating on the next spell she would use. She flung out her hands and shouted a dozen words.

A wind of near-searing heat blew past me and the trolls.

"No slobber!" the trolls began to cry in panic. The powerful spell spun them about and pressed them to the mud.

But my beloved had miscalculated. The heat from this new spell was so great that it began to dry the morass entrapping my captors' feet. One by one, they began to pull themselves free of the imprisoning muck.

"Slobber!" one said tentatively.

"Slobber! Slobber!" another added with much greater authority.

I once again found myself grasped by a myriad of troll hands.

"No!" I protested.

A bunch of flowers fell out of my shirt.

What? For an instant, my confused mind searched for meaning in the daisies about my feet. Then I remembered the hat. Norei had told me it might be reactivated during periods of extreme magic! And there was extreme magic all about me now!

"Yes!" I cried.

A bunch of scarves fell into the mud.

The wind buffeted the trolls back again. Some of them even lost their hold upon my person. Oddly enough, I did not feel the wind as strongly as I had before. Somehow, Norei was modulating her spell so that it affected the trolls much more than it affected me!

Still, though, it was not enough for the trolls to release me completely from their collective death grip. However, what would happen if there were some further distraction? It was certainly worth the attempt. Perhaps it just might work!

"Perhaps!" I shouted. "Perhaps! Perhaps! Perhaps! Perhaps and perhaps!"

"Eep!

"Eep eep eep!"

"Eep eep eep eep eep!"

An army of ferrets leaped from my shirt front.

The trolls were overwhelmed. The wind spell alone they might have weathered. The ferrets by themselves they would probably have laughed at. But the two together were far too much for the trolls' small brains to deal with.

"No slobber!" the trolls shrieked. "No slobber!" Covered with ferrets, they beat a hasty retreat to the dungeon gate.

I found myself suddenly troll-free.

"Norei!" I called. I ran, as best as I could, into the arms of my beloved.

"Oh, Wuntvor," Norei chided as she pushed away from me. "I know you are glad to see me, but we are still in dire peril!"

I regarded my beloved with some concern. She looked much more worn than I had ever seen her before.

"Oh, I am quite all right!" She smiled weakly as she saw the concern on my face. "I'm just a little tired. It took all of my magical skills to help free you from the trolls. Now I need to recover. Our current position is too well known by the forces of the Netherhells! We must leave this place as quickly and quietly as possible." I had Norei lean against me as we turned to walk up the corridor that would lead us back to the Netherhells mall. With my beloved by my side, I felt my own strength return every time I took a step. Together we would persevere!

"Wuntvor!" Norei cried with alarm. "There's something coming!"

She was right! There was a sound like two hundred small feet pounding against the phosphorescent moss.

"Eep!"

"Eep eep!"

Dozens of small, furry things rushed to follow us. With the trolls gone, the ferrets had begun to gather around me again.

"Eep eep! Eep eep!"

"Well," Norei amended as we picked our way through the gladly crying, nuzzling horde. "At least we can go quickly."

There seemed to be no signs of pursuit as we moved rapidly along the glowing green corridor. I asked Norei how she had managed to get away.

"Easy enough," she answered. "Once that short, loud demon left the Collectors, it was simplicity itself to hit them with a confusion spell and simply walk out of their claws. The Collectors are vicious, but they are not very bright."

That was my Norei, ready for any challenge! I kissed her chastely upon the cheek.

"Oh, Wuntvor!" Norei frowned again. "Is that all you can think of at a time like this? Here we are, still in dire peril, waiting for perhaps the entire might of the Netherhells to descend upon us, and I am stuck walking down a corridor with an amorous apprentice and his three-score trained ferrets!"

"Norei?" I whispered, quite taken aback. "If you feel that way, why did you rescue me?"

My beloved glanced at me and her exhausted countenance broke into a genuine smile. "Oh, you know how I feel about you, you big oaf. It's only that your behavior isn't always as appropriate to the situation as it might be!" She glanced at her feet. "Besides, it's annoying having to look down constantly so you won't trip over a ferret!"

I smiled, filled with an inner peace. What did it matter what befell us now, so long as we were together? My beloved loved me still!

"Wait!" Norei placed a cautionary hand upon my shoulder. "I sense someone ahead."

I looked beyond the sea of ferrets that surrounded us. We had come almost to the end of the corridor. I could see the window displays of the stores mere paces before me. But something was wrong. There were no beckoning torches lit to lure unwary customers, and those stores I could see clearly were dark inside. It looked like a Netherhells trap. Oh, what I would do for a weapon now, even Cuthbert, my cowardly sword!

"There they are!" a voice cried from the gloom ahead. "Doom!"

Five figures stepped into the space where the corridor met the mall.

"Who?" Norei fell back automatically into a basic conjuring position.

"Hold!" I cautioned her. "I believe these are our compatriots."

"Wuntvor?" a timorous voice inquired. "Could it be you?"

I noticed then that the tallest of those before us held aloft a gently glowing sword.

"Yes, it is I!" I called in return. "And I have brought Norei with me!"

"Oh, Wuntvor! Wuntvor!" Cuthbert yelped with glee. "I'm so glad to see you! Now I can be returned to my rightful master! You don't know what a trial it's been to be possessed by this big fellow in black!" Cuthbert shivered in the Dealer's hands. "Why, he wants to fight all the time!"

The Dealer smiled at that. "We've been hewing demons of late."

"Oh, hew, hew, hew!" Cuthbert wailed. "He had me cutting anything and everything! There was ichor flying everywhere!"

"Yes," the Dealer agreed. "It was quite lovely, wasn't it?"

Zzzzz the demon stepped forward, a large grin upon his wizened face. "We've been revitalizing!"

"Doom!" Hendrek added.

"Ob, give me back to Wuntvor!" Cuthbert pleaded. "I

showed you where to find him. What else could you ask a magic sword to do?"

"Well..."the Dealer began.

"I know! I know!" the sword wailed. "But it is Wuntvor who should decide! After all, I was given to him by the wizards!"

"Oh, all right," the Dealer said with some reluctance. He handed Cuthbert and the scabbard to me. "It's back to strangling, then. But it's become so boring. I mean, where's the sport?"

"You were whistling a different tune when you met the Collectors!" Snarks remarked. "It isn't such a piece of cake when your victims have no necks!"

"Snarks?" I questioned. "You're still here?"

"You mean, after betraying you?" The demon waved his hands about in a helpless gesture. "You know I couldn't help myself. I have to tell the truth, no matter what the cost!"

"Doom!" Hendrek remarked. "Then he and Brax went off and joined the forces of the Netherhells!"

Snarks took a step backwards. "Well, it was sort of expected of us. Here we were, with the Collectors staring us in the face, and if we weren't against them, we had to be with them!"

"Yeah!" Brax stepped forward, waving his cigar. "But wait 'til you hear what we found out! Have we got a deal for you!"

"You!" Norei said in a voice filled with ice.

"Beg pardon?" Brax turned to the young witch. "Oh, the woman we absconded with. I didn't recognize you. You should hit me on the head once or twice. Then I'd know you right away!"

"What is this fiend doing in our midst?" Norei demanded.

"Now hold onto your spells there for a moment!" Brax chided. "Who do you think made it possible for you to escape? Rule number one of the successful sales supervisor: Never leave Collectors out on their own! Without proper supervision, those fellows can't collect their way out of a paper bag!"

"So you allowed me to escape?" Norei's voice was heavy with sarcasm. "I have you to thank for everything?"

"No question about it," Brax replied. "I couldn't be too obvious, you know. If I just said, 'Okay, lady, time to escape!' it would have blown my cover sky high!"

"Don't be too harsh on him," Snarks added. "I know he's

a worthless salesdemon, and I have yet to discover any of his good points, but he did have his uses. Between the two of us, we discovered the whereabouts of Vushta!"

I looked back and forth between Brax and Snarks. Could we truly trust these demons?

"Listen," Snarks said when he saw my skepticism. "Let me tell you everything that happened, so you can see I haven't really changed and I'm still the sincere, truthful demon that I always was!"

I looked to the others in our party.

"You are wondering, perhaps, why these demons are still alive?" the Dealer asked. "I had decided to wait a bit before I kill them. We are in a strange place among strange creatures. I thought it best not to strangle them until we had time for some discussion." The large man flexed his hands absently. "In addition, you know the way I feel about demons." The Dealer made a muscular face. "They squish."

"Doom," added Hendrek.

"Revitalize them all!" Zzzzz cried. "Oh, when they tore down my home to build a Slime-O-Rama, I never realized it would be so much fun!"

"Hold it right there!" Snarks protested. "I never wanted to be involved in this in the first place. I could have spent the rest of my life in relative happiness, worshiping an extremely minor deity at Heemat's retreat. But no, I get dragged along with you folks to save the world!"

"Doom," Hendrek remarked again. "The demon is right. Let him speak his piece."

"Good," Snarks replied, his voice a good deal calmer than before. "I'm glad to see at least one human shows a little common sense. So here we are, confronted by Collectors, demanding to know if we are for or against the Netherhells! Well, what could we say?"

"I told them about the Netherhells that used to be!" Brax said, patriotic fervor once again rising in his voice. "The quiet beauty of a lava flow at night, the pristine cries of the perpetually tormented, the glorious feeling when you get up in the morning and fill your lungs with that first breath of fetid waste! That's what the Netherhells is all about!"

"And I kept my mouth shut," Snarks added. "Brax was doing enough talking for the both of us!"

"But wait!" I interjected. "There were three demons here. What happened to Zzzzz?"

"They ignored me," the elder demon answered. "They always ignore me. Everybody always ignores me. Revitalize them all!"

"To continue with my story," Snarks said quickly, "the Collectors told us to go to this demonic aid station just up the road—"

"And may I add," Brax put in, "when the Collectors tell you to do something, you do it!"

"If I might?" Snarks remarked peremptorily. "Thank you. Anyway, we thought it best to comply with the Collectors' request. And I must admit that I had a further motive. The Netherhells, after all, was where I was born and raised, and I harbored some lingering homesickness for what I used to know!"

"The feel of burning sulfur beneath your feet!" Brax rhapsodized. "The joyous agony of being bathed, head to foot, in slime!"

"If you don't mind!" Snarks spoke haughtily to his fellow demon. "Thank you. Is there anyone here who wishes to add anything further? No? Very good. I shall proceed."

The demon cleared his throat. "As I was saying, I felt some nostalgia for the Netherhells that was. We were going to a place where demons rested and recovered from their ills. Perhaps, I thought, there would be a park where the old ways were still preserved. I could see a sulfur pool or two, maybe a bit of flowing magma. But no!"

Brax seemed about to speak. Snarks glared at him for an instant before he continued.

"I think I realized from the first that I would never find an answer to my longing. But this!" The demon shuddered. "The aid station was indistinguishable from the rest of the mall, full of multicolored torches, and that faint, insidious music urging us on. I found myself wanting to wrap myself in bandages, or use half a dozen crutches simultaneously! And then the worst happened..." Snarks paused, as if what occurred next was almost too horrible to remember.

The demon took a deep breath. "They fed us Slime Burgers!" he managed at last.

"Ah, yes!" Brax intoned, the patriotic fervor still in his voice. "It's not like the Netherhells cuisine of yesteryear. Remember how good a real Sweet Demon Pie tastes? Ah, the way those brambles stick to your gums!"

"Indeed," I remarked. "But you mentioned that you had found a way to Vushta?"

Snarks nodded. "Vushta, it appears, is all the talk among demon kind. What they see in a dull city full of human beings is beyond me! Then again, anything must be better than life in an intercity mall!"

Now that Snarks had confessed his transgression, the acid tone was once again flowing back into his voice. He sounded just like the demon that we knew and...Well, he sounded just like the demon that we knew. Perhaps Snarks had been telling the truth all along.

"Anyway," the demon continued, "they've transported Vushta to the city of Upper Retch, Netherhells knows why. And, according to a chart on the station wall, there is a passageway that will lead us directly to that city a mere few minutes' walk from here!"

So we were closer to Vushta than I had thought. We might triumph yet!

"Indeed," I said. "Then we are nearing our destination. What say we get on with it?"

The others in our party agreed that it was time to go.

Doom," Hendrek added as we began to march. "I still carry your horn." He handed me the sack that contained Wonk, the horn of persuasion. I tied it to my belt opposite Cuthbert's scabbard.

"What are these?" The Dealer of Death looked at my army of ferrets. There seemed to be a strange longing in his eyes.

"So soft," he whispered, "so warm. They're not much like a wild pig, but they're more like a wild pig than a demon is!" The Dealer looked at me hopefully.

"You wouldn't mind if I strangled just one?"

I looked over the sea of brown that followed our procession. "I would very much! These are my ferrets!"

"Yes, I suppose you are right." The Dealer sighed. "I know I should only strangle for a cause. But I can't help myself! How was I to know wild pigs would become addictive?"

I was troubled as well. Only with the Dealer's question had I come to realize how much my ferrets meant to me.

"Here we are!" Snarks shouted.

"Doom!" Hendrek cried, war club at the ready. "Where?"

Brax and Snarks struggled together to lift a large plate from the ground.

"On the road to Vushta!" Snarks explained.

I walked to the edge of the hole they had uncovered. It appeared to be some sort of chute, going straight down.

"Here?" I asked, a bit of doubt in my voice.

Snarks nodded. "Upper Retch is directly below our current location."

"Upper Retch is below us?" I asked. Had I accepted the demons back among us too soon!? Was this some sort of Netherhells trick?

"I'm afraid so." Snarks smiled happily.

"Then why do they call it Upper—"

"It's the way demons think," Snarks replied. "Down you go!"

With that, the demon gave me a hearty push.

I yelped as I fell in the hole, sliding down the chute into darkness.

CHAPTER THIRTEEN

When there appears to be no hope; when all around you are screaming like lost souls and every spell you try fails to work; when it appears that chaos and evil will at last triumph over good—then it is truly time for a vacation.

—from The Teachings of Ebenezum, Volume XXXV

I dropped at what seemed to be tremendous speed through total blackness. I heard other noises above me. One sounded like a woman's yell, another a deep-throated "Doom" that reverberated down the shaft. Could the demons have thrown my compatriots down the chute as well?

The sides of the passageway through which I slid were utterly sleek. There seemed no chance of me finding a handhold to stop or even slow my progress. I heard a cry of terror. I thought for a moment that it came from my own throat, until I realized it really came from the scabbard at my belt. For the briefest instant I considered drawing Cuthbert to throw some light on this total gloom, but I was traveling so fast that I feared the sword would be torn from my grasp. I was falling so rapidly now that I would surely be crushed the next time I hit something solid. I silently apologized to my master for dying in such a stupid way and consequently being unable to rescue Vushta.

Then, as suddenly as I had dropped into darkness, I found myself flying through the strange greenish glow of the Netherhells. I landed in a huge pile of phosphorescent moss, then tumbled down to rest where the moss met the floor of the cave.

"Doo—oof!" came the cry above me. I quickly scrambled out of the way to avoid the great bulk now rolling down the mossy slope. I heard Norei's cheerful yell as I stood up and brushed myself off, then looked up to see the Dealer's large form sail silently through the air. Three small figures followed in rapid succession, the demons Zzzzz, Brax, and Snarks.

Then perhaps this wasn't a Netherhells plot! But then exactly what was going on?

"Gangway!" Snarks said, leaping from the top of the mossy pile. "Ferrets coming through!"

The sky rained small, brown furry things.

"Good!" Snarks exclaimed as he looked about. "Looks like everyone's accounted for."

"Ah," Brax said with a grin. "The Netherhells express. I ask you—is there any other way to travel?"

I approached the cigar-smoking demon. "Is that what it's called? The Netherhells express?"

"What else would you call it?" Brax said with some surprise.

"I could think of a couple things," I replied. "But that's beside the point. Why didn't you warn us what was going to happen?"

"Would you have jumped as readily into that hole if we did?" Snarks reasoned.

"Besides," Brax confided, "we heard voices from farther down the corridor. Three voices talking in unison."

"The Dread Collectors!" the Dealer of Death rumbled.

"Yeah!" Zzzzz broke in. "I wanted to stay there and revitalize them!"

"But you know what happened the last time we attempted to fight the Collectors," Snarks reminded us. "So we decided that rescuing Vushta was more important."

"Vushta!" I repeated the name of that fabled city and the old wonder crept back into my voice. "Are we near?"

"If my calculations are correct," Snarks said, "and they always are, we should be able to see Vushta as soon as we climb the next rise!"

So I would see Vushta at last!

"Maybe it is time to contact Ebenezum," Norei suggested.

She was right. We were about to enter Vushta and confront the dread Guxx Unfufadoo. Now was the moment we really needed the wizard's expertise.

I drew Cuthbert from its scabbard.

"What!" the sword screamed. "You don't need me already, do you? I still haven't recovered from all the hewing that big fellow did!"

I explained to the sword in my calmest tone that we needed to contact the wizard Ebenezum.

"Oh. Why didn't you say so? I can be quite reasonable, if properly informed. But no, you let me go on and on..."

"You know," I mentioned to Norei, "I could give this sword back to the Dealer."

"Magical communication!" the sword cried. "Magic you want, magic you get! Coming right up! We aim to please, yes, sir!"

"Indeed," I replied. "We need to talk with Ebenezum again, in East Vushta."

"My extreme pleasure!" Cuthbert answered. "You know the routine. Swing away!"

I swung the sword three times, until the point of light had again become a window to the surface world.

This time, the window opened on the interior of the extension school, perhaps the front hallway. The image blurred and shifted and we were in the Great Hall.

"In theory," Snorphosio shouted, "there is no reason why our plan to save Vushta won't—"

"Theory, hah!" Zimplitz retorted. "Magic is only proved through practice! Before a spell can truly work, it has to be baptized in a magician's blood!"

"If what you are saying was true, Vushta would be littered with dead magicians. Only through theory can—"

I cleared my throat. "Excuse me."

Both magicians' heads snapped around to the window.

"What!" Snorphosio cried.

"Why, 'tis the apprentice!" Zimplitz waved in my direction.

"I see it's the apprentice," Snorphosio rejoined peevishly. "I was just wondering what he wanted!"

Zimplitz smiled cruelly. "You were wondering what he wanted in theory, eh?"

"I will not have you make fun of my craft!" Snorphosio

screamed. "I am more than capable of talking with the apprentice! Why don't you go outside and play some of your dirty little magic tricks!"

"Dirty!" Zimplitz fumed. "Little! Why, you..."

The magicians grappled with each other and fell upon the floor.

"Excuse me," I tried again.

"Yes, yes, be with you in a second!" one of them hollered.

"If this fool would just listen to reason!" the other retorted. With them rolling about the floor like that, it was difficult to tell them apart.

"Please!" I called. "Just answer one question. Where is my master, Ebenezum?"

One of the mages pulled free of the other's grasp. As he dusted himself off, I saw he was Snorphosio.

"Ebenezum sits on the dais behind—ulp!" Snorphosio fell as Zimplitz grabbed him around the knees. I looked above the two struggling sorcerers to the dais. Yes, there was my master, still wearing his worn and tattered robes. He lay full out upon the marble. He appeared to be sound asleep.

"Master!" I called.

Ebenezum snored peacefully.

"Let me try," Cuthbert suggested cheerfully. He emitted a loud whistle. "Oh, magician!"

There was no response from the sleeping mage.

"No," the Dealer of Death said from behind me.

"You need something really loud to wake a mage from so profound a sleep." He made a sound like a dozen bull elephants engaged in a screaming contest.

My master rolled on his side and snored even louder.

"There is only one way to wake the mage!" Norei informed us. "We must all shout as one!"

All of us screamed together, our noise echoed by the squeals of sixty exuberant ferrets.

My master scratched absently at one eyebrow. His snoring continued unabated.

It was a dire problem; so close to Vushta and unable to confer with the greatest magician in all the Western Kingdoms. What could I do to wake my master? Even our combined shouting was not enough. What could possibly be loud enough to break through my master's slumbers?

Then the answer came to me.

"Cover your ears," I told the others. "I fear I will have to use Wonk."

The magicians stopped wrestling.

"Wonk?" they both cried.

"Oh, you need to wake your master!" Zimplitz exclaimed, as if it were the most novel idea in the world.

"Let us do it for you!" Snorphosio was all smiles as well.

"Yes, we'll be more than happy to!" Zimplitz climbed the steps to the left of the dais.

"All you have to do is ask. After all, you're the hero around here." Snorphosio climbed the steps to the right.

Snorphosio and Zimplitz each shook one of Ebenezum's shoulders.

"No, no," the magician mumbled. "I know they look like rats but—What? What is the matter?" The mage sat up as both Zimplitz and Snorphosio pointed toward the magic window.

"Wuntvor!" My master smiled as he rubbed the sleep from his eyes. "You've contacted us again!"

Ebenezum yawned. "Excuse me. I had the strangest dream. The world had become overrun with ferrets. But we don't have time to discuss that now. You must have called for a reason."

I told my master that indeed I had. We had reached the outskirts of Vushta and wanted to tell those above about our current position.

"Also," I added, "we would not frown on any last-minute advice you might have to offer."

"Indeed," Ebenezum said. "I am glad that you have been able to keep in touch. Knowing you are so close to your goal will help facilitate the final plan. So far, you seem to have done well enough. Is that the Dealer of Death I see behind you? No, don't explain. There will be time enough for explanations when Vushta is back where it belongs. Be sure to follow the original instructions and I'm sure everything will go splendidly."

I quickly went over the plan in my head. I was to locate

Guxx and, through the use of the special spell Ebenezum had given me, along with my magic weapons, I was to remove a single nose hair from the demon's proboscis. It seemed simple enough in theory. To maximize our chances, I should take time beforehand to memorize the spell.

"Oh, tell him about Klothus!" Snorphosio giggled. "Indeed," Ebenezum frowned. "I do not think this is the time to go into—"

"Your master may be a qualified wizard," Zimplitz called to me, "but sometimes he can be a little reserved. Let me tell the story. It seems that Klothus, miffed at his lack of success in clothing your master, insisted that he could make ducks and bunnies look somewhat like moons and stars!"

"It was not a pretty sight!" Snorphosio added.

"What!" I asked. "The ducks and bunnies?"

"No, no," Snorphosio chortled. "Klothus, when your master was done!"

"I wanted to tell him about that!" Zimplitz yelled.

Snorphosio laughed. "Well, for once you weren't quite fast enough, were you? And you call yourself the Action Wizard!"

"I've had enough of you!" Zimplitz shrieked. "I'm going to cram all your theories down your throat!" Once again he leaped for the skinny wizard.

Alea walked into the room, stepping around the two mages rolling on the floor. She spoke to Ebenezum:

"Hubert seeks an audience. He has a few new verses for the song. Oh, hello, Wuntie—"

The picture blinked out.

"I told you about vaudeville," Cuthbert said curtly.

I had had enough of this sword. I twirled Cuthbert back toward where the Dealer stood.

"Then again," the sword said, "perhaps I've never given vaudeville the chance it truly deserves."

"So she still calls you Wuntie." Norei gazed at me icily.

Perhaps, I thought, I should curb my anger. Cuthbert may have eliminated the window at the best possible moment.

"On to Vushta!" I cried. "We cannot falter now!"

We began the march up the hill where we would first see the city of a thousand forbidden delights.

There was a loud noise behind us. I turned. It was coming from the chute Brax had termed the Netherhells express. It took me a moment to realize it was voices echoing down the shaft. They seemed to be saying one thing over and over again.

I paused, attempting to make it out.

"We we we come come come to to to col col col lect lect lect."

"Doom!" Hendrek shouted.

I waved at the others to follow me. It appeared that we would enter Vushta at something more than a stately walk.

CHAPTER FOURTEEN

When one first arrives in Vushta, one should beware of street sellers offering forbidden delights near the outskirts of town. These first delights are far more shoddy in nature than those to be had in the Inner City, and can be actively unpleasant if you do not have an affinity for goats.

—from *Vushta on Twenty-five Pieces of Gold a Day* by Ebenezum, Greatest Wizard in the Western Kingdoms, revised, updated fourth edition

We were too close to our goal to be stopped by the Dread Collectors! I reached the top of the hill, the rest of the party on my heels.

And I saw Vushta.

I wish that I had had time to stand there and savor it. I saw glimpses of multicolored pastel towers as I ran, structures that appeared to be three times taller than anything I had seen, even in East Vushta! A dozen banners rose above the city walls, as bright in color as the towers were subtle. And there seemed to be people everywhere on the city's winding streets!

I learned a valuable lesson bounding down that hill: It is very difficult to gape and escape at the same time. Could I help it if Vushta's magnificence filled my eyes so that I could not watch my feet? Somewhere about halfway down the hill I found something they could not bound across. I tripped and swiftly rolled to the city gate.

"Hey, watch it there, fella!" a tall, rather unkempt man shouted as he scurried out of my way.

I apologized as I rose to my feet. A quick check showed that I still carried both my weapons.

"Doo—oof!" Hendrek cried as he, too, rolled to a spot not far from where I had landed.

"Are there more where you come from?" The unkempt man squinted up the hill.

"There's a few," I replied, "but I think they'll all be on foot."

The Dealer of Death reached us next, his great legs leaping more than running down the hillside. He pulled up next to us, breathing as if he had merely had a summer stroll.

"Sorry I am late," he apologized, "but I do not like to roll."

Norei arrived next, followed by the three demons. "Good heavens!" the unkempt man exclaimed. "Are you a tour group?"

"Indeed," I said. If we could put this Vushta native at ease, perhaps we could get some information from him. "After a fashion."

"Say." The man smiled. Half his teeth seemed to be gone. "Have you ever seen a forbidden delight?"

"Indeed," I said. "I understand there are a thousand of them within these city walls."

"More or less," the man agreed. "But most of them aren't as interesting as one I know. Would you like to come and see?"

I frowned. "Well, perhaps later, if we have the time. I have to wait for the rest of our group to arrive."

"The rest of your group?" The unkempt man rubbed his hands together in anticipation.

"Indeed," I answered. "Here they come now. You can hear their cries as they top the hill."

"Eep!"

"Eep eep!"

"Eep eep eep!"

Our little companions swept down the hill like some great, brown wave.

"Ferrets?" The unkempt man looked at the hill in horror. "You travel with ferrets?"

"Indeed," I replied. "In fact, in a way we are personally related. Now, about this forbidden delight—"

"Forget it!" the man stated as he walked away. "I can see I misjudged you. You're way out of my league. Ferrets? Personally related? Maybe you'll find something to your taste inside those walls. But I think you're going to have to go all the way to the Inner City!"

"Indeed?" I said to the man's rapidly retreating back. I turned to the others. "I had heard that Vushta was different. Apparently the natives here have strange customs. We shall have to do better with the next person we meet."

The ferrets at our heels, we walked through the great gates that led into Vushta.

A short, fat man walked our way. "Ah hah, I perceive you are strangers!" he called. "Have you ever seen a forbidden delight?"

I explained to this man that we were new to town.

"I thought so!" the man chortled. "And I imagine you'd like somebody who can show you around? Well, fortune has smiled upon you today. Honest Emir is at your service!"

"Honest Emir?" Brax muttered darkly. I realized that our demonic companion, in his guise as used weapons seller, had often attached the word "honest" to his name as well. Perhaps Brax was aware of the word's true and inner meaning, at least in a business context.

"Eep!"

"Eep eep!"

"Eep eep eep!"

Three-score ferrets ran rapidly through the gate, all crying with joy that they had found me again.

"What is this?" Honest Emir's belly shook as he laughed. "So you are new to town and you just happen to be traveling with an army of ferrets! Now who is fooling who?"

I opened my mouth to speak, but I was not quite sure what to say. Once again we seemed to be having problems communicating. It must have something to do with living in a large city. Perhaps words common in the countryside took on an entirely different meaning among the urban throngs.

I decided the best thing to do was to be as truthful as possible.

"Indeed," I began in a low voice. "We are not your ordinary travelers. We are here to rescue Vushta!"

"Ah hah!" Emir cried. "I thought as much! Wait a moment! Rescue Vushta from what?"

I wished Emir wouldn't talk so loudly. Others in the street were beginning to stare. Of course, the large number of ferrets around us seemed to be drawing some attention as well. I began to wonder how long we could keep our mission a secret.

"From the Netherhells!" I whispered.

"Oh," Emir replied, a tinge of disappointment in his voice. "You're evangelists, then. I'm afraid it's useless. Vushta has been going to the Netherhells for years!"

"No! You don't understand! Vushta has been taken captive by the Netherhells!"

Emir looked at me as if I had told him the sun always rises at midnight. "No, it couldn't be. Are you still kidding me? Vushta is so full of jokers. Captured by the Netherhells?" He glanced aloft at the gloom that reached to the upper recesses of the cave. "Well, come to think of it, it has been a little dark around here lately."

"Doom!" Hendrek interjected. "You mean you failed to see that Vushta has been taken over by demons?"

"Well," Emir said defensively, "what's so odd about that? A lot of stranger things take place in Vushta every day, let me tell you!"

"Doom," Hendrek repeated.

"Indeed," I remarked. Rescuing Vushta might be more difficult than I had thought. Perhaps it would be best to contact some of the local wizardry. "Do you think you might be able to take us to someone in charge?"

"Oh, you want to go to the Inner City!" Emir exclaimed, brightening perceptibly. "Ah hah! I thought you brought those ferrets for a reason! You can tell me. You're really a new forbidden delight, traveling incognito!"

Norei stepped forward before I could deny Emir's accusation. "Our mission is of the utmost secrecy!" she said. "We will reveal it to you," she added in a whisper, "when we reach our destination."

"Ah hah!" Emir rubbed his hands together gleefully. "So, when you reach your destination, all will be"—he paused meaningfully—"revealed?"

"Indeed," I said a bit doubtfully.

"Oh, permit me to be your guide!" Emir insisted. "No, no! I will not accept any gold for my services! I consider it an honor to be able to lead you to your"—he paused meaningfully again—"revelation!"

"So why do we tarry?" Norei demanded.

"Speak and I shall obey!" Emir responded. "All of you! Follow me to the Inner City!"

And so we began our walk through the streets of Vushta. And what streets they were! I had thought I had seen colors before, but other fabrics and paints and building stones, even people themselves, all were but pale imitations of the true colors of Vushta. I had thought I had heard sounds before, but no music had ever sounded so sweet as that we heard in passing from open windows high above and no laughter ever sounded so inviting as that which drifted from side streets as we walked.

The streets themselves were narrow and crowded for the most part, full of little stalls with people selling everything imaginable, and some things beyond imagining. Not so different, I supposed, from the never-ending Netherhells mall, except that the spirit here was the complete opposite. Back in the Netherhells, you were somehow impelled by useless music to buy useless things for useless places. Here, though, it was different. If you spent your money in Vushta, you were buying life!

And there were women here, also! I had thought I had seen women before, but—well, in this, even my powers of description fail me!

My companions had fallen silent as we walked. The others in our party seemed as overwhelmed as I. Only the Dealer of Death was constantly on the move, jogging from one side of our little group to the other, looking high and low, his every muscle alert—ready, I imagined, for any sudden danger that might confront us.

The Dealer moved with the grace of a panther up to the front of the line. Emir looked at him curiously.

"Pardon me," he said mildly, "but might I ask you a question?"

"Of course!" Emir enthused. "I will be glad to be of any

service whatsoever! One hand washes the other, if you catch my"—he paused significantly—"meaning."

"Oh." The Dealer flexed his massive shoulders. "I was wondering—er—if you might know the whereabouts of any— um—wild pigs?"

"Wild pigs?" Emir appeared to be getting truly excited. "Both ferrets and wild pigs? This is much better than I ever imagined!" The portly man winked in the Dealer's direction. "You can find anything in Vushta if you look long enough. But why am I telling you this?" He paused meaningfully. "You should be the one telling me!"

"Doom!"

We stopped in our tracks at Hendrek's cry. The vast warrior's arm shook as he pointed with his cursed war club to a sign directly ahead.

The place before us looked as if it had been dropped here from somewhere else, certainly someplace other than Vushta. Instead of the customary Vushtan building materials of bright stone or brick, this structure was made of something dark and shiny, some metal perhaps. Instead of having an open front like all the other stalls in the street, this building was enclosed, with a large, brightly lit window to entice you within. I thought I heard faint but compelling music emanating from somewhere nearby.

"So now do you believe our story?" Norei demanded of Emir.

The portly man stared dumbly at the large sign before us, carved in letters three feet high:

SLIME-O-RAMA!

Home of the Famous Slime Burger!

"I know this all fits in somehow." Emir frowned. "Ferrets and wild pigs and Slime Burgers? I had noticed this new group of establishments appearing all over town. Good heavens! We have been invaded by the Netherhells!"

"At last!" Snarks sighed. "I should have realized that this whole thing was going to be more difficult than I thought. I forgot that, when we went to rescue Vushta, we would be forced to deal with humans!"

Emir shrugged. "Well, it's a natural mistake. I mean, so we've been captured by the Netherhells! There's so much going on in Vushta, who would notice the difference?"

"Indeed," I replied. "So now will you get us to the Inner City with all speed?"

"With all speed!" Emir declared. Before he turned to lead us on, he added, a twinge of disappointment in his voice: "Does this mean you're really not a forbidden delight?"

"I'm afraid not," I admitted.

"Have you thought about going into that line of work?" Emir asked hopefully. "Let me tell you, you have all the ingredients for a real success!"

"We don't have time for that now!" Norei exclaimed. "We must rescue Vushta!"

"Oh, yes." Emir turned with some reluctance. "Rescuing Vushta. Well, I suppose, if it has to be done."

He led us on through the teeming streets.

"Hold!" the Dealer of Death cried a moment later. "I hear something ahead!"

We paused, but all I could hear were the noises of the ongoing bazaar surrounding us.

"It is still some distance away." The Dealer flexed his ears. "Let us move cautiously."

Norei glanced at me questioningly. I nodded to her and told the Dealer to take the lead. His assassination-trained senses might mean the difference between success and capture by the forces of the Netherhells.

As we moved, I began to hear the noises, too. It was a low sound at first, as if some great beast rumbled beneath the earth. But we were already beneath the earth! What other horrors might there be even farther underground?

But there was another noise as well, some magically amplified voice calling out and an entire crowd of voices responding. I wondered if we should avoid this situation altogether and ask Emir if there was a somewhat more circuitous route into the Inner City. Still, we owed it to ourselves to check the origins of this commotion. Who knew? Perhaps it was created by the very leaders of Vushta I sought!

We turned a corner in the winding street and the sound became suddenly clearer. I could now make out every word the amplified voice was saying:

We can do just what we please,
For humans will be on their knees!

And the crowd replied: "Guxx! Guxx! Guxx! Guxx!"

Doom," Hendrek intoned. "We have found Guxx Unfufadoo."

Apparently we had. I urged the other members of our group to caution. While we had located Guxx, I did not yet wish Guxx to locate us.

We moved quickly but quietly through the crowd, which rapidly shifted from being almost all human to almost all demon. Some of the sickly looking fiends were carrying signs. A chill ran through my entire being as I read one of the placards:

GUXX UNFUFADOO FOR SUPREME DICTATOR OF THE WORLD!

We had apparently stumbled upon some sort of political rally. All the other placards the demons carried seemed to be in much the same vein, although some of them said simpler things like "Guxx is the Greatest!" and "Let Guxx Dictate!"

"Brax!" I whispered. "Snarks! Do you know anything about this?"

Brax whistled from behind his cigar. "I knew Guxx was a marketing genius, but this is the big time. He captures the most important city from the surface, he's about to rule the surface world as well, and he uses that one-two punch to corner the highest elected office in all the Netherhells! What master planning!" An involuntary shiver coursed through the demon's frame. "Thank vileness he never sold used weapons!"

"Oh, no," Snarks moaned, close to my side. "This is worse than I thought."

He pointed ahead of us, across the crowd. There, on a raised platform, stood Guxx Unfufadoo in his full ugliness, clothed in a robe of muddy brown, black, gray, and livid purple.

"What is he wearing?" I whispered.

"Oh," Snarks said dismissively. "Those are just the Netherhells colors. I mean that thing behind him!"

I looked beyond Guxx and his platform to a huge, shining structure made of some gray metal. The low, rumbling sound was louder here. It seemed to originate from the structure.

"What is it?" I asked urgently.

"It is a slimeworks," Snarks replied grimly.

"A slimeworks?" I swallowed although my mouth was dry. "What do they do in a slimeworks?"

"You do not wish to know," Snarks said even more grimly than before. "Only now do I realize how serious Guxx really is. If we do not act quickly, the surface world is doomed to a future filled with Slime Burgers!"

There was a commotion on the stage. Some of Guxx Unfufadoo's followers had clambered up to be closer to their hero. Guxx had rapidly retreated and had to be coaxed back to the front of the stage by his aides, who said things like "Don't worry, it isn't her," and "There isn't an old lady within miles of here!" in extremely soothing tones.

Guxx stepped to the edge of the stage again and smiled, the very picture of demonic confidence. He began to speak again.

Now it is my honor and the time

To dedicate this edifice to slime!

The demonic audience cheered mightily and waved their placards.

"See what I mean?" Snarks complained. "Oh, why did I let Ebenezum talk me into this? Being banished from the surface world is better than the slimeworks. Maybe I could have learned to like living in the upper air!"

"You should be ashamed of yourself!" Brax rejoined. "And you call yourself a demon! Giving up so easily when there is so much to regain! Don't you remember the Netherhells of yesterday, where a demon was a demon and a slimepit was a pit of slime? Remember going out on vacation to laugh and make fun of the doomed souls? Remember taking your first drink of hot magma and really burning the roof of your mouth? Remember how, the first time you ate Sweet Demon Pie, you got too many brambles in your mouth and they hooked your lips together? Oh, I know, such memories of yesterday are sweet! But the Netherhells can be like that again! They can be a place where a demon was proud to be a used weapons dealer!"

Brax paused, overcome with emotion. "I think it is time for another inspirational cheer."

I know a place, and it sure is swell,

The hot, foul, and dirty Netherhells!

He wiped away a tear. "The Netherhells forever!"

"Wait!" The Dealer of Death spoke urgently. "There is something else!"

Again we paused and listened. Perhaps, I hoped wildly, this might be whatever the mighty Guxx was so afraid of. But again I heard nothing but the noises immediately around me: the chanting of the crowd; the political rhymes of Guxx Unfufadoo; the deep rumble of the slimeworks.

"It is behind us!" the Dealer said.

I heard it then. It was the sound of marching feet, and three voices, calling as one:

"We come to collect!"

I had forgotten all about the Dread Collectors! What a time for them to catch up to us, with our quarry almost within our grasp! Whatever we did, we could not let them catch us!

"Doom," Hendrek intoned, echoing my sentiments. "What do we do now?"

"There is only one way to go," the Dealer of Death remarked. "Toward our quarry." And with that he began to run full speed toward the slimeworks.

"He's right!" Norei agreed.

"Doom!" Hendrek chimed in.

"Revitalization!" Zzzzz rejoined.

"The Netherhells forever!" Brax exclaimed.

"Eep! Eep eep! Eep eep eep!" the ferrets chorused.

"Oh, why am I doing this?" Snarks yelped.

"Excuse me, but I have pressing business elsewhere," Emir muttered.

All but Emir began to run through the demonic crowd. What else could I do but join them?

CHAPTER FIFTEEN

There is the truth, and there are lies, and there is nothing on Earth or in the Netherhells that does not fall under one of these two headings, with the exception of politics.

—from The Teachings of Ebenezum, Volume LXXXVIII

I drew my sword as I ran.

"Not again!" Cuthbert wailed. "Oh! Watch out! There are demons everywhere!"

"We will collect you for Guxx!" The Collectors' voices reverberated above the crowd. They seemed much closer than before. The demons were milling around in confusion. I pushed a placard roughly out of the way and muscled my way through the crowd with all speed. I couldn't let the Collectors get me!

"We will catch you with our claws!" the Dread Collectors said in unison.

"Oh, no!" Cuthbert moaned. "Not them! Not more ichor!"

A gaggle of demons, surprised by the talking sword, leaped out of the way. I found my path clear for a dozen paces. Perhaps Cuthbert had his uses after all.

"Listen," the sword said in a more confidential tone. "Have you ever thought of other ways I might be employed? I have many fine uses besides fighting, you know. Not only am I good at magical communication over great distances and glowing in the dark, but I am excellent at cutting cheese!"

I booted aside a small green demon who had had the misfortune to wander in my path, then swung my sword above my head as with as much menace as possible. Another dozen demons scattered before me.

"Yes," Cuthbert continued, "I'm actually capable of over one hundred and one common household uses, but does anyone ever think of me that way? No, sir! It's always Cuthbert, slash this, Cuthbert, hack that!"

A loud voice boomed over the crowd:

Who are these interlopers who toward me plow?

Stop them, my followers! Stop them now!

So Guxx had noticed us at last.

"So it's the really big demon!" the Dealer of Death cried. "I lost you when we fell into the Netherhells! Now, though, I get another try!"

The Dealer glanced at me, all boyish enthusiasm. "I know that demons squish, but I've never been able to strangle a really big one! Who needs a wild pig? Maybe this rhyming fellow can squish enough to be really satisfying!" He turned and ran for Guxx's platform, clearing clumps of demons with every bound.

Guxx screamed again to his followers:

We are many! Together we stand!

We must drive these invaders from our land!

"Doom!" Hendrek swung his enchanted war club before him, dispensing with a dozen demons at every blow. Those too fast for the warrior's club ran in any direction they could save for the one in which we were going. The path between us and the platform was clearing rapidly.

I detected a note of panic in Guxx's next rhyme:

Oh, supporters, I am on my knees!

Protect your dictator elect! Please?

"Quickly now!" Norei called to the rest of our little band. "We have them on the run! Now the attack truly begins!" Her hands flew through a half dozen quick conjures. Small buckets of water appeared above what few demons still barred our way. Two dozen wet demons screamed and fled. There was no one between Guxx and our force now. Nothing could stop us!

"Have no fear!" three voices called from much too close. "We will collect them all!"

"Can't you humans move?" Snarks screamed in terror. "They're gaining on us!" He ran past me, followed closely by Brax and Zzzzz. I never knew demons could move so fast.

"This is the one who escaped!" three voices shouted

seemingly in my ear. "We will collect him now! We will give him to Guxx!"

No! I was too close to fail now! I would confront their leader with Ebenezum's spell! Then I would be safe from the Dread Collectors forever!

But there were other complications as well. The demonic hordes had become aware of the Collectors' presence and had paused in their flight. It was only a matter of seconds before they turned around and joined the attack.

I reached the steps that led up to the platform. The Dealer had already climbed to the top and Hendrek was in close pursuit. Our demon allies ringed the bottom of the stairs, each holding whatever weapon they had managed to find. Snarks still carried the metal pole he had found in the decimated shop and Zzzzz had grabbed hold of a sharp-edged placard. Brax had redrawn his dagger, while in the other hand he held his lit cigar. I knew they would hold off our enemies for as long as they could. If Guxx Unfufadoo were triumphant this day, it meant the end of their way of life.

The three demons were, of course, surrounded by an army of bright-eyed ferrets.

"Oh, no!" Cuthbert shrieked. "We're in for it now!"

With a bloodcurdling yell, the demonic hordes ran toward us, the Dread Collectors at their front, all claws and fangs and fury, moving with unbelievable speed.

"We will collect!" the monsters bellowed.

I glanced at Norei, still by my side. If we were going to die, at least we would die together!

"To the platform!" we cried as one and quickly ran up the stairs. I held Cuthbert aloft, ready for any attack from above. With my free hand, I fished within my shirt for the piece of parchment that held the spell that was the key to our defeat of Guxx Unfufadoo.

All I found were pieces of hat. I cursed my luck. It must have fallen in with the remains of my earlier aborted attempts at magic. Unless—oh, of course! How foolish of me! This shirt had a pocket.

Norei and I reached the top of the platform to see Guxx

Unfufadoo and the Dealer of Death but a few paces apart. The Dealer would take a step forward and Guxx would take a step back. This drama would not last long. The large demon was very close to the platform's edge.

Guxx shouted as he backed away.

I have ripped the heart from many a man
When I have fought them hand to hand!

"Then why do you run?" The Dealer smiled. "You have nothing to fear from me, or so you say. After all, I only want to feel how your neck squishes."

"Doom!" Hendrek called. "Be careful! His strength grows with every rhyme he makes!"

Of course! That must be the fiend's foul strategy! He would keep the Dealer at bay until he had rhymed so much that he was practically unstoppable!

"Hold, Dealer!" Norei shouted from where she stood by my side. "Wuntvor has a spell from Ebenezum, guaranteed to keep Guxx at bay!"

I nodded grimly and walked across the platform until I stood by the Dealer's side, Cuthbert the sword still in my right hand, ready for any treachery on the part of Guxx.

"You don't scare me with your talk of spells!" Guxx retorted. "For I will send you straight to…" The demon paused and shook his foul head. "No. That doesn't work. You're already there! Let's try this one: You don't scare me with your sorcery, for I can stop you with my force—er—that one isn't very good either, is it?"

"Don't worry!" Snarks yelled encouragingly. "He's nothing without his speechwriters!"

We had Guxx now! Without his rhymes, he could not increase his strength and the Dealer could defeat him easily. I reached into my pocket in triumph, ready to deal the final blow to this would-be demonic dictator.

But my pocket was empty.

Where was the parchment?

I had a sudden, clear vision of a small red card and another small, white piece of parchment fluttering to the ground in a dungeon many miles away. A troll had picked up the card. I knew now what had been on the piece of paper.

"Wait! I've got it!" Guxx Unfufadoo cleared his demonic throat.

You don't scare me with your magic

And now your end will be very tragic!

Guxx grinned in triumph.

"Let me take him!" the Dealer growled. He leaped forward, but Guxx pushed him back with a flick of demonic claws. The demon had become too powerful!

"Wuntvor!" Norei said. "Your spell?"

Still holding my sword aloft as inadequate protection against the advancing demon, I glanced at my beloved. How could I tell her that I had lost the only spell that would save us?

"Oh, no!" Cuthbert moaned. "Can't we talk this over?"

Guxx Unfufadoo smiled as he bore down upon me.

"Now I'll defeat you! The Netherhells knows, for with every rhyme my great strength—ferrets?"

Yes, once again my army of ferrets had come to the rescue! With a great chorus of eeps, they leaped upon the advancing demon.

"Norei!" I cried. "The spell is gone!"

"Watch out!" Snarks called from below. "The Collectors!"

"Doom!" Hendrek remarked.

"Revitalize everything!" Zzzzz added.

"What can we do?" Norei shouted.

The Dread Collectors' attack had forced our demonic allies to retreat to the platform. Now the Collectors were climbing the stairs with amazing speed.

"There's only one thing to do!" Cuthbert screamed. "Run!"

For once, Cuthbert was right.

"But where can we go!?" Norei asked.

Guxx had shaken off the ferrets as a dog might shake off rainwater. He stepped toward us again.

"We will collect you now." The Collectors were almost to the top of the stairs.

The platform was far too high. If we jumped, it would be to our deaths.

I looked around rapidly and saw a silver door at the rear of the platform that apparently led into the building beyond.

"We must go through there!" I pointed. "Into the slimeworks!"

"Doom!" Hendrek said as he followed us in.

CHAPTER SIXTEEN

Ebenezum: There are a number of ways of dealing with extreme stress. For example, when all about you is going wrong and it looks as if you might not survive your current circumstances, it is often helpful to think of a pleasant thought.

Interviewer: Do you mean, for example, how good it will feel to strangle, pummel, and utterly destroy my enemy?

Ebenezum: Well, no, you do not quite have the spirit of it. Think rather of a flower, or rather, a group of flowers. Picture bright yellow daisies, perhaps, or stately red roses, full and fragrant. And now that you have this thought in your mind, think how lovely those flowers will look on the grave of your enemy once he has been strangled, pummeled, and utterly destroyed. It is only in this way that the besieged wizard may find inner peace.

—from Conversations with Ebenezum; A Series of Dialogues with the Greatest Wizard in the Western Kingdoms, fourth edition

"**M**y mother didn't raise me to go into a slimeworks," Snarks said behind me.

"Quiet!" I demanded. "We have to keep our wits about us! It is the only way we can escape!"

I led the others quickly through the dimly lit corridor we had found at the other side of the door. There was barely enough light to see. Still, I was reluctant to use Cuthbert's glowing ability. After all, I could think of no better beacon than a shining sword to guide our enemies to us.

I have mentioned that I heard a low rumble as I approached this great gleaming building. Now that we were within the structure, I no longer so much heard the rumbling as felt it beneath my feet with every step I took. I thought about asking Snarks about the nature of the noise, but was afraid of the answer I would get.

I still held Cuthbert before me, in case of another demonic attack. Norei was immediately to my rear, then Hendrek and the Dealer, followed by our three demonic cohorts. I thought I also heard another noise beneath the rumbling, like dozens of tiny feet scrambling against metal. So perhaps some of my ferrets were with us as well! It was astonishing how quickly I had become attached to the little creatures. But then again, in a certain way, I was responsible for every single one of them!

"Ouch!" Cuthbert cried. "Watch it there!"

I seemed to have bumped my sword against a door.

"Hold!" I said quietly to those behind me. I pushed at the door. It swung away easily.

"We are going through," I told the others. "Keep together and keep quiet. There's no telling what's out there!"

"I know what's out—" Snarks began.

"Quiet!" I repeated. "There will be time enough for talk once we get out of this place!" And I stepped through a door onto another platform.

Voices drifted up to me from far below.

"And this is where we make our special sauce!"

I looked down. The platform we had stepped out on overlooked a huge room filled with enormous vats. All the vats appeared to be filled with liquid, gray and bubbling. In one corner of the room stood a group of demons gazing in wonder at the process before them. It was from this group that the voices drifted.

"We here at Slime-O-Rama are very proud of our sauces!" said a demon who faced all the others. "Our special sauce has made Slime Burgers what they are today!"

The huge gray vats continued to bubble and belch. As long as we kept our voices low, for the moment we were safe from detection.

"What's going on?" Norei whispered.

"It's a guided tour of the new slimeworks," Snarks interjected. "It's part of something they call the Slime-O-Rama

Outreach Program. When I was in school, they used to bring us to a slimeworks every year." Snarks shivered. "I still remember their slogan: 'Helping hands through slime!' "

"Then you know the design of such a building?" I asked, the excitement causing me to speak more loudly than I should. I glanced nervously down at the demons in the other corner of the room, but they still seemed busily involved in a discussion of the vatting process. I continued in a whisper:

"You can tell us what everything is! And you can find us a way out of here!"

"Unfortunately," Snarks replied, "I know everything that goes on within these walls far too well. 'We are now in the boiling room, where the liquid slime is boiled down to its proper gooey, stick-to-the ribs quality that Slime Burger lovers love to eat!' I can repeat every word they're saying down there!"

"Yes," Norei urged, "but can you find a way out of here?"

Snarks considered her question. "The fact that they are conducting guided tours gives us a slight chance. Perhaps we can disguise ourselves as tourists and get past the guards. If that doesn't work, there's only one way we're getting out of here!"

"And how is that?" I prompted.

Snarks pointed down at the vats. "As slime."

"Doom," Hendrek said. "We leave as slime?"

Snarks nodded his small, green head. "That's the thing about slime. No matter what you put into it—mud, demons, humans—it still comes out slime."

"Doom," Hendrek repeated.

But I could not believe we did not have a chance. There had to be other ways to escape, and ways to get at Guxx as well, if only we could think of them. My master had said that I was gifted with luck. If I ever needed that gift, it was now!

I turned to my beloved. "Norei. Misfortune has caused me to lose the spell that would have enabled us to capture one of Guxx's nose hairs. But you are a full-fledged witch. Surely you know some spell we can use."

"Oh, dear," she replied, frowning. "That may be something of a problem. We lived on a farm, you know. I can perform a great deal of household magic, and I know more than a few crop spells, plus a few specialized things I memorized before I left home to meet you. But I'm afraid, throughout my magical training, as much as I would like to tell you otherwise, I have had very little dealing with nose hair."

Oh, how I hated to see my beloved frown so! "Do not worry!" I said. " 'Tis only my desperation that made me ask such a thing of you! We will just have to find some other means to succeed."

Norei looked thoughtful. "Still, Wuntvor, I may be able to come up with something."

There was a substantial commotion behind us. I hoped for one mad instant that it was only the ferrets. But I knew, as I heard their cheerful eeps all around, that it had to be something far worse.

Four words reverberated down the metal corridor through which we had escaped.

"We come to collect!"

"This is getting a little tiresome," Snarks commented. "Couldn't those guys come up with something else?"

"Maybe we can sell them some new material," Brax suggested. "I think it may be time I got out of the used weapons business."

"I think it may be time we got out of the Netherhells altogether," Snarks replied.

A set of Collector claws sheared through the door behind us.

"There is one consolation," the Dealer of Death remarked softly. "I will have a second opportunity to find if these creatures have necks." He smiled grimly. "Or I shall die trying."

"We come to destroy!" the Collectors cried as one.

"Now see," Snarks mused. "They used a new word. That at least shows a little originality. Maybe these monsters don't have to be totally boring after all."

"We come to maim!" the Collectors screamed. "To torture! To kill!" Claws shredded what little was left of the door and the entranceway around it.

"You know," Snarks said, "I think an awful lot of this is done just for effect."

"We've got to get out of here!" Cuthbert insisted. And again the sword was right.

There was a set of narrow stairs that wound down between the vats. I raised Cuthbert in the air and yelled for the others to follow me.

I walked quickly but carefully down the stone stairs. Every third step seemed to hold a puddle of slime, and it would do no good to slip and fall now. We needed all our wits about us if we were to have any chance of success.

A railing began where the steps curled around one of the vats. I put my hand on it to give me stability, but pulled it away as soon as I touched its wet, gooey surface. I absently sniffed my fingers. It was slime all right.

I was reminded of the thick gray sludge between two pieces of bread I was offered as part of my dungeon torment. This is what the demons were doing to Vushta! And they would bring Slime-O-Rama to the surface world as well if we failed in our task. I had a clear, horrifying vision of Wizard's Woods, where I was born and raised, entirely covered by slime.

While I was alive, that would not happen!

I could no longer hear demonic voices on the floor below us. The tour must have moved on to the next room. That meant one complication at least was out of the way. Now all we had to do was lose the Dread Collectors, somehow temporarily immobilize Guxx Unfufadoo long enough to prune a nose hair, and escape back to the surface world without being caught. I swallowed again, though I did not remember having any saliva in my mouth since I had entered the Netherhells. We would have to face each of our problems as we came to them.

The gloom was far deeper between the vats. I asked Cuthbert to give me a little light. The sword obliged with hardly any comment. I pointed it down to guide me to the floor.

"Glurph!" the sword exclaimed.

In Cuthbert's light, I could see I had reached the bottom of the steps, except that, instead of dry floor beneath me, there was a layer of slime.

I lifted Cuthbert's point out of the gray muck.

"I thought there was nothing worse than ichor!" the sword wailed. "I was wrong!"

How deep was the slime? Could we still walk out of here or

would we have to swim? There was only one way to find out. I planted my feet on the last step above the liquid.

"Have you no compassion?" Cuthbert protested as I immersed it once again in slime.

The sword submerged only halfway before I hit something solid.

"Quickly!" I called to the others. "There's a layer of slime on the floor that will slow us down. Get off the stairs as fast as you can!"

With that, I jumped to the ground. My feet oozed downwards in slime. And I heard an all-too-familiar voice from the platform above.

Get them, Collectors, for they are mine!

Don't let them escape through the slime!

"We will collect for Guxx!" the Collectors screamed as they rushed down the steps.

The other members of my band splashed down around me. I walked on as best as I could, intent on getting as far away from the Collectors as possible. It was rather like walking through soup, except that the smell that rose about us made me think that perhaps the soup was a few days too old. I had to be careful to plant my feet firmly every time I took a step, or I might slip entirely below the gray muck.

"Doo—oof!" Others in my party seemed to be having similar problems. Hendrek picked himself back up, his body now half-covered with slime.

"Snarks!" I called. "Come up here with me. Which is the best way to go?" Even as I spoke, though, I was still moving. I saw a large archway ahead filled with light. Noise seemed to come from there as well. Until Snarks told me otherwise, I decided that arch was our destination. Whatever lay beyond had to be better than slime.

I risked a look above us. Guxx still watched from his vantage point atop the platform, but the Collectors, with their horrible speed, were already over halfway down the stairs. I did my best to redouble my pace.

Snarks was saying something as he swam up to meet me, but it was lost in the growing noise that emanated from the archway ahead. I could make out some sort of voices; chanting perhaps, or periodic yells or cheers. It was hard to tell more than that because of the other noise that came from there as well, a steady roaring sound that grew louder with every step, under laid with a rhythmic crunching noise. There was an odd familiarity about that crunching, until I realized that its rhythms were the same as the rumbling sound I had heard even before we had entered this building. We would finally get to see what would make such a colossal noise.

Something pulled at my sleeve. I turned to see Snarks looking more frightened than he had ever before.

"No!" The truth-telling demon shrieked over the noise. "We don't want to go in there."

I tried to explain that we had to. The Collectors were almost on top of us. If we turned around, they would catch us for sure.

"No, you don't understand!" Snarks insisted. "We don't dare go in there! That's the grinding room."

The grinding room? I stopped my forward flight and paused to listen more carefully to the sounds coming from the room ahead. Perhaps those voices weren't chanting, or even yelling. In fact, the closer I got to it, the more it sounded like screaming.

"We collect you now!" I spun about to see all three Dread Collectors reaching the foot of the stairs. What could we do? There was no place for us to go!

And then the Collectors leaped into the slime.

"Get out of their way!" Norei yelled as they slid toward us. My beloved had spotted their weakness! In their eagerness to collect us, the monsters had entered the slime at full speed. Now there was no way for them to stop.

I pulled Snarks up close against one of the vats. The three Collectors sped past us, all sliding uncontrollably on the slime.

"We have gone too far!" all three cried as they slid beyond us into the grinding room.

It was then that I really heard the screams. I wondered if it were the Dread Collectors making the noise, or other things in that grinding room that were waiting to be ground. Whatever it was, I had no wish to investigate it further. With the Collectors out of our way, perhaps there was some way we could overpower Guxx.

"Turn around!" I called to the others. "Back up the stairs!"

The rest of my party eagerly complied.

"Dealer!" I shouted. "Hendrek! We must detain Guxx!"

"My pleasure," the Dealer responded, leaping up the stairs four at a time.

"Doom," Hendrek remarked as he rapidly lumbered behind.

Guxx raged overhead:

You try to capture me, you dunces!

Well, I'll no longer pull my punches!

"Dunces and punches?" Snarks called from by my side. "Do you call that a rhyme?"

Guxx growled, even more furious than before.

"Now you question my rhyming talent!

"Well, I will throw you off this planet—er—no, I know that one doesn't work either. See here, you've got me upset. I can never rhyme properly when I'm upset." The fearsome demon leader pointed at Snarks. "I know who you are! I knew there was a reason we banished you. Just wait a minute while I get my strength back. Let's see..."

Now you question my rhyming skill.

Well, I know someone I can—urracht!

The Dealer had launched himself straight for Guxx Unfufadoo's neck. Guxx still had enough strength to at least partially break away and draw a ragged breath. The two of them rolled about on the platform above us.

"Quickly!" I said to the others. "We must join them as well!"

"Watch your step!" Cuthbert called as I hurried up the stairs. "Say, I tell you what. How about I keep giving you this nice, modulated light, and we can watch the others beat up that big demon thing? Doesn't that sound like a good idea?"

I did not bother to answer. Instead, I called to Norei, who had already climbed halfway up the stairs.

"Have you thought of any spells?"

"I'll come up with something!" she called back. "I only have to think what demons and farming have in common!"

The commotion became even louder above us.

"Now I have it! I've broken free!" Guxx screamed overhead. "Now we'll see who the winner will—urk!"

The demon leader had temporarily bested the Dealer of Death, but he had forgotten completely about Hendrek, who had managed to connect with a vicious blow of the doomed club Headbasher.

"Who? What?" Guxx queried, temporarily under the dread Headbasher's fearsome spell. "Oh, that's right. I'm Guxx Unfufadoo, soon to be the Supreme Ruler of Everything!" His senses once again about him, the demon deflected a second blow with a well-placed set of claws.

Norei was on the platform now. Her hands flew as she uttered a quick spell. A cloud appeared immediately above Guxx and almost as immediately let loose with a torrent of water.

Guxx glared at her, somewhat dampened but otherwise unfazed.

You try to stop the mighty Guxx with water.
But from my task I shall not falter!

I reached the platform then, with Snarks hot on my heels.

"Grab him now!" Snarks cried. "He can't possibly be gaining any strength with rhymes like that!"

The Dealer approached Guxx, more cautiously this time, but with no easing of his deadly purpose. Perhaps, I thought, we really could subdue Guxx this time!

And then three voices called from down below:

"We are back from the grinding room!"

Oh, no! The Dread Collectors had somehow survived. Even now I could hear them coming up the stairs.

Guxx laughed evilly.

"Now we will kill you all!" he shouted and launched into another rhyme:

While it may not yet be June,
You will never see the moon,
For it is your death I croon,
And we will eat you with a spoon!

The Dealer of Death attacked Guxx then, but it was already too late. The demon leader pushed the Dealer aside with a flick of his claws. He laughed again.

"We have you now!" he yelled. "The old rhyme schemes are always the best!"

So we would die now. There appeared to be no other choice. I turned to the edge of the stairway. I would face the rapidly climbing Collectors, sword in hand. Perhaps I could at least wound one before my demise.

"What are you doing?" my sword shrieked.

I calmly outlined my death plan.

"But couldn't you do something else?" Cuthbert begged.

And then I realized, of course I could! Cuthbert was not my only weapon. And this time I still had Wonk, the horn of persuasion, tied to my belt!

I quickly undid the sack as the Collectors reached the platform's edge.

"We collect you no—" they began.

I put Wonk to my lips and blew.

The Collectors froze in their tracks. I moved toward them, still blowing relentlessly. The monsters looked about wildly, seeking some means of escape. But I had stepped around them and now stood between them and the stairs.

The three Dread Collectors looked at each other for a single instant, then jumped as one off the platform.

"We are slime!" they screamed in unison. And they plunged into the vats below.

I looked to those of us remaining on the platform.

Everyone, Guxx included, was cowering where they stood, ears covered.

Norei came over and leaned heavily against me. She looked deep into my eyes.

"Wuntvor?" she whispered. "Could you do one thing for me?"

"Anything, my beloved!" I replied.

She smiled sweetly. "Unless you absolutely have to, promise me you'll never blow that thing again."

"Indeed," I agreed. "Let us see if we can get what we need from Guxx!"

"Thank the Netherhells you stopped!" Snarks moaned.

"Another moment of that noise and I would have opted for slime as well!"

"Come," I said. "We must take Guxx now!"

CHAPTER SEVENTEEN

Wizards should not go seeking revenge, killing, or death in general. After all, revenge, killing, and death in general have a way of showing up whether you are looking for them or not.

—from The Teachings of Ebenezum, Volume I

Guxx Unfufadoo staggered to his feet as we approached. He shook his head and frowned with pain. All his fangs showed when he grimaced. His voice shook as he spoke.

You think to beat me with the horn,
But you shall soon be tossed and—

I blew Wonk again, only a short blast this time, but it was enough to drive Guxx to his knees.

"I thought I asked you not to do that again!" Norei cried from my side. She appeared to have fallen to her knees as well.

"Indeed," I replied. "It could not be helped. If we can get a nose hair, I will never have to do it again." With my free hand, I drew forth Cuthbert.

"What do you want now?" the sword shrieked.

"Don't worry," I said reassuringly. "You won't have to kill anyone this time."

"Oh, thank goodness!" the sword exclaimed, greatly relieved. "There's been too much happening lately. My nerves are all on edge!"

"This will all be over soon," I assured the sword. "All we have to do is cut out a single one of this demon's nose hairs."

"You want me to go in there?" Cuthbert screeched. "Inside a demon's nose? Have you no code of honor?" "Come on now!" I chided. "It won't be so bad. A single snip and you're done."

"That's easy for you to say!" the sword complained. "You

don't have to go into some strange creature's orifice! Heavens knows where it's been!"

I could see this was going to be more difficult than I had expected. And, realistically, Cuthbert had a point. He was a fairly broad sword and, as large as Guxx was, his nose wasn't really huge. It would be a delicate operation at best. There had to be a better way.

Guxx began to stir again.

"A single move," I warned, "and you will hear the horn."

"Don't move!" everyone urged fervently. "Please don't move!"

And then I had an idea.

"Norei," I asked, "you say you are most familiar with household and farming spells?"

"Yes?" she replied.

"Then you could know some simple growth spells!" "Of course," she answered. "Why?"

"Is it possible to apply one of those spells to a single nose hair?"

"Oh!" She brightened as she caught my idea. "It would be simplicity itself!"

She made three small gestures, combined with a short string of magic phrases. Something black and coarse poked its way from Guxx's nostril.

"This is a little disgusting," Norei admitted.

"Hey," Snarks retorted. "It's the Netherhells. What did you expect?"

The hair continued to grow. I waited until a good foot of it was exposed to the open air.

"All right," I said to Cuthbert. "Now we will cut." "If we have to," the sword replied as I set to work. "Ouch! Ooh! Hey boss, this just isn't going to work!"

Cuthbert was right. No matter how I chopped or sliced, it made no dent. Guxx Unfufadoo was a virtually indestructible demon. That meant that his nose hair was indestructible as well!

"You mean there's no way you can cut this?" I said in alarm.

"Sorry," Cuthbert answered. "I may be magic, but I'm not perfect."

A great shout came from deep within the corridor we had used to enter the slimeworks.

"Uh oh," Snarks said. "It sounds like reinforcements! We have to get out of here!"

"Doom!" Hendrek added. "But what about the hair?"

I had to make a quick decision. "We have to keep the growing spell going! Norei, can you reinforce the spell in any way? Cuthbert, we need to contact my master!"

Guxx laughed from where he sat.

You will never cut my hair

And my reinforcements are almost—

His voice died in his throat as I pointed at Wonk. I handed the horn to Norei. "It will work as well in her hands," I warned the demon. "We may not be able to get all of your hair, but at least we'll take one end!"

With that, I swung the sword about my head three times and the magic window opened. It once again showed the great hall of the East Vushta academy and two wizards dressed in red.

"I can see you talking about theory while demons eat you!" Zimplitz said.

"I can see you with your simple, practical spells, totally inadequate for dealing with the Netherhells!" Snorphosio retorted.

"Would you people be quiet!" I shouted.

Snorphosio peered through the window. "Oh, dear. 'Tis the apprentice. We're not always like this, you know. You see us at our worst. It's the stress, I'm sure—"

"I don't care what it is!" I cried. I rapidly outlined our situation. "Is there some way to get us out of here?"

"Certainly," Zimplitz agreed. "A simple retrieval spell."

"Well," Snorphosio added, "I don't know how simple that would be. There are a lot of variables..."

The noises from the hallway were getting louder. They seemed to come from a great many very angry demons.

"If it's not simple enough to retrieve us right now," I insisted, "I don't think you'll see us again!"

"Well..." Snorphosio began.

"Put your hands together!" Zimplitz directed. "We'll get you out!"

The window disappeared as I placed Cuthbert back in its scabbard. I carefully wrapped a couple of feet of nose hair around my wrist and told all those going with me to join hands. Brax and Zzzzz both politely refused.

"If you can defeat Guxx," Brax added, waving his cigar, "I can go back to my day job. Hendrek, I'll be seeing you soon about a payment!"

"Doom," the warrior replied.

"I can't leave this place now!" Zzzzz responded. "You've given my life new meaning. Revitalization forever!"

With that, the horde of angry demons burst into the room.

Would the magician's spell come too late? I held Norei's hand even tighter than before. Perhaps I could say some final words before the end.

"Norei, I..." I began.

But the rest of my words were lost to the wind. A wind that seemed to spring from nowhere, that surrounded us and lifted us aloft, over the platform and vats, then out of the slimeworks. We seemed to be moving at tremendous speed. I caught a single glimpse of the pastel towers of Vushta, then another of the garish colors of the Netherhells mall, then we were plunged into darkness.

The wind ceased. We had returned to light. I blinked. We all sat on the floor of the large hall of the wizards' extension school.

"Is that a spell"—Zimplitz beamed—"or is that a spell?"

I looked about the room. Snorphosio stood by Zimplitz's side, still looking skeptical. The wizards were flanked by their students, plus a couple of newcomers in sorcerous gear.

"Where is Ebenezum?" I asked.

"He is on his way," Zimplitz replied. "You did arrive rather suddenly, after all. In the meantime, the rest of us are ready. Do you have the nose hair?"

I proudly showed them the strand still wrapped around my knuckles. The hair, apparently, had not been broken by Zimplitz's magic. Instead, it stretched out of the hall into the foyer and, I imagined, far beyond that.

"We were unable to cut it," I explained.

Something nuzzled my knee. It was small and covered with slime.

"Eep!"

"Eep eep!"

"Eep eep eep!"

So Zimplitz's spell had rescued the ferrets as well! Well, at least some of the ferrets. I had never had time to pause and make an accurate count.

"Do you mean," Snorphosio's voice cut through my reverie, "that one end of this nose hair is still attached to Guxx Unfufadoo?"

I nodded. " 'Twas the best we could do under the circumstances."

"Men!" Snorphosio cried. "We must be more than ready! We will be attacked at any second!"

The earth began to shake. As dazed as my party was, we regained our feet. We all realized that this would be the final battle.

The newly refinished floor of the Great Hall burst asunder. A mighty voice cried above the roar:

I can follow my hair wherever it grows.

I will teach humans to pick my nose!

And Guxx appeared in our midst, leading a demon horde!

Demons seemed to be everywhere! I fell back by the line of student wizards, all busily conjuring, thinking their protection would give me a moment to collect myself. But a great purple and green demon appeared from nowhere to sweep them from their feet before they could complete a single spell.

Grimly, I drew Cuthbert from its scabbard.

"Not again!" it began.

"Quiet!" I instructed the sword. "If we lose this battle, you'll be owned by demons!"

The purple and green creature turned to me. It was easily twice my height. I barely ducked beneath its sweeping claws.

"Watch out!" Cuthbert warned.

I had watched the thing's claws, but I had forgotten about its heavily barbed tail! It whistled through the air as it descended to crush my skull. Perhaps it was instinct, or perhaps it was the magic sword actually doing its job for a change, but Cuthbert met the tail as it fell and neatly sliced it in two. The barbs flew away, missing me completely. Dark ichor sprayed from the wound. Cuthbert, to its credit, did nothing but whimper.

The huge creature cried in rage and pain, and spun to attack me again. But a dozen small, slime-covered shapes streaked between us, attaching themselves to various parts of the demon's anatomy. The monster screamed as it fell, thrashing about in a vain attempt to rid itself of ferrets.

My small charges had once again given me a moment to think. If only I had Wonk to hand, I could rout these demons in an instant. But I had given the horn to Norei. Would she think to use it? I could not see her in the battle. All I could see were demons.

"Doom!"

"Urk!" Hendrek's enchanted war club, Headbasher, dispatched a demon that had been flying straight for my head.

"Urracchhtt!"

"Urracchhtt!"

The Dealer of Death strode through the room, strangling demons with one hand or the other as he passed.

"Men!" I cried to the two of them. "Forget these other demons! We must take Guxx!"

"Doom," Hendrek said, clubbing his way to my side.

"My pleasure," the Dealer remarked, nonchalantly strangling a demon or two as he walked my way.

I looked quickly about the room. Guxx stood upon the dais, facing Zimplitz. Snorphosio lay in a heap at Guxx's feet.

"I'll drink his blood to slake my thirst!" Guxx cried over the unconscious mage. "He should not have talked. He should conjure first!"

This was worse than I thought. Guxx seemed to be back in prime rhyming form!

But Zimplitz was unabashed. "All right, fiend!" he cried. "Let's see how you deal with practical magic!"

Guxx reached out and flicked Zimplitz from the dais before the mage could complete his mystic gesture!

Your magic is dead, your end is near,
There is nothing left for Guxx to—
"Where is that pest!?" An elderly, cracked voice broke
through Guxx's rhyme.

"No!" the demon lord screamed. "Not her!"

Using her umbrella for support, a gray-haired old lady
pushed herself out of the hole through which the demons had
arrived.

"There he is!" she cried in triumph as she waved her
umbrella aloft.

"Mother!" Tomm the sorcery student cried.

"Get her, demons!" Guxx shrieked. "Whatever you do, get
her!"

The demonic horde leaped for the old lady.

"Mother!"

Tomm and his fellow students followed the horde.

Guxx grinned as he saw the umbrella disappear under a
pile of demons.

I've now gotten rid of one more fool,
For in this place Netherhells will rule!
The demon lord laughed evilly.

The demon horde was occupied. It was time to confront
Guxx.

"The Netherhells will never rule here!" I shouted. "Guxx,
you are defeated!"

At a sign from me, the Dealer, Hendrek, and I rushed the
dais.

Guxx grabbed Headbasher in one hand and the Dealer's
throat in the other. He threw both warriors away as if they were
pieces of parchment. He smiled at me as he spoke:

So this is what you call defeat.
Victory is not this sweet!
He reached forward to crush my head in his claws.

"No!" I screamed.

A bunch of daisies fell from my shirt. There must be a
magical overabundance here. The pieces of magic cap within
my shirt were working again.

"No!" I shouted. "Yes! No! Yes! No! Yes!" Thousands of

daisies and scarves exploded outward, straight into Guxx's face.

The demon lord screamed with rage.

You try this demon to distract!

Now I will kill you! That's a fact!

But not until I had exhausted every weapon in my arsenal! Holding Cuthbert before me for what small protection the sword still afforded me, I took a deep breath.

"Perhaps!" I cried. "Perhaps! Perhaps! Perhaps! Perhaps! Perhaps!"

Guxx was attacked by a legion of ferrets.

The demon lord tossed every single one aside.

Now at last we are all alone.

I'll drink your blood and crunch your bones!

Guxx Unfufadoo grinned broadly as he approached.

There was a crash. The hall's huge oak door had been pushed open by some colossal force.

"Indeed," a deep voice rumbled behind me.

It was my master, Ebenezum, greatest wizard in all the Western Kingdoms!

Guxx's smile faltered as he looked beyond me to the mage.

I have defeated you once before—

I will gladly oblige if you want some more!

Ebenezum raised his hands. A mighty wind sprang up, pushing Guxx against the dais.

"Wuntvor?" my master asked calmly. "Do you have the nose hair?"

"Yes!" I answered. One end was still wrapped around my knuckles.

"If I might have it?" the wizard requested.

I unwrapped the strand from about my hand and passed it to my master.

"Guxx is immune to any magic!" the demon cried as he struggled to rise from the dais. "Try it and your end is tragic!"

"Indeed," my master replied. "I think not."

He took one end of the demon's nose hair and lifted it to his own nostril. And then the wizard sneezed.

Guxx laughed hideously.

You sneeze at magic no matter what you do!
And now Guxx will use his claws—wahhhchooo!
And Guxx began to sneeze as well.

My master quickly blew his nose on what looked to be a new set of robes and said a quick series of spells. Guxx's sneezes doubled and redoubled.

"No!" The demon sneezed. "I am not—" Guxx sneezed again. "I will rhyme—" And sneezed again. "Well, perhaps maybe I am—"

My master intoned another group of mystic words. Guxx seemed about to sneeze, but breathed in instead. He seemed about to sneeze again, but inhaled some more. A look of panic came over his countenance.

Ebenezum snapped his fingers. The room was filled with a mighty roar.

When the dust had cleared, there was a hole where the demon lord had stood. Guxx Unfufadoo appeared to have sneezed himself back down to the Netherhells. Demons screamed in terror and leaped into the hole to follow their leader.

Dragon fire came through the windows to singe what few fiends remained. They quickly ran to join the others.

"Master?" I called.

"Indeed," the mage reflected. "Guxx Unfufadoo now finds, should he contact anything having to do with the surface world, that he will sneeze uncontrollably."

And then my master began to sneeze as well.

CHAPTER EIGHTEEN

And what is the professional wizard's greatest reward for completing a particularly arduous and dangerous task? Is it the accolades of a grateful populace? Is it huge amounts of gold and silver tossed about his feet? Is it the complimentary vacation in the pleasure gardens of Vushta, or his official removal from the tax rolls? Although all these other factors are important for the wizard to feel truly honored, they pale before the professional wizard's basic and oh-so-necessary demand: The stipulation that he never has to repeat that particularly arduous and dangerous task, or one even remotely like it, for as long as he shall live.

Truly professional wizards, after all, must set priorities.

—from How to Hire a Wizard and Still Profit from the Upcoming Netherhells Crisis, by Ebenezum, Greatest Wizard in the Western Kingdoms (book still in progress)

Someone knocked on the door of my sleeping room. Groggily, I asked who it was.

Norei opened the door.

"You have slept the clock around!" she called. "Get up! We will have dinner shortly!"

Dinner? How long had I slept? I pushed myself to a sitting position as Norei left the room. Now that she mentioned it, I was rather hungry.

It all seemed like a bit of a blur now. Once I realized that Norei had managed to alert Ebenezum and Hubert the dragon of the danger from the Netherhells, and the two combined to send the fiends back where they had come from, what energy I had left seemed to vanish completely.

Oh, I had not gone to sleep immediately. I managed to

stay awake long enough to wash most of the slime from my
body and to watch them retrieve Vushta and put it back where
it belonged. But watching the city of forbidden delights being
set back into place had completely done me in. I didn't even
remember making it to my bed. I remembered nothing, indeed,
before Norei's knock.

My clothes were laid out on a chair. Apparently, someone
had cleaned them while I slept. I had to admit, as I slipped them
on, they felt much more comfortable than they had for quite
some time, but I found I missed the torn bits of hat I used to
keep within my shirt.

There was a scratching at the door as I moved about my
room. I pulled it ajar.

"Eep!"

"Eep eep!"

"Eep eep eep!"

The room was suddenly filled with adoring ferrets. I
laughed as they nuzzled my knees and ankles. I hoped Norei
would understand my need to keep these creatures near me.
Perhaps we could put them in pens so they could still be close
and not underfoot.

I walked from the room with a hundred ferrets at my heels.

"Ah, there you are, Wuntvor!" Snorphosio called. "Glad to
see you're up and about. There's so many things to organize,
you know. Eventually, we'll even have a dinner in everybody's
honor, as soon as we can get everybody together!"

I asked after my master.

"Oh," Snorphosio confided in a whisper, "he is in the Great
Hall, being cured by the greatest wizards in all of Vushta."

I thanked the old wizard and walked down the corridor to
the great oak door beyond which Ebenezum was receiving his
cure. I heard repeated, muffled sneezing. Apparently, they had
not yet made it to the final stage. It would probably be best if I
did not bother my master just yet.

I walked through the foyer and stepped outside.

"Oh, Wuntie!" Alea waved to me. She stood between the
dragon Hubert and one of the student wizards. I walked over
to meet them.

"Wuntie!" Alea repeated breathlessly. "Have you met Tomm?"

I smiled in a vague sort of way before I remembered. That was right! He was the one who gave up a life of tinking! Well, I supposed he was a decent enough chap with which to pass the time of day. We exchanged pleasantries.

"Wuntie," Alea breathed, impulsively grabbing the tinker's hand, "Tomm and I are going to be married!"

I could not believe my ears! The beautiful Alea was going to marry this lout? For a moment, I was taken aback. I wondered what she could see in someone as big and stolid as that. What had the two of them done, while I had been risking my life in the Netherhells?

"Yes," Tomm beamed. "My mother is very happy."

I mumbled my congratulations.

"But we have even better news!" Hubert added. "We realize now that our original efforts describing your journey may have been a little downbeat. So we've brightened up the song considerably and made it a real hum-along tune!"

The dragon blew an enormous smoke ring. He looked as if he could no longer contain his excitement. "I suppose we could give him a little sample. Hit it, damsel!" Alea once again sang in her clear, high soprano:

Wuntvor the apprentice, he's our kind of guy!

Awkward as he was, he still somehow survived!

I thanked them quickly, before they could get any farther, and told them I would rather wait and hear the entire song cycle at once, so that I might get the proper effect. To my great relief, they agreed and then began to tell me of the festivities in some detail. It seemed that, after one final discussion with my master, Klothus had decided to become a weaver. As soon as he finished three more robes in a certain silver moon-and-star design, Hubert assured me, he would straightaway begin a series of ceremonial costumes for damsel, dragon, and the guests of honor who would make the festivities grander still.

I began to think that, on the night of my honorary dinner in the Great Hall, I might find something to eat in Vushta.

I hailed Snarks and Hendrek, who had just stepped from the college.

"A beautiful day," the vast warrior said, looking aloft. "Doom."

"So everything's back to normal," Snarks added. "And as dull as ever!"

A great commotion came from a clump of trees beyond the college. "I found one!" a mild yet strong voice cried. "A wild pig at last!"

"Like I said," Snarks continued, "just like normal. I see they've got your master stuck in the big room over there. Is it going to do him any good?"

I assured the truth-telling demon that these were the greatest mages in all of Vushta. True, Ebenezum's malady was. a little different from their everyday problems, but they would surely find a cure!

I walked below a nearby window that led to the Great Hall, anxious to hear these great wizards weaving their curative spells. Oddly enough, there seemed to be even more sneezing than before.

"Doom," Hendrek said. "So what do we do now?"

I assured Hendrek that, once my master was cured, he would quickly be able to remove the curse from Headbasher. Snarks, it appeared, had been offered a post at the extension school as resident expert on the Netherhells.

And then I thought, what would I do? Eventually, I imagined, go back to the Western Kingdoms with my master, study, and become a full-fledged wizard. But all of that could wait a day or two. I was but a few minutes' walk away from Vushta, city of a thousand forbidden delights. Even though I had walked the Vushtan streets, it had been at a time of crisis, and I had had no time for sightseeing, much less going down one of those side streets where a single errant glance might doom a man for all eternity.

But I could correct all that now. It appeared that Snorphosio was in charge of arranging the dinner in our honor. If that was the case, I had all the time in the world. And the time to see Vushta was now!

"Anyone interested in an afternoon stroll?" I asked the others.

"Wuntvor!" a woman's voice called to me before either of

my compatriots had a chance to answer. Norei walked rapidly across the lawn to meet us.

"I saw you out here with the dragon and that—damsel." There seemed to be an edge to her voice.

I quickly told Norei about Alea's happy announcement.

"Really?" The news seemed to cheer her considerably. "Still, I feel a bit sorry for the tinker. But that is none of my affair. Wuntvor, may I speak to you for a moment?"

We excused ourselves from the others.

"Wuntvor," Norei said softly as she gazed deep within my eyes. "Do you have any plans for this afternoon?"

I mentioned that I had thought about going to Vushta.

"Vushta?" Her lower lip trembled ever so slightly. "But this might be the last afternoon we can spend together for a long time. Who knows what will happen after they cure your master?" Her fingers, somehow, had managed to intertwine with my own.

"Oh," I said. What was Vushta when I had my beloved by my side?

Then again, I remarked, perhaps I didn't want to go to Vushta after all.

Suddenly, there came a bout of sneezing so great that the outer walls of the Great Hall shook, as if not only my master but every single wizard in the room with him had sneezed at once.

"Then again," I added, "we may be here for quite some time."

We walked hand in hand toward the privacy of the trees.

"Wuntvor," Norei said sweetly. "I only have one question. Isn't there some place you could put these ferrets? At least for a little while?"

About the Author

Craig Shaw Gardner is the author of more than thirty novels and fifty-odd short stories (some of them very odd.) His novelization of BATMAN was a New York Times bestseller, and he's a past president of the Horror Writers Association. He's written reviews and articles for numerous periodicals, ranging from THE WASHINGTON POST to RAMPAGE WRESTLING, and (far more importantly) he serves as the perennial co-host (with Eric Van) of the "Kirk Polland Memorial Bad Prose Competition" every July at Readercon. He lives just north of the Center of the Universe (a.k.a. Cambridge, MA) with his wife and their two cats, George and Gracie.

Curious about other Crossroad Press books?
Stop by our site:
http://store.crossroadpress.com
We offer quality writing
in digital, audio, and print formats.

Enter the code FIRSTBOOK
to get 20% off your first order from our store!
Stop by today!